BEDHEAD
TED

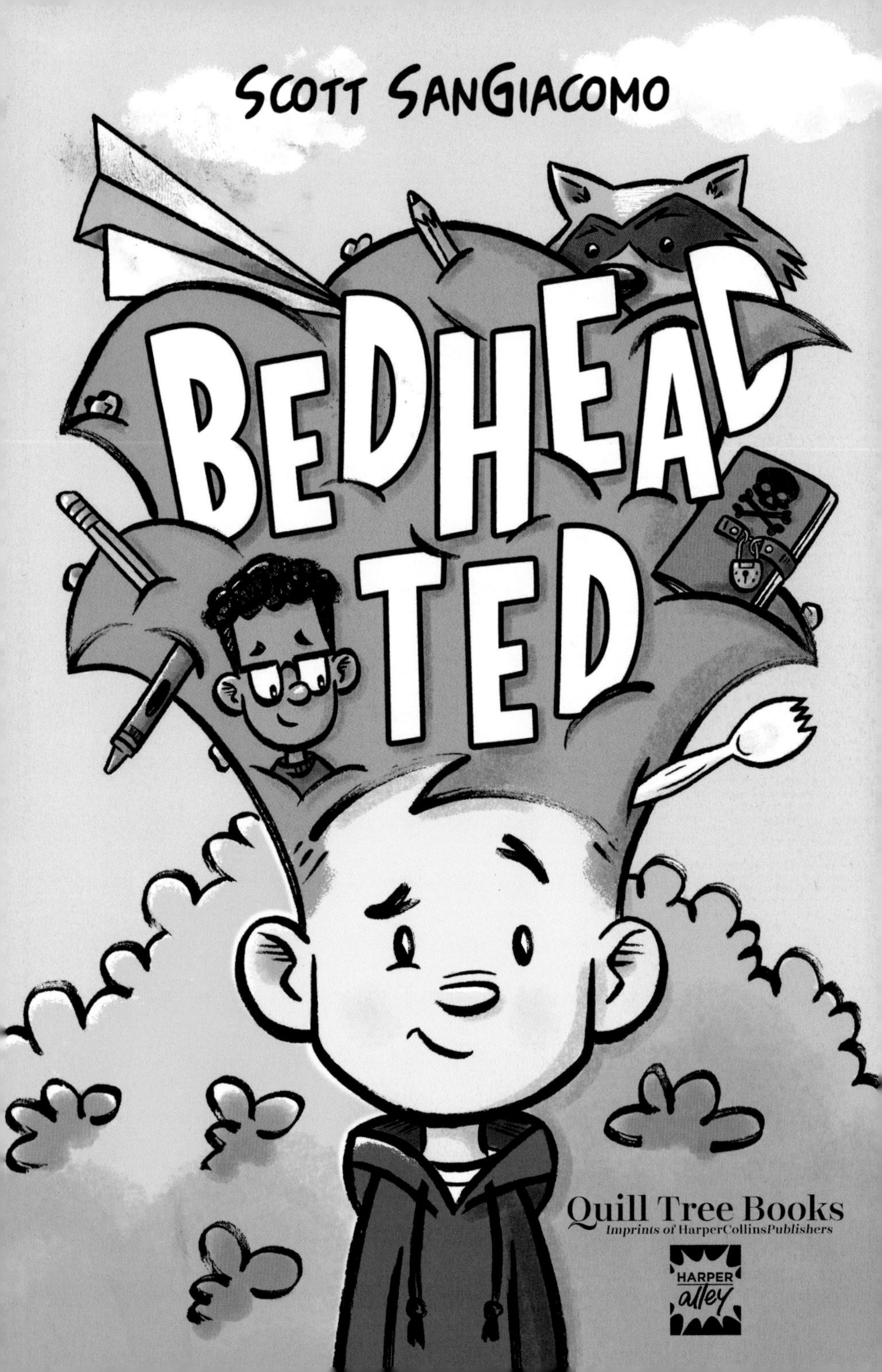
SCOTT SANGIACOMO
BEDHEAD TED
Quill Tree Books
Imprints of HarperCollinsPublishers
HARPER alley

Quill Tree Books is an imprint of HarperCollins Publishers.
HarperAlley is an imprint of HarperCollins Publishers.

Bedhead Ted
Copyright © 2021 by Scott SanGiacomo
All rights reserved. Printed in Spain.
No part of this book may be used or reproduced in any manner whatsoever
without written permission except in the case of brief quotations
embodied in critical articles and reviews. For information address
HarperCollins Children's Books, a division of HarperCollins Publishers,
195 Broadway, New York, NY 10007.
www.harperalley.com

Library of Congress Control Number: 2021930180
ISBN 978-0-06-294132-9 — ISBN 978-0-06-294130-5 (pbk.)

The artist used a combination of traditional and digital media
to create the illustrations for this book.
21 22 23 24 25 EP 10 9 8 7 6 5 4 3 2 1
First Edition

For my mom, Elizabeth SanGiacomo

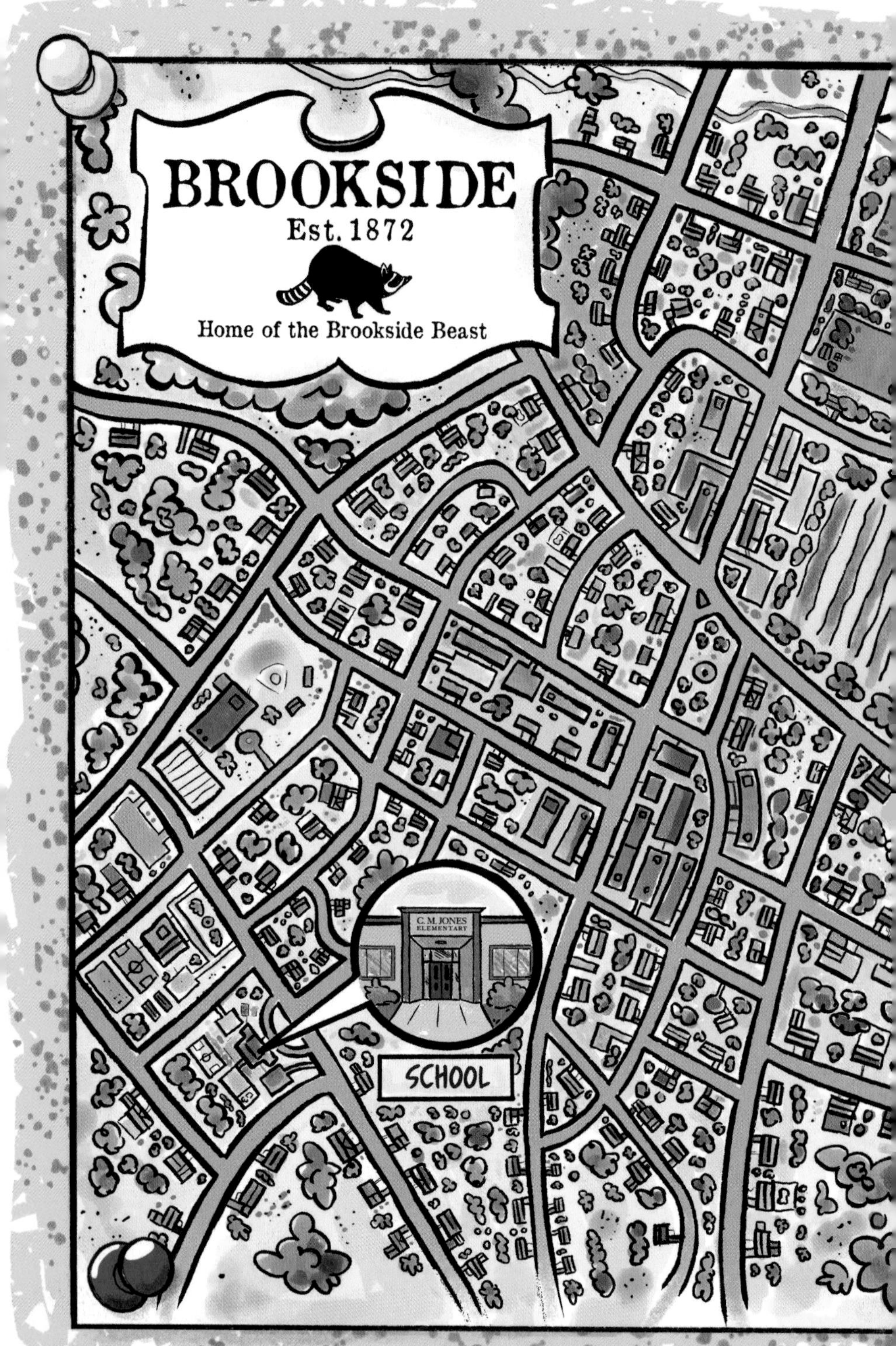
BROOKSIDE
Est. 1872
Home of the Brookside Beast
C. M. JONES
ELEMENTARY
SCHOOL

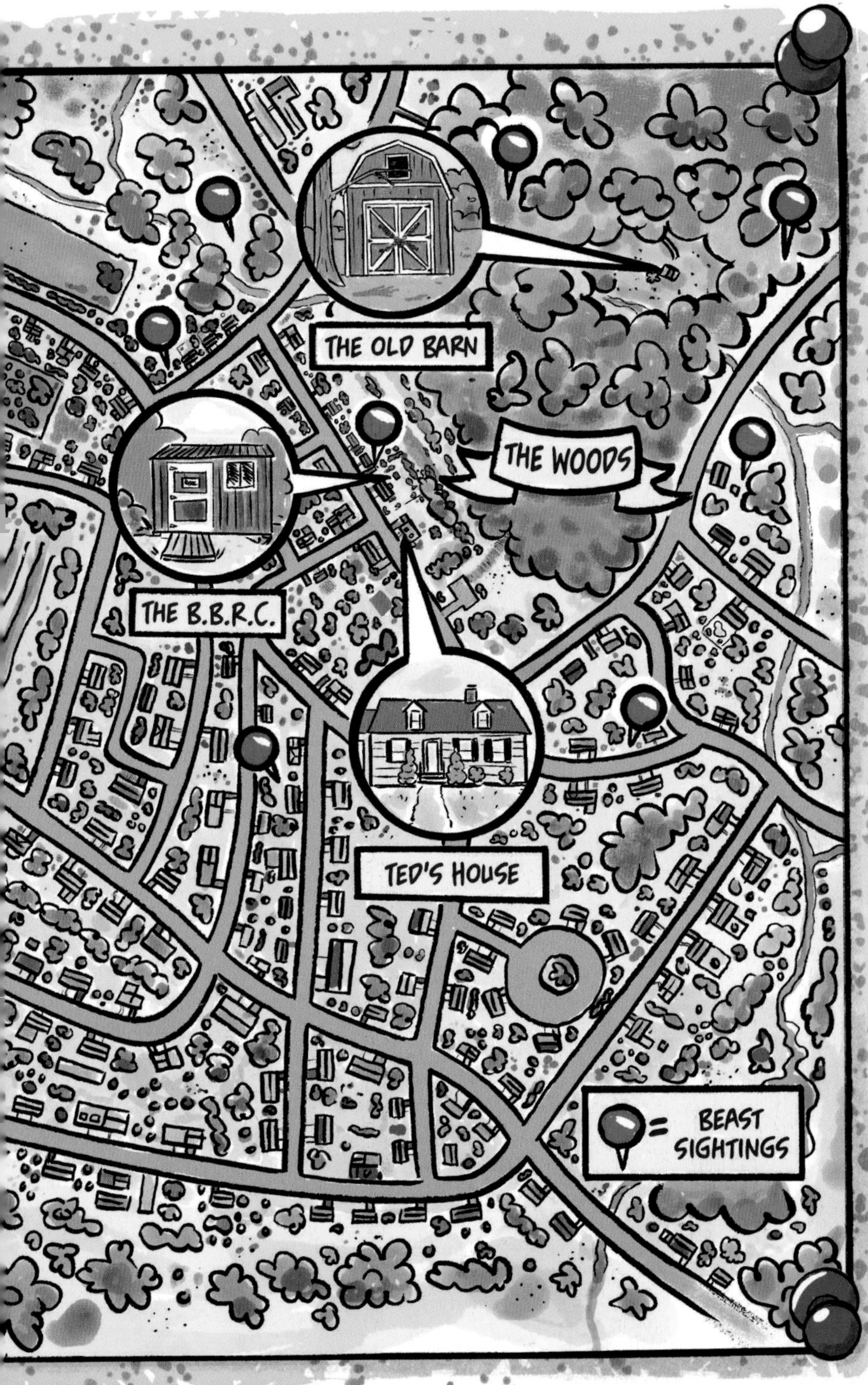
THE OLD BARN
THE WOODS
THE B.B.R.C.
TED'S HOUSE
= BEAST SIGHTINGS

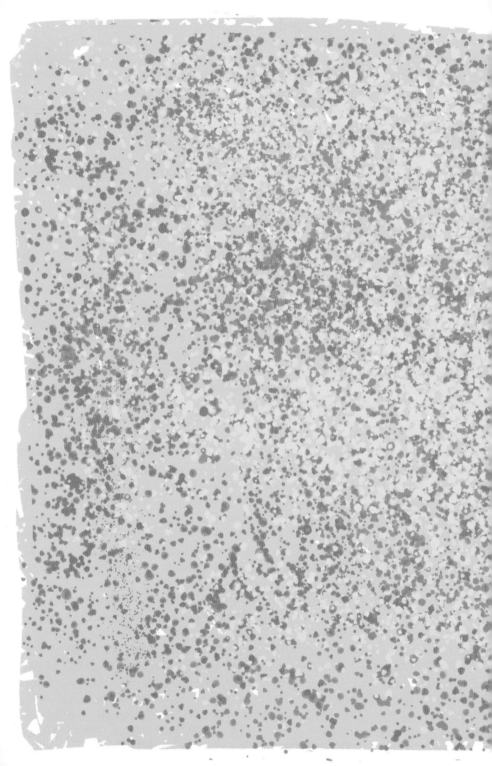

CHAPTER 1:

THE WORST NICKNAME EVER

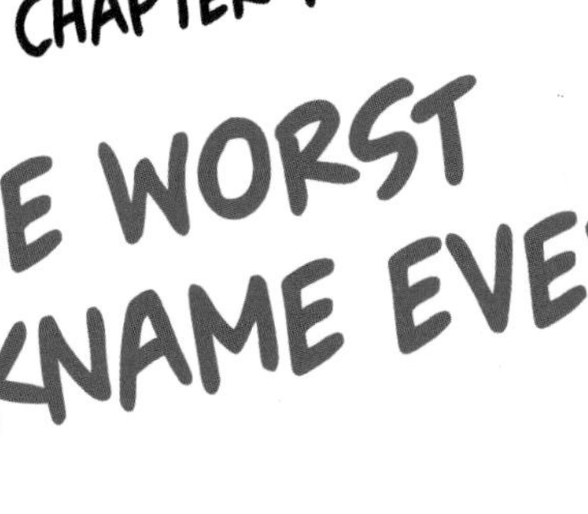
ha ha

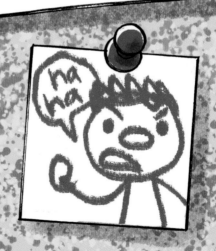

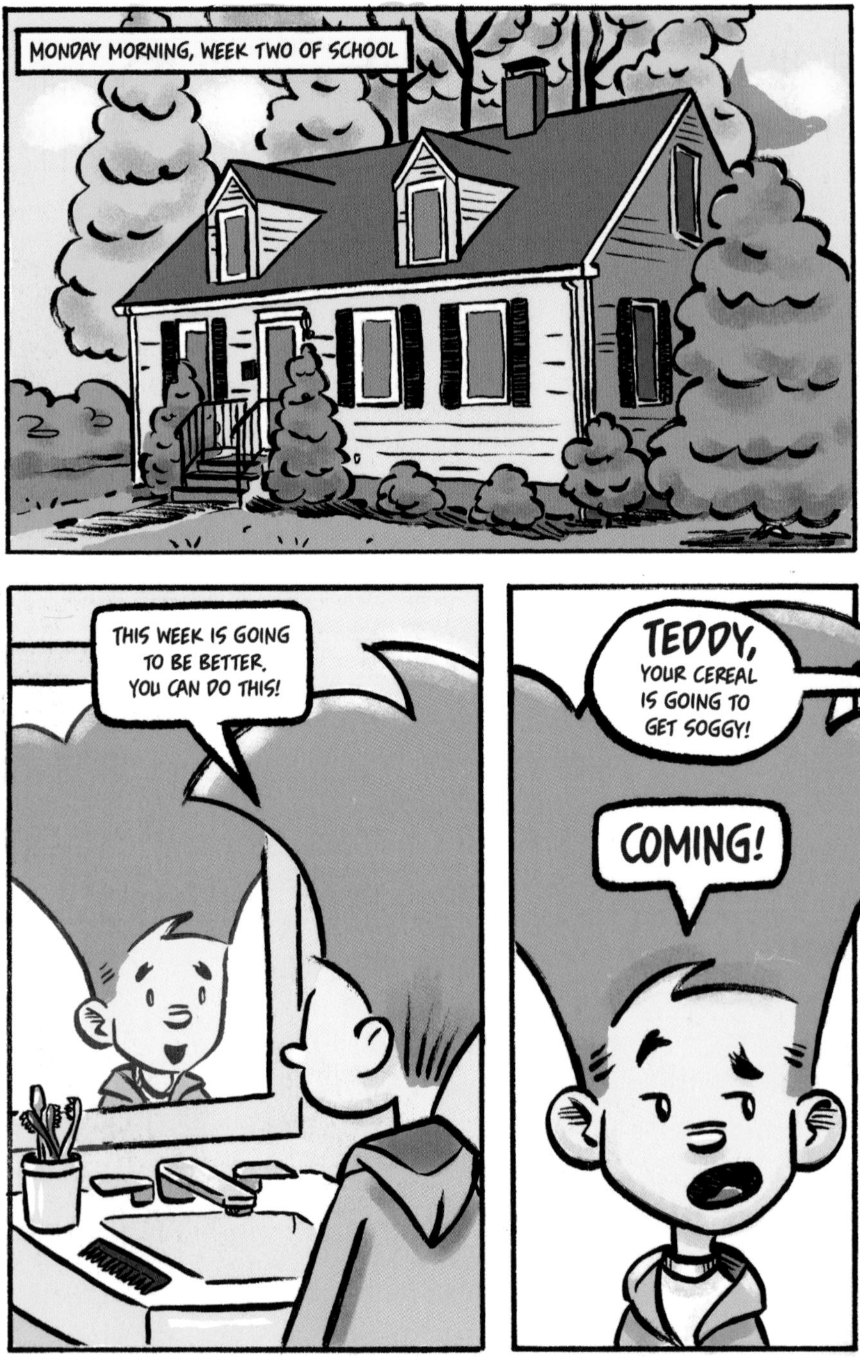
MONDAY MORNING, WEEK TWO OF SCHOOL
THIS WEEK IS GOING TO BE BETTER. YOU CAN DO THIS!
TEDDY, YOUR CEREAL IS GOING TO GET SOGGY!
COMING!

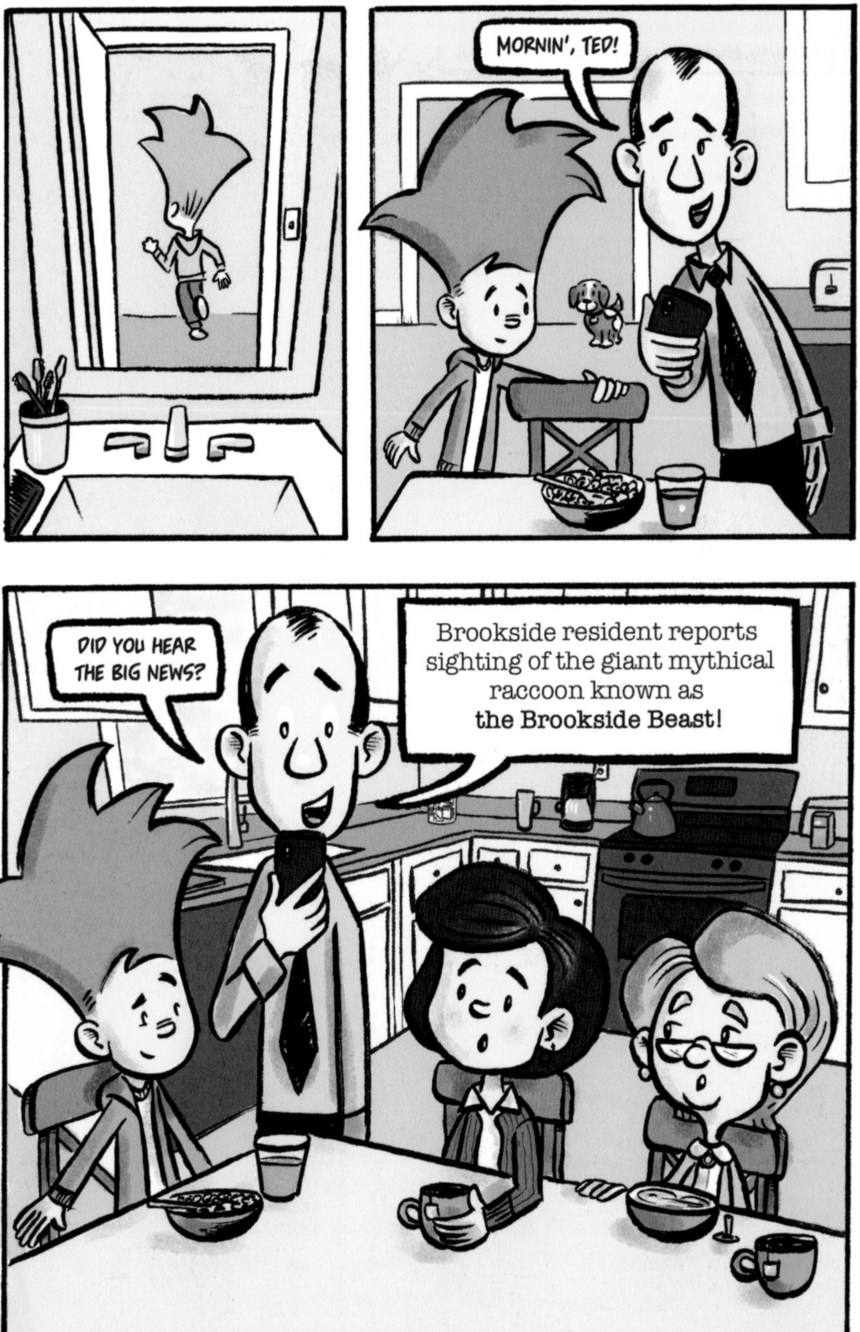
MORNIN', TED!
DID YOU HEAR THE BIG NEWS?
Brookside resident reports sighting of the giant mythical raccoon known as **the Brookside Beast!**

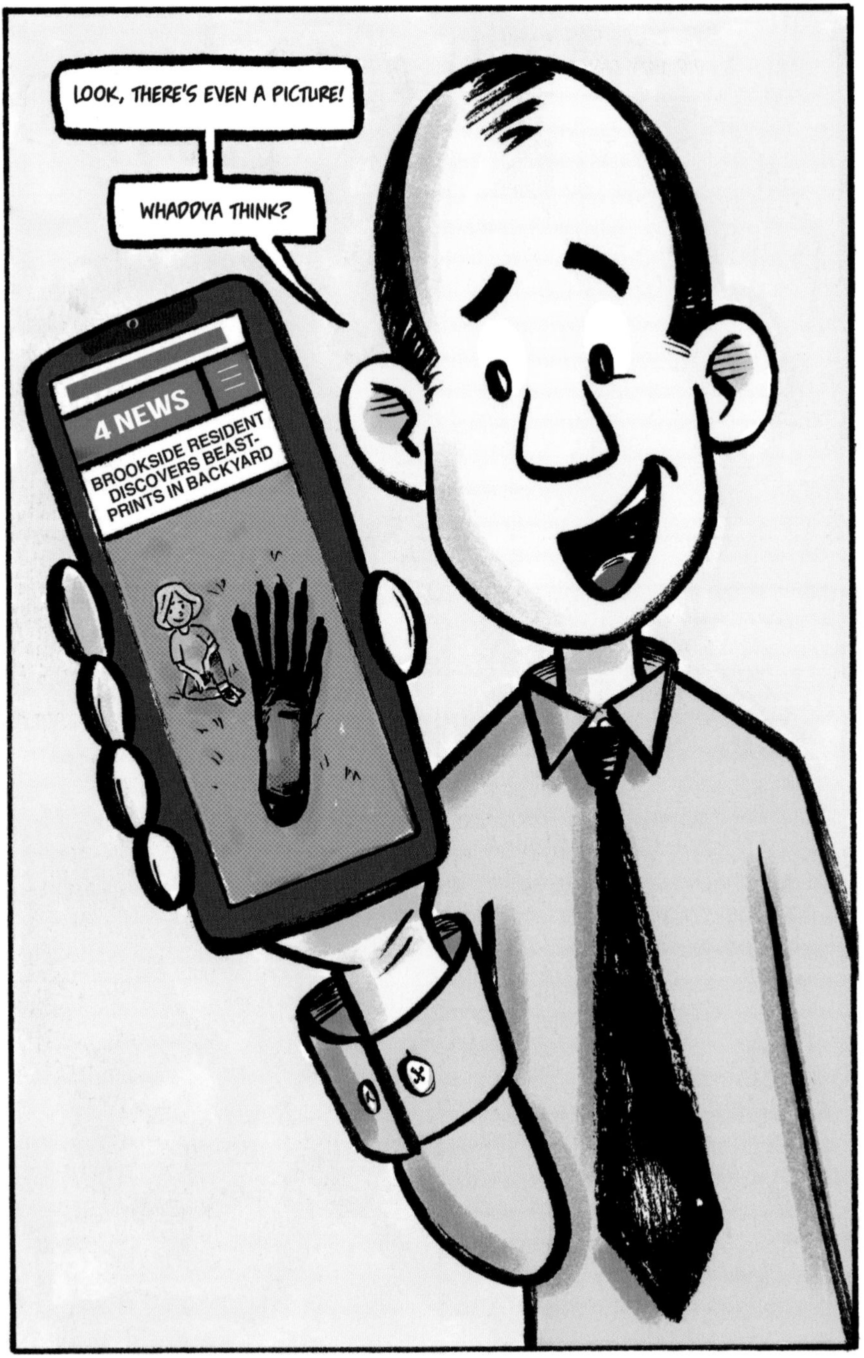
LOOK, THERE'S EVEN A PICTURE!
WHADDYA THINK?
4 NEWS
BROOKSIDE RESIDENT DISCOVERS BEAST-PRINTS IN BACKYARD

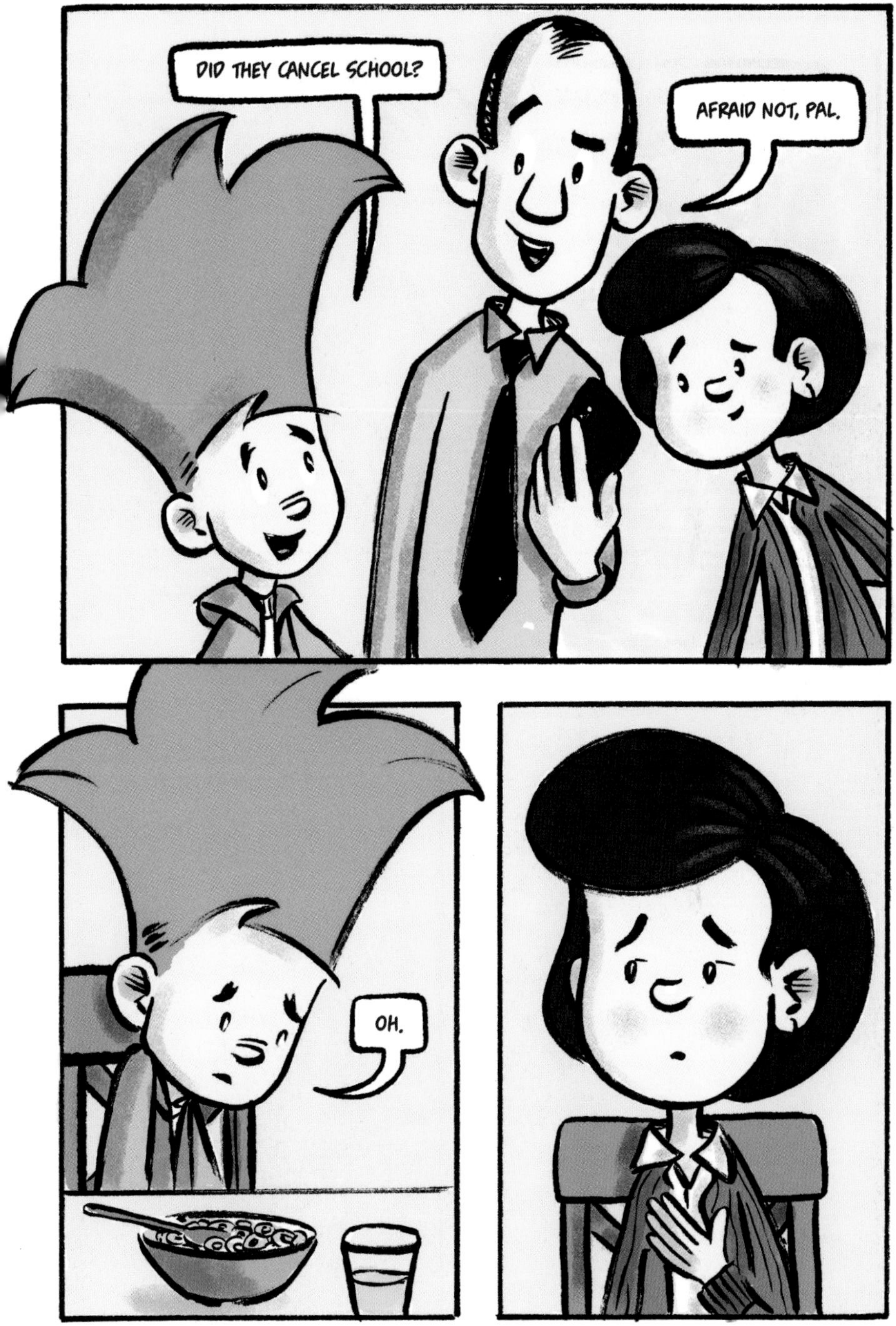
DID THEY CANCEL SCHOOL?
AFRAID NOT, PAL.
OH.

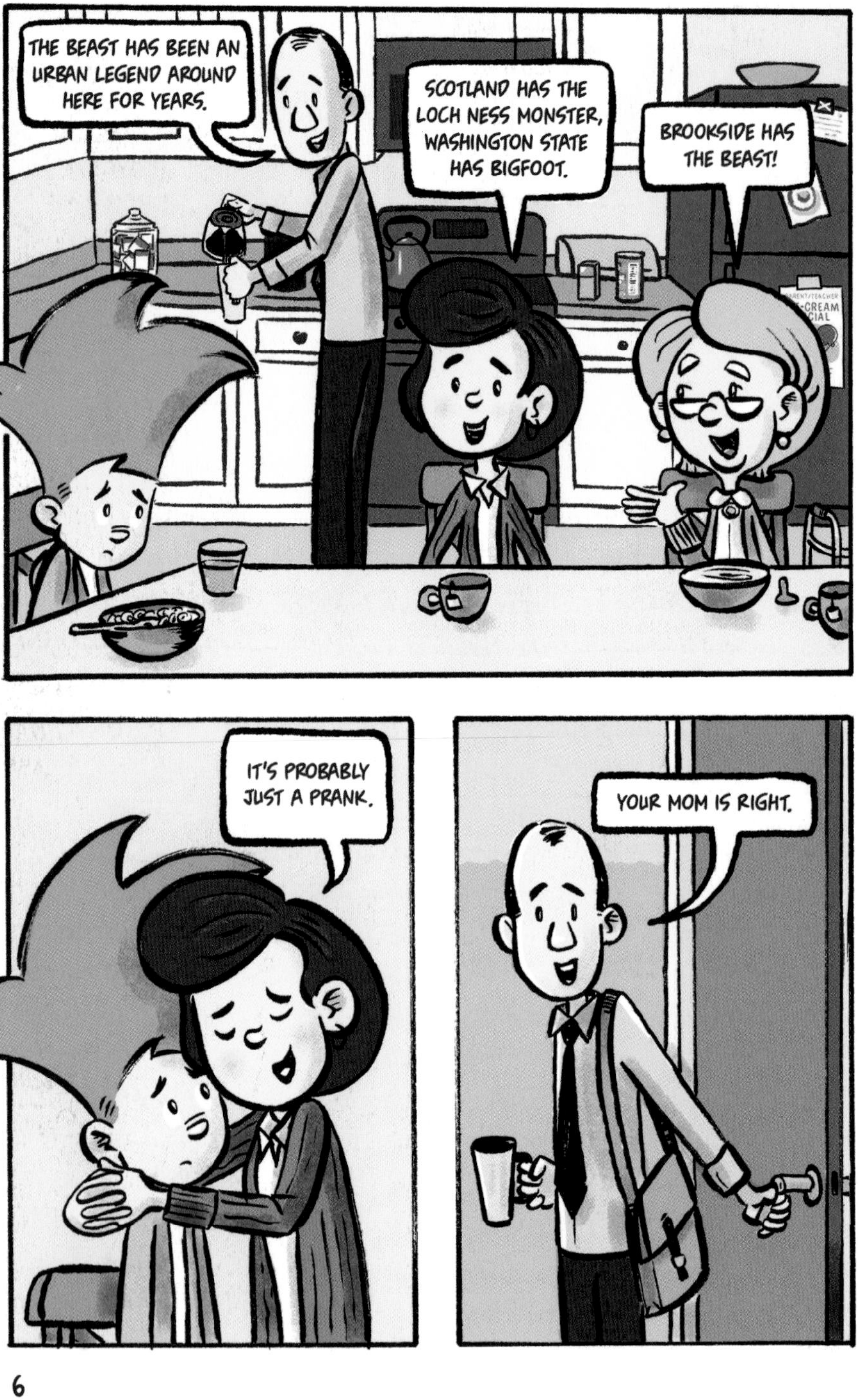
THE BEAST HAS BEEN AN URBAN LEGEND AROUND HERE FOR YEARS.
SCOTLAND HAS THE LOCH NESS MONSTER, WASHINGTON STATE HAS BIGFOOT.
BROOKSIDE HAS THE BEAST!
IT'S PROBABLY JUST A PRANK.
YOUR MOM IS RIGHT.

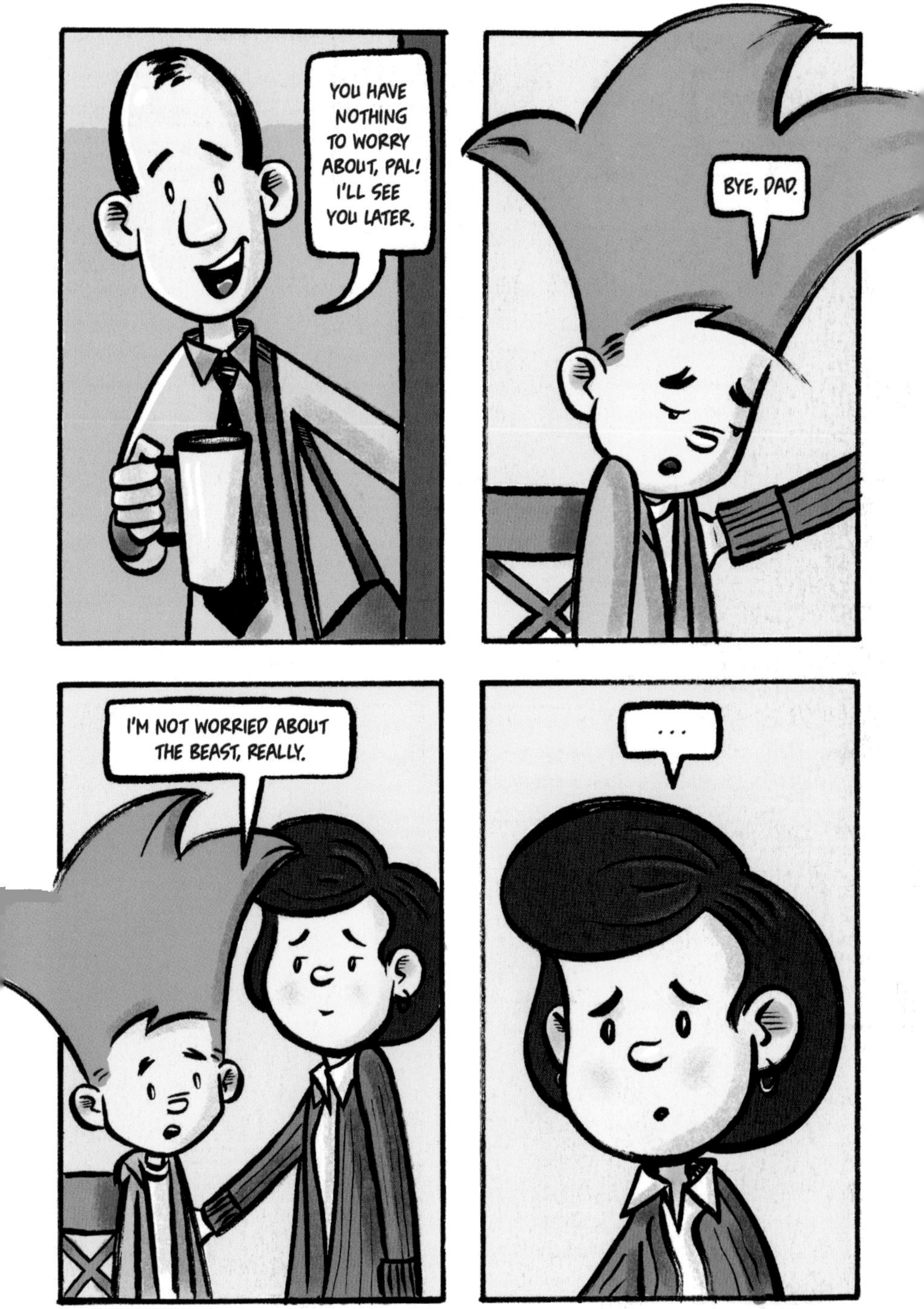
YOU HAVE NOTHING TO WORRY ABOUT, PAL! I'LL SEE YOU LATER.
BYE, DAD.
I'M NOT WORRIED ABOUT THE BEAST, REALLY.
...

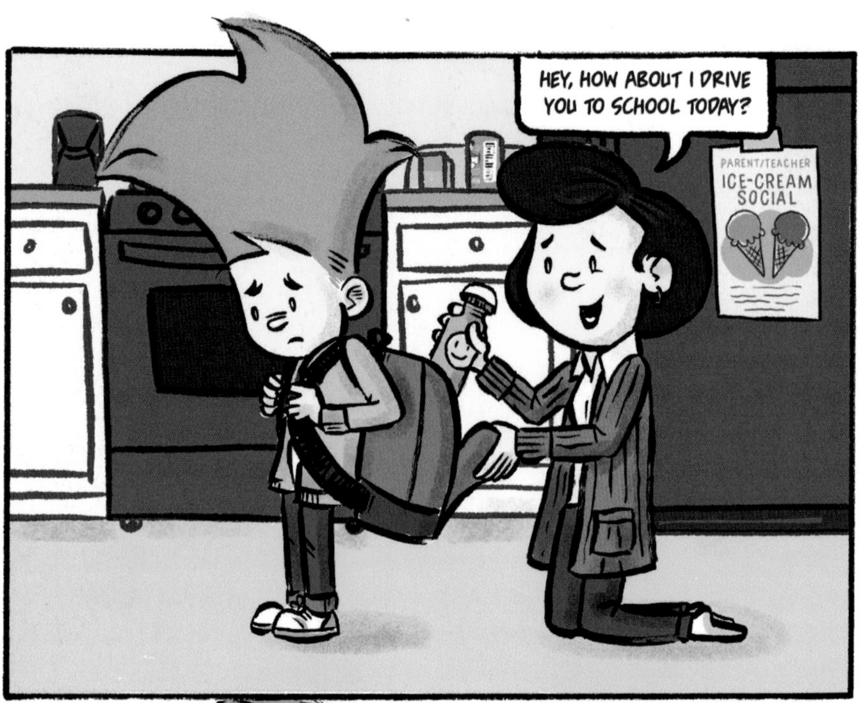
HEY, HOW ABOUT I DRIVE YOU TO SCHOOL TODAY?
PARENT/TEACHER ICE-CREAM SOCIAL

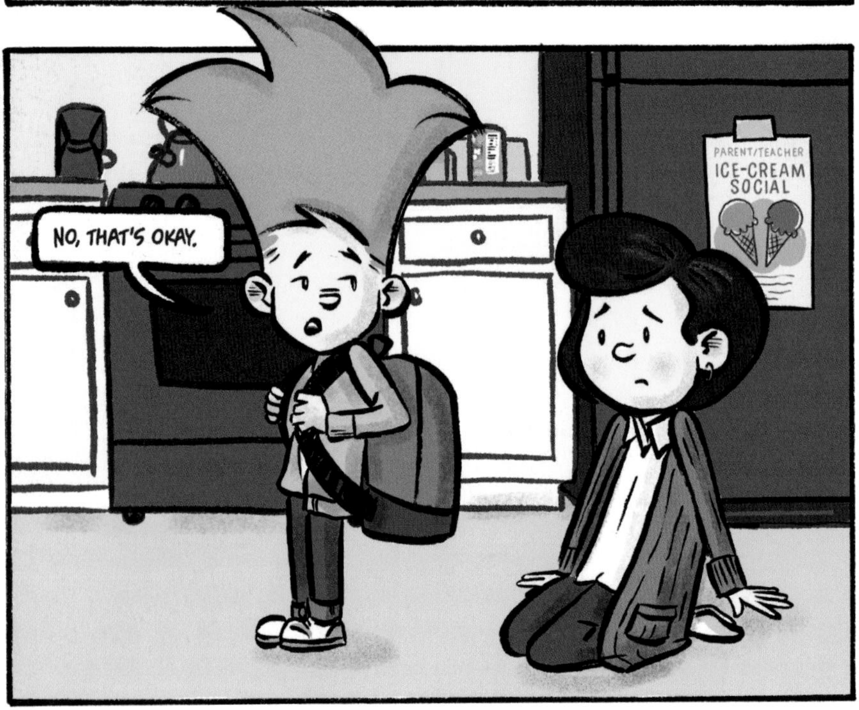
NO, THAT'S OKAY.
PARENT/TEACHER ICE-CREAM SOCIAL

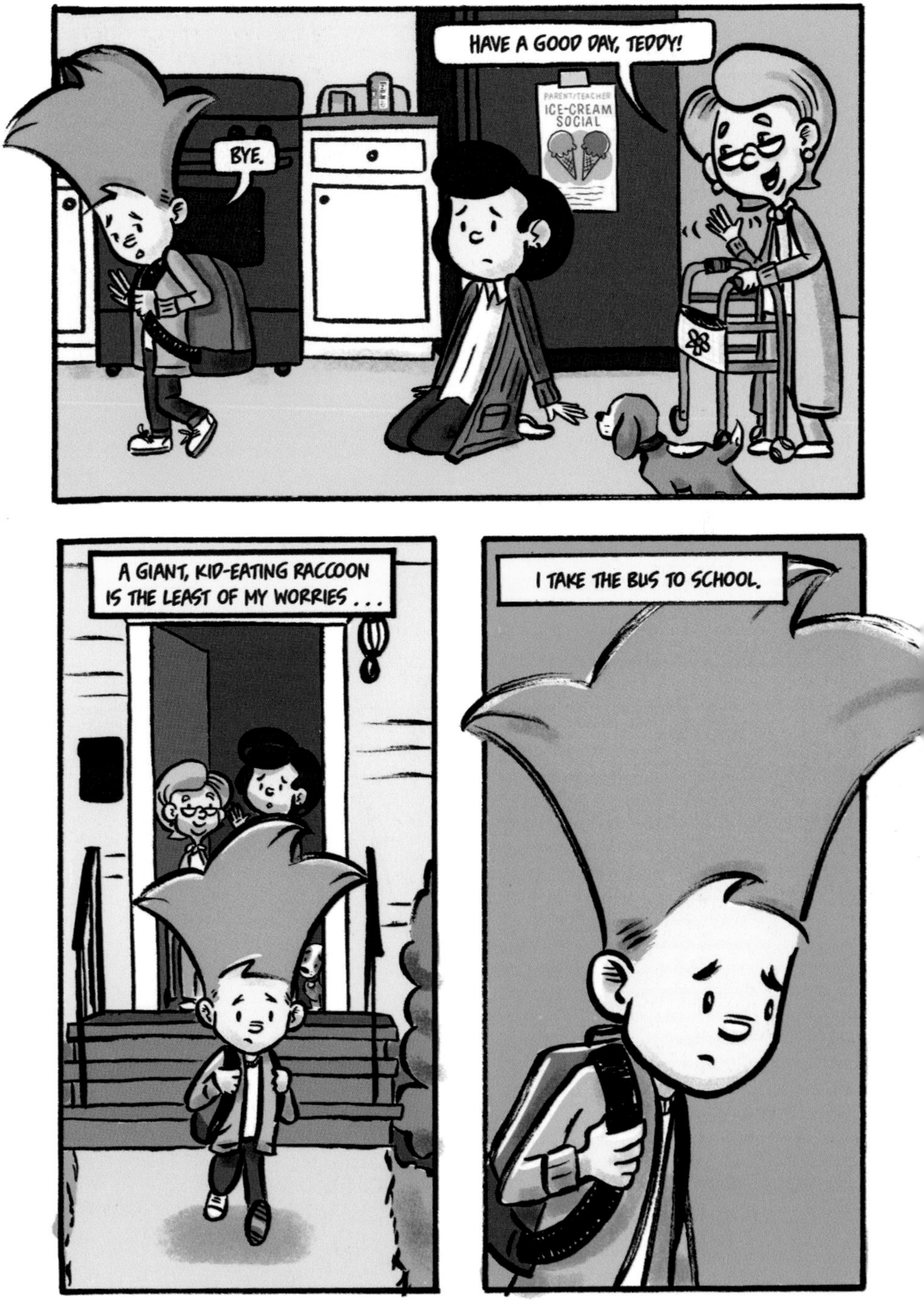
BYE.
HAVE A GOOD DAY, TEDDY!
PARENT/TEACHER
ICE-CREAM
SOCIAL
A GIANT, KID-EATING RACCOON
IS THE LEAST OF MY WORRIES . . .
I TAKE THE BUS TO SCHOOL.

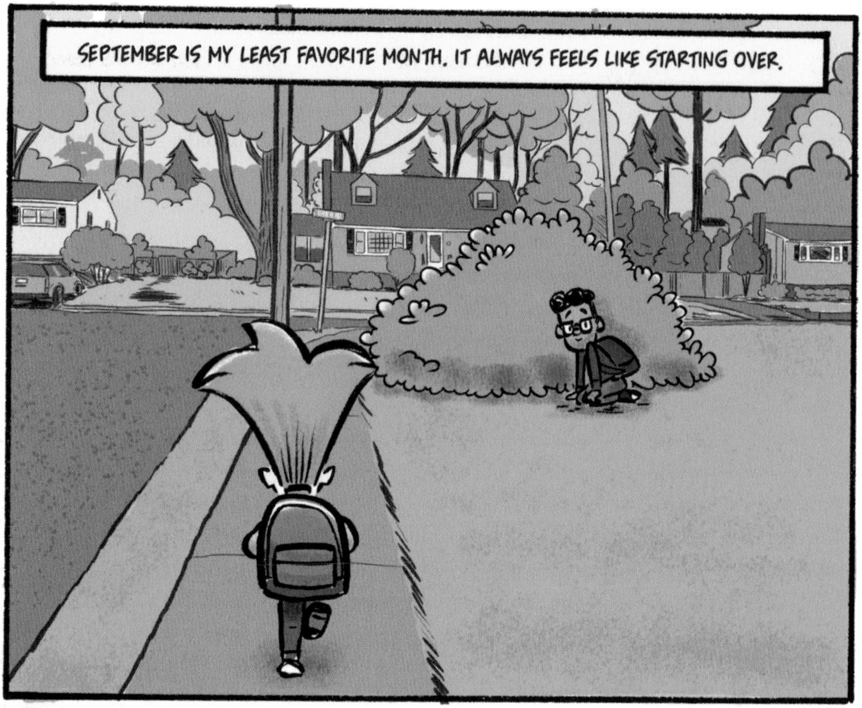
SEPTEMBER IS MY LEAST FAVORITE MONTH. IT ALWAYS FEELS LIKE STARTING OVER.

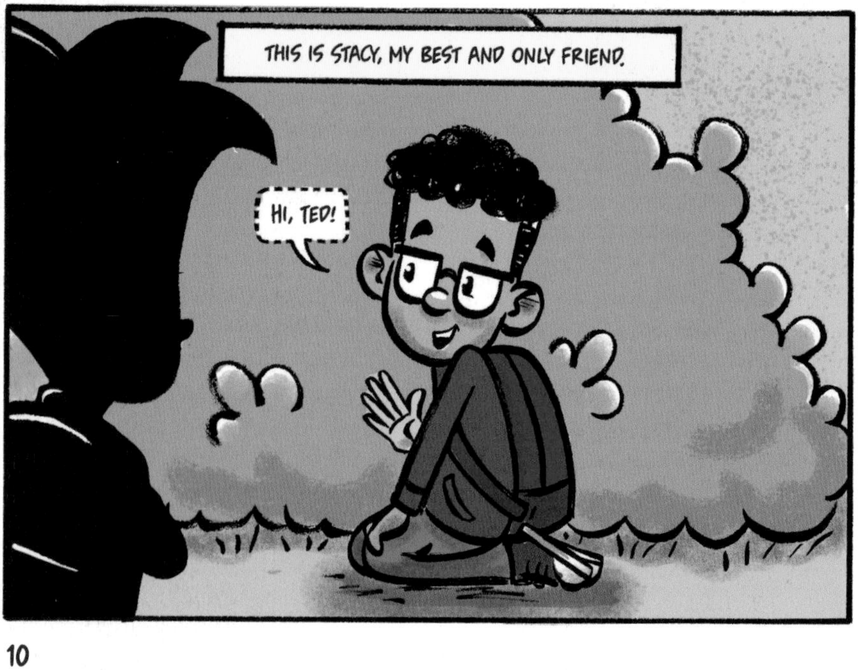
THIS IS STACY, MY BEST AND ONLY FRIEND.
HI, TED!

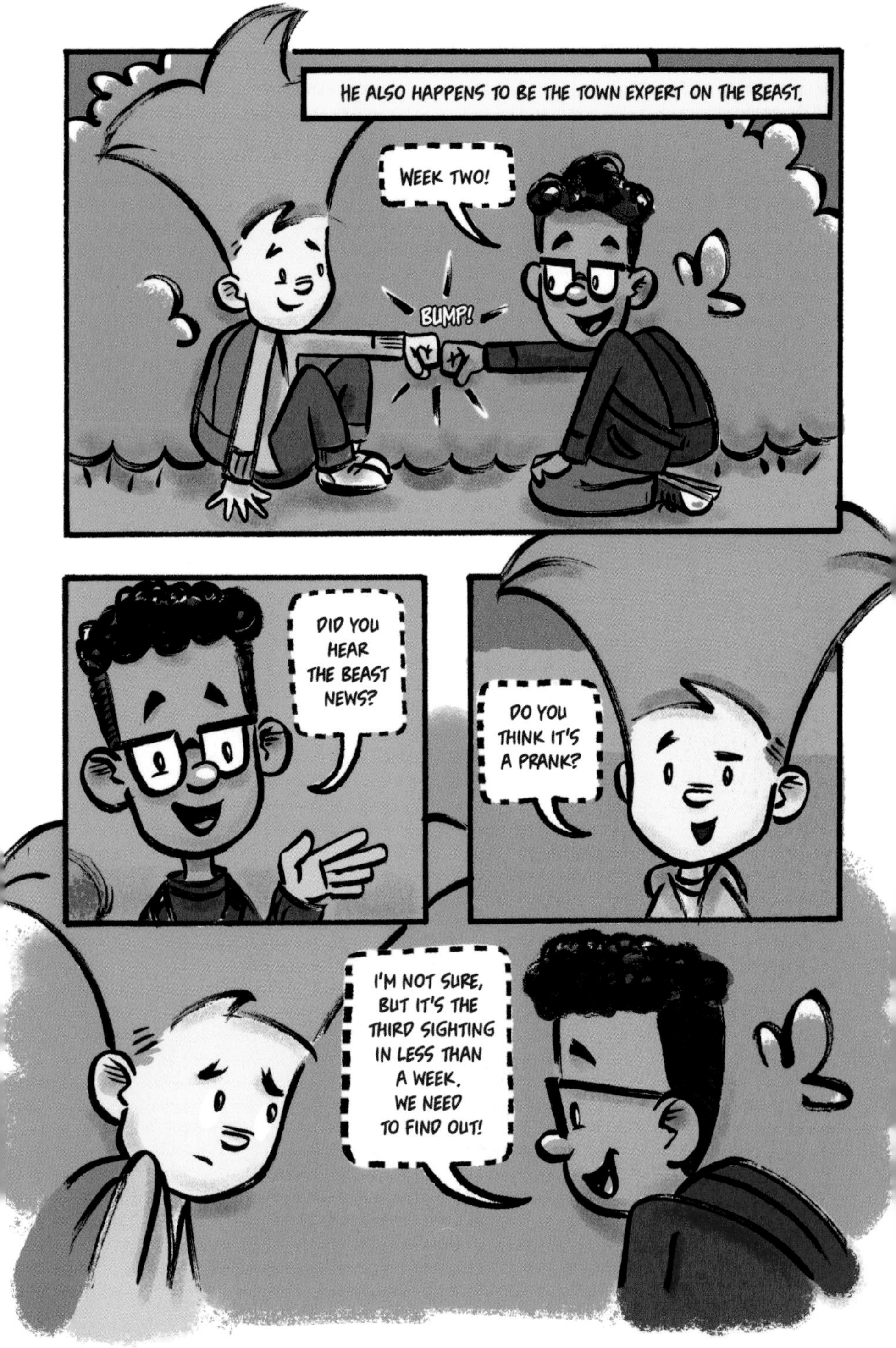
HE ALSO HAPPENS TO BE THE TOWN EXPERT ON THE BEAST.
WEEK TWO!
BUMP!
DID YOU HEAR THE BEAST NEWS?
DO YOU THINK IT'S A PRANK?
I'M NOT SURE, BUT IT'S THE THIRD SIGHTING IN LESS THAN A WEEK. WE NEED TO FIND OUT!

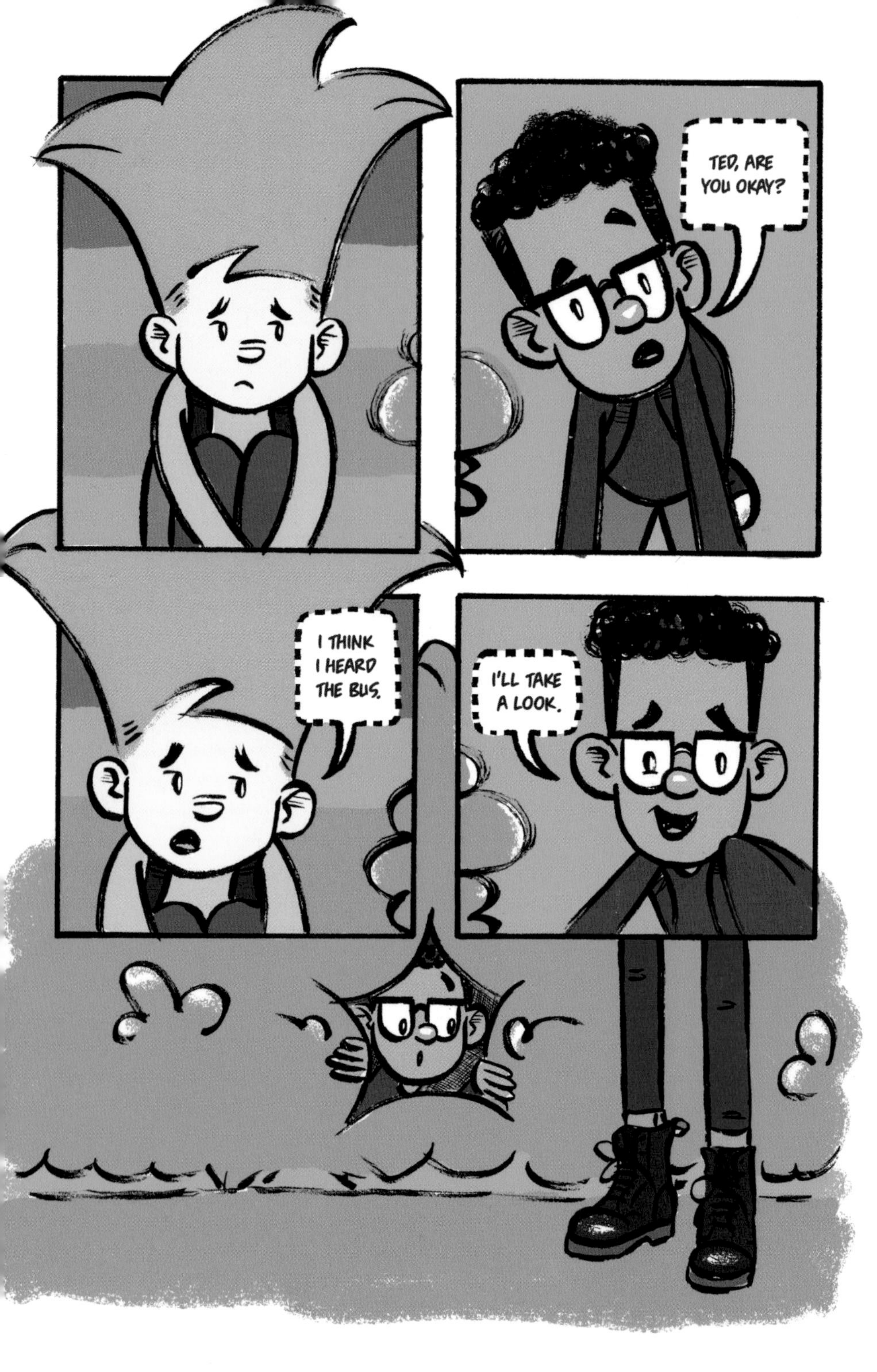
TED, ARE YOU OKAY?
I THINK I HEARD THE BUS.
I'LL TAKE A LOOK.

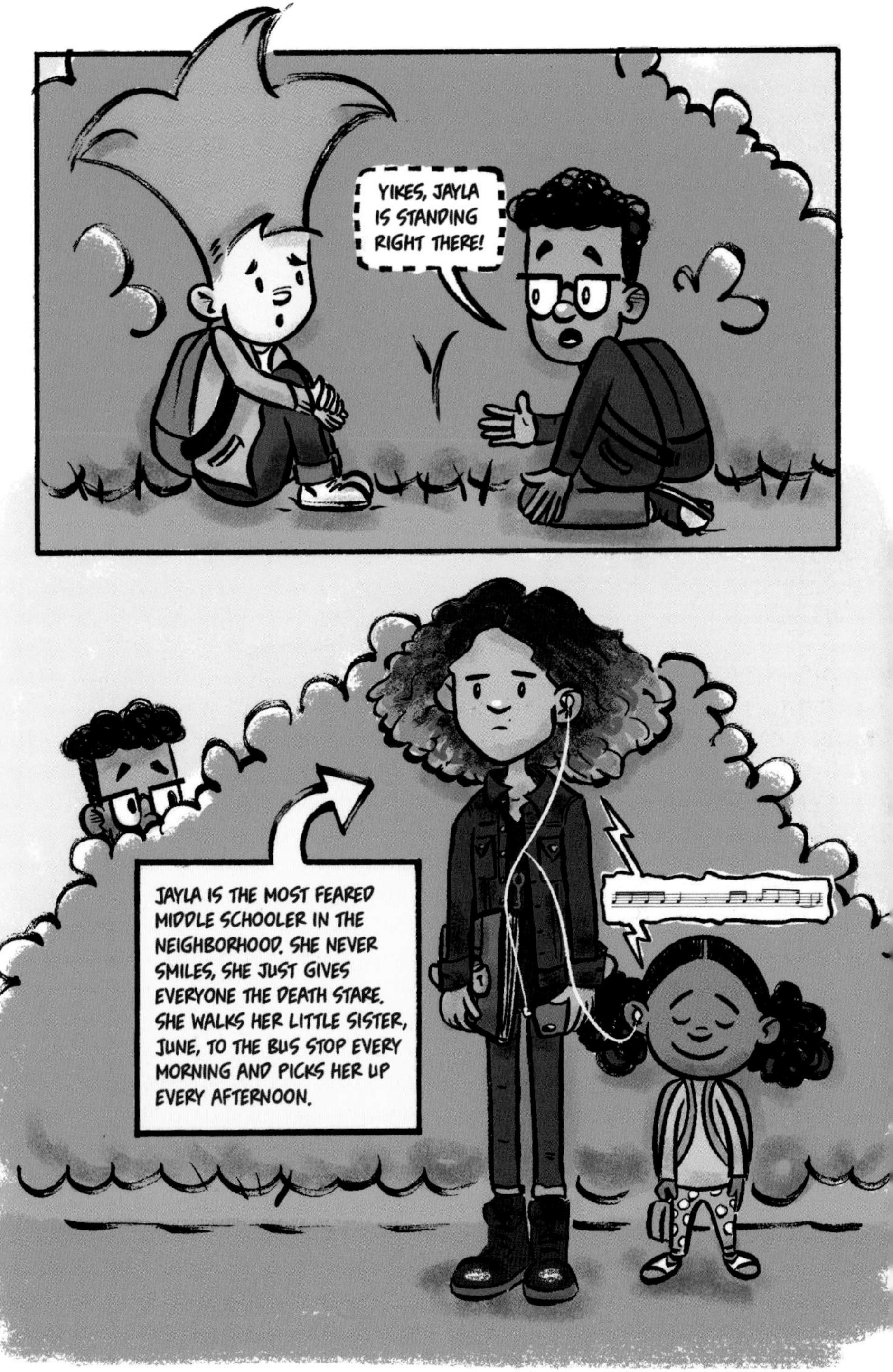
YIKES, JAYLA IS STANDING RIGHT THERE!
JAYLA IS THE MOST FEARED MIDDLE SCHOOLER IN THE NEIGHBORHOOD. SHE NEVER SMILES, SHE JUST GIVES EVERYONE THE DEATH STARE. SHE WALKS HER LITTLE SISTER, JUNE, TO THE BUS STOP EVERY MORNING AND PICKS HER UP EVERY AFTERNOON.

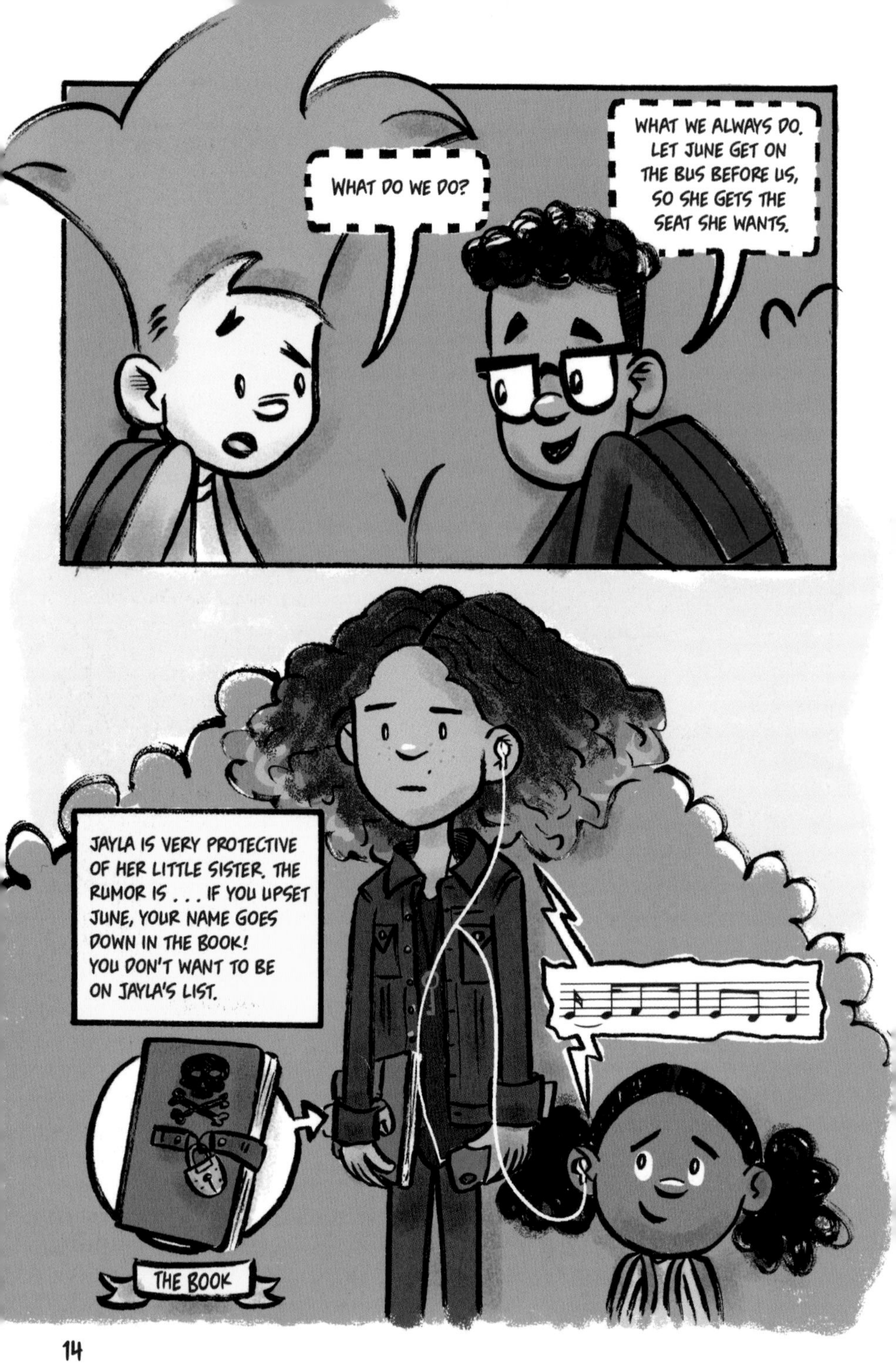
WHAT DO WE DO?
WHAT WE ALWAYS DO. LET JUNE GET ON THE BUS BEFORE US, SO SHE GETS THE SEAT SHE WANTS.
JAYLA IS VERY PROTECTIVE OF HER LITTLE SISTER. THE RUMOR IS . . . IF YOU UPSET JUNE, YOUR NAME GOES DOWN IN THE BOOK! YOU DON'T WANT TO BE ON JAYLA'S LIST.
THE BOOK

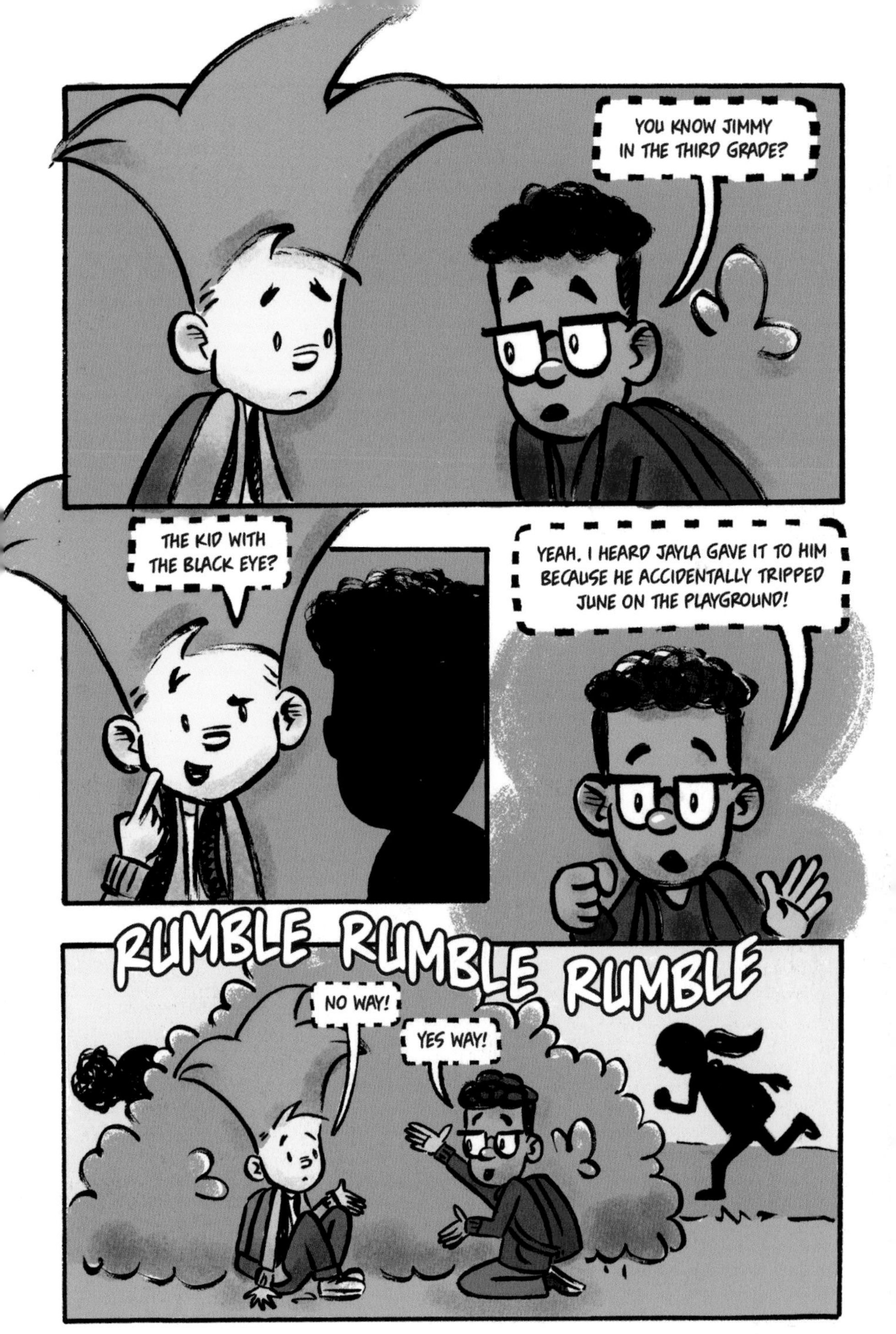

YOU KNOW JIMMY IN THE THIRD GRADE?
THE KID WITH THE BLACK EYE?
YEAH. I HEARD JAYLA GAVE IT TO HIM BECAUSE HE ACCIDENTALLY TRIPPED JUNE ON THE PLAYGROUND!
RUMBLE RUMBLE RUMBLE
NO WAY!
YES WAY!

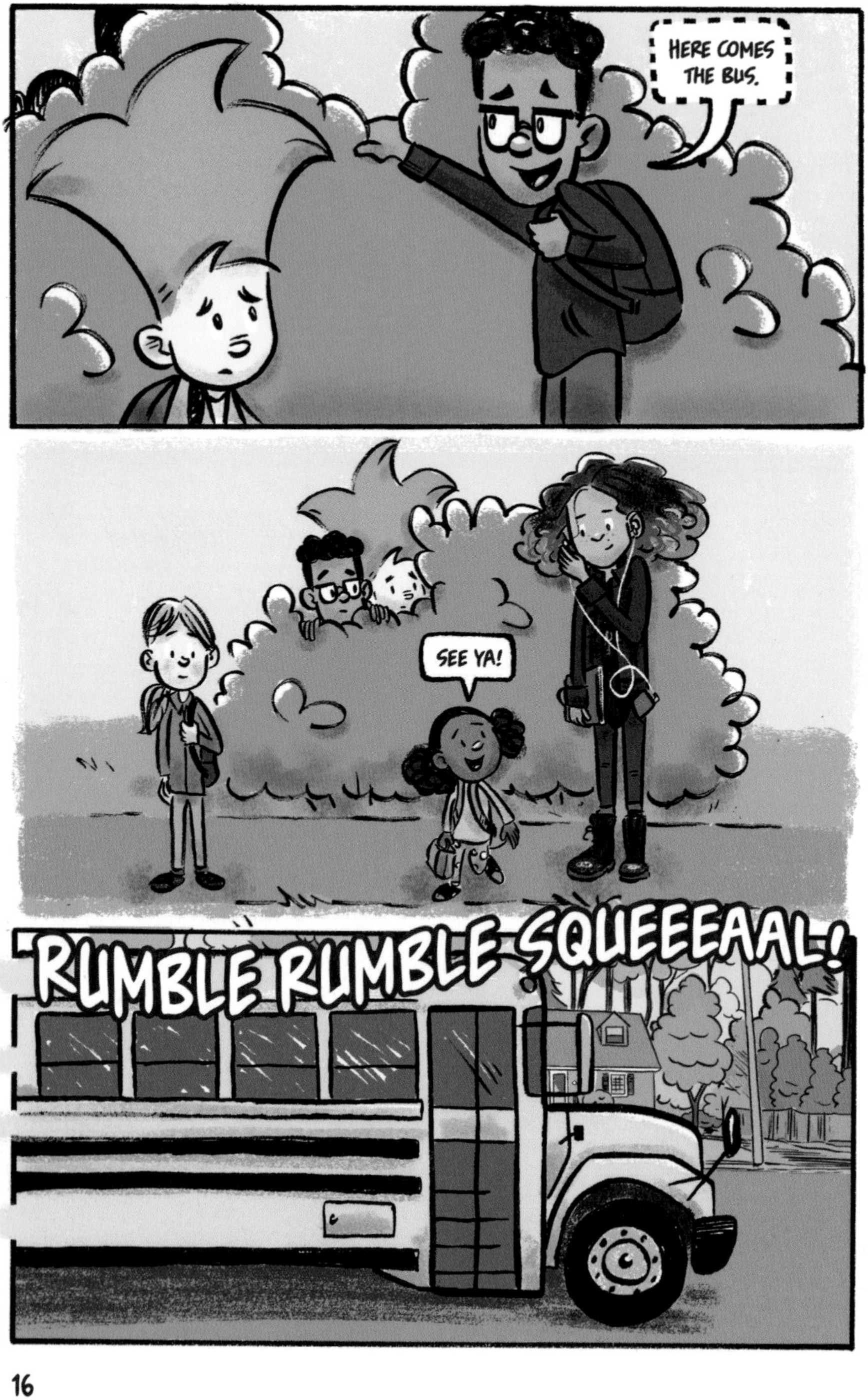
HERE COMES THE BUS.
SEE YA!
RUMBLE RUMBLE SQUEEEAAL!

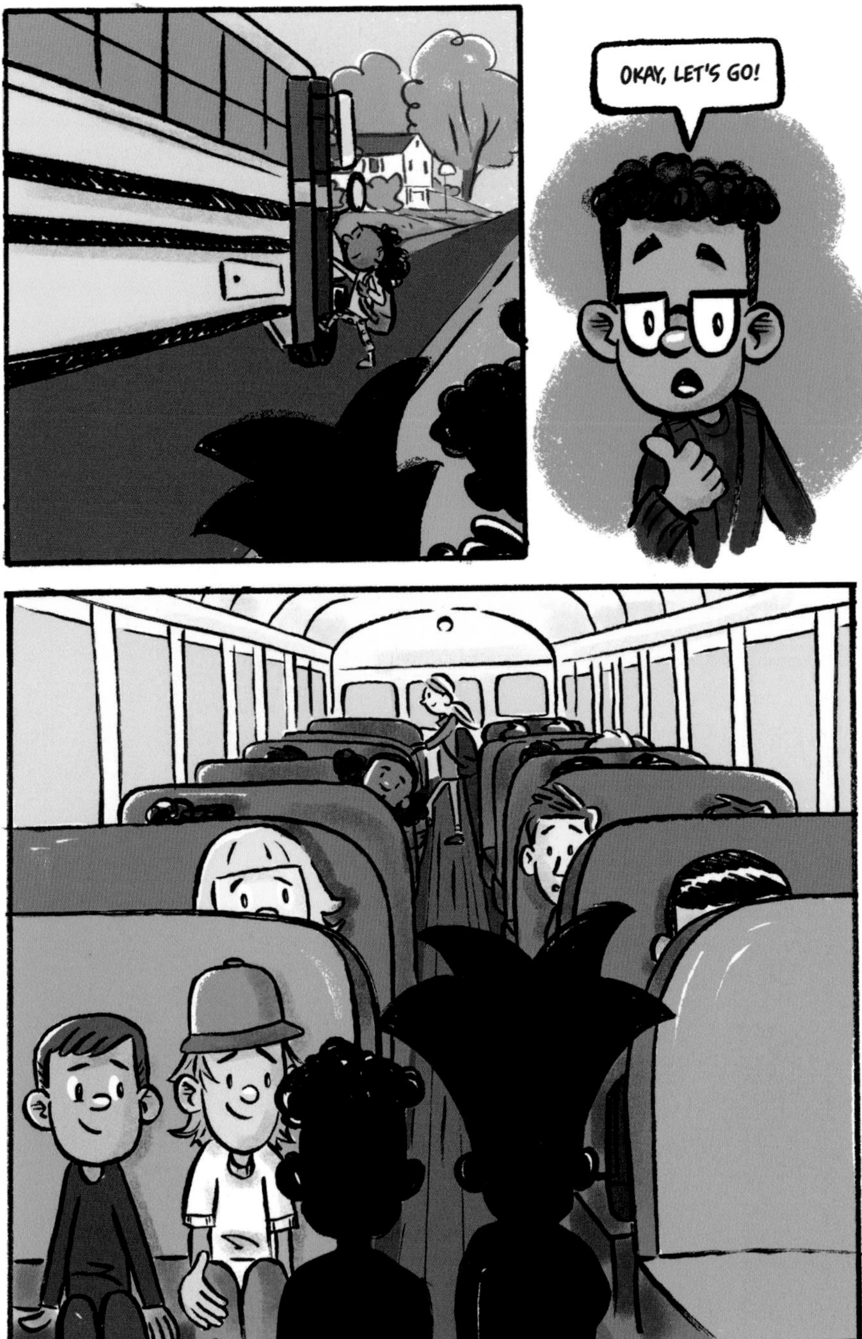
OKAY, LET'S GO!

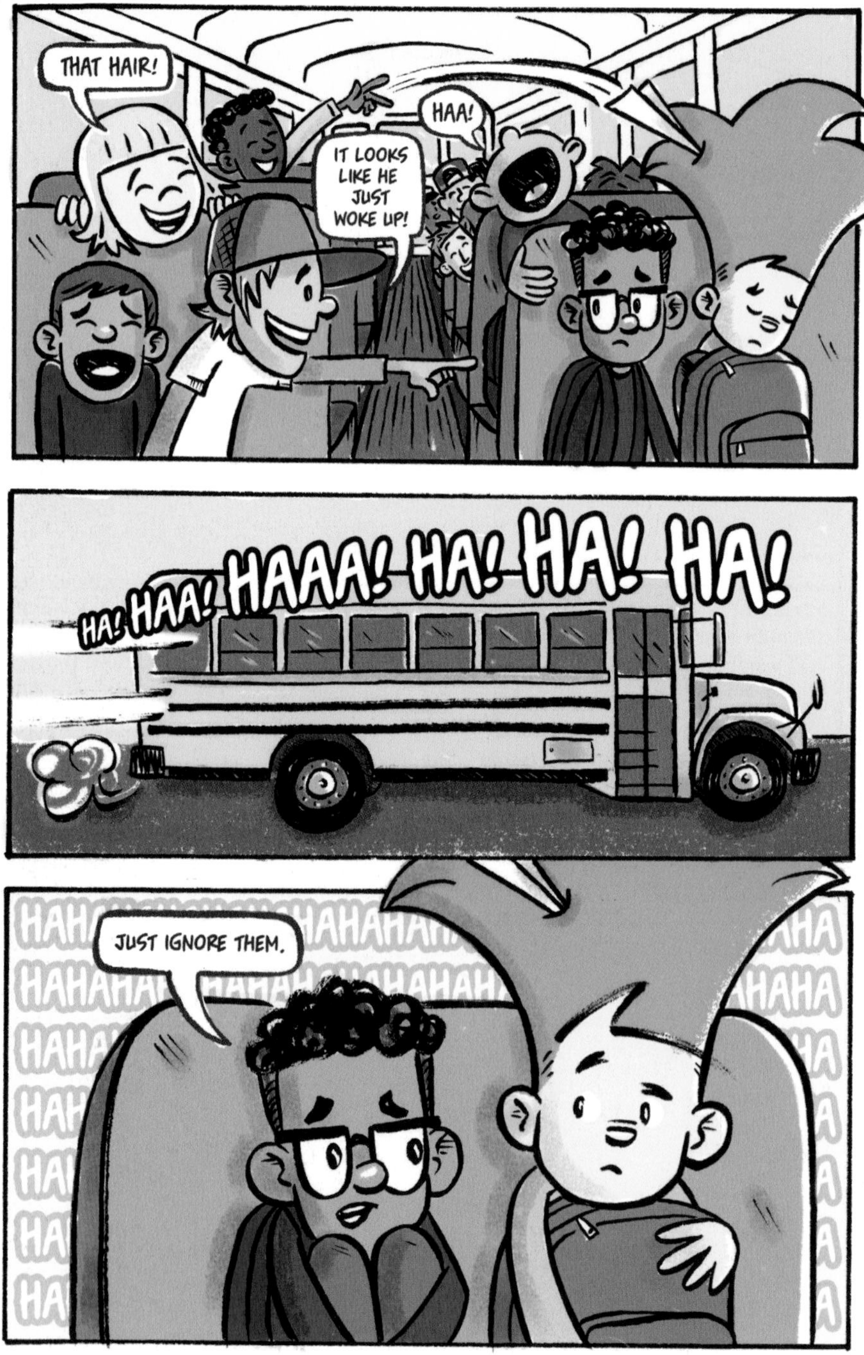
THAT HAIR!
IT LOOKS LIKE HE JUST WOKE UP!
HAA!
HA! HAA! HAAA! HA! HA! HA!
JUST IGNORE THEM.

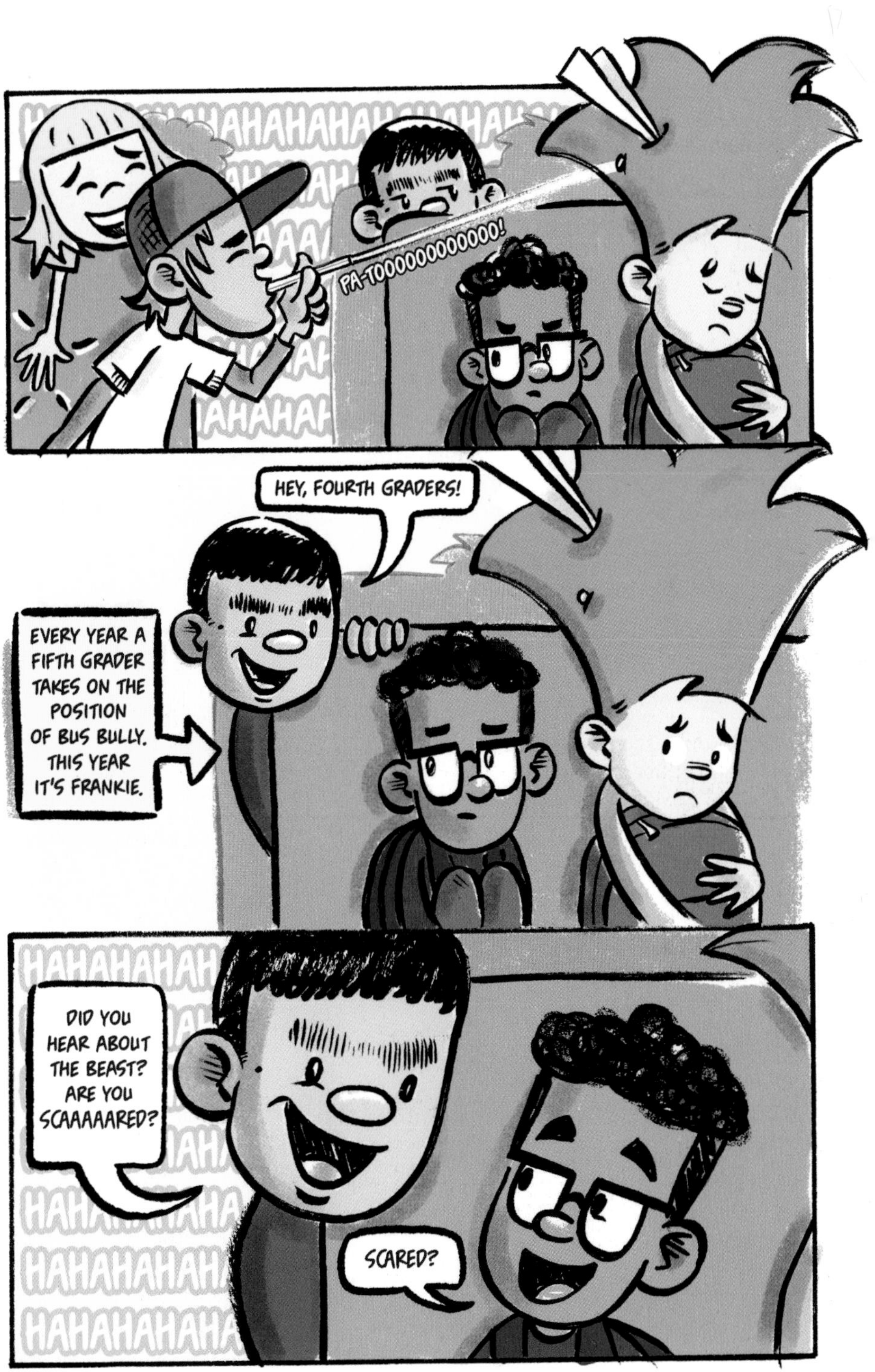
HAHAHAHAHAHAHAHAHA
PA-TOOOOOOOOOOOOO!
HEY, FOURTH GRADERS!
EVERY YEAR A FIFTH GRADER TAKES ON THE POSITION OF BUS BULLY. THIS YEAR IT'S FRANKIE.
HAHAHAHAH
DID YOU HEAR ABOUT THE BEAST? ARE YOU SCAAAAARED?
SCARED?
HAHAHAHAHA

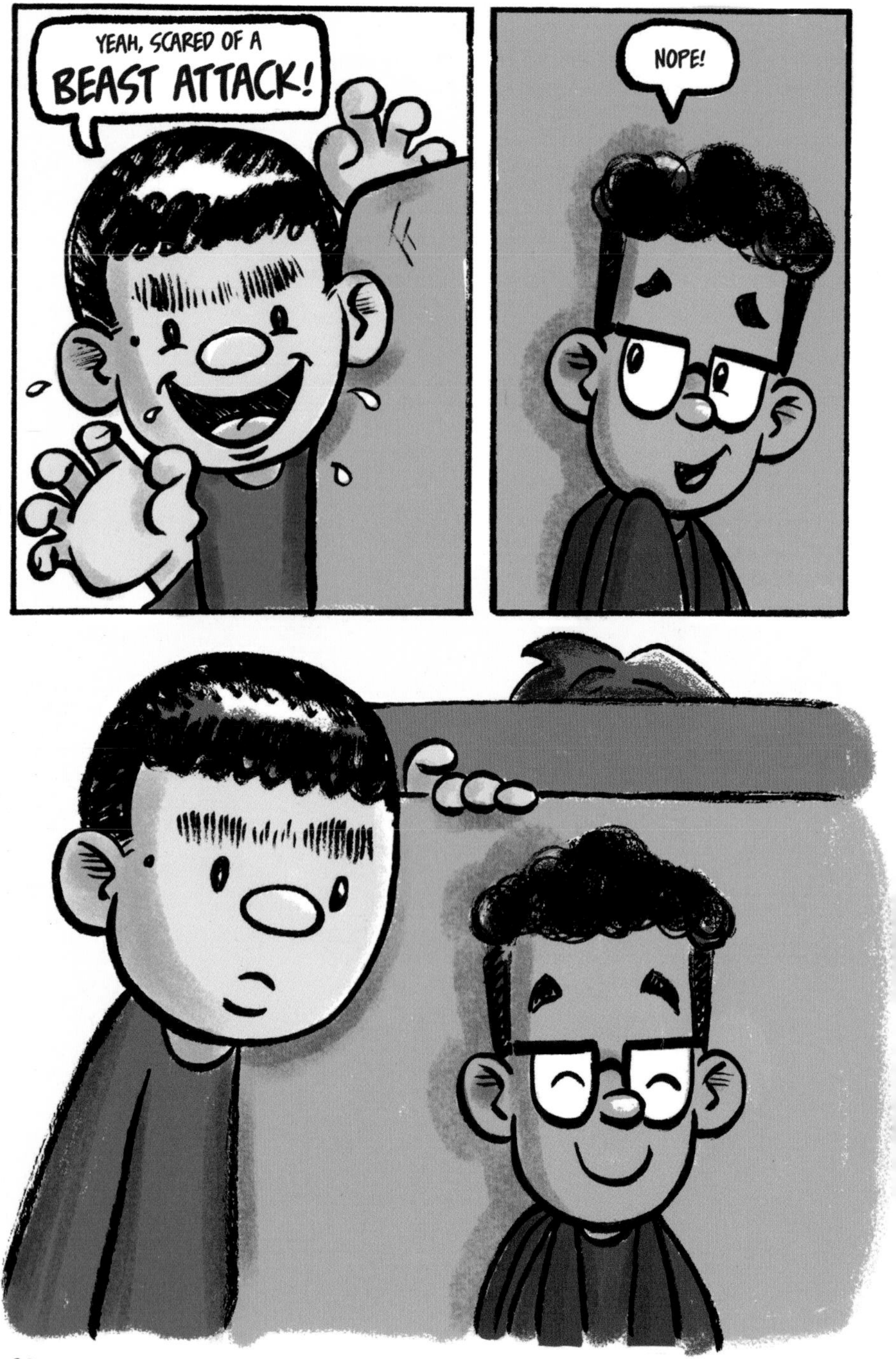
YEAH, SCARED OF A
BEAST ATTACK!
NOPE!

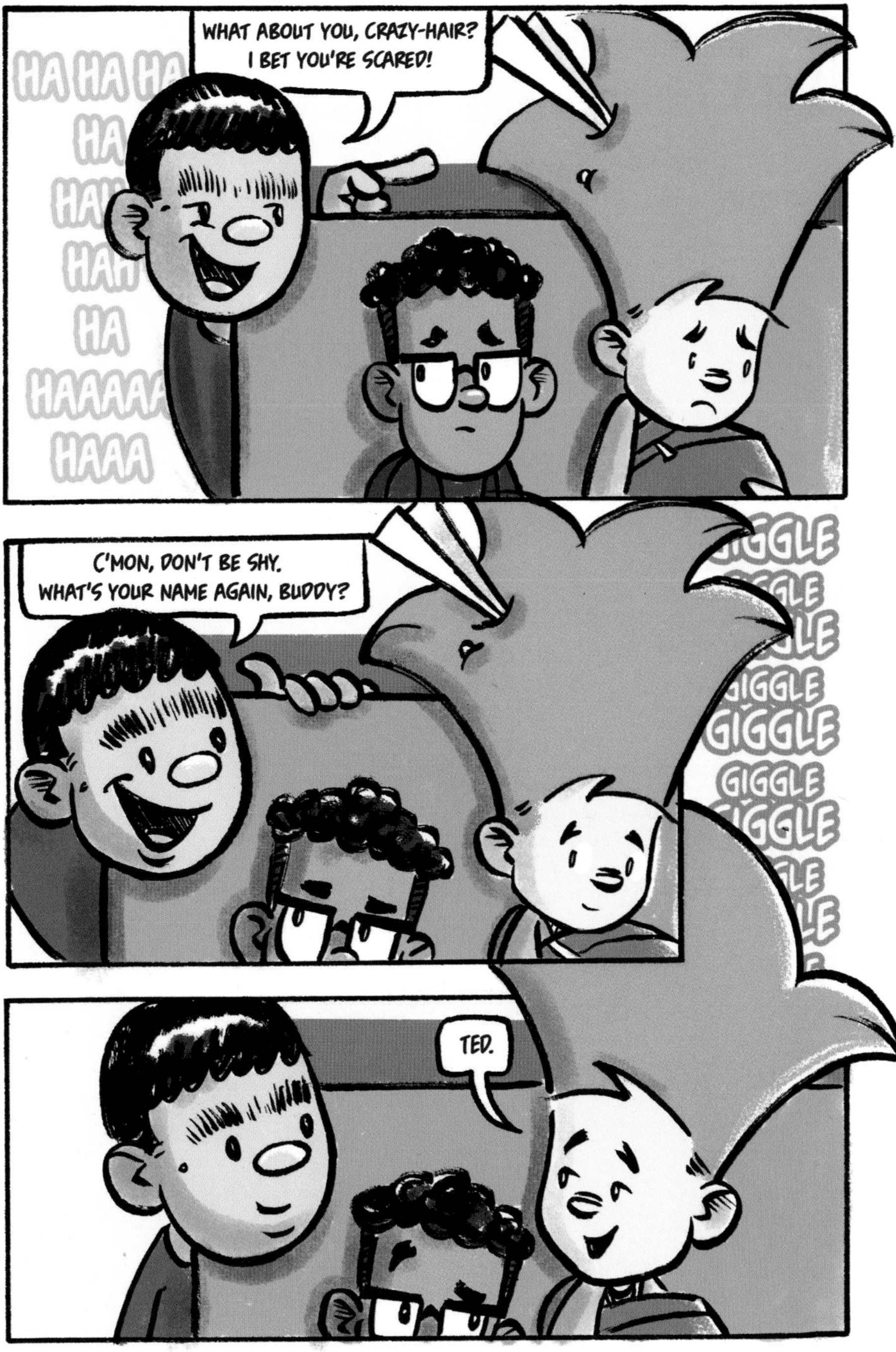
HA HA HA
HA
HA
HA
HA
HAAAAA
HAAA
WHAT ABOUT YOU, CRAZY-HAIR? I BET YOU'RE SCARED!
C'MON, DON'T BE SHY. WHAT'S YOUR NAME AGAIN, BUDDY?
GIGGLE
GIGGLE
GIGGLE
GIGGLE
TED.

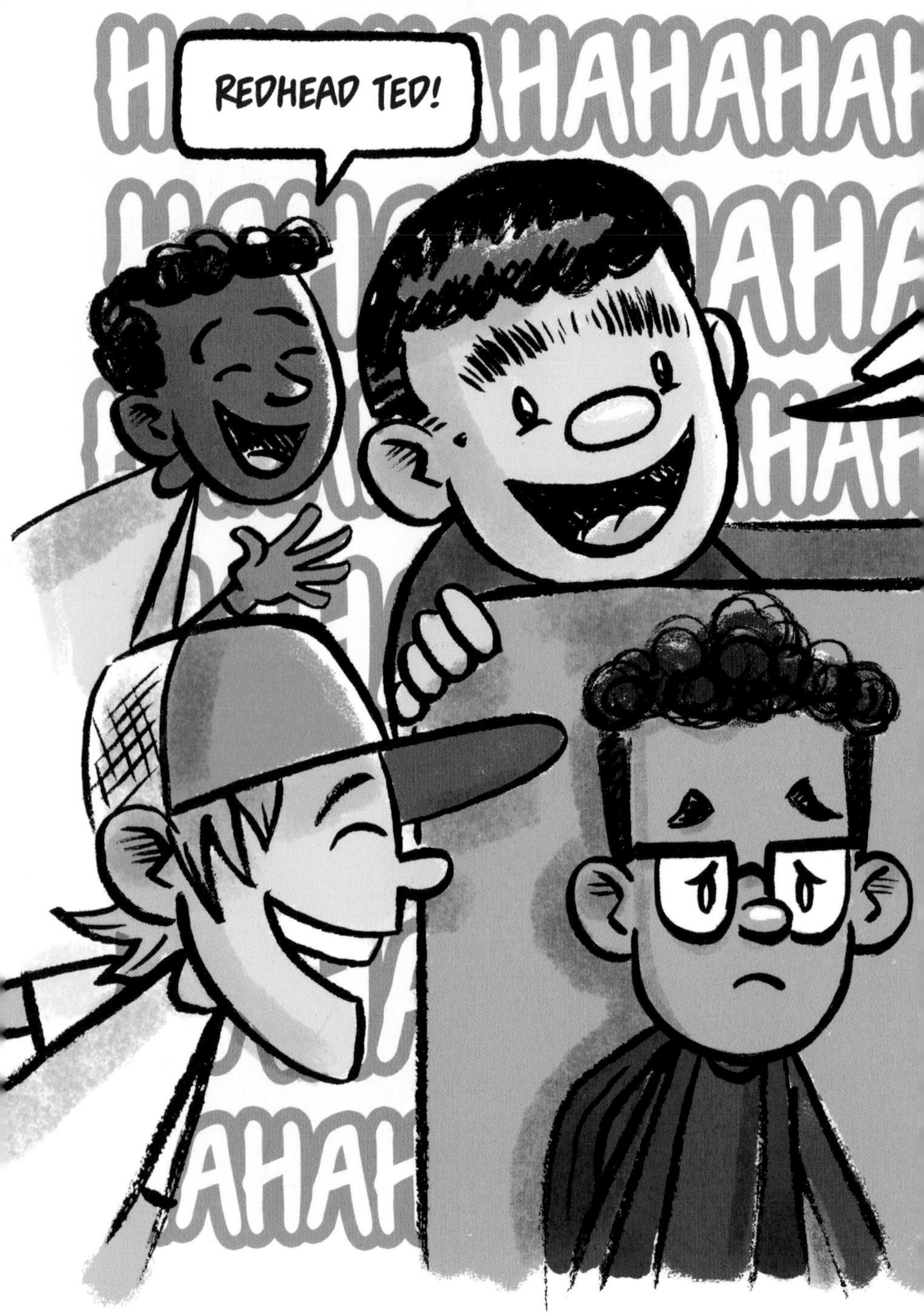
HAHAHAHAHAH
REDHEAD TED!
AHAH

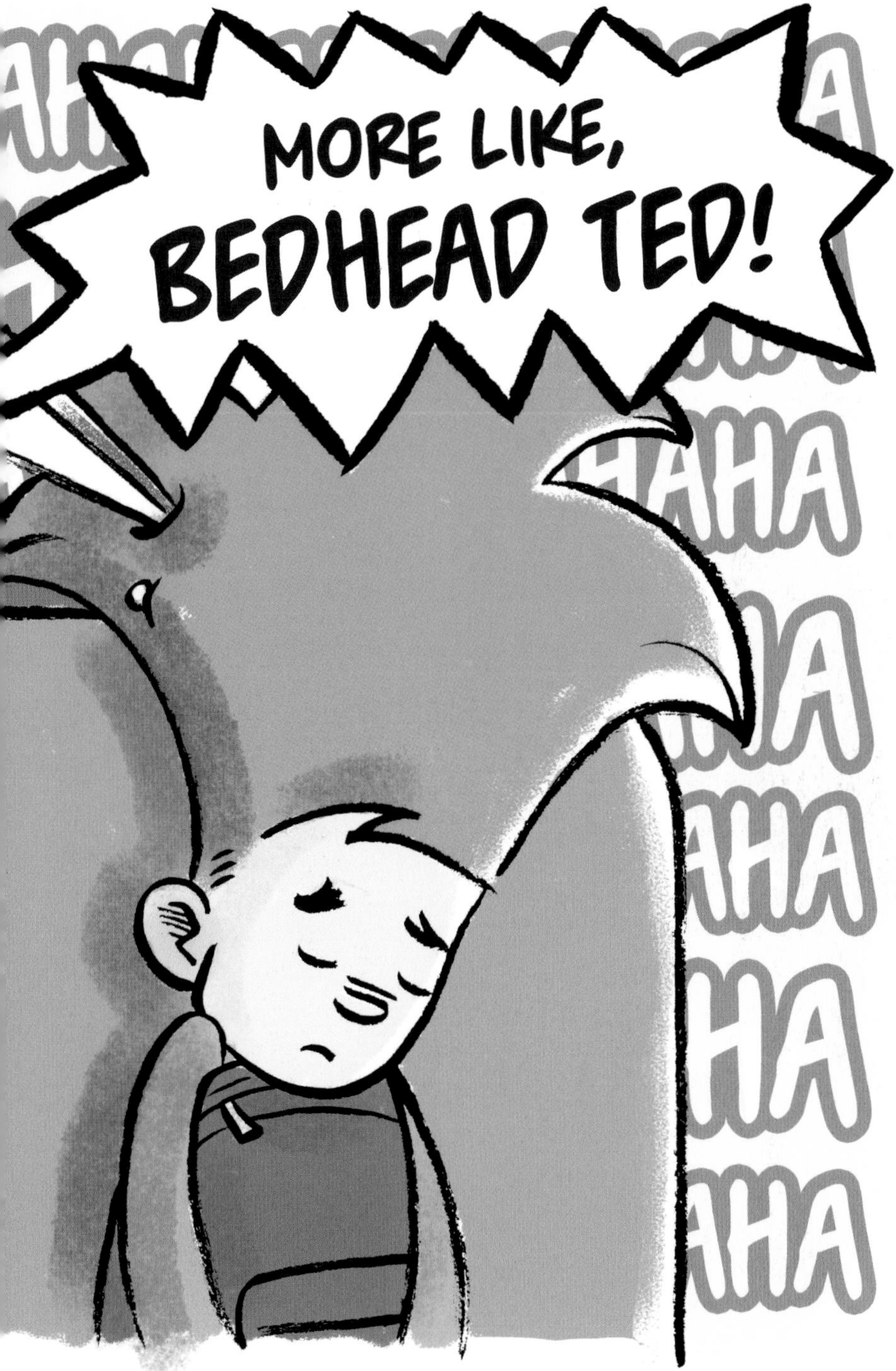
MORE LIKE,
BEDHEAD TED!
HAHA
HAHA
HAHA
HAHA
HAHA
HAHA

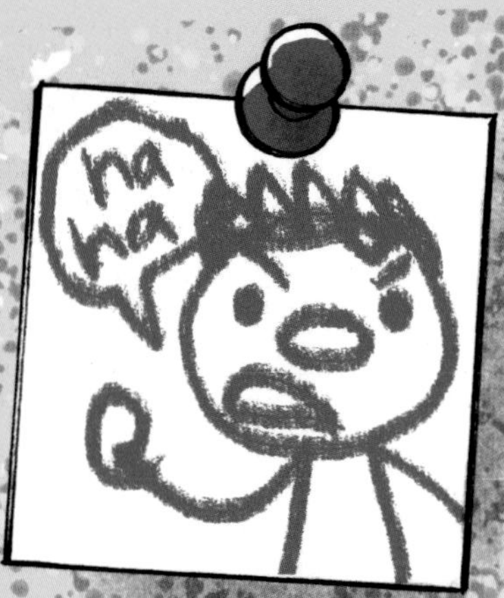
ha ha

CHAPTER 2:

SAME OLD, SAME OLD

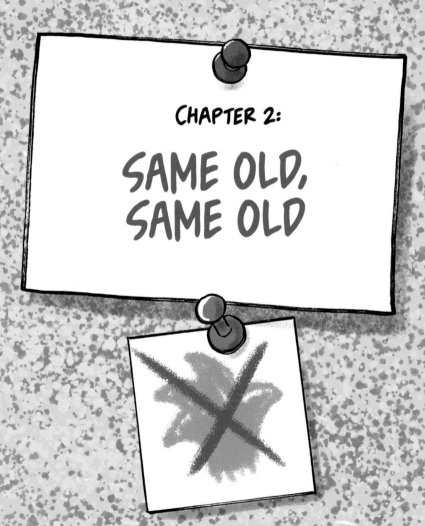

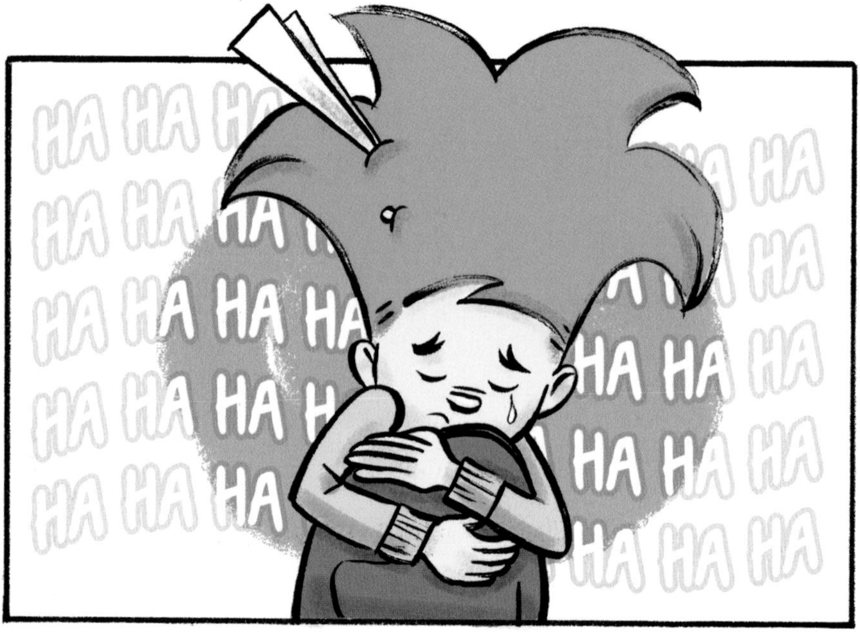
HA HA HA HA
HA HA HA HA
HA HA HA HA HA
HA HA HA HA HA
HA HA HA HA HA
HA HA HA

THIS WASN'T THE FIRST TIME I'D BEEN LAUGHED AT, BUT IT DIDN'T MAKE IT ANY EASIER. THIS HAS BEEN HAPPENING SINCE DAY ONE!

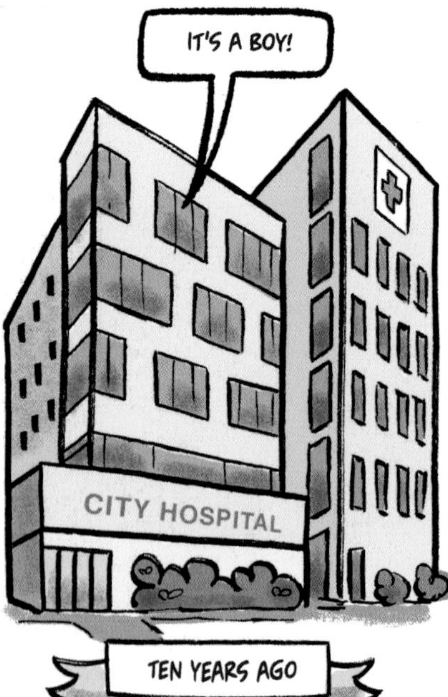
IT'S A BOY!
CITY HOSPITAL
TEN YEARS AGO

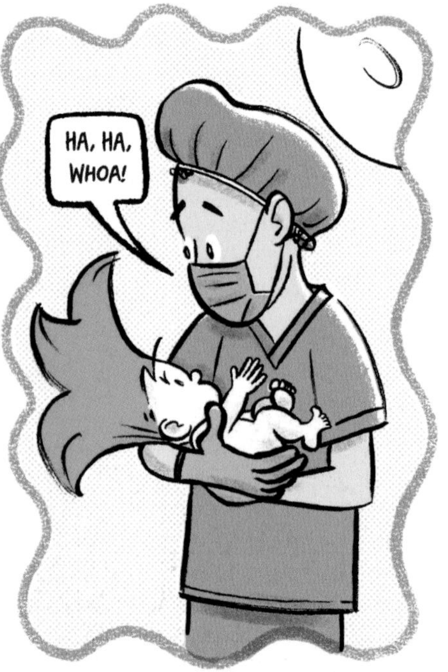
HA, HA, WHOA!

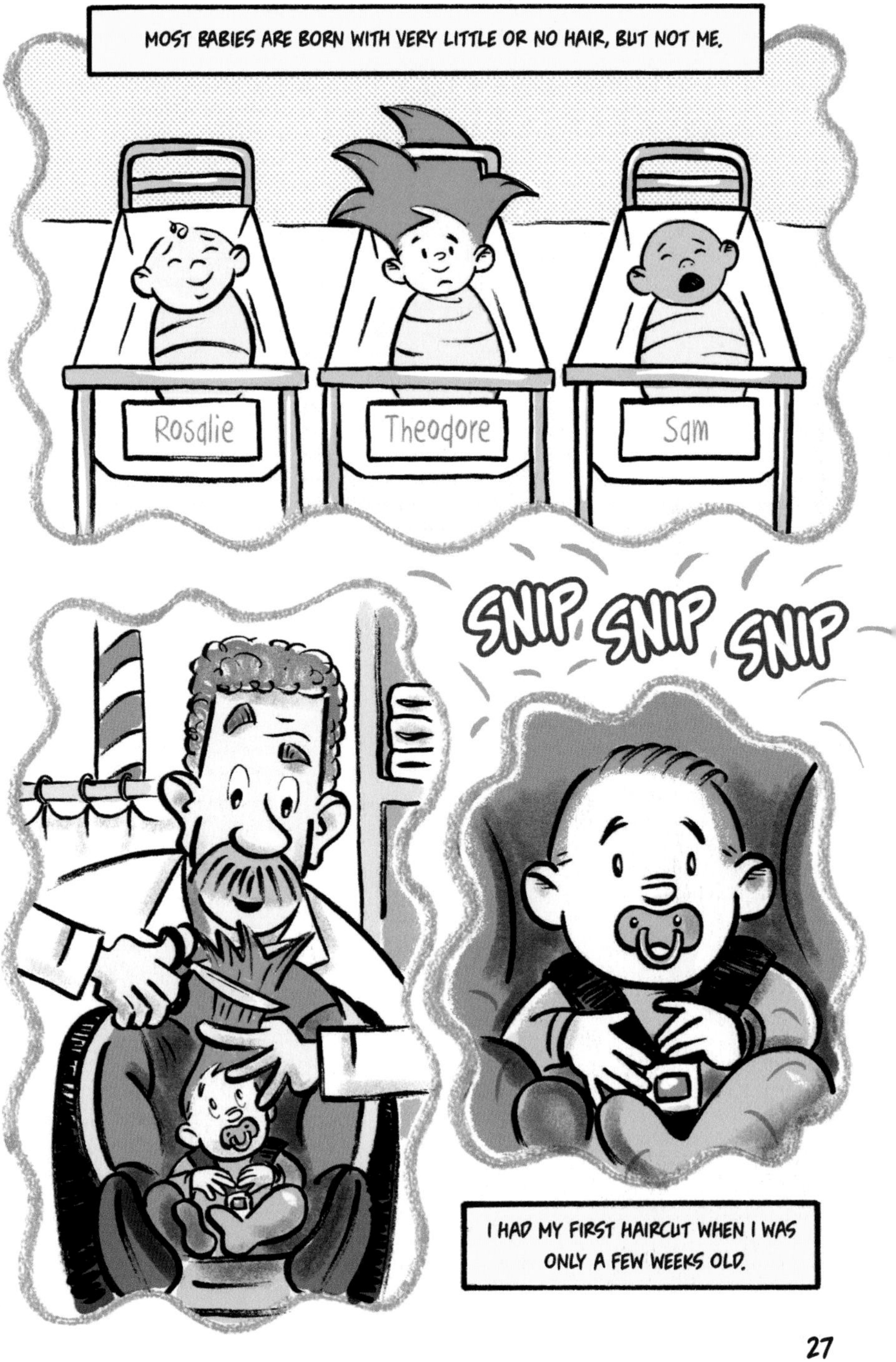
MOST BABIES ARE BORN WITH VERY LITTLE OR NO HAIR, BUT NOT ME.
Rosalie
Theodore
Sam
SNIP SNIP SNIP
I HAD MY FIRST HAIRCUT WHEN I WAS ONLY A FEW WEEKS OLD.

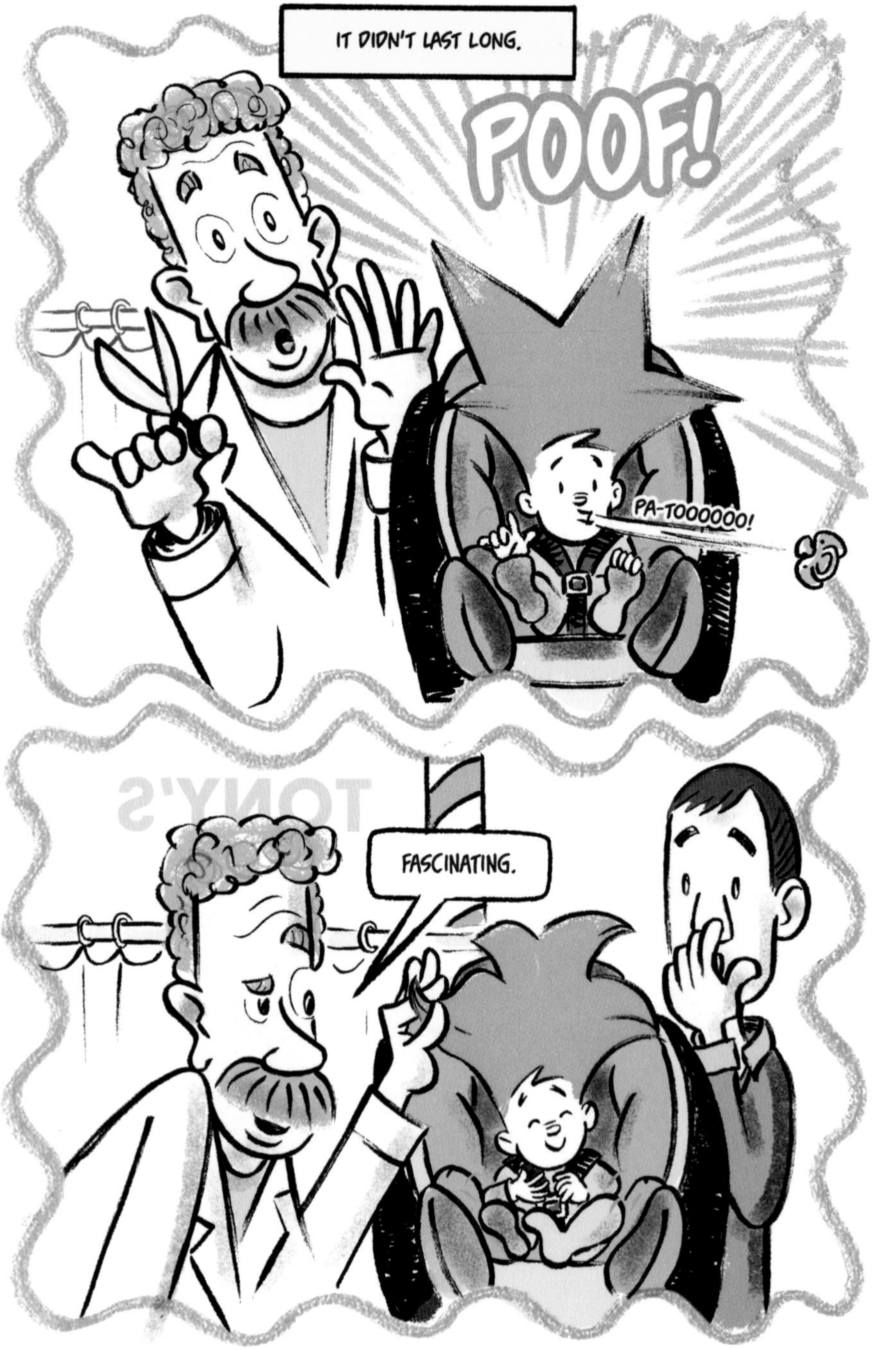
IT DIDN'T LAST LONG.
POOF!
PA-TOOOOOO!
TONY'S
FASCINATING.

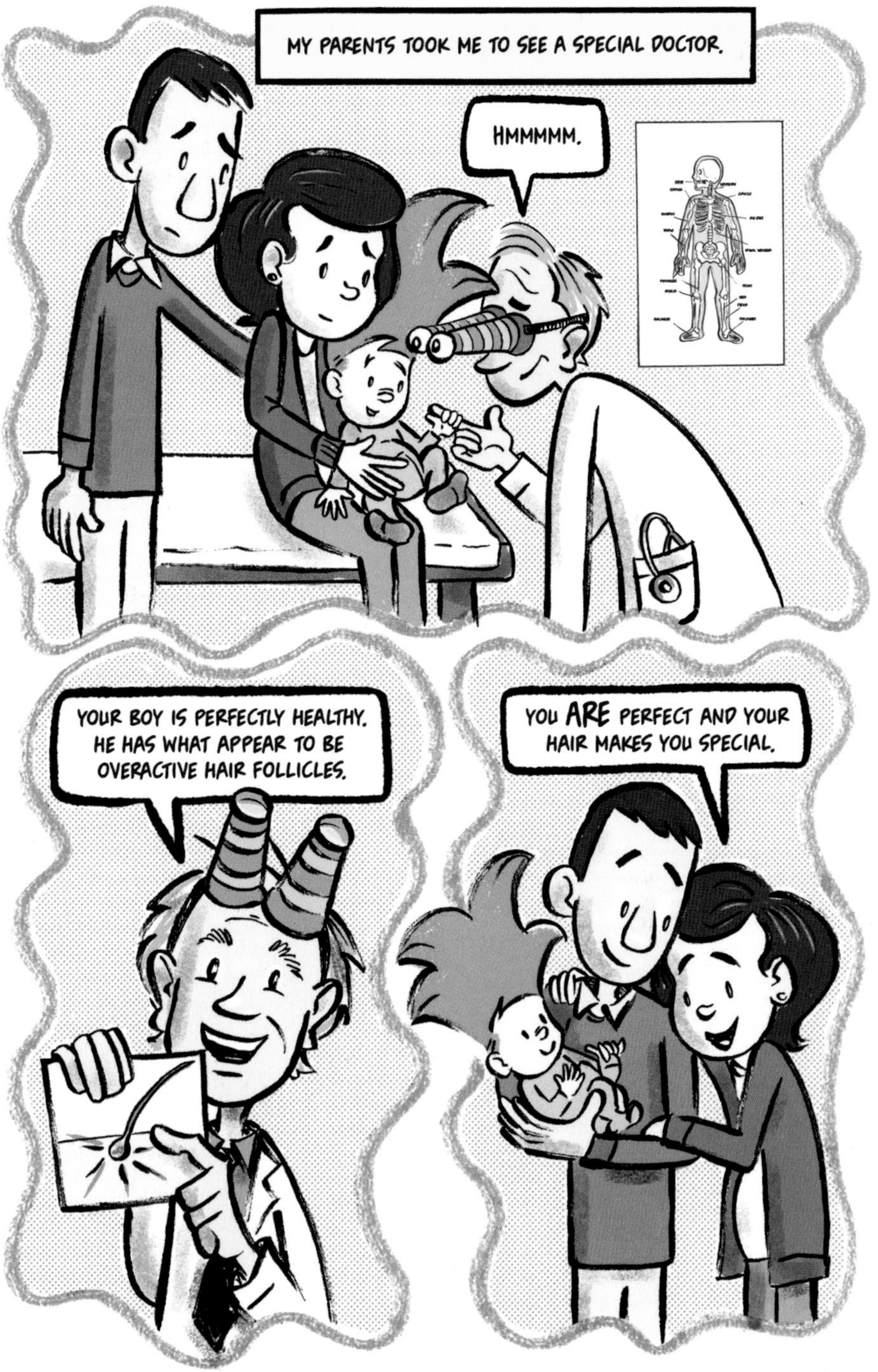
MY PARENTS TOOK ME TO SEE A SPECIAL DOCTOR.
HMMMMM.
YOUR BOY IS PERFECTLY HEALTHY. HE HAS WHAT APPEAR TO BE OVERACTIVE HAIR FOLLICLES.
YOU ARE PERFECT AND YOUR HAIR MAKES YOU SPECIAL.

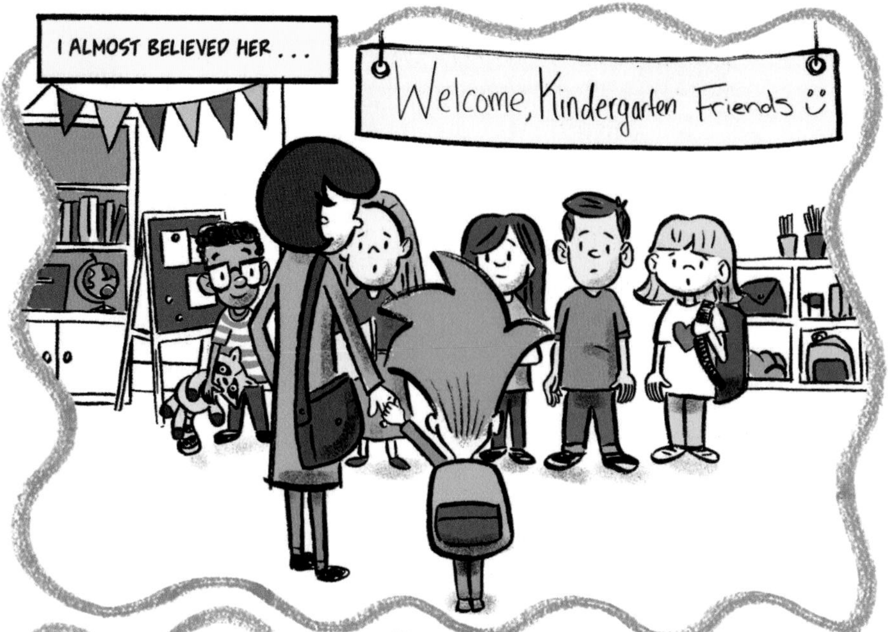
I ALMOST BELIEVED HER . . .
Welcome, Kindergarten Friends

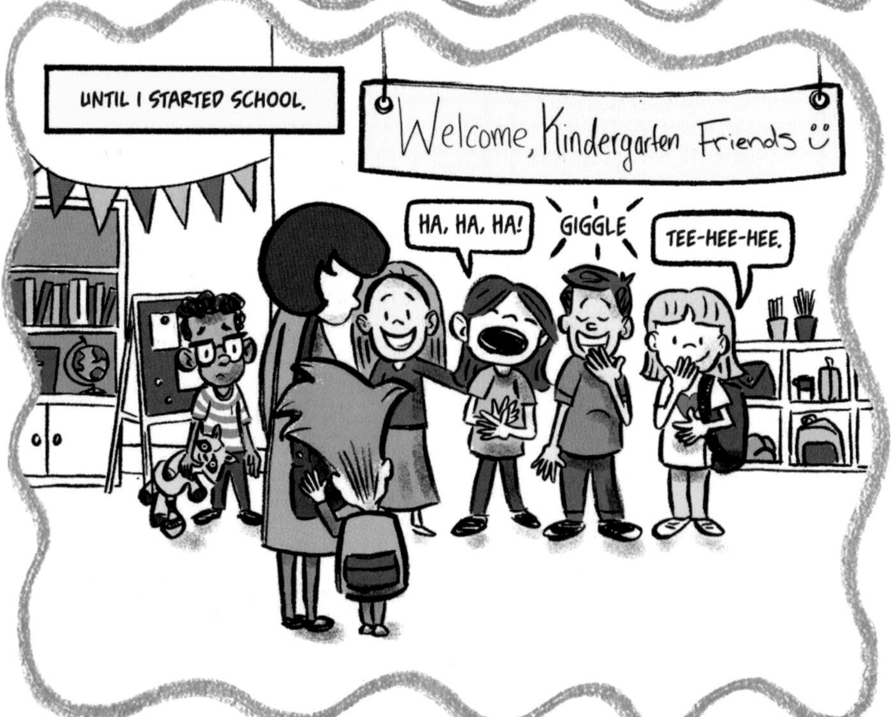
UNTIL I STARTED SCHOOL.
Welcome, Kindergarten Friends
HA, HA, HA!
GIGGLE
TEE-HEE-HEE.

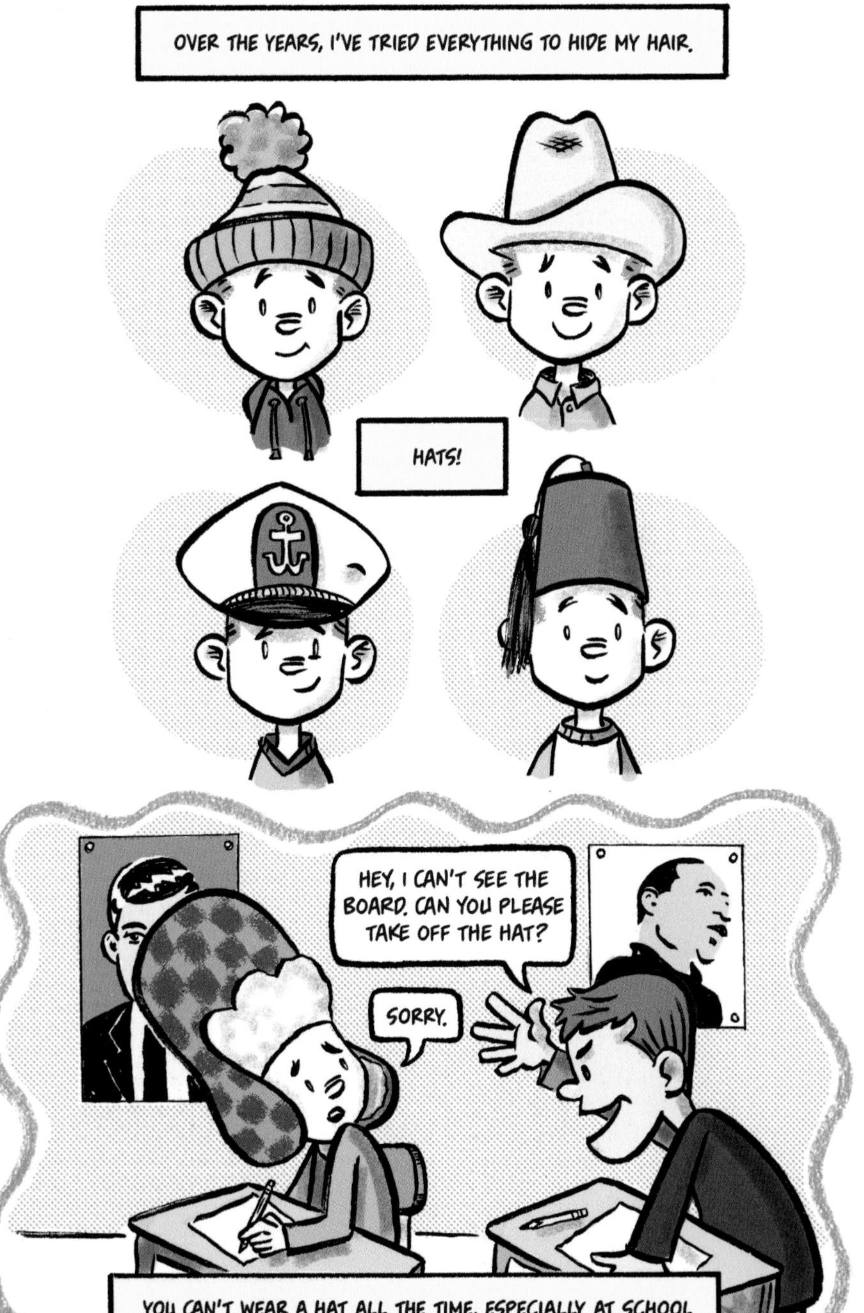
OVER THE YEARS, I'VE TRIED EVERYTHING TO HIDE MY HAIR.
HATS!
HEY, I CAN'T SEE THE BOARD. CAN YOU PLEASE TAKE OFF THE HAT?
SORRY.
YOU CAN'T WEAR A HAT ALL THE TIME, ESPECIALLY AT SCHOOL.

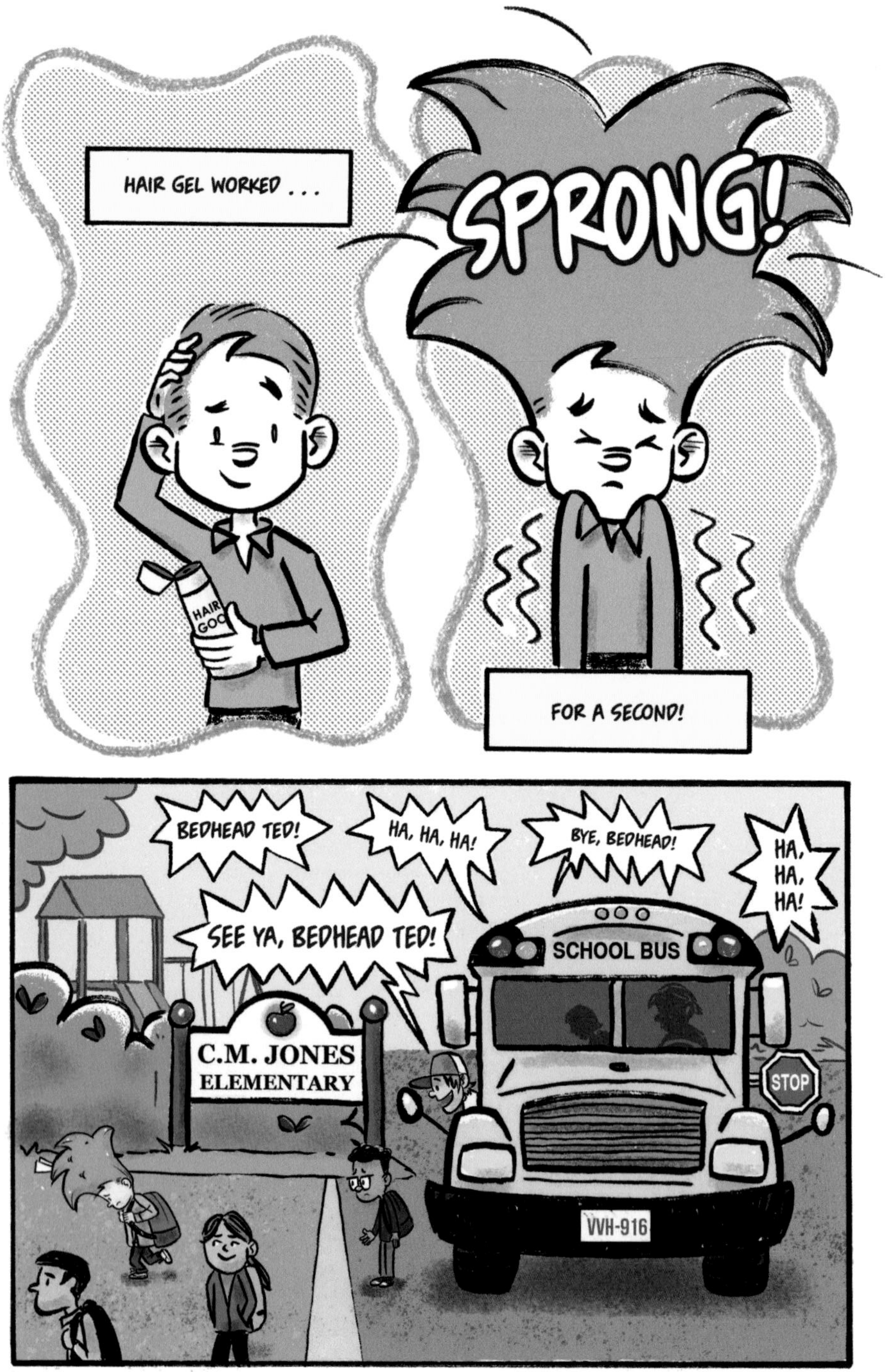

HAIR GEL WORKED . . .
HAIR GOO
SPRONG!
FOR A SECOND!
BEDHEAD TED!
HA, HA, HA!
BYE, BEDHEAD!
HA, HA, HA!
SEE YA, BEDHEAD TED!
SCHOOL BUS
C.M. JONES ELEMENTARY
STOP
VVH-916

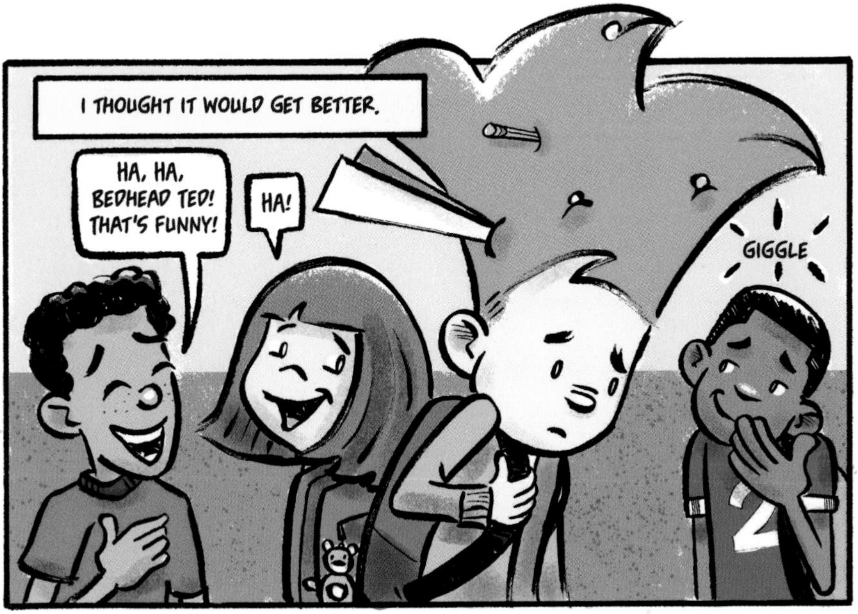
I THOUGHT IT WOULD GET BETTER.
HA, HA, BEDHEAD TED! THAT'S FUNNY!
HA!
GIGGLE

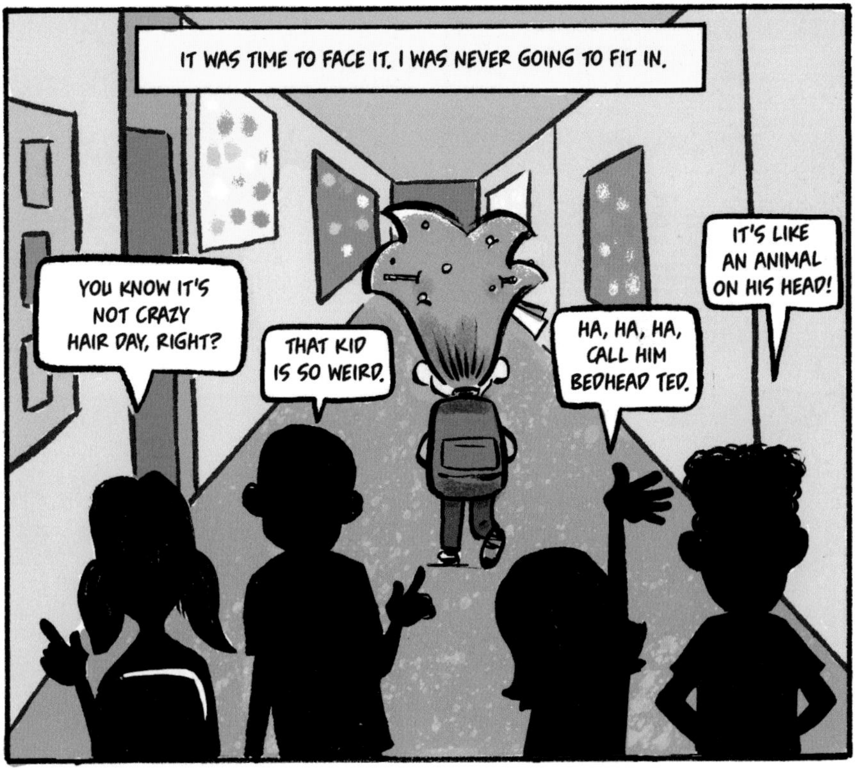
IT WAS TIME TO FACE IT. I WAS NEVER GOING TO FIT IN.
YOU KNOW IT'S NOT CRAZY HAIR DAY, RIGHT?
THAT KID IS SO WEIRD.
HA, HA, HA, CALL HIM BEDHEAD TED.
IT'S LIKE AN ANIMAL ON HIS HEAD!

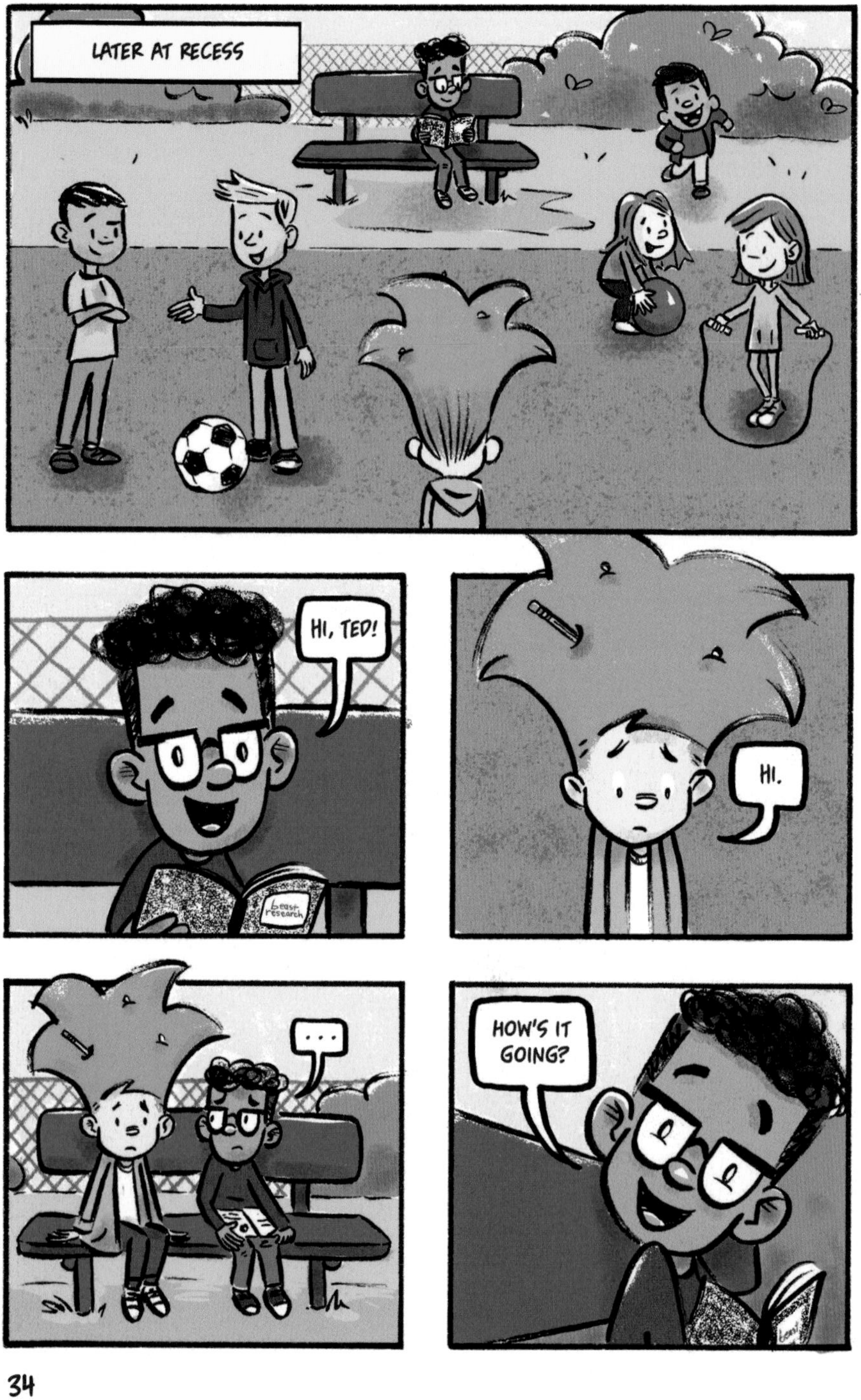
LATER AT RECESS
HI, TED!
HI.
...
beast research
HOW'S IT GOING?

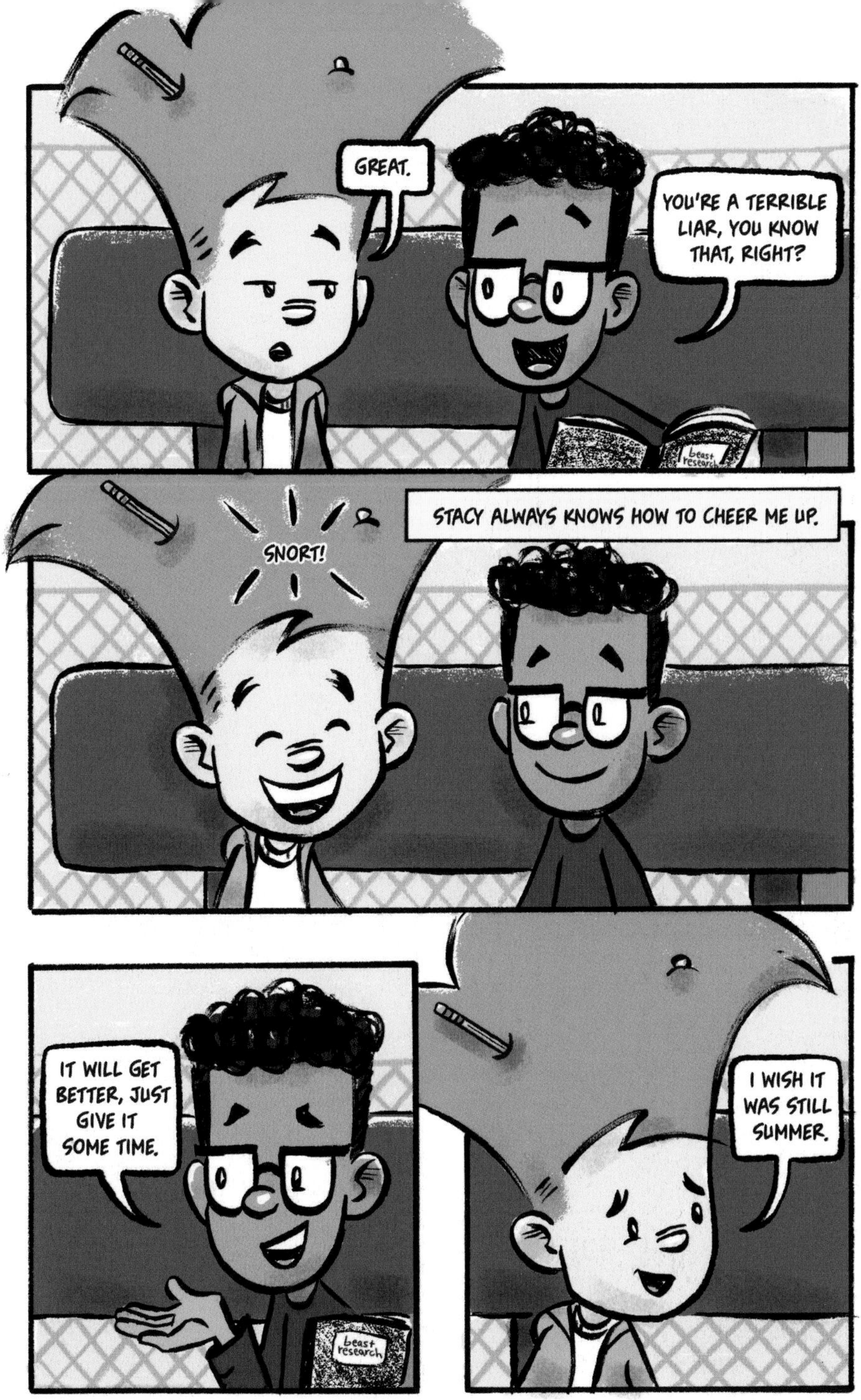
GREAT.
YOU'RE A TERRIBLE LIAR, YOU KNOW THAT, RIGHT?
beast research
STACY ALWAYS KNOWS HOW TO CHEER ME UP.
SNORT!
IT WILL GET BETTER, JUST GIVE IT SOME TIME.
beast research
I WISH IT WAS STILL SUMMER.

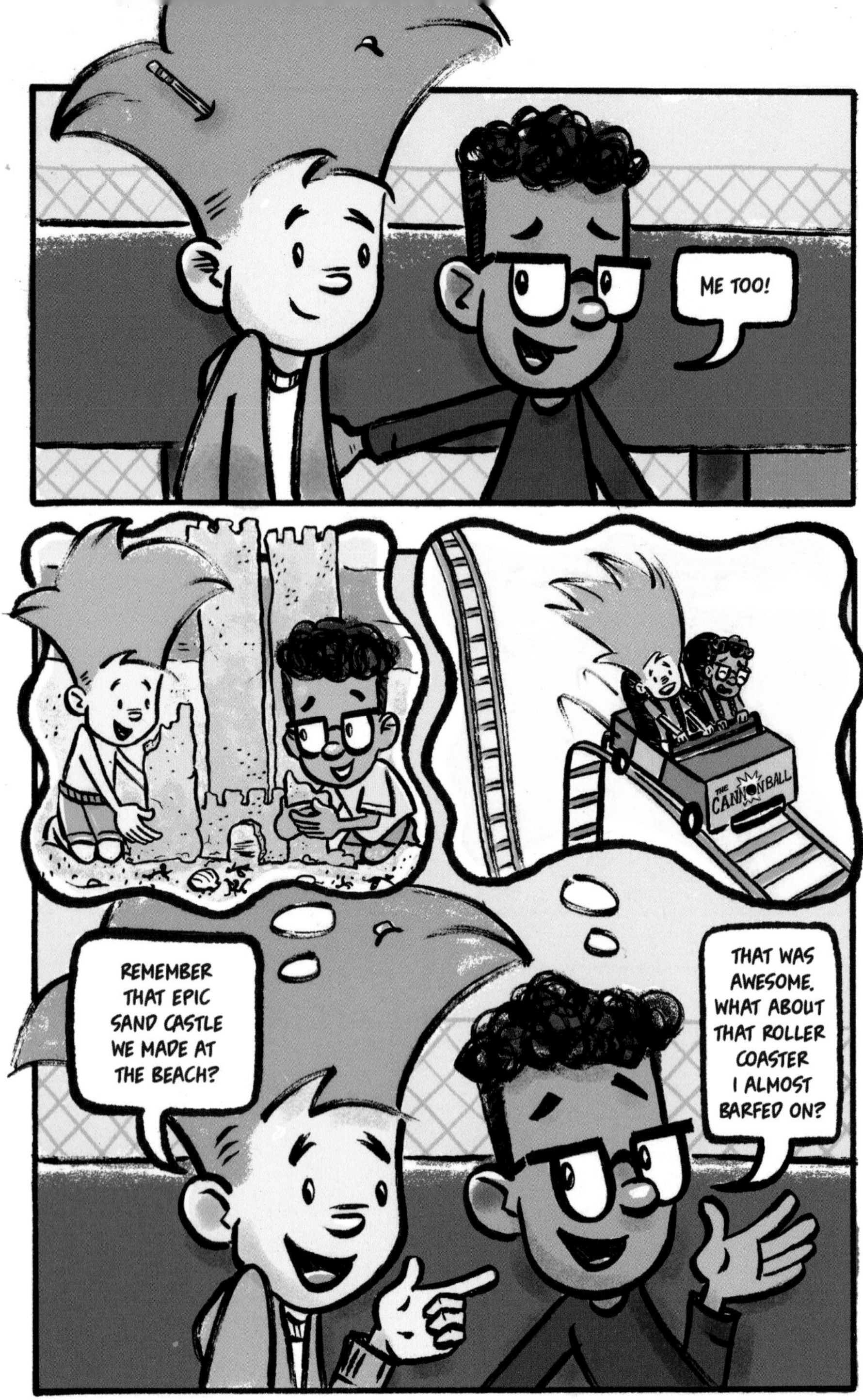
ME TOO!
THE CANNONBALL
REMEMBER THAT EPIC SAND CASTLE WE MADE AT THE BEACH?
THAT WAS AWESOME. WHAT ABOUT THAT ROLLER COASTER I ALMOST BARFED ON?

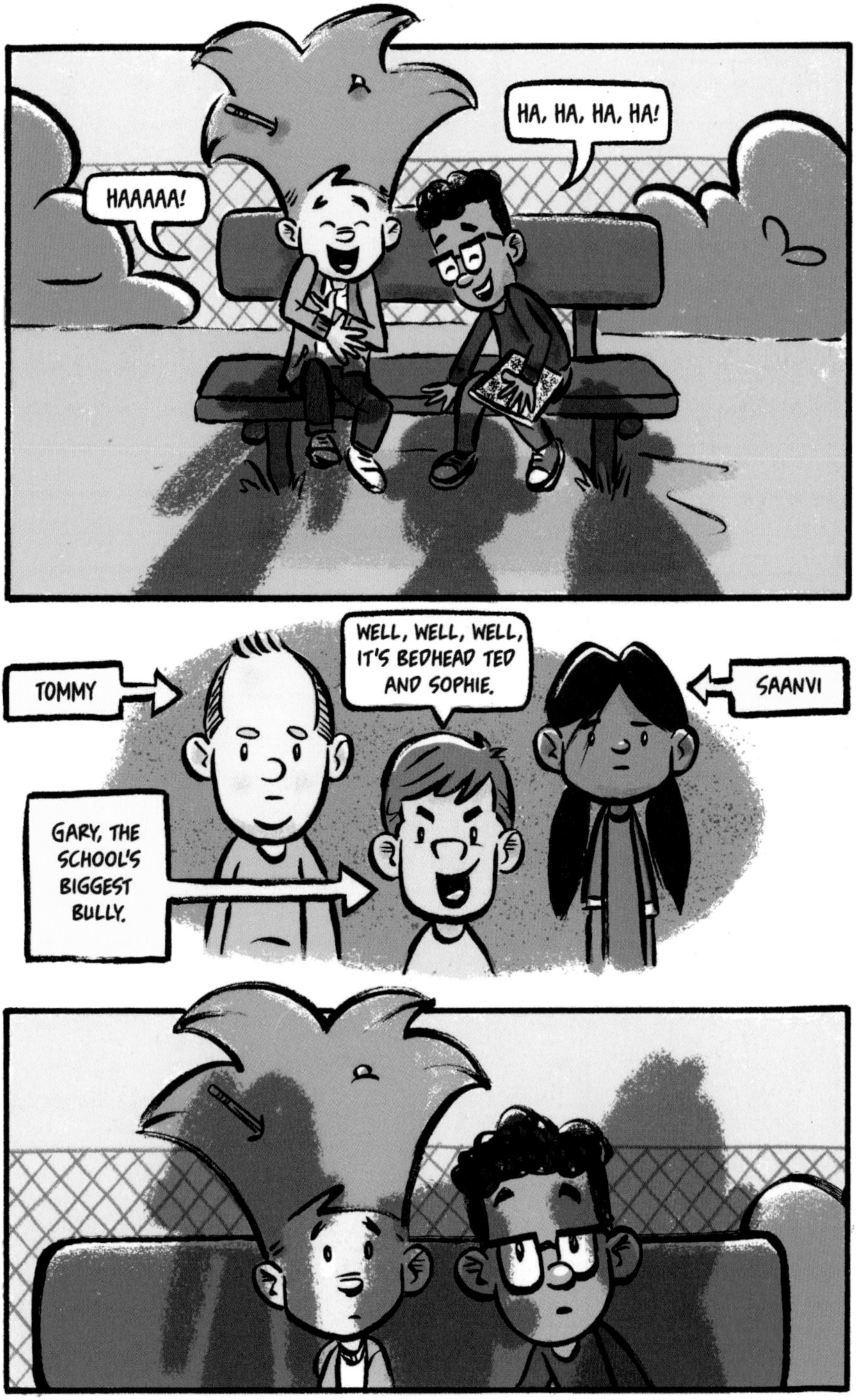
HAAAAA!
HA, HA, HA, HA!
TOMMY
WELL, WELL, WELL, IT'S BEDHEAD TED AND SOPHIE.
SAANVI
GARY, THE SCHOOL'S BIGGEST BULLY.

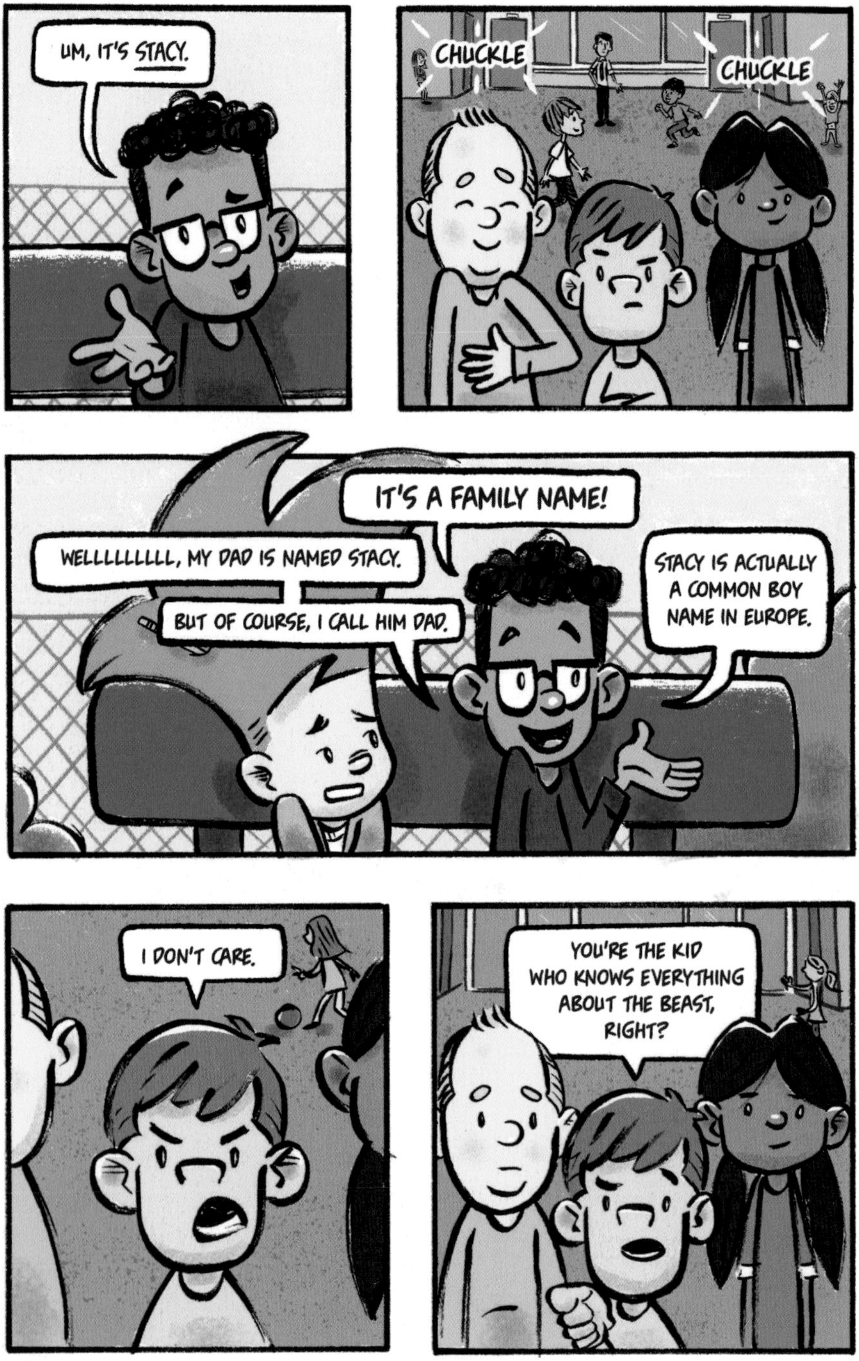
UM, IT'S STACY.
CHUCKLE
CHUCKLE
IT'S A FAMILY NAME!
WELLLLLLLLL, MY DAD IS NAMED STACY.
BUT OF COURSE, I CALL HIM DAD.
STACY IS ACTUALLY A COMMON BOY NAME IN EUROPE.
I DON'T CARE.
YOU'RE THE KID WHO KNOWS EVERYTHING ABOUT THE BEAST, RIGHT?

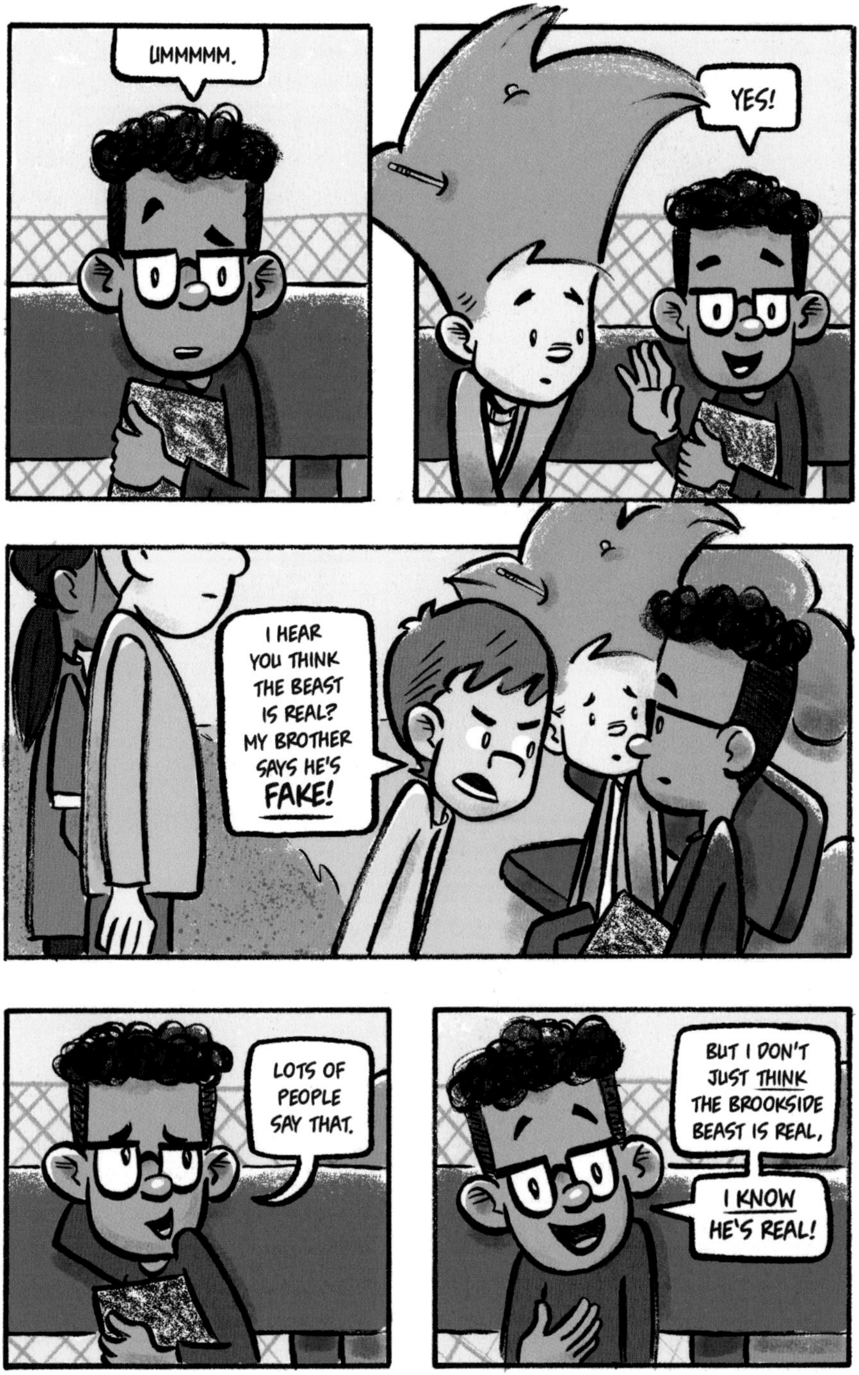
UMMMMM.
YES!
I HEAR YOU THINK THE BEAST IS REAL? MY BROTHER SAYS HE'S FAKE!
LOTS OF PEOPLE SAY THAT.
BUT I DON'T JUST THINK THE BROOKSIDE BEAST IS REAL,
I KNOW HE'S REAL!

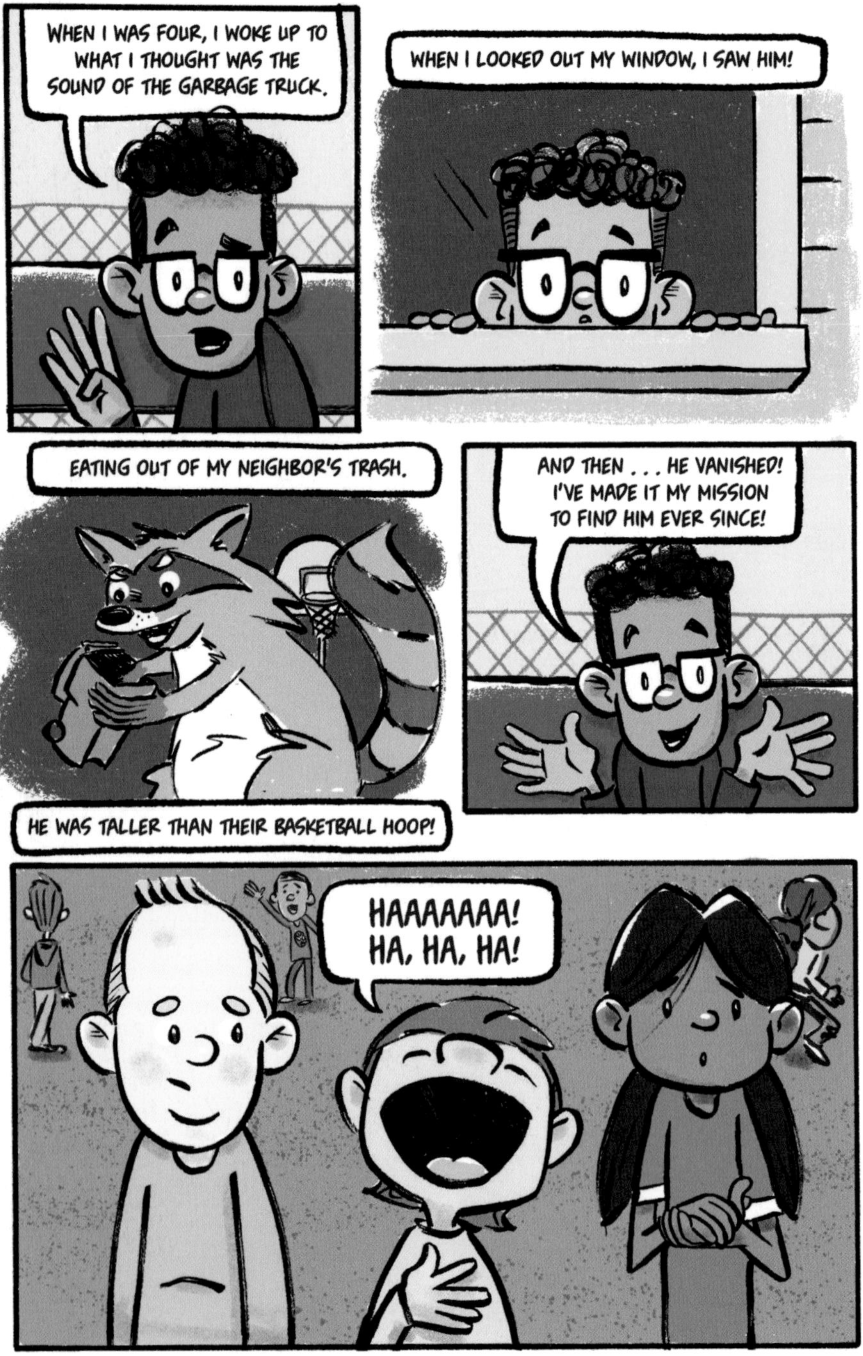
WHEN I WAS FOUR, I WOKE UP TO WHAT I THOUGHT WAS THE SOUND OF THE GARBAGE TRUCK.
WHEN I LOOKED OUT MY WINDOW, I SAW HIM!
EATING OUT OF MY NEIGHBOR'S TRASH.
HE WAS TALLER THAN THEIR BASKETBALL HOOP!
AND THEN . . . HE VANISHED! I'VE MADE IT MY MISSION TO FIND HIM EVER SINCE!
HAAAAAAA! HA, HA, HA!

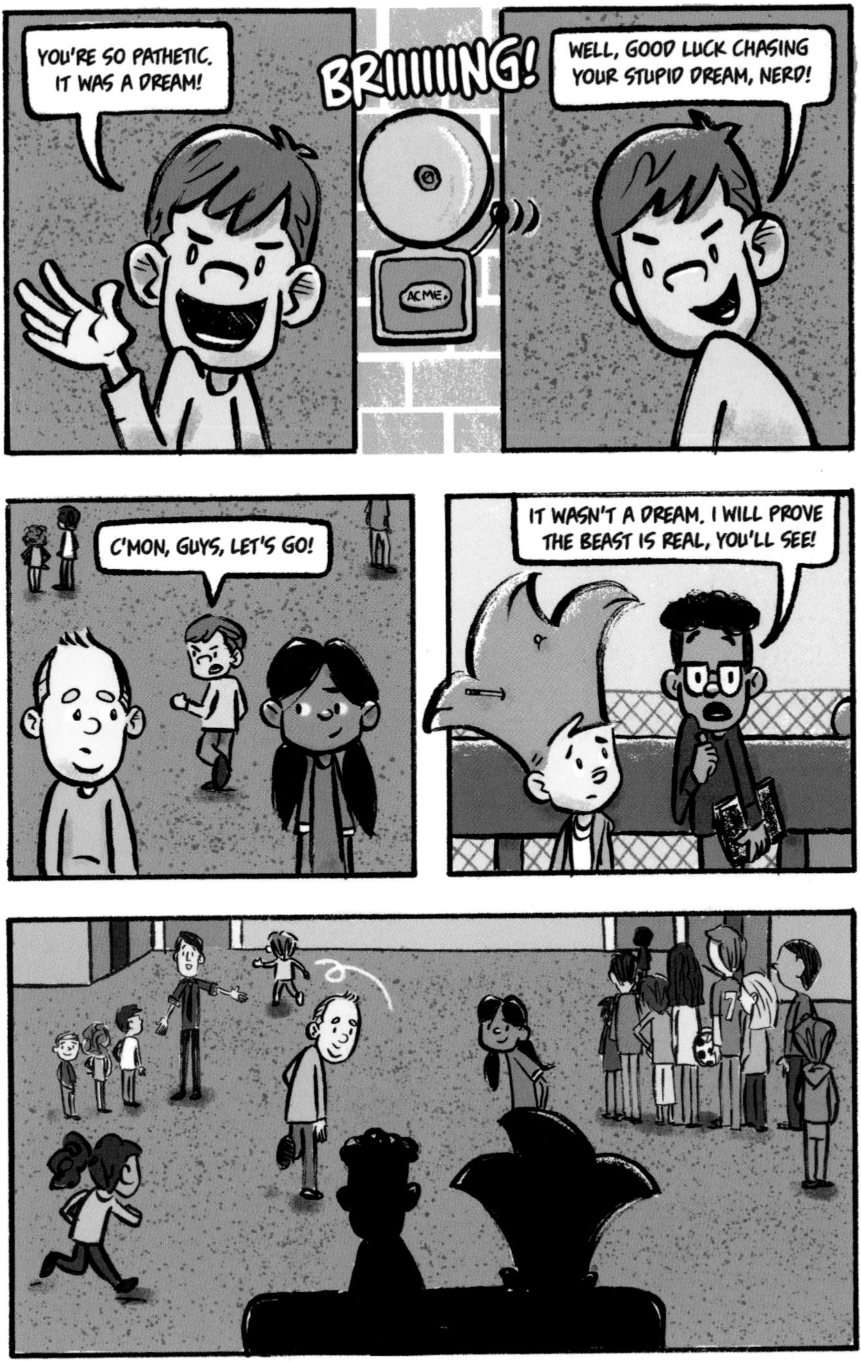
YOU'RE SO PATHETIC. IT WAS A DREAM!
BRIIIIIING!
ACME
WELL, GOOD LUCK CHASING YOUR STUPID DREAM, NERD!
C'MON, GUYS, LET'S GO!
IT WASN'T A DREAM. I WILL PROVE THE BEAST IS REAL, YOU'LL SEE!
7

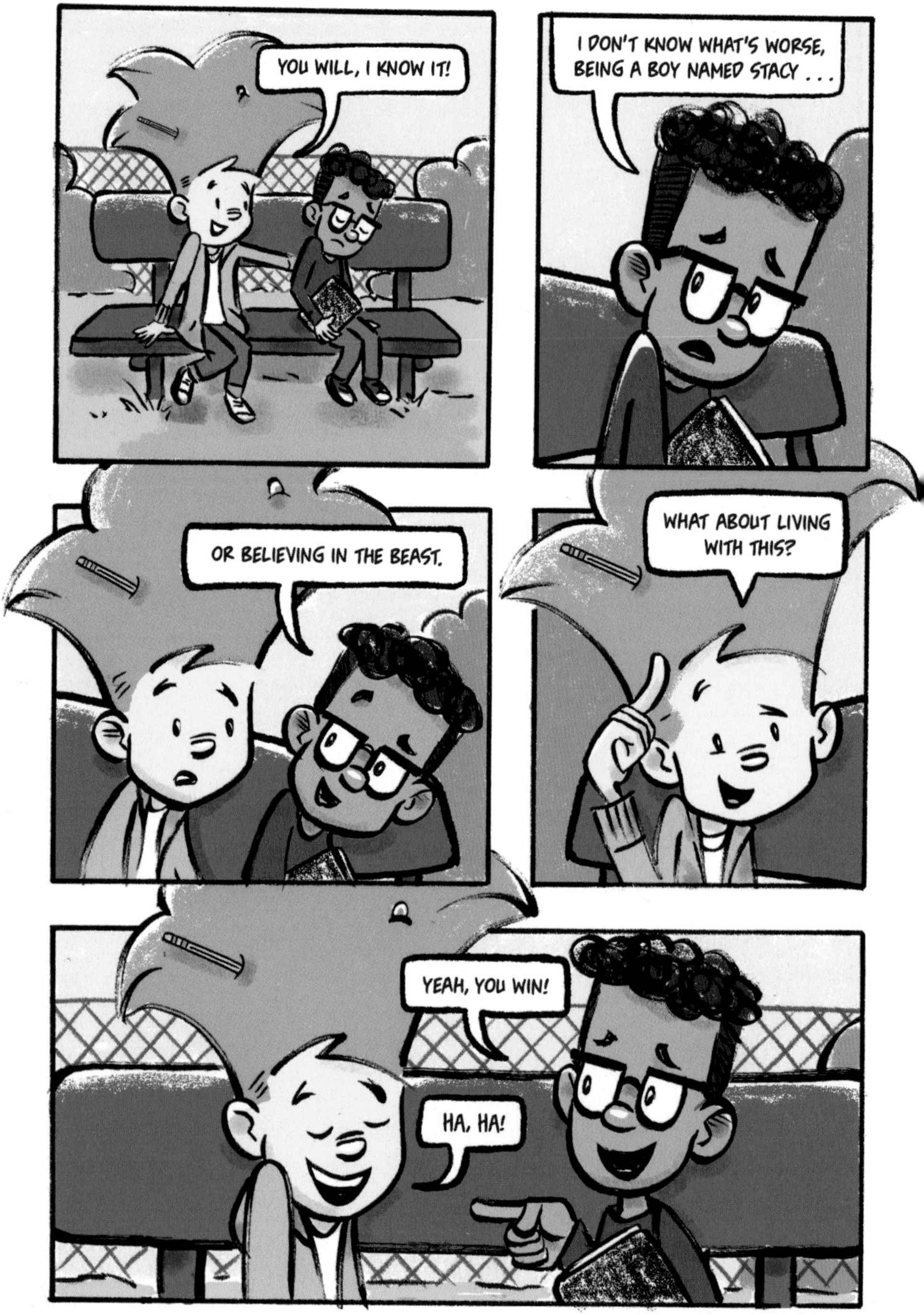
YOU WILL, I KNOW IT!
I DON'T KNOW WHAT'S WORSE, BEING A BOY NAMED STACY . . .
OR BELIEVING IN THE BEAST.
WHAT ABOUT LIVING WITH THIS?
YEAH, YOU WIN!
HA, HA!

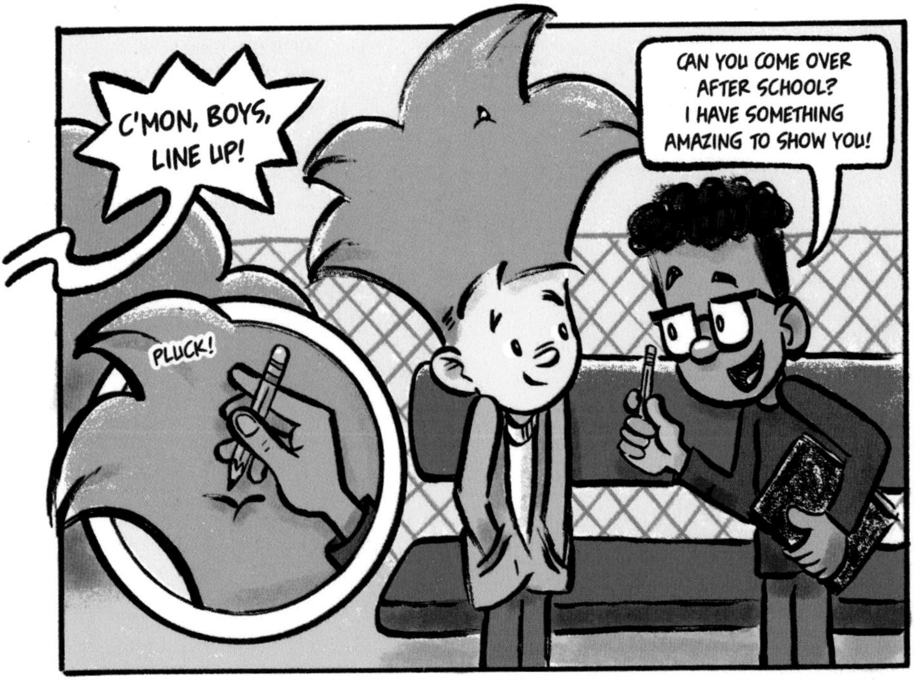
C'MON, BOYS, LINE UP!
CAN YOU COME OVER AFTER SCHOOL? I HAVE SOMETHING AMAZING TO SHOW YOU!
PLUCK!

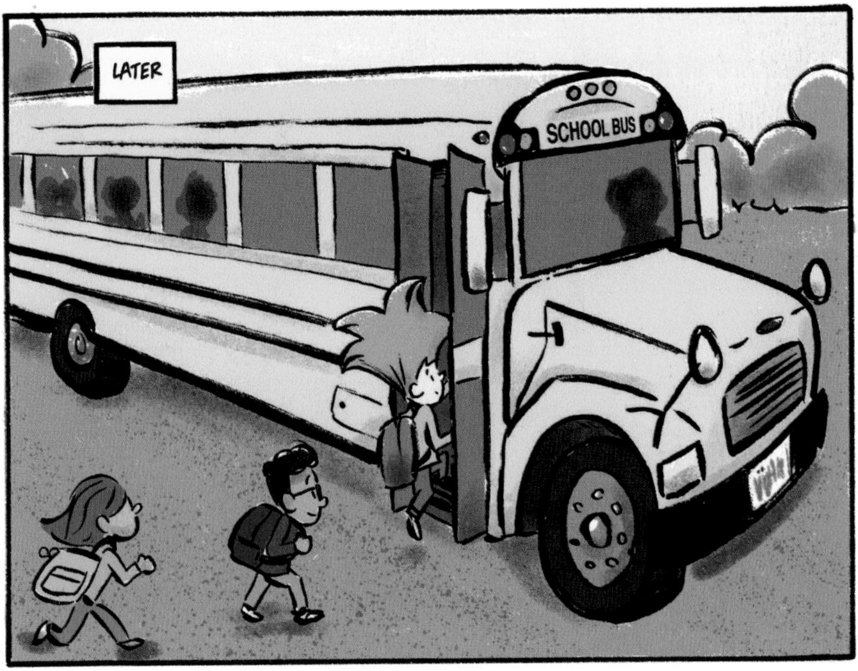
LATER
SCHOOL BUS

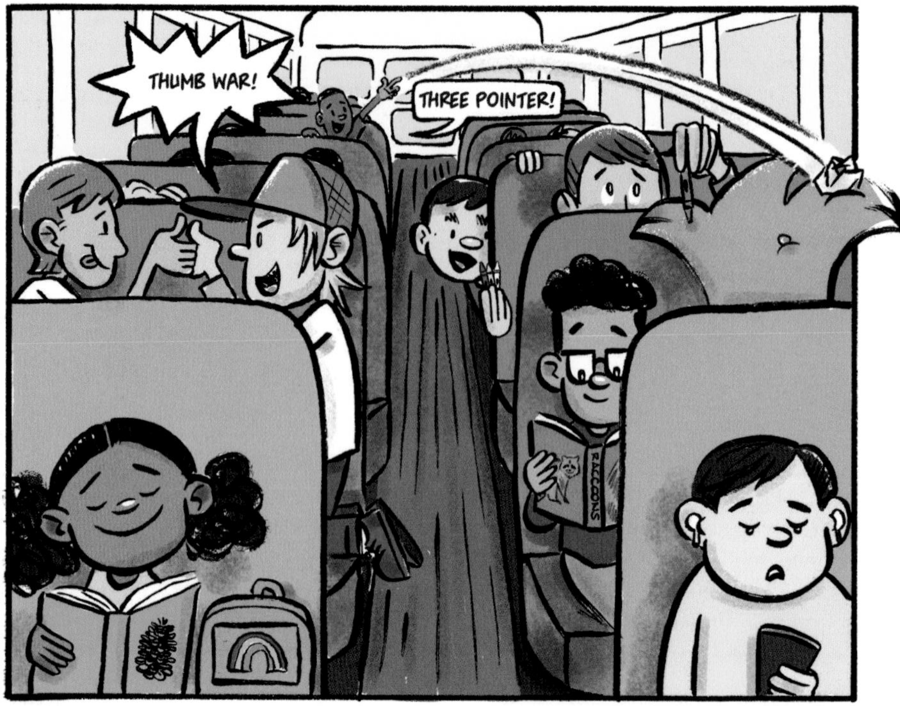
THUMB WAR!
THREE POINTER!

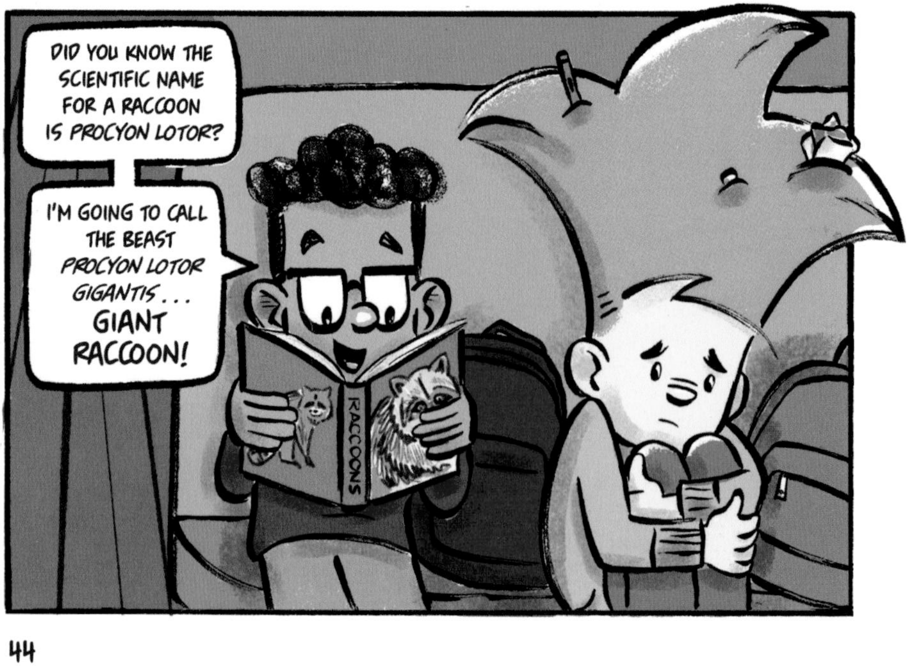
DID YOU KNOW THE SCIENTIFIC NAME FOR A RACCOON IS *PROCYON LOTOR*?
I'M GOING TO CALL THE BEAST *PROCYON LOTOR GIGANTIS* . . . GIANT RACCOON!
RACCOONS

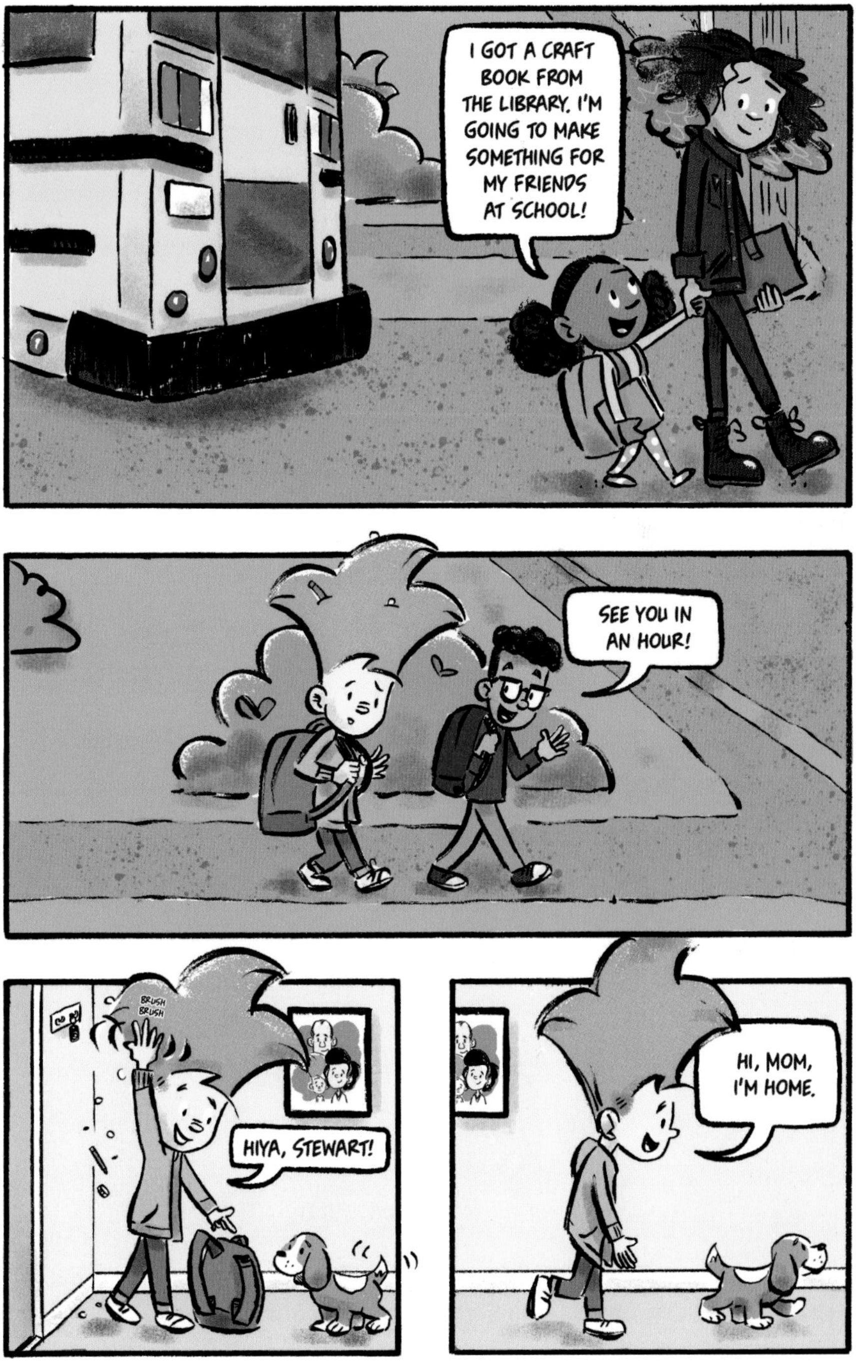
I GOT A CRAFT BOOK FROM THE LIBRARY. I'M GOING TO MAKE SOMETHING FOR MY FRIENDS AT SCHOOL!
SEE YOU IN AN HOUR!
BRUSH BRUSH
HIYA, STEWART!
HI, MOM, I'M HOME.

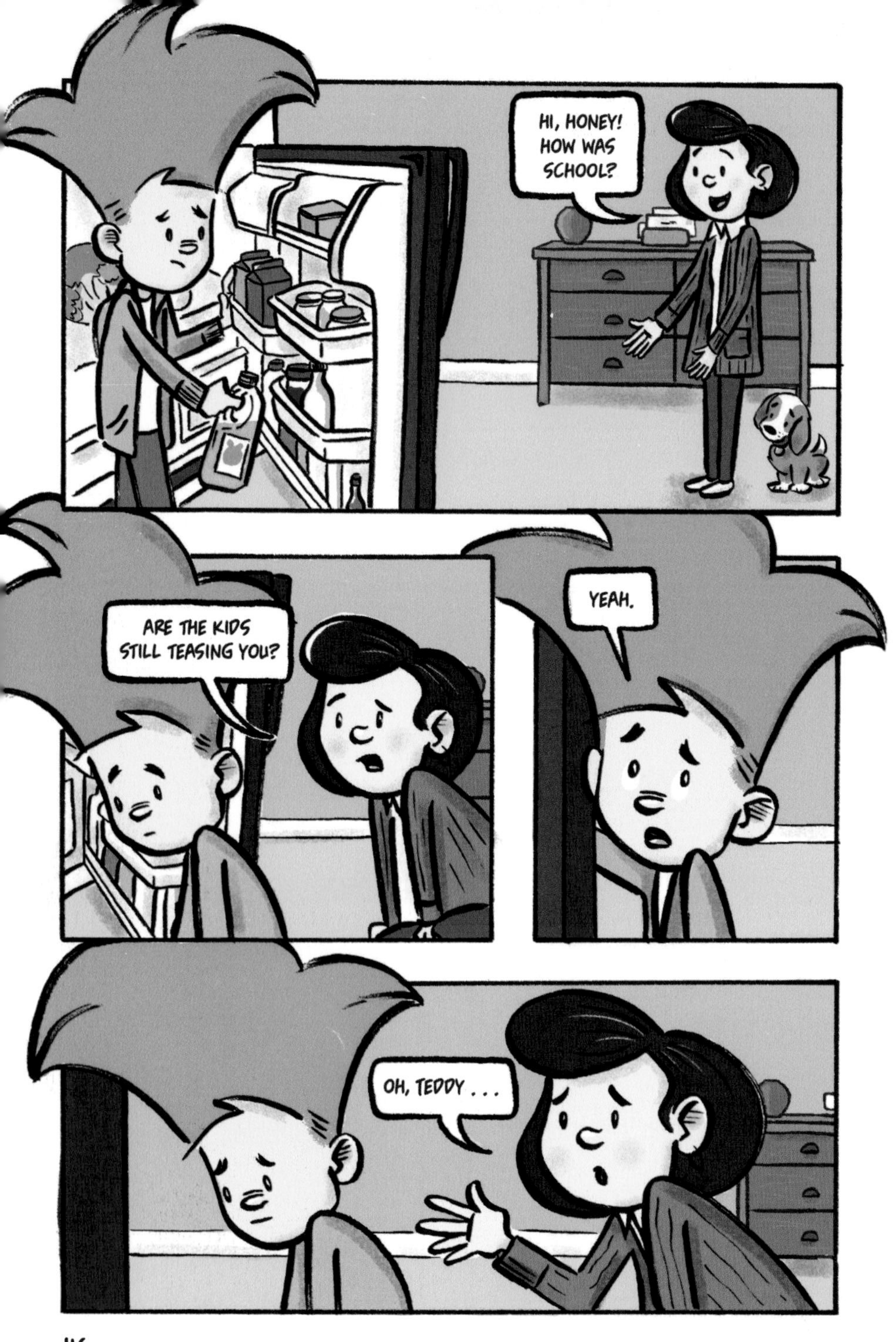
HI, HONEY! HOW WAS SCHOOL?
ARE THE KIDS STILL TEASING YOU?
YEAH.
OH, TEDDY . . .

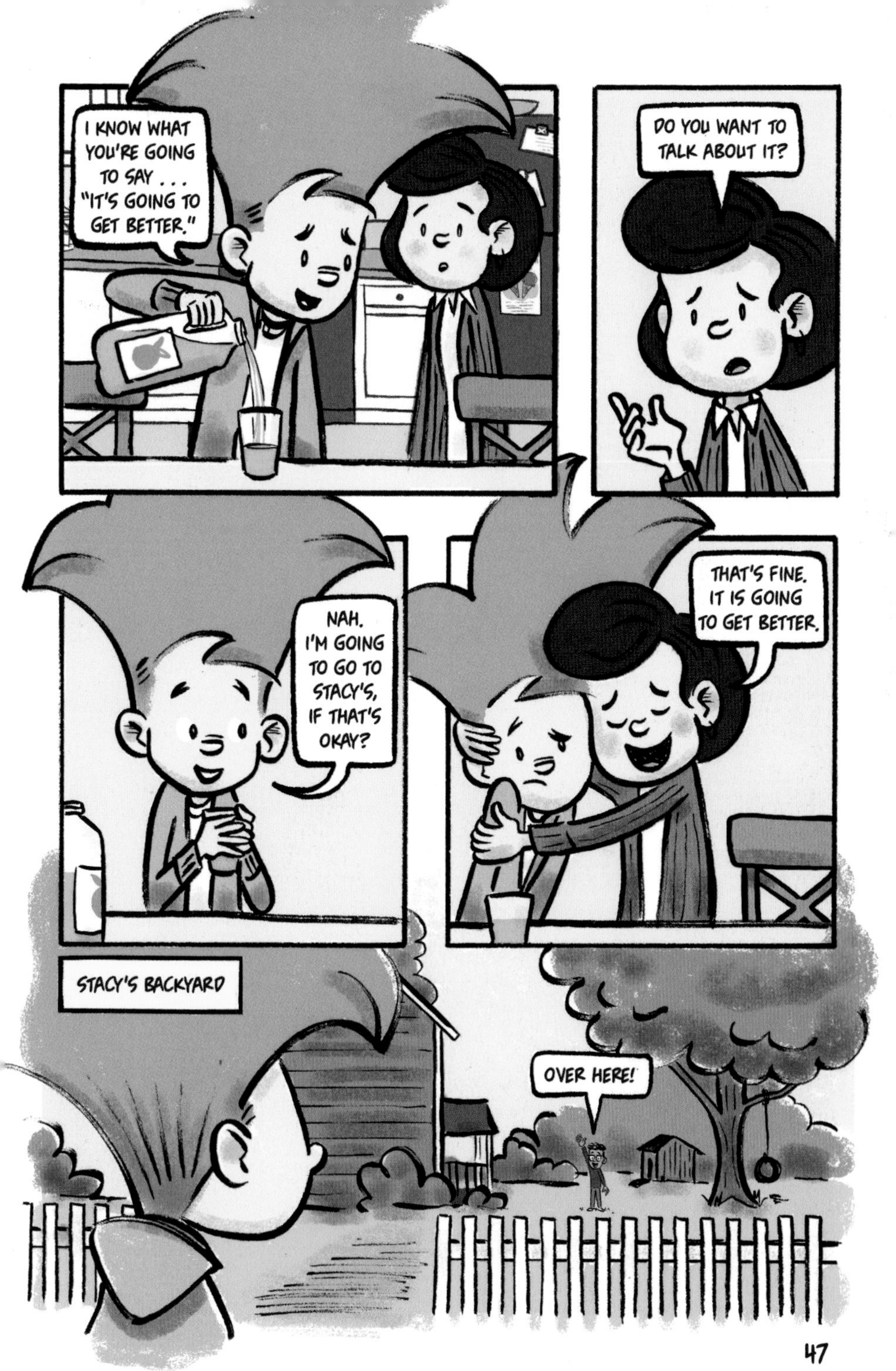
I KNOW WHAT YOU'RE GOING TO SAY . . . "IT'S GOING TO GET BETTER."
DO YOU WANT TO TALK ABOUT IT?
NAH. I'M GOING TO GO TO STACY'S, IF THAT'S OKAY?
THAT'S FINE. IT IS GOING TO GET BETTER.
STACY'S BACKYARD
OVER HERE!

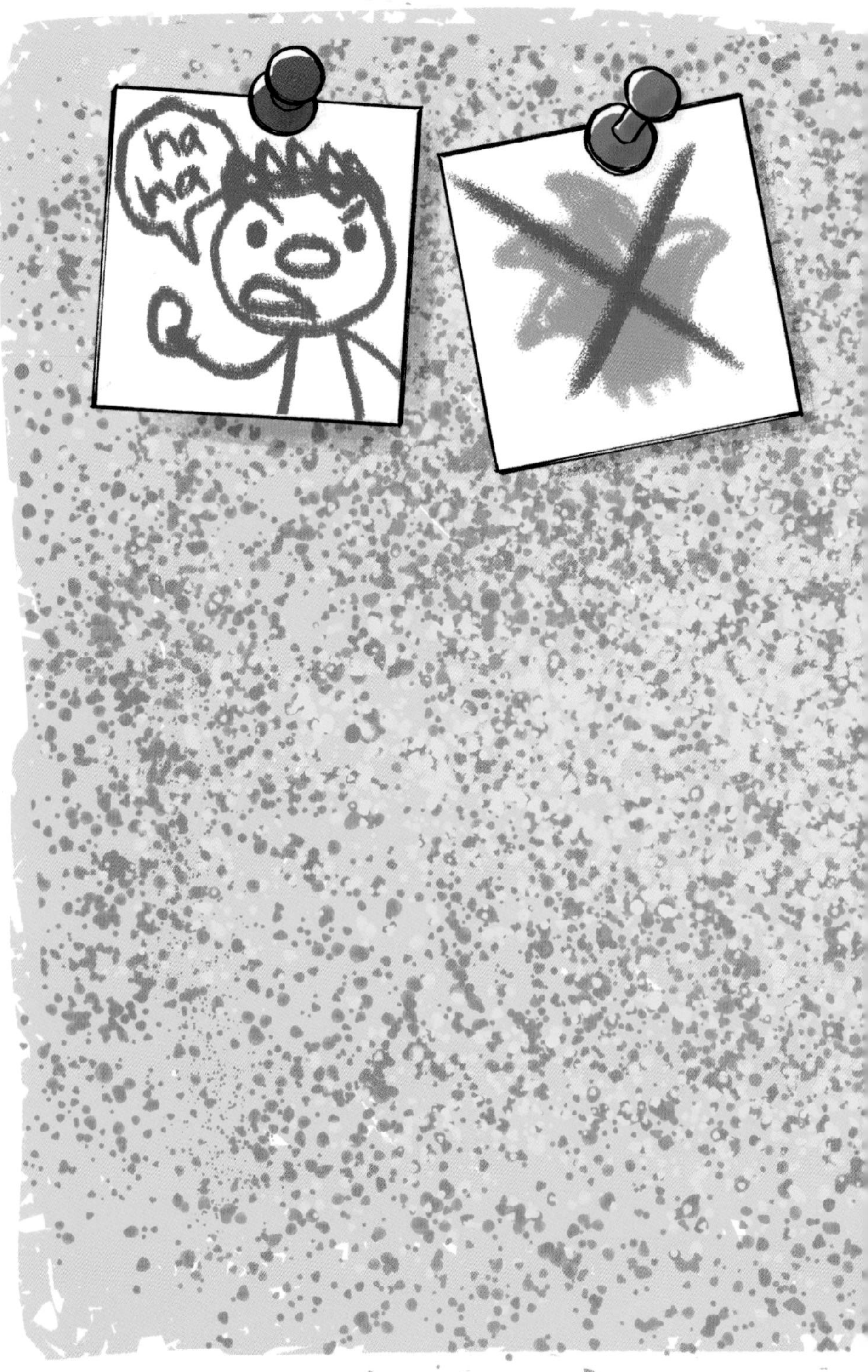
ha ha

CHAPTER 3:
HAIR-POWER

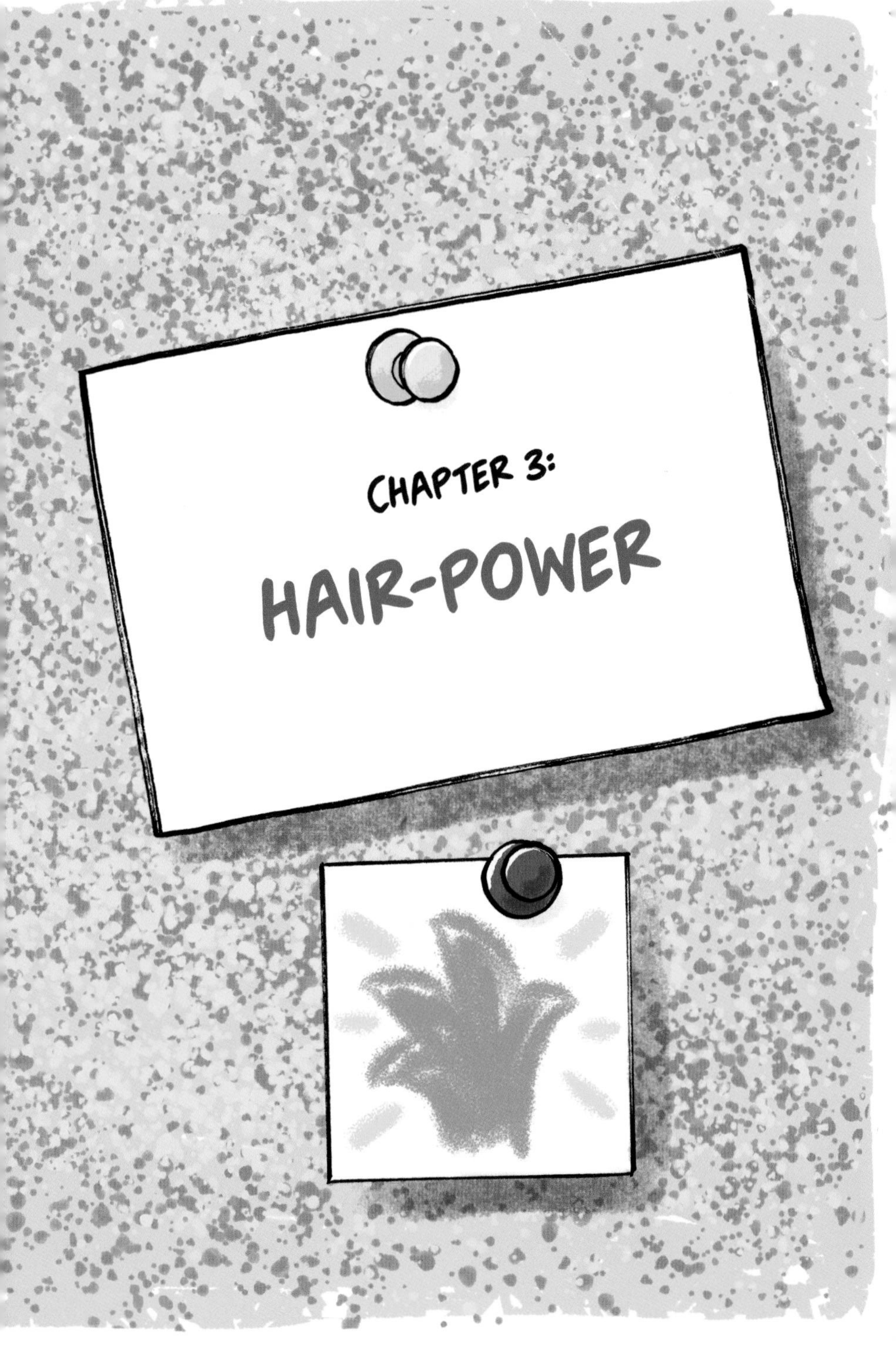

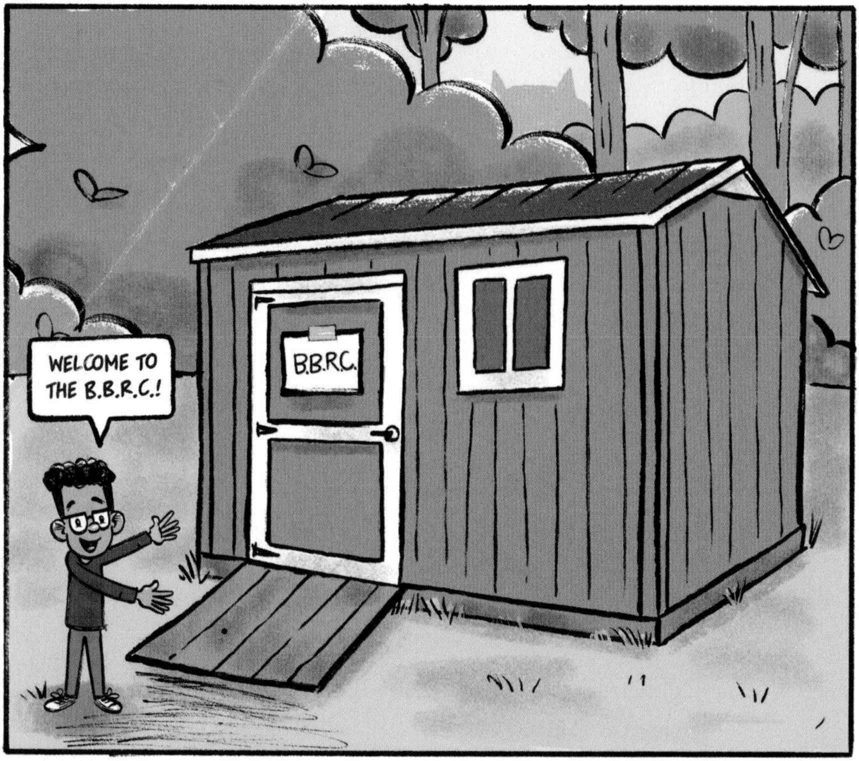
WELCOME TO THE B.B.R.C.!
B.B.R.C.
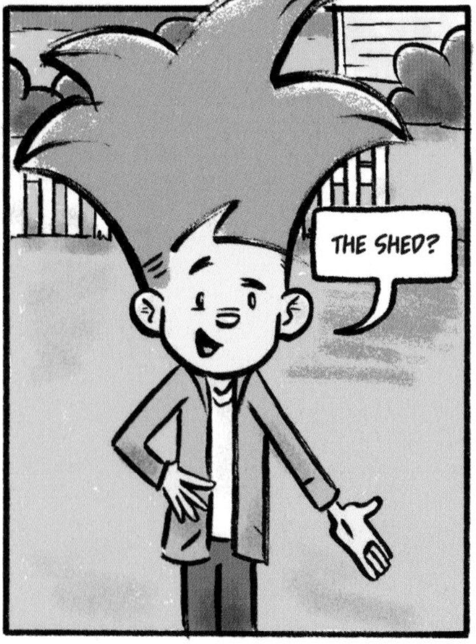
THE SHED?
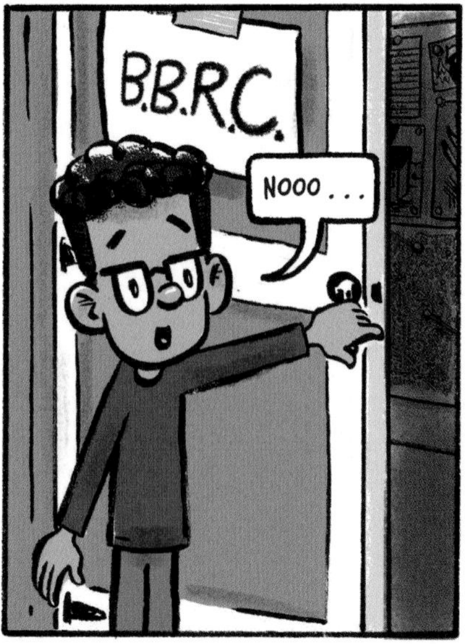
B.B.R.C.
NOOO . . .

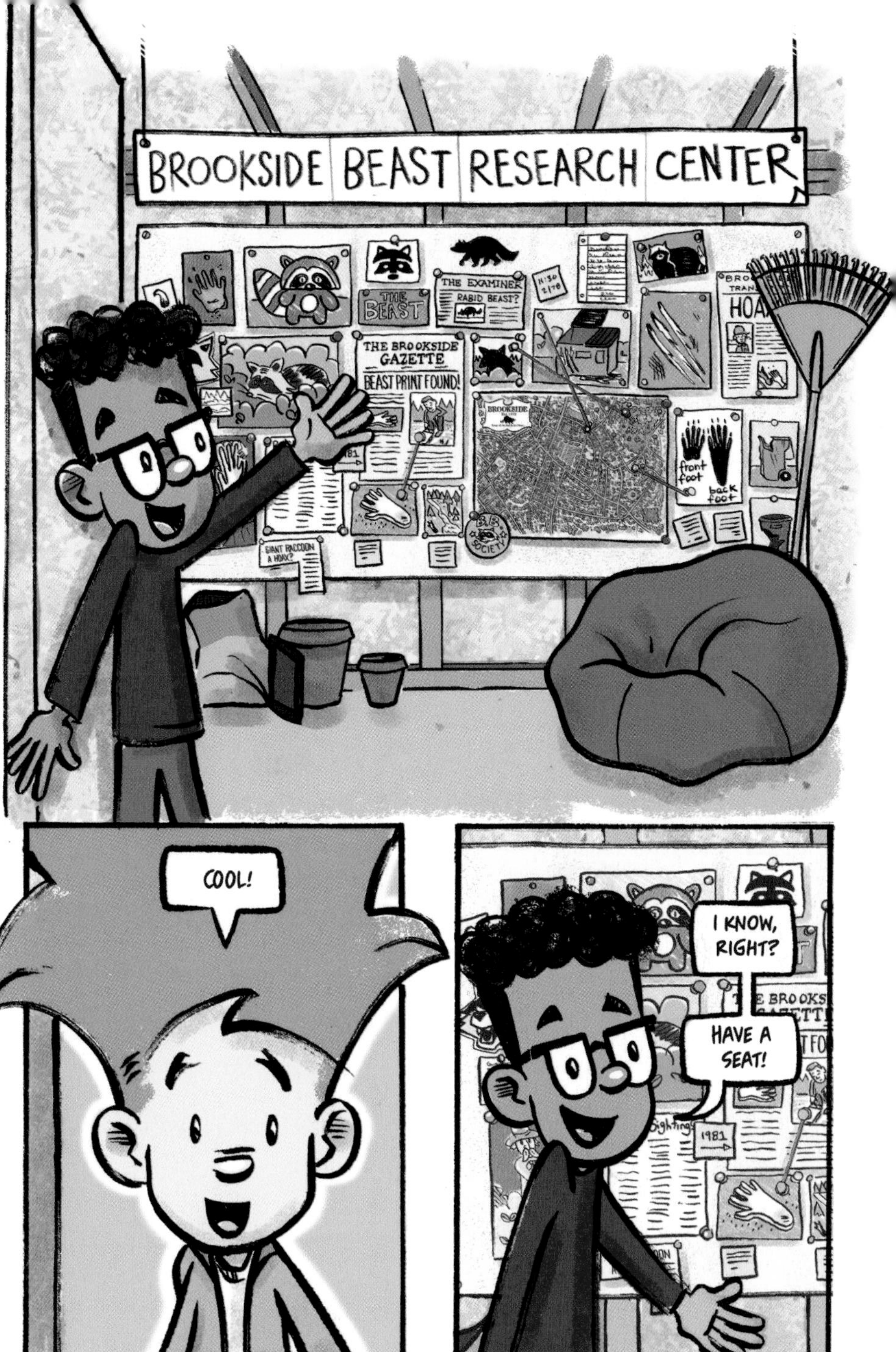

BROOKSIDE BEAST RESEARCH CENTER
THE EXAMINER
RABID BEAST?
THE BEAST
THE BROOKSIDE GAZETTE
BEAST PRINT FOUND!
front foot
back foot
GIANT RACCOON A HOAX?
COOL!
I KNOW, RIGHT?
HAVE A SEAT!

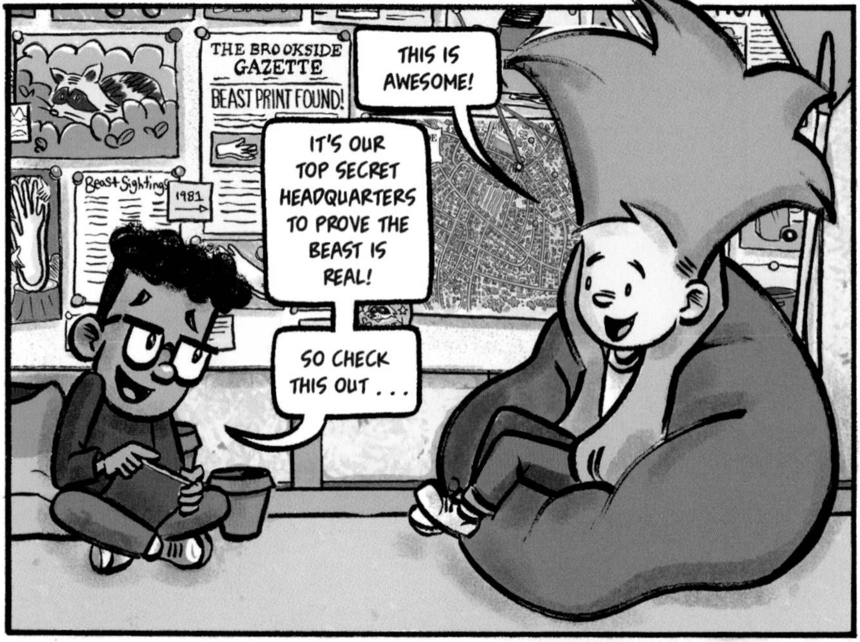
THE BROOKSIDE GAZETTE
BEAST PRINT FOUND!
Beast Sightings
1981
THIS IS AWESOME!
IT'S OUR TOP SECRET HEADQUARTERS TO PROVE THE BEAST IS REAL!
SO CHECK THIS OUT . . .

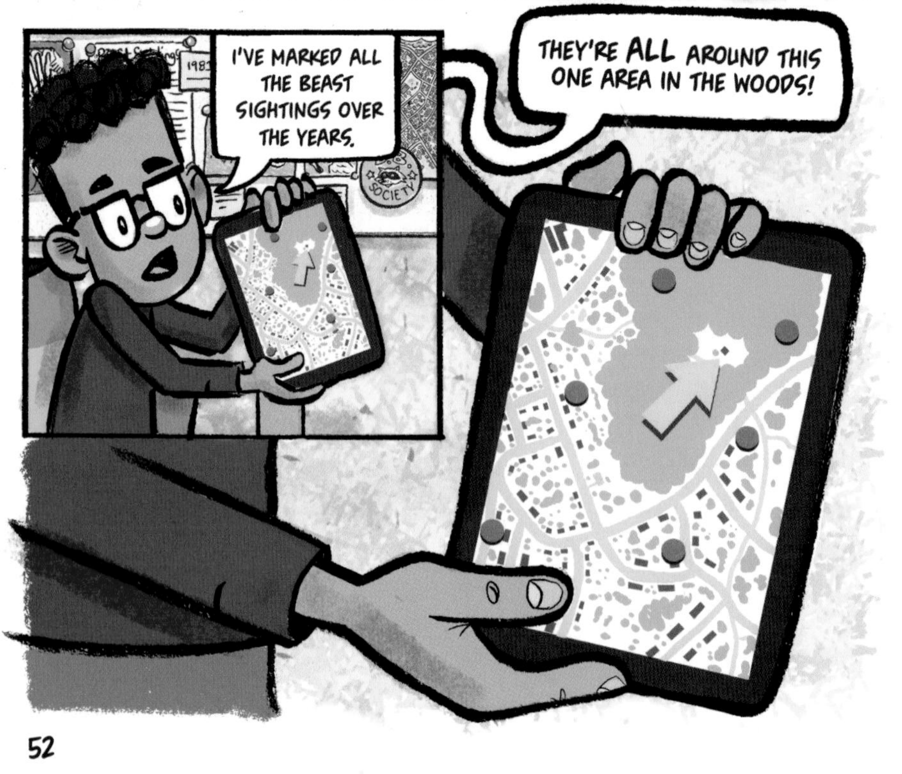
I'VE MARKED ALL THE BEAST SIGHTINGS OVER THE YEARS.
THEY'RE ALL AROUND THIS ONE AREA IN THE WOODS!
SOCIETY

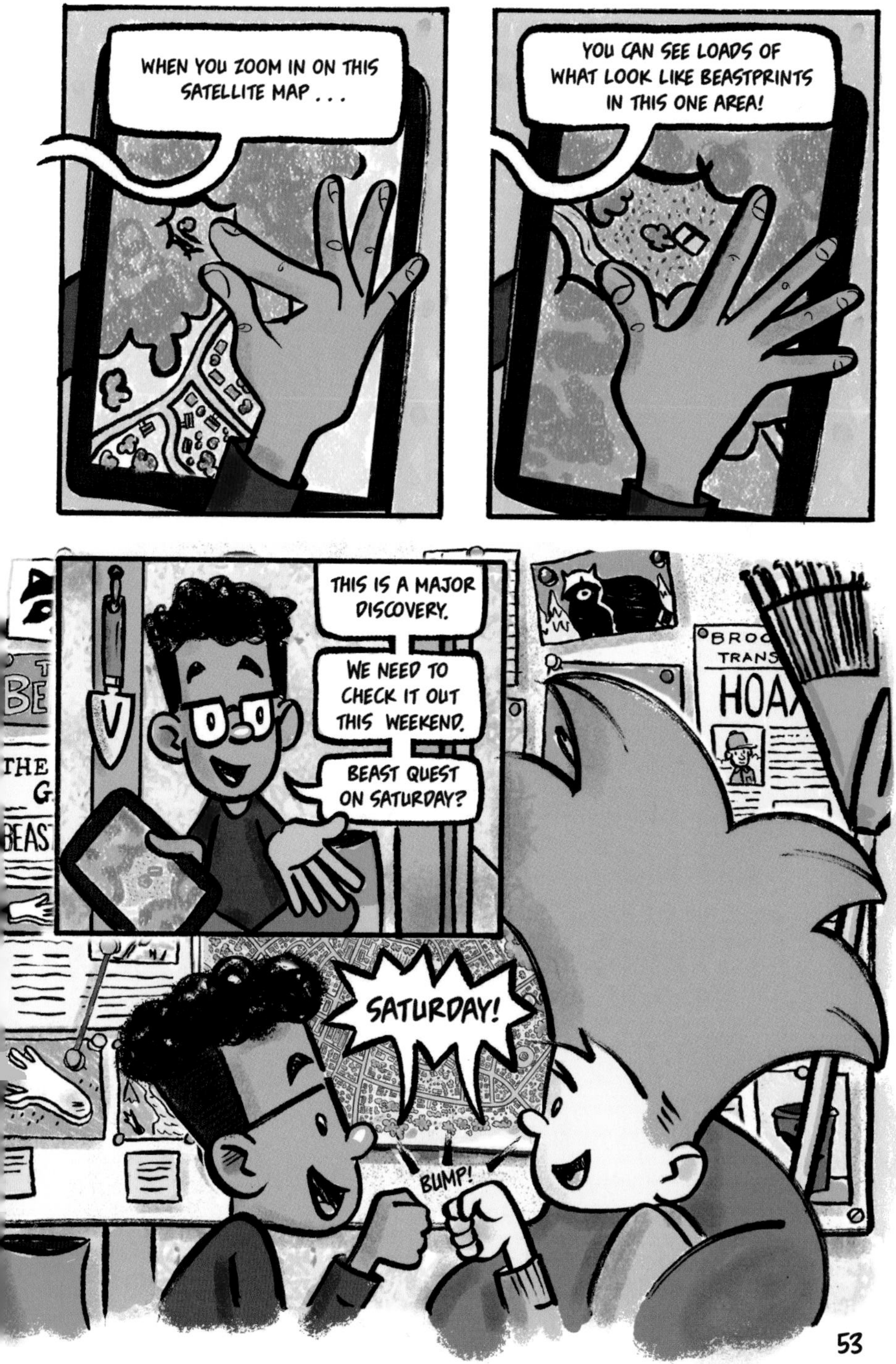
WHEN YOU ZOOM IN ON THIS SATELLITE MAP . . .
YOU CAN SEE LOADS OF WHAT LOOK LIKE BEASTPRINTS IN THIS ONE AREA!
THIS IS A MAJOR DISCOVERY.
WE NEED TO CHECK IT OUT THIS WEEKEND.
BEAST QUEST ON SATURDAY?
SATURDAY!
BUMP!
HOAX

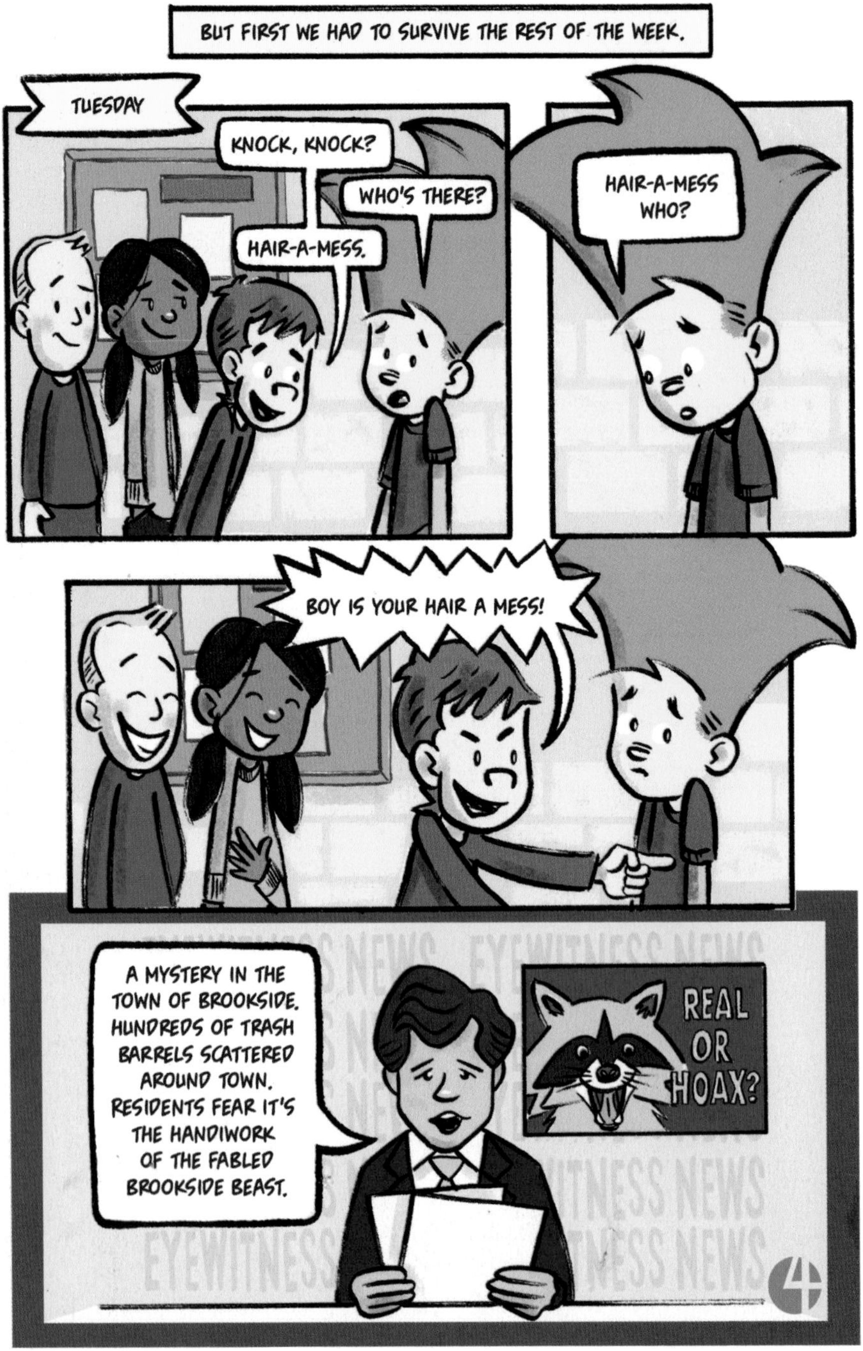
BUT FIRST WE HAD TO SURVIVE THE REST OF THE WEEK.
TUESDAY
KNOCK, KNOCK?
WHO'S THERE?
HAIR-A-MESS.
HAIR-A-MESS WHO?
BOY IS YOUR HAIR A MESS!
A MYSTERY IN THE TOWN OF BROOKSIDE. HUNDREDS OF TRASH BARRELS SCATTERED AROUND TOWN. RESIDENTS FEAR IT'S THE HANDIWORK OF THE FABLED BROOKSIDE BEAST.
REAL OR HOAX?
EYEWITNESS NEWS
4

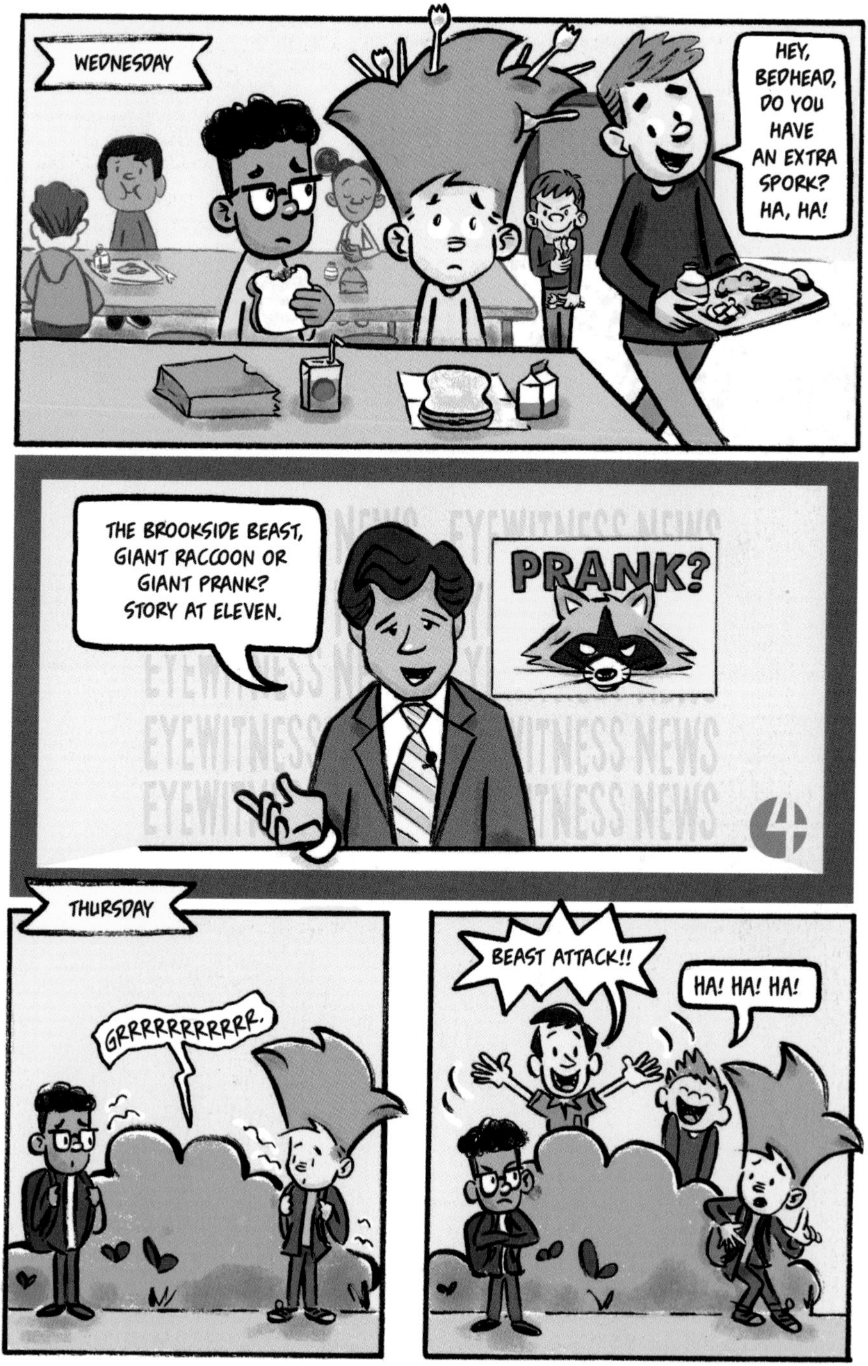
WEDNESDAY
HEY, BEDHEAD, DO YOU HAVE AN EXTRA SPORK? HA, HA!
THE BROOKSIDE BEAST, GIANT RACCOON OR GIANT PRANK? STORY AT ELEVEN.
PRANK?
EYEWITNESS NEWS
4
THURSDAY
GRRRRRRRRRR.
BEAST ATTACK!!
HA! HA! HA!

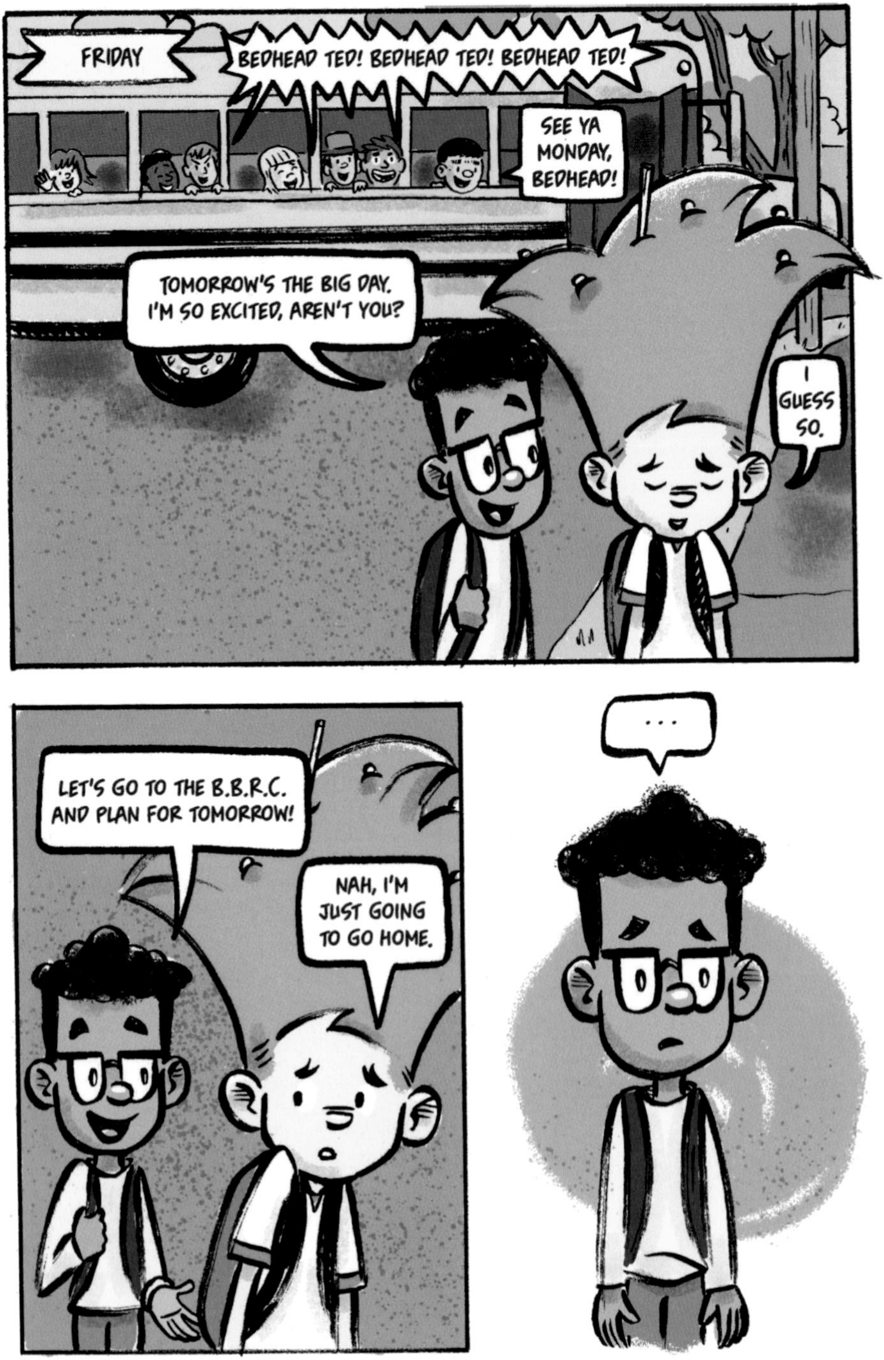
FRIDAY
BEDHEAD TED! BEDHEAD TED! BEDHEAD TED!
SEE YA MONDAY, BEDHEAD!
TOMORROW'S THE BIG DAY. I'M SO EXCITED, AREN'T YOU?
I GUESS SO.
LET'S GO TO THE B.B.R.C. AND PLAN FOR TOMORROW!
NAH, I'M JUST GOING TO GO HOME.
...

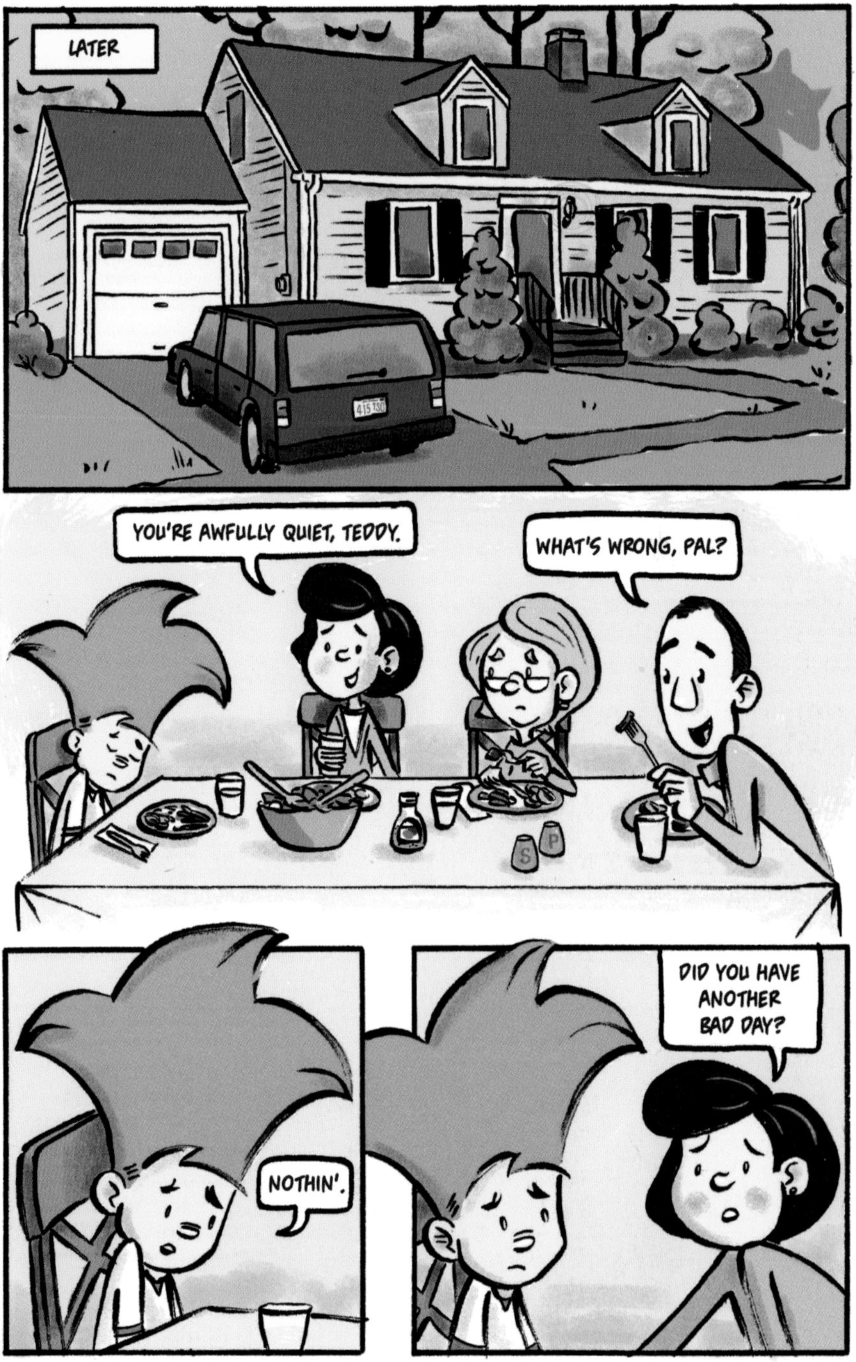
LATER
YOU'RE AWFULLY QUIET, TEDDY.
WHAT'S WRONG, PAL?
NOTHIN'.
DID YOU HAVE ANOTHER BAD DAY?

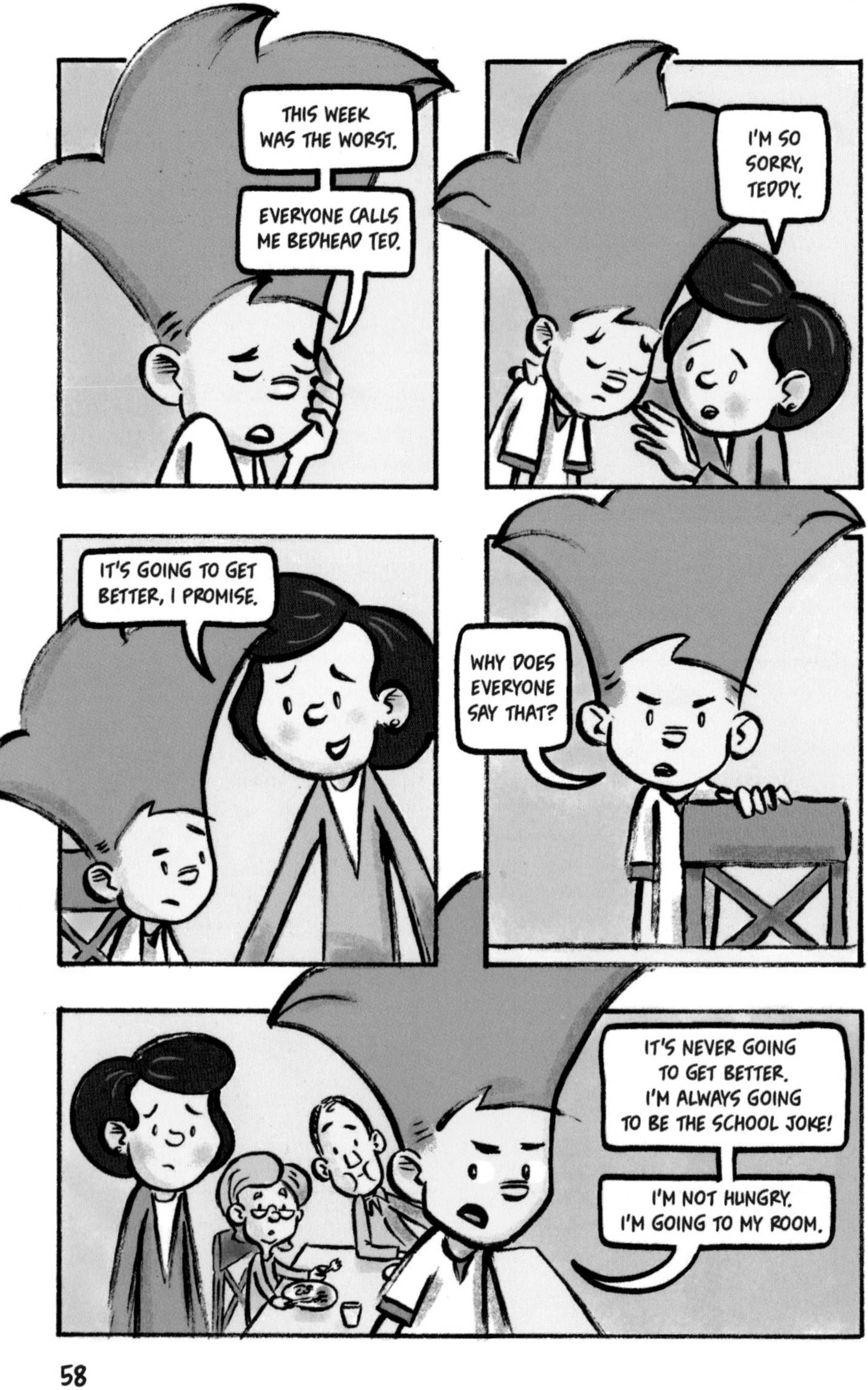
THIS WEEK WAS THE WORST.
EVERYONE CALLS ME BEDHEAD TED.
I'M SO SORRY, TEDDY.
IT'S GOING TO GET BETTER, I PROMISE.
WHY DOES EVERYONE SAY THAT?
IT'S NEVER GOING TO GET BETTER. I'M ALWAYS GOING TO BE THE SCHOOL JOKE!
I'M NOT HUNGRY. I'M GOING TO MY ROOM.

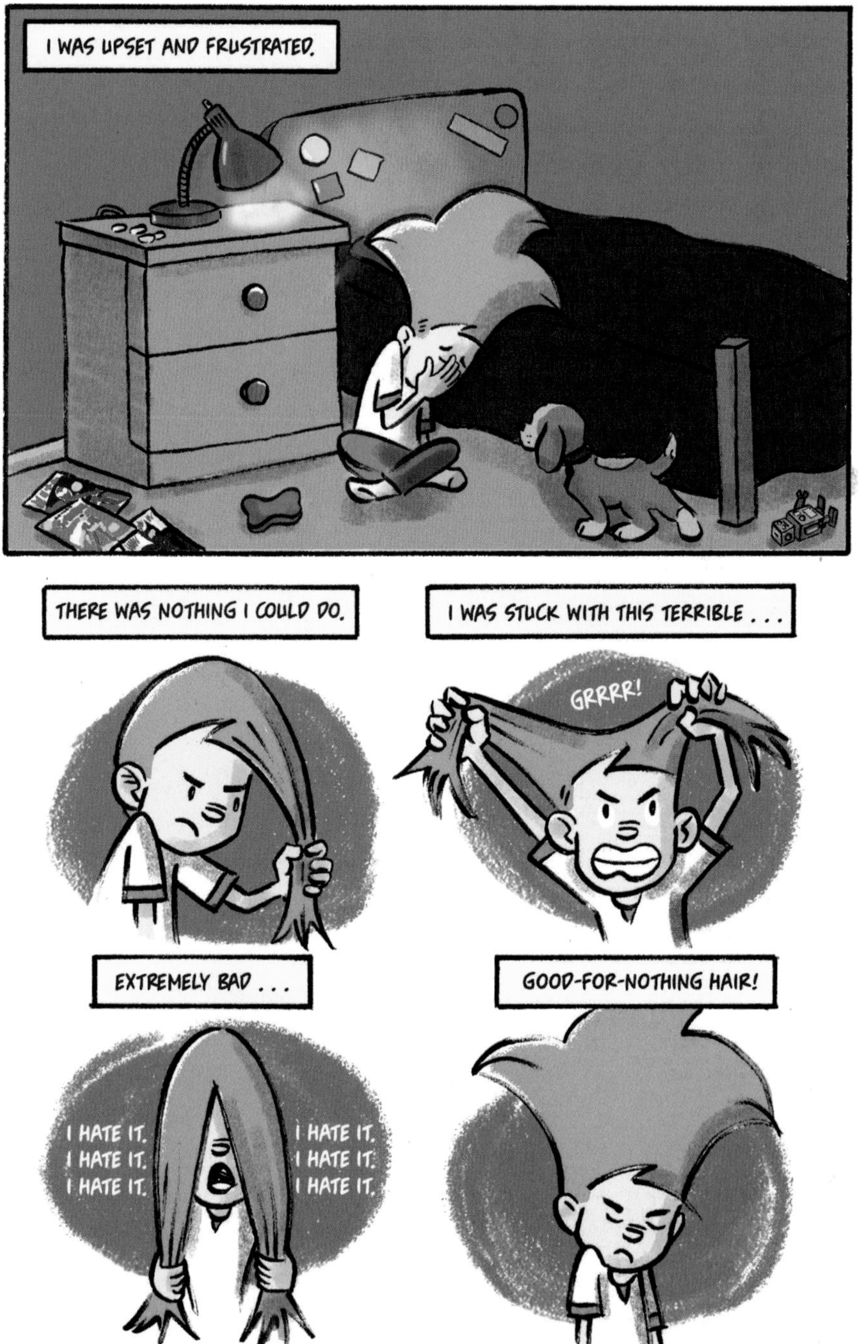
I WAS UPSET AND FRUSTRATED.
THERE WAS NOTHING I COULD DO.
I WAS STUCK WITH THIS TERRIBLE . . .
GRRRR!
EXTREMELY BAD . . .
GOOD-FOR-NOTHING HAIR!
I HATE IT.
I HATE IT.
I HATE IT.
I HATE IT.
I HATE IT.
I HATE IT.

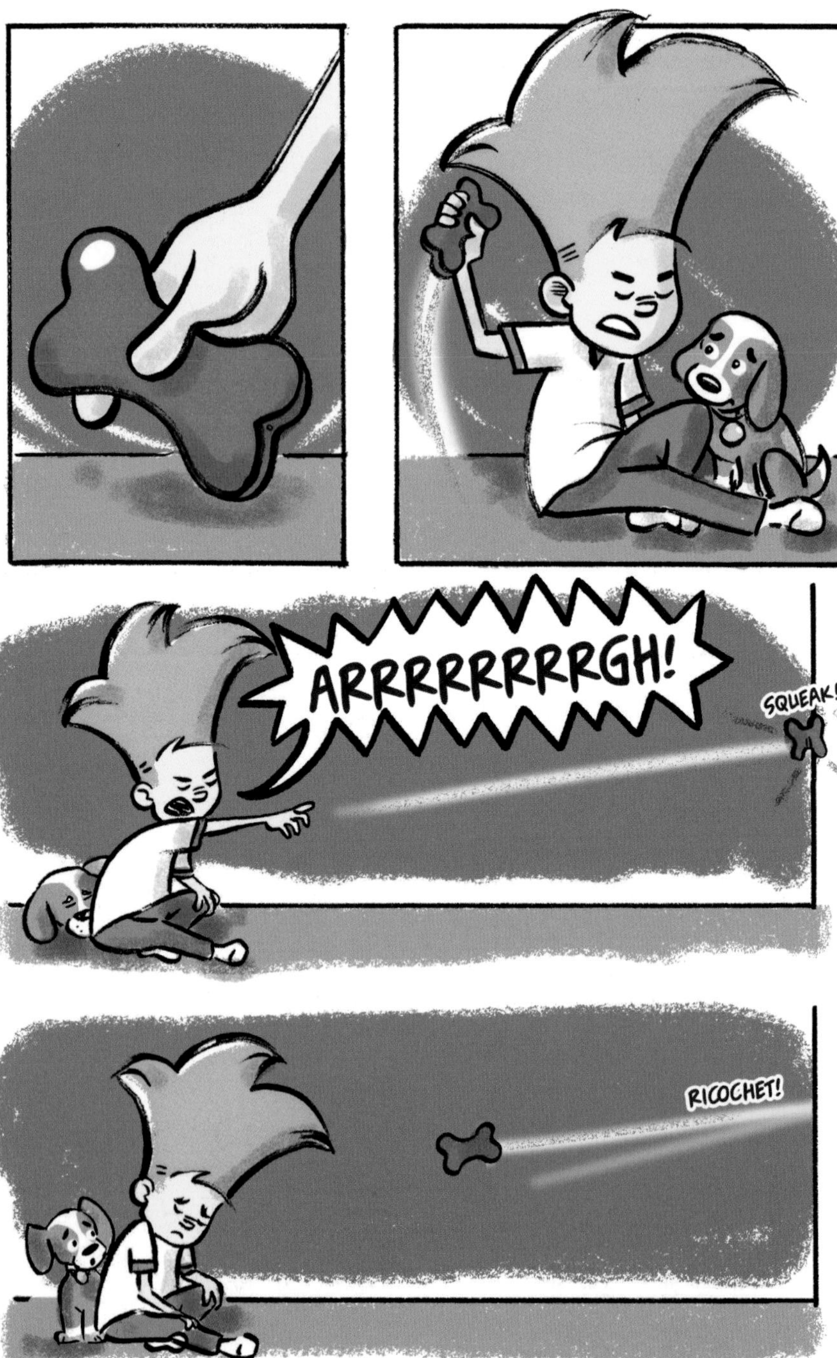
ARRRRRRRRGH!
SQUEAK!
RICOCHET!

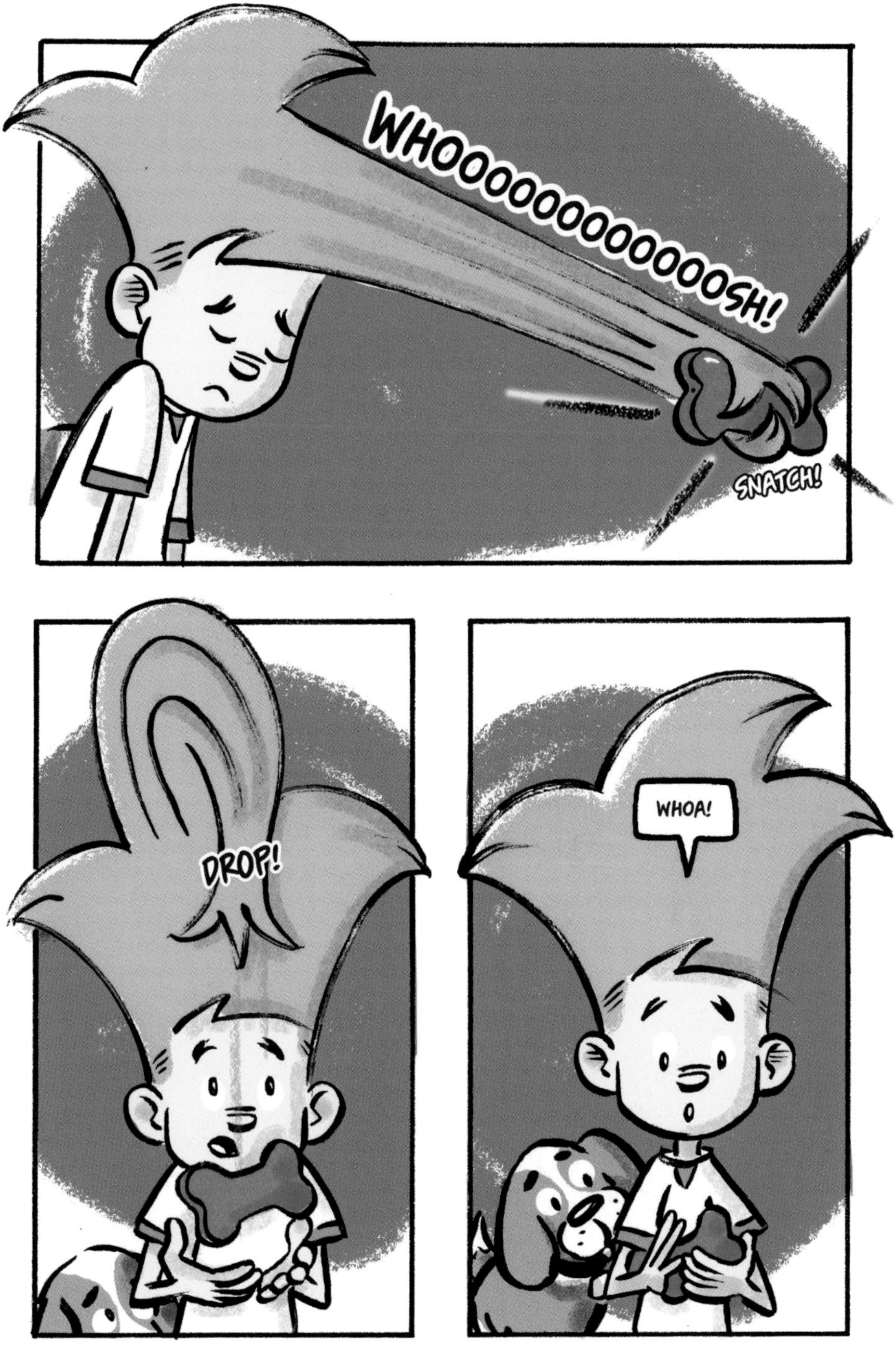
WHOOOOOOOOOOOOOOSH!
SNATCH!
DROP!
WHOA!

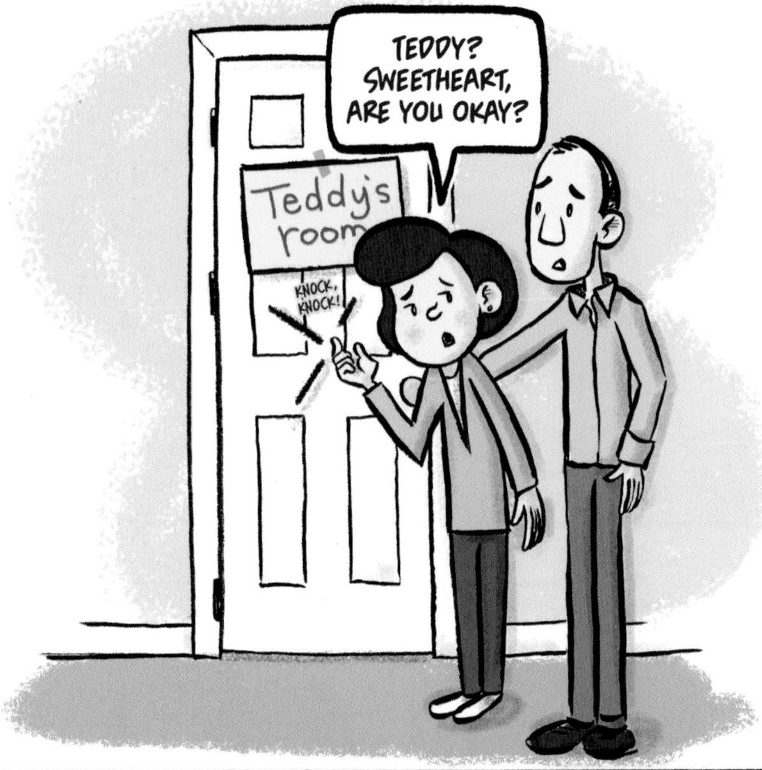
TEDDY? SWEETHEART, ARE YOU OKAY?
Teddy's room
KNOCK, KNOCK!

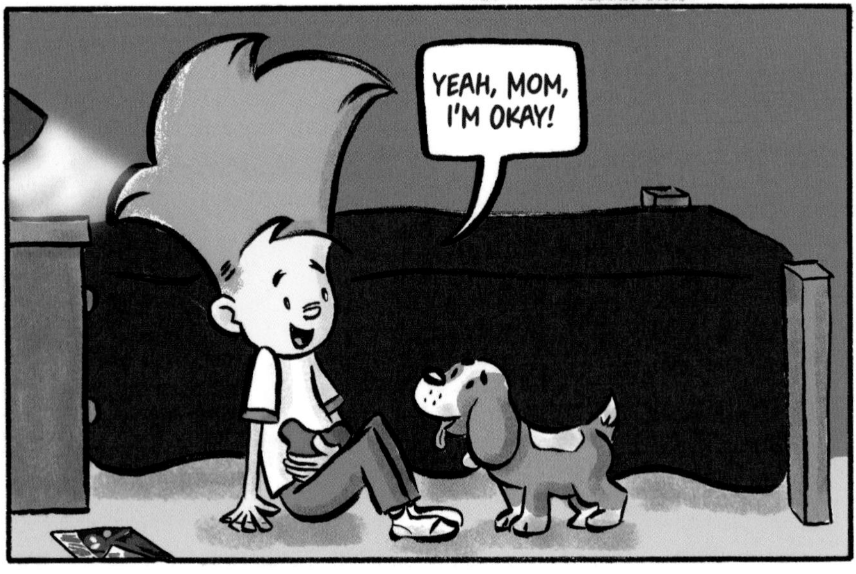
YEAH, MOM, I'M OKAY!

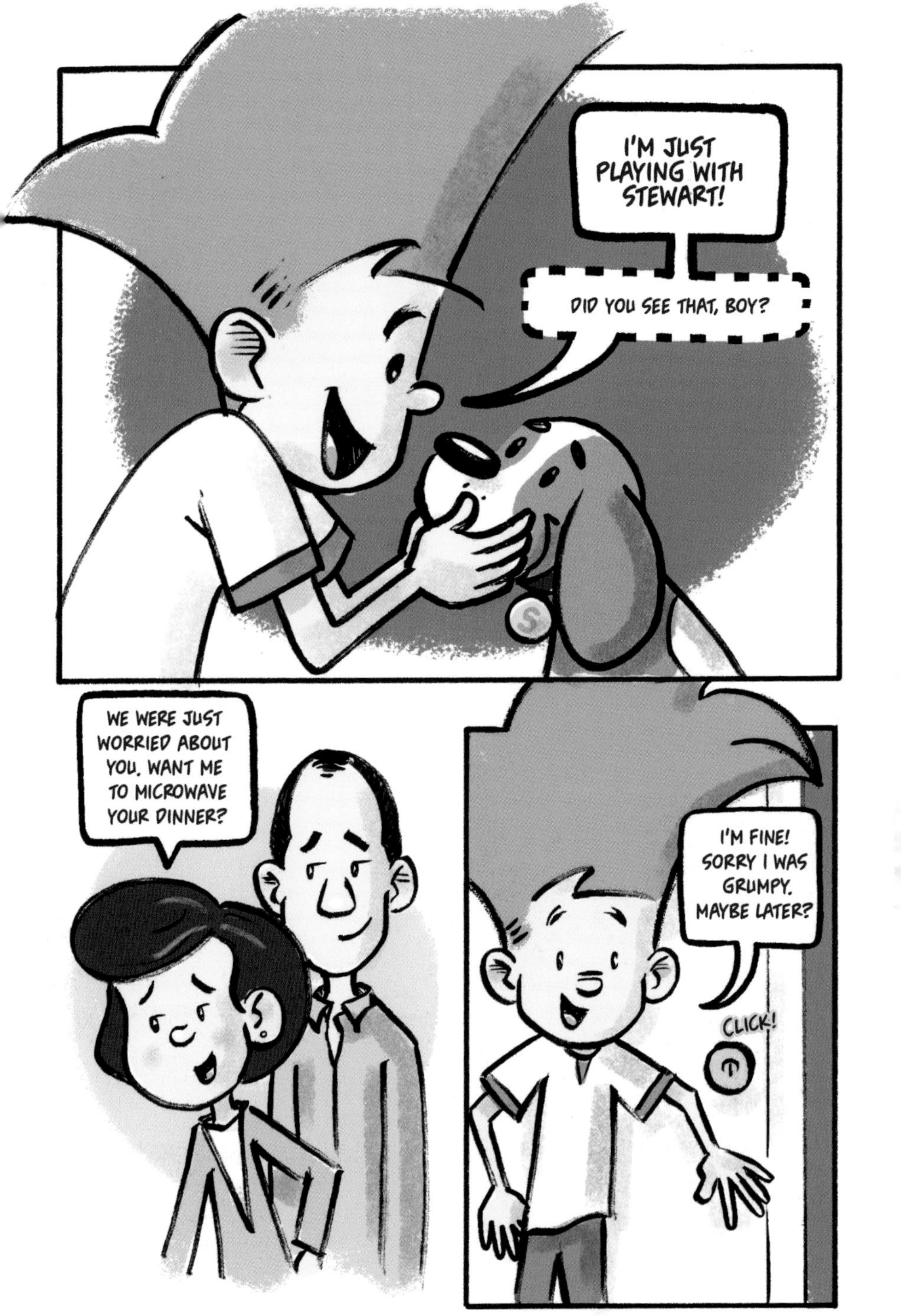
I'M JUST PLAYING WITH STEWART!
DID YOU SEE THAT, BOY?
WE WERE JUST WORRIED ABOUT YOU. WANT ME TO MICROWAVE YOUR DINNER?
I'M FINE! SORRY I WAS GRUMPY. MAYBE LATER?
CLICK!

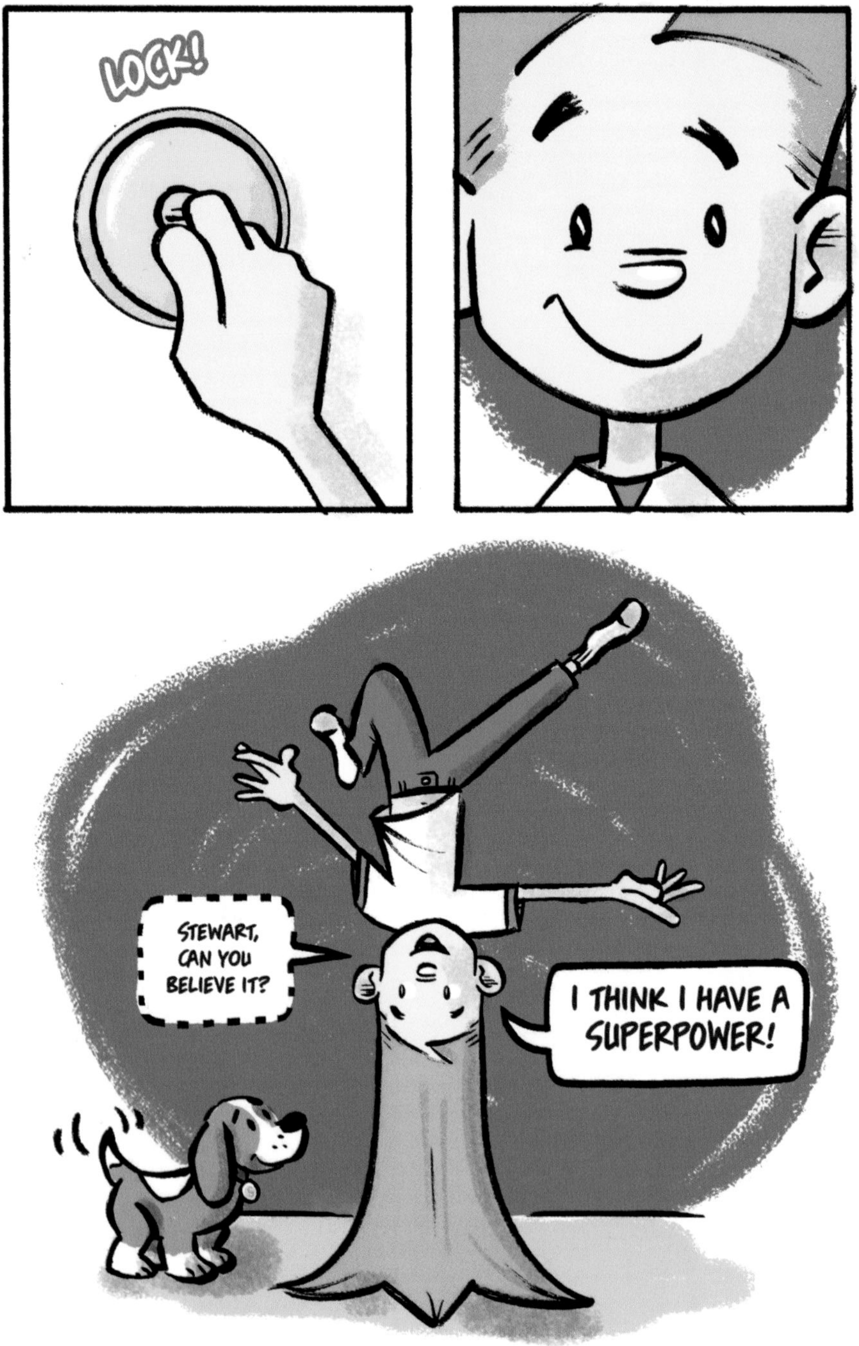
LOCK!
STEWART, CAN YOU BELIEVE IT?
I THINK I HAVE A SUPERPOWER!

I SPENT THE REST OF THE NIGHT TESTING WHAT MY HAIR COULD DO.

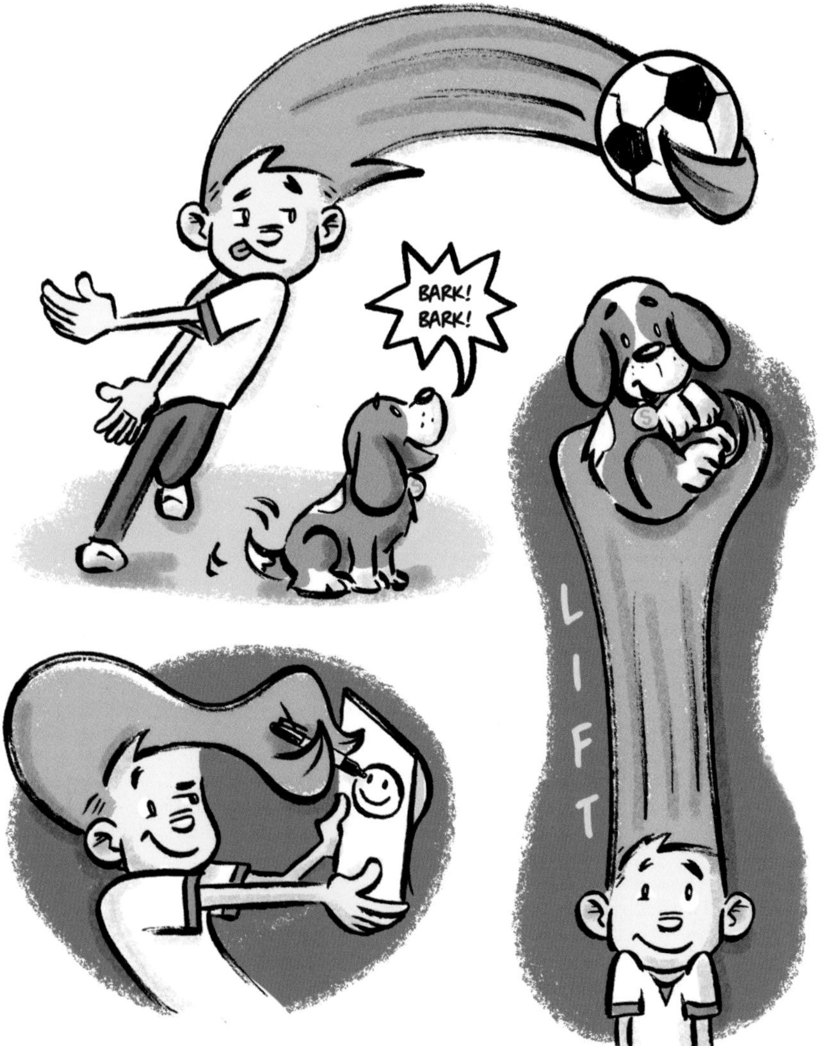
BARK! BARK!
LIFT

IT WAS INCREDIBLE!

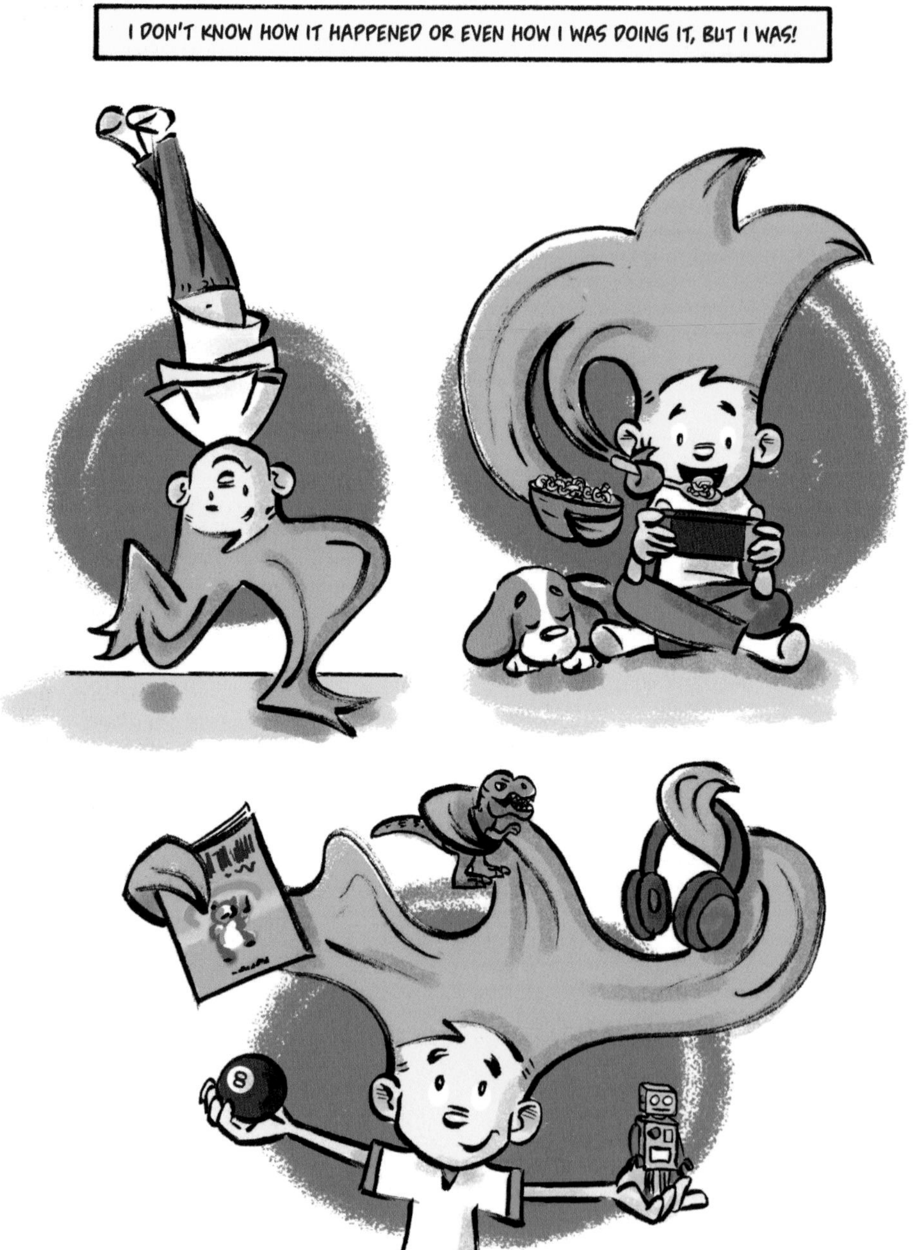
I DON'T KNOW HOW IT HAPPENED OR EVEN HOW I WAS DOING IT, BUT I WAS!

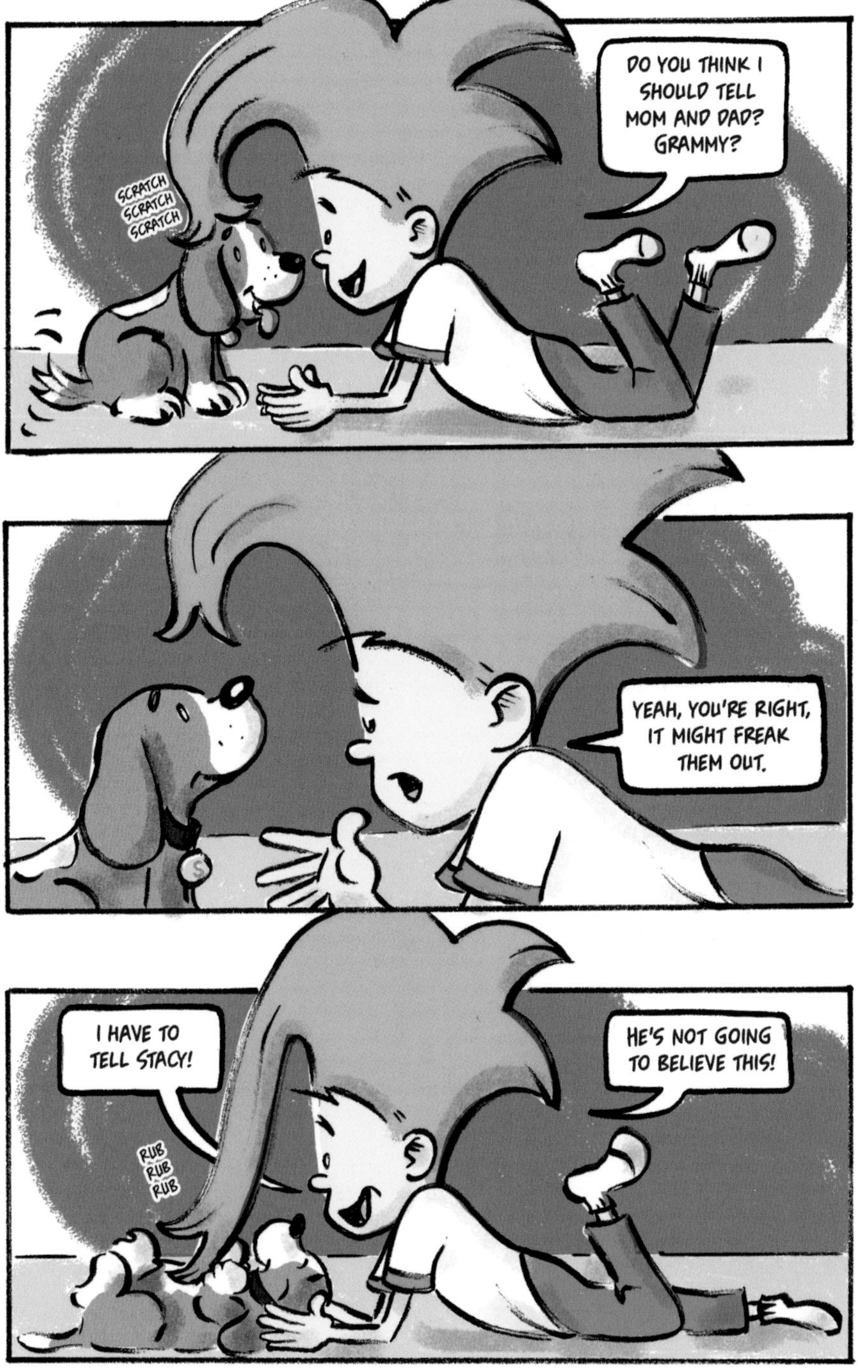
DO YOU THINK I SHOULD TELL MOM AND DAD? GRAMMY?
SCRATCH SCRATCH SCRATCH
YEAH, YOU'RE RIGHT, IT MIGHT FREAK THEM OUT.
I HAVE TO TELL STACY!
HE'S NOT GOING TO BELIEVE THIS!
RUB RUB RUB

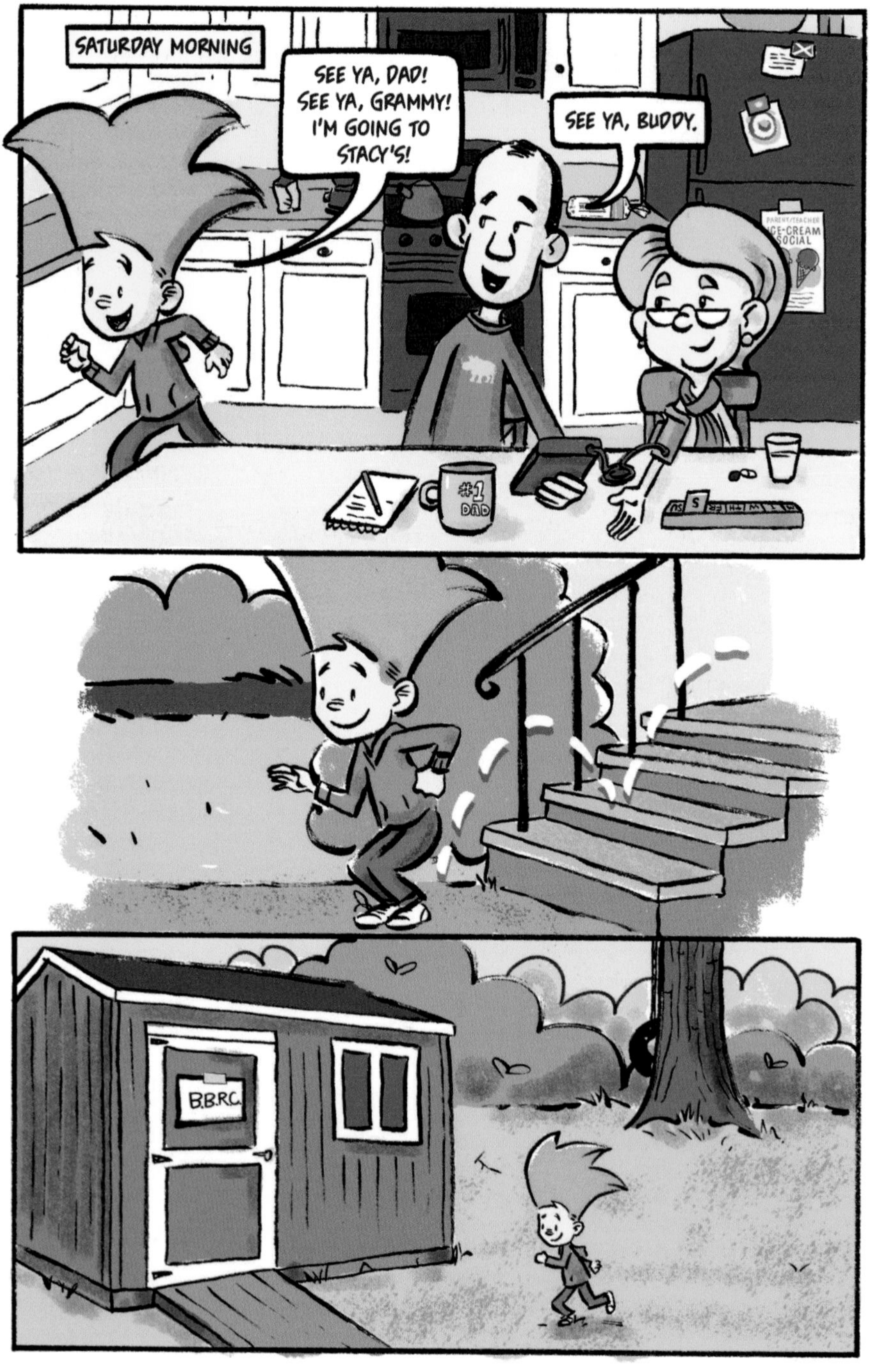
SATURDAY MORNING
SEE YA, DAD! SEE YA, GRAMMY! I'M GOING TO STACY'S!
SEE YA, BUDDY.
PARENT/TEACHER ICE-CREAM SOCIAL
#1 DAD
B.B.R.C.

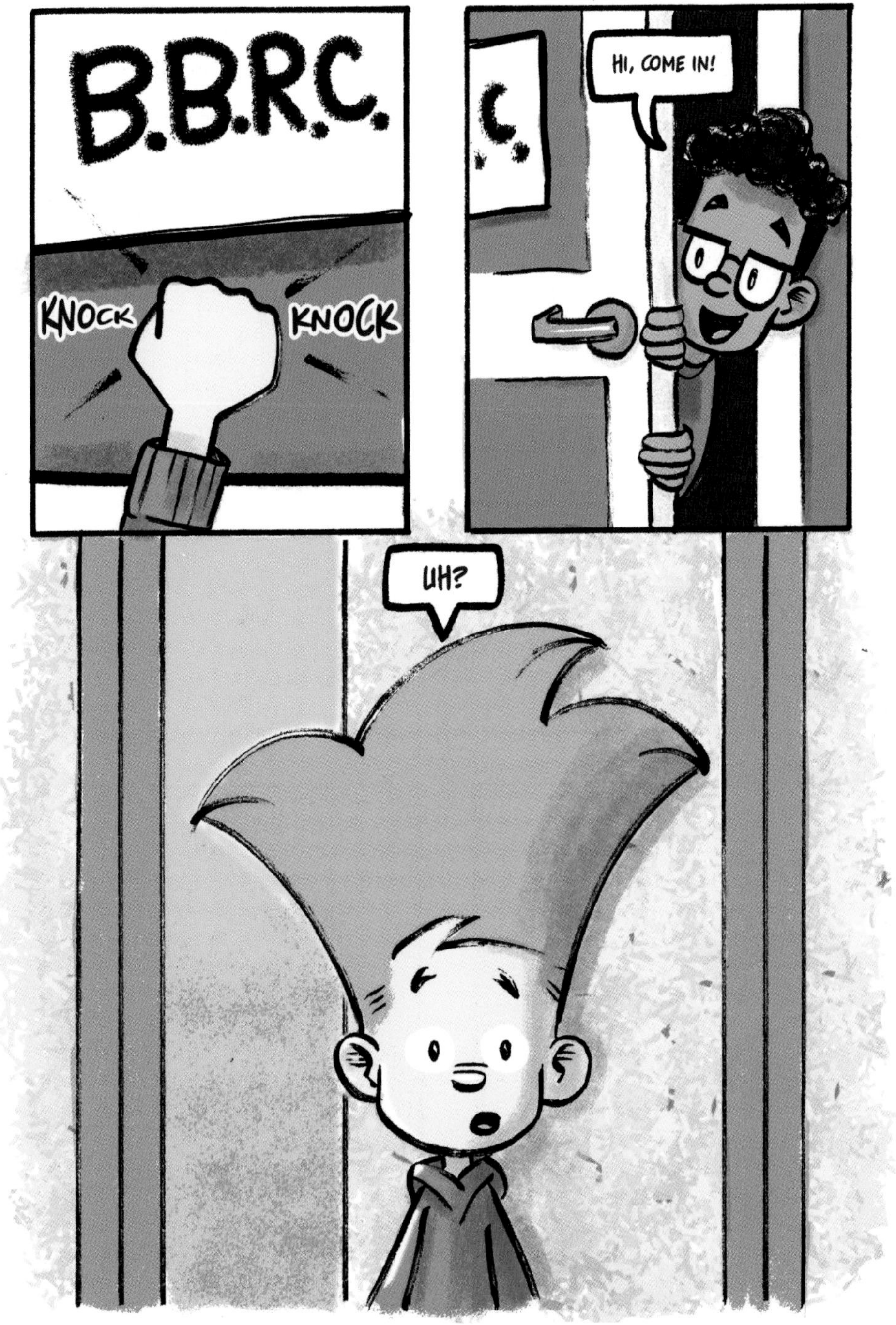
B.B.R.C.
KNOCK
KNOCK
HI, COME IN!
UH?

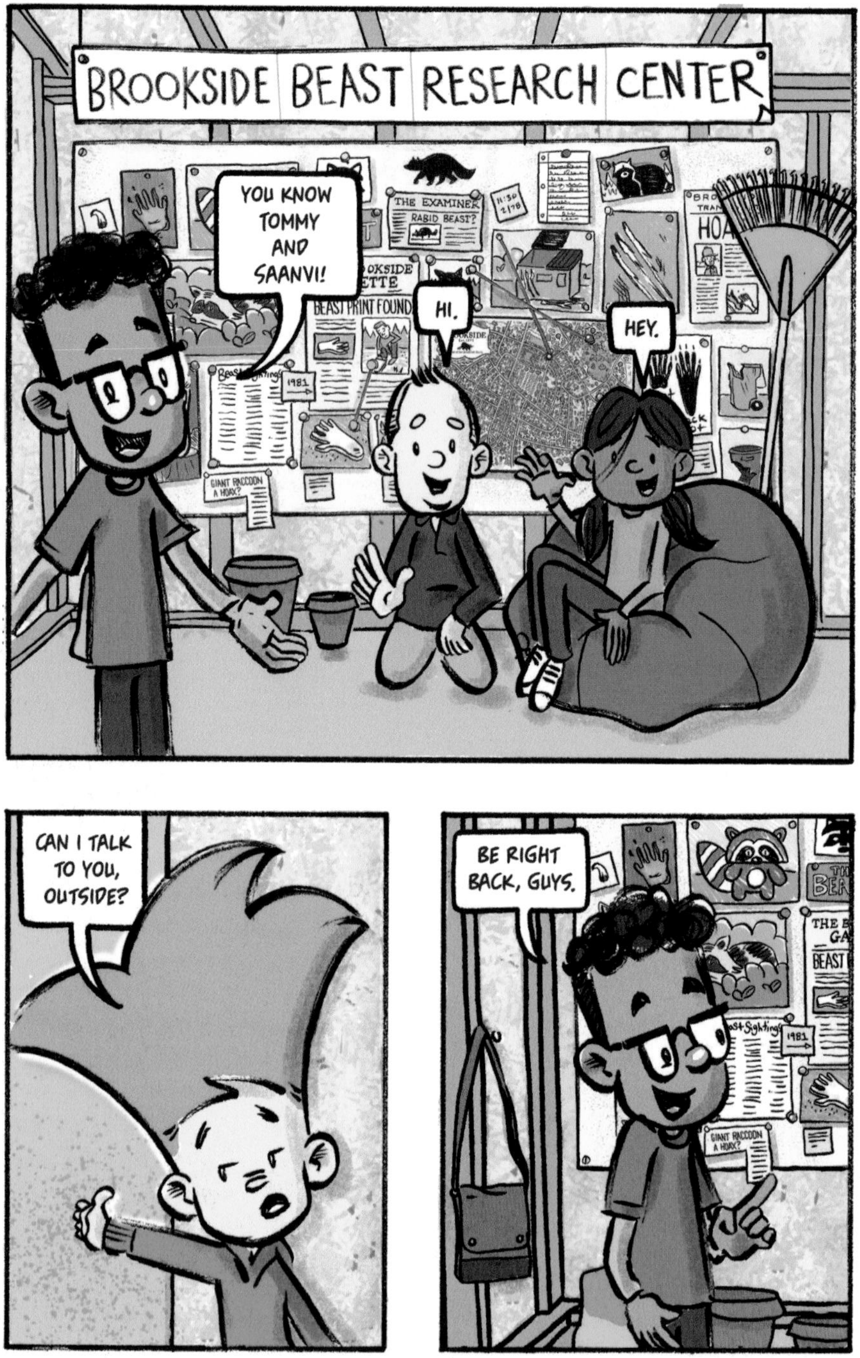
BROOKSIDE BEAST RESEARCH CENTER
THE EXAMINER
RABID BEAST?
BEAST PRINT FOUND
1981
GIANT RACCOON A HOAX?
YOU KNOW TOMMY AND SAANVI!
HI.
HEY.
CAN I TALK TO YOU, OUTSIDE?
BE RIGHT BACK, GUYS.

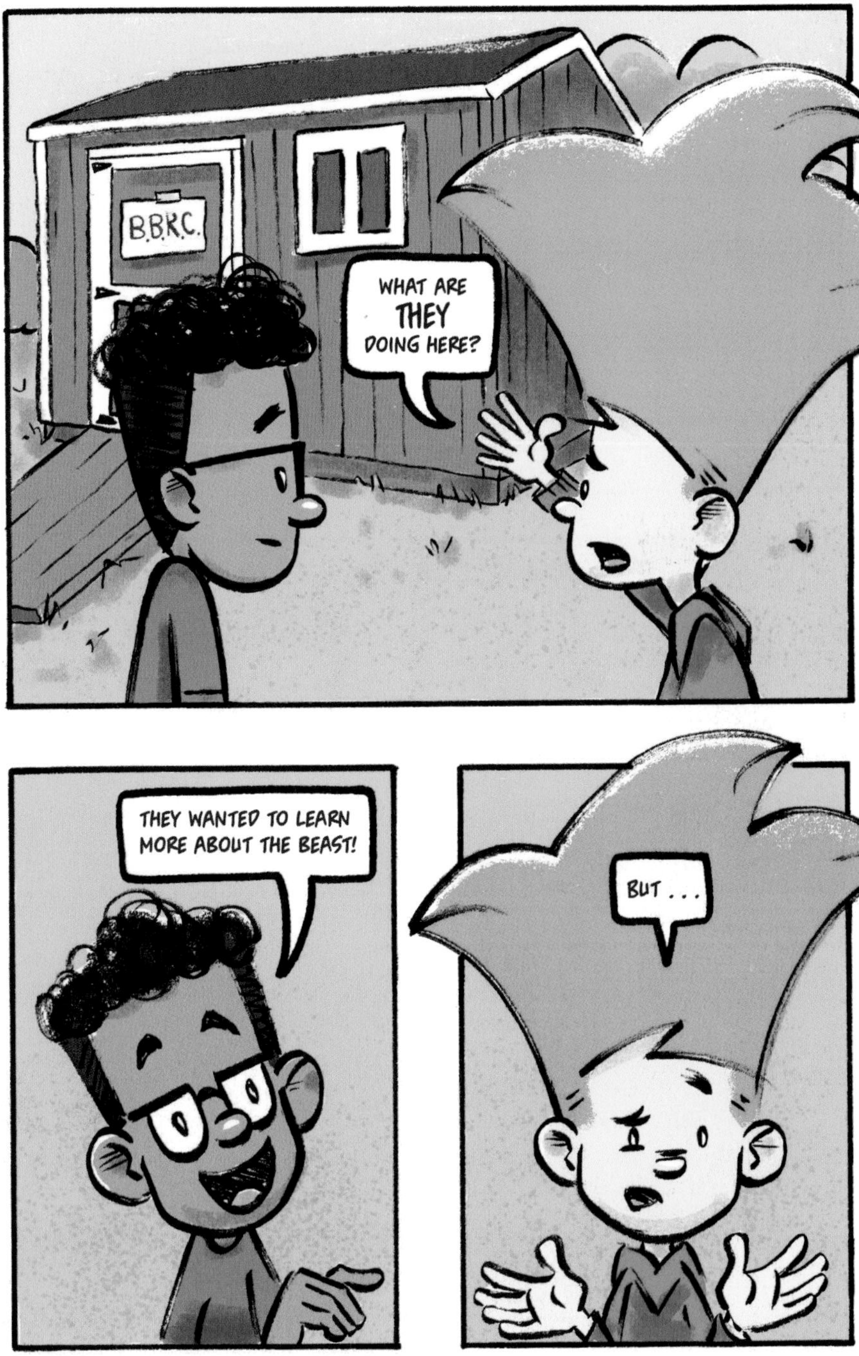
B.B.R.C.
WHAT ARE THEY DOING HERE?
THEY WANTED TO LEARN MORE ABOUT THE BEAST!
BUT . . .

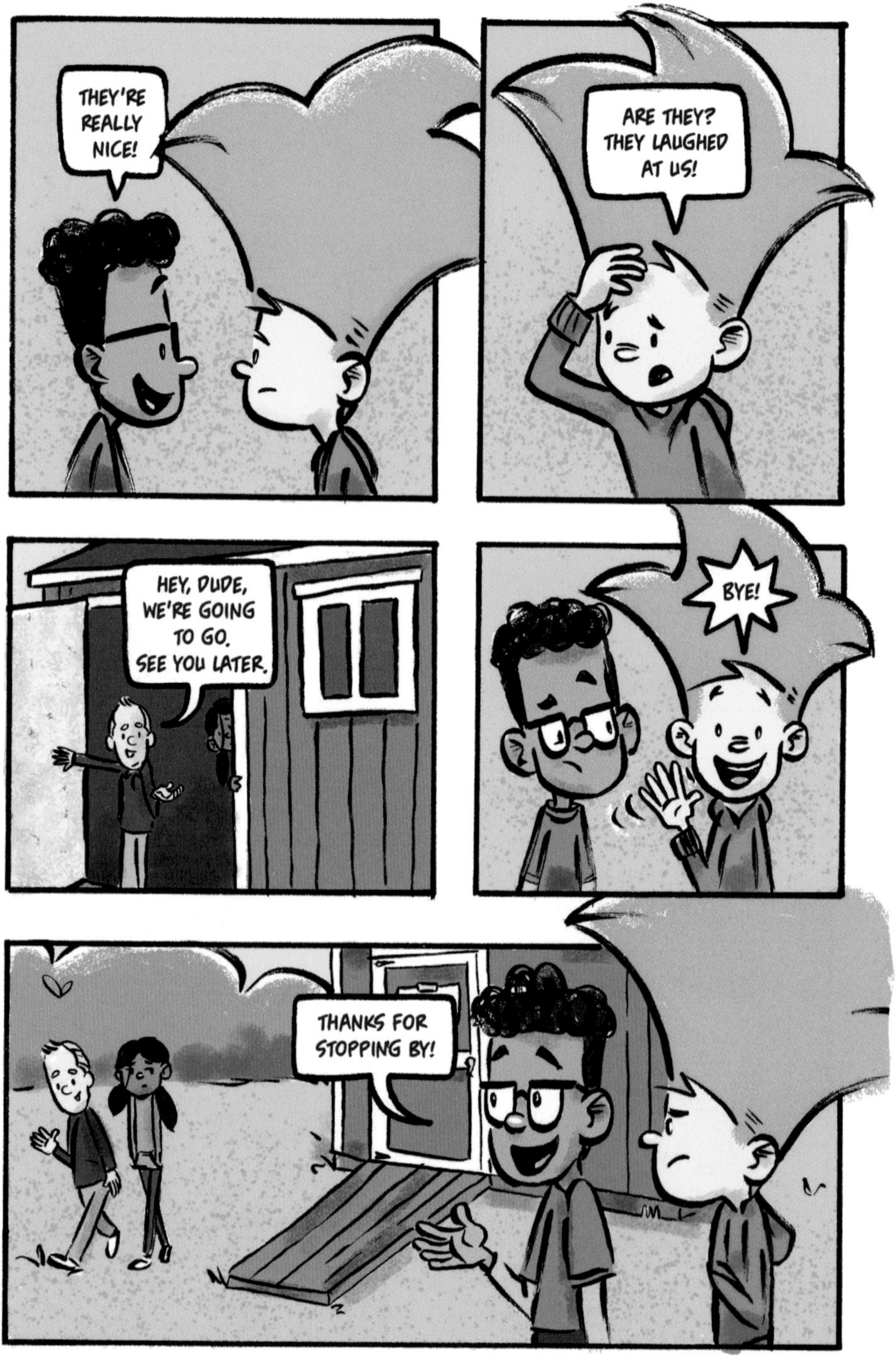
THEY'RE REALLY NICE!
ARE THEY? THEY LAUGHED AT US!
HEY, DUDE, WE'RE GOING TO GO. SEE YOU LATER.
BYE!
THANKS FOR STOPPING BY!

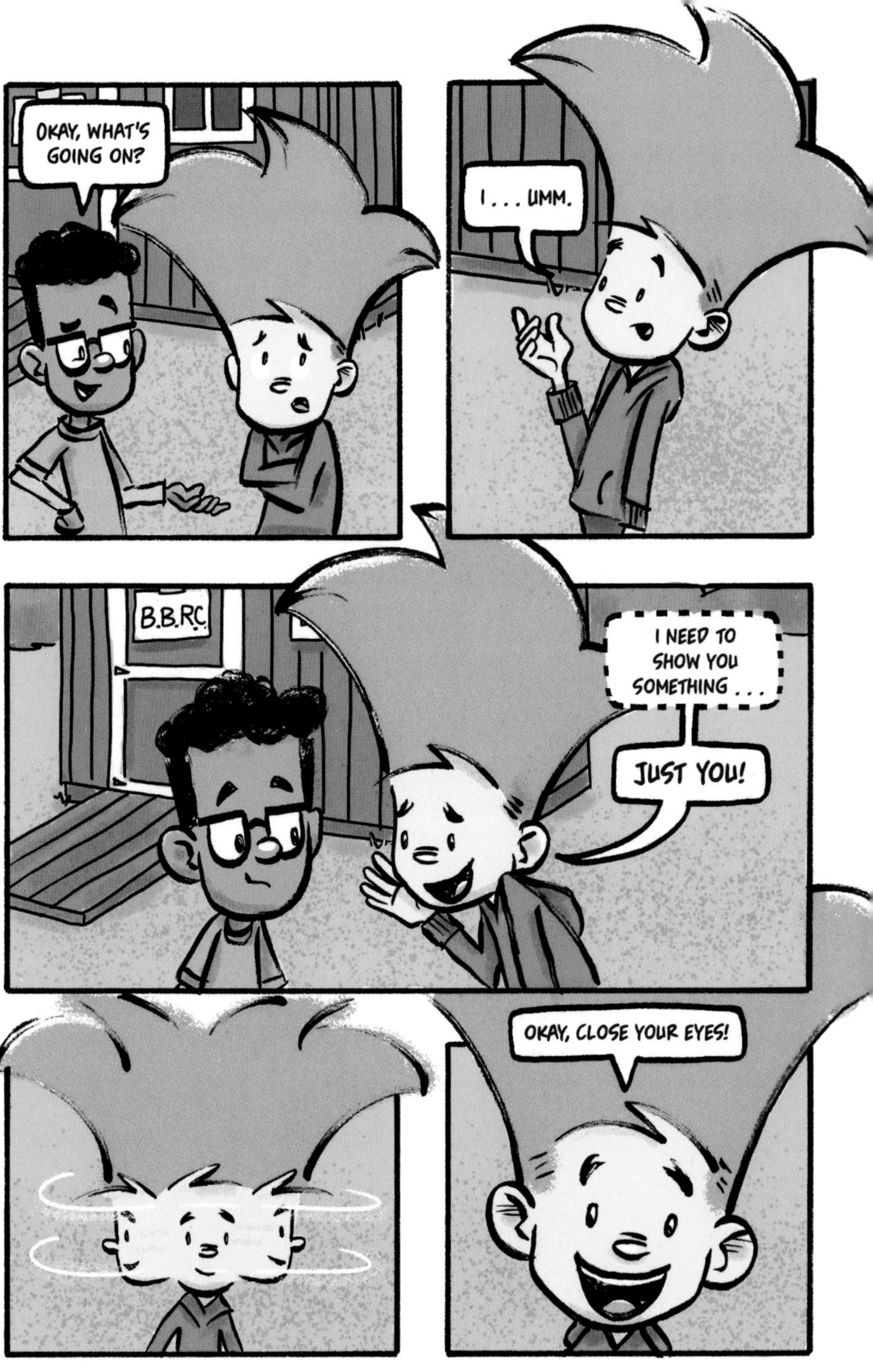
OKAY, WHAT'S GOING ON?
I . . . UMM.
B.B.R.C.
I NEED TO SHOW YOU SOMETHING . . .
JUST YOU!
OKAY, CLOSE YOUR EYES!

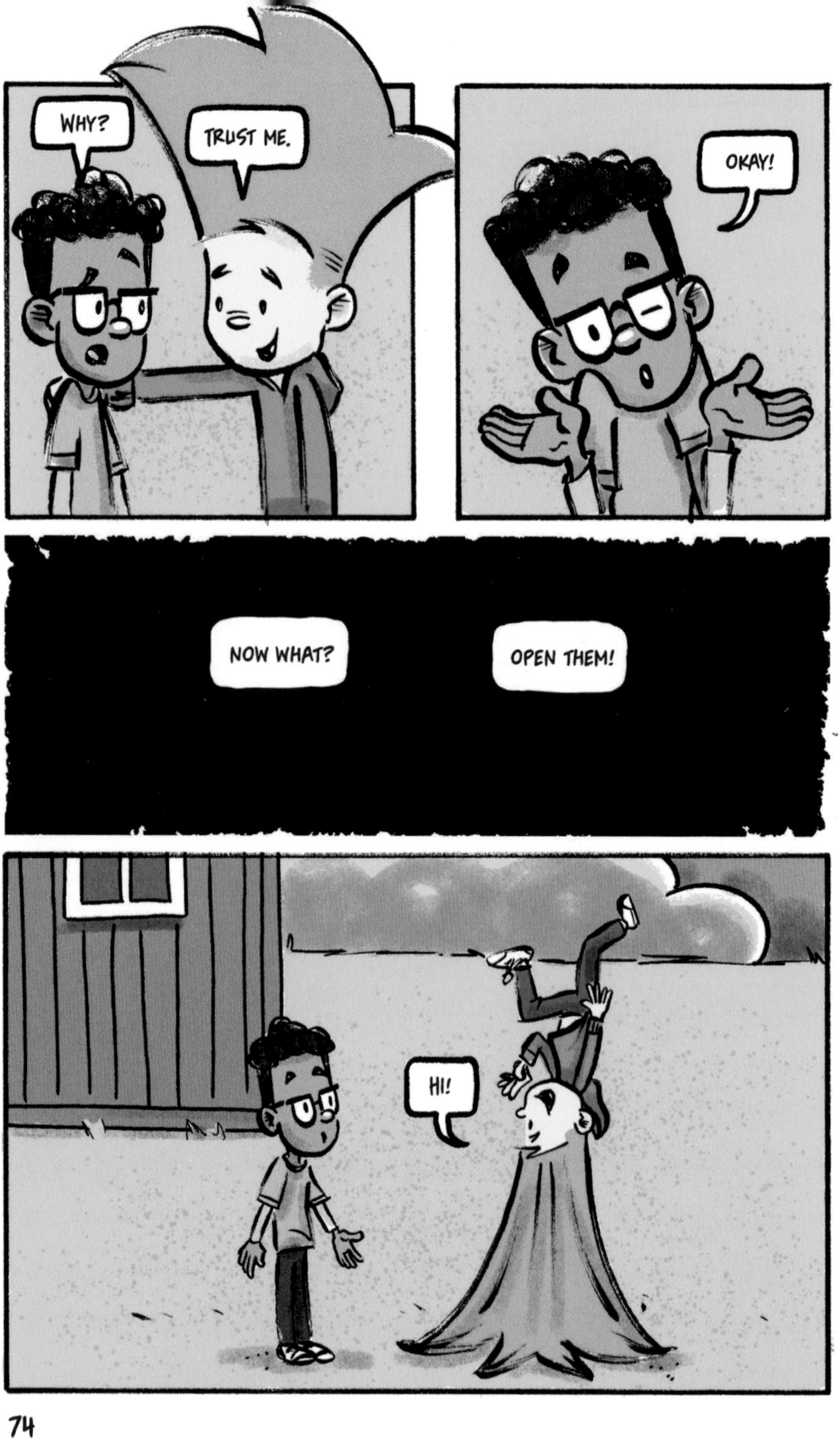
WHY?
TRUST ME.
OKAY!
NOW WHAT?
OPEN THEM!
HI!

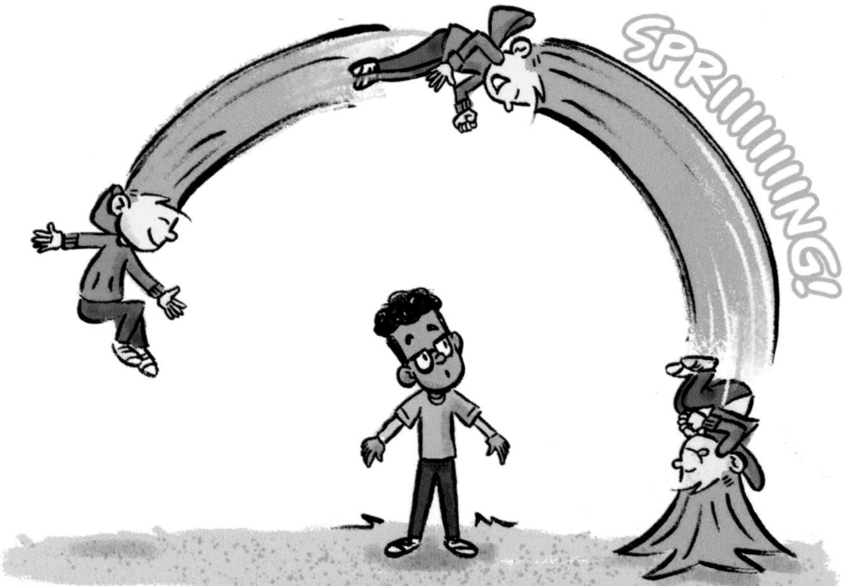
SPRIIIIIING!

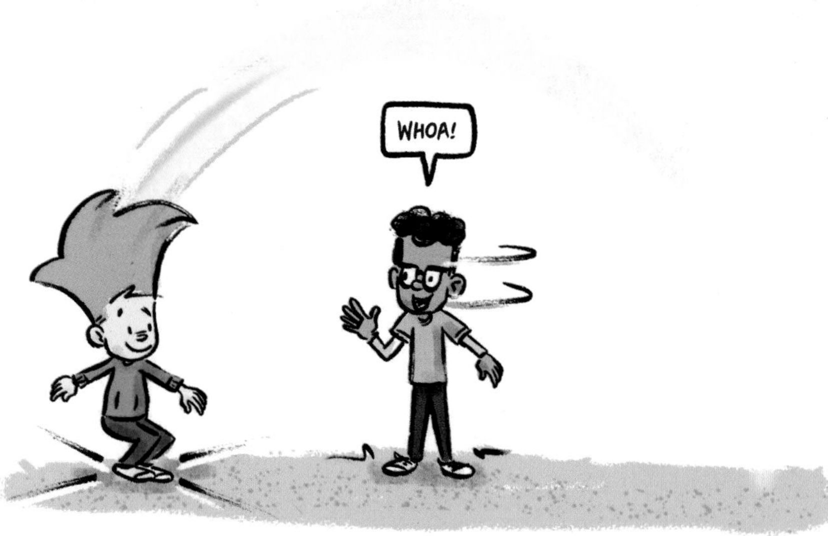
WHOA!

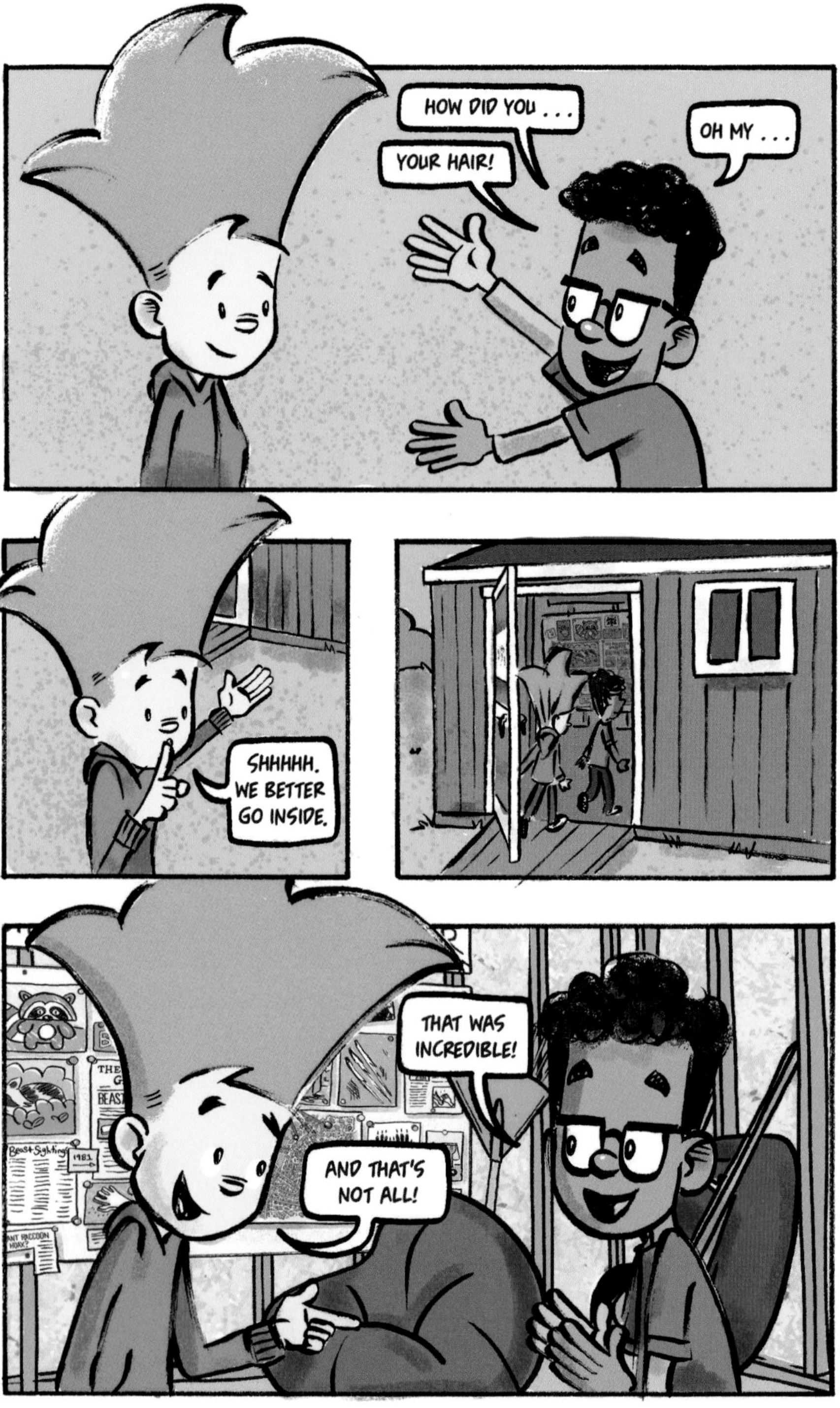
HOW DID YOU . . .
YOUR HAIR!
OH MY . . .
SHHHHH. WE BETTER GO INSIDE.
THAT WAS INCREDIBLE!
AND THAT'S NOT ALL!

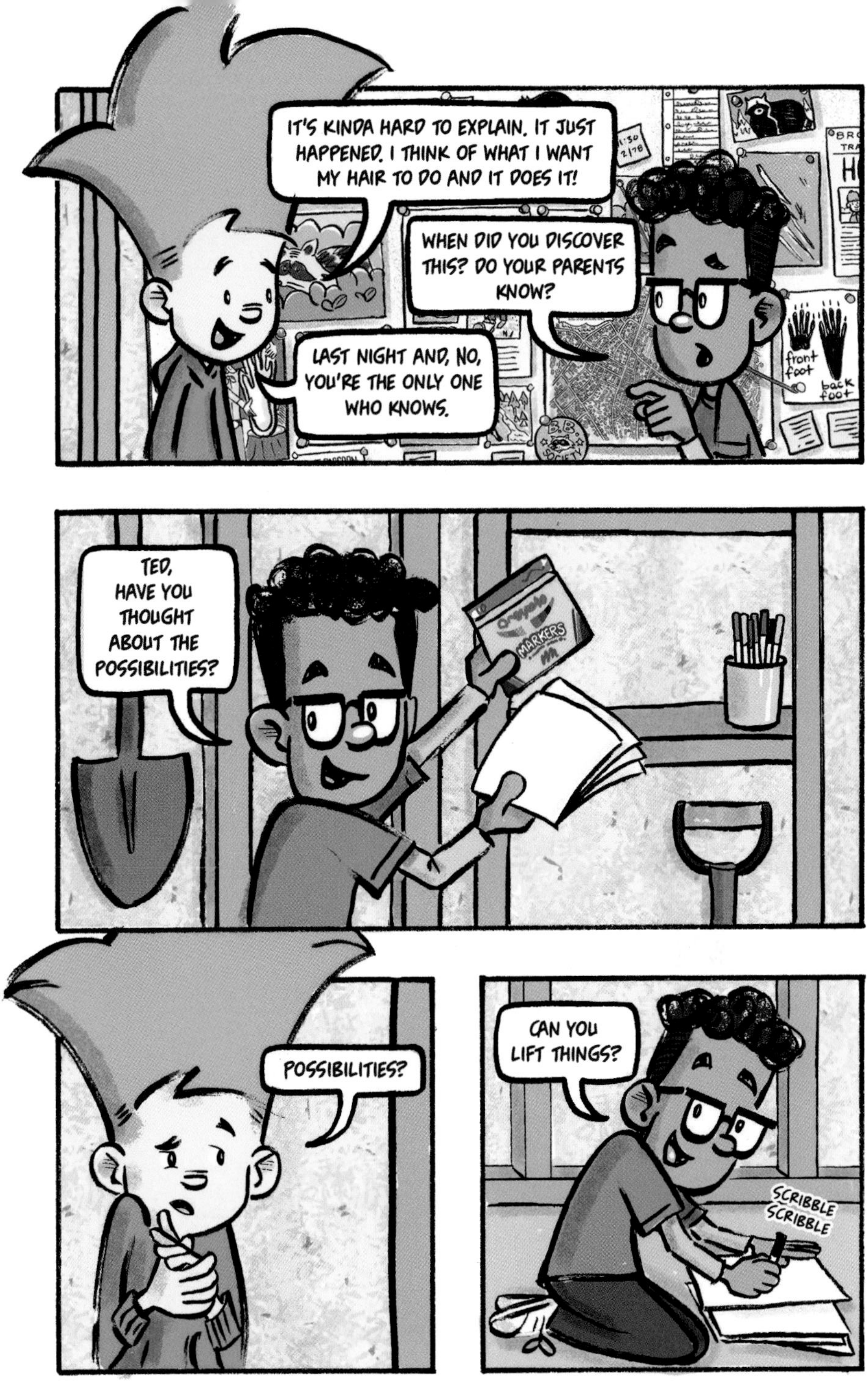
IT'S KINDA HARD TO EXPLAIN. IT JUST HAPPENED. I THINK OF WHAT I WANT MY HAIR TO DO AND IT DOES IT!
WHEN DID YOU DISCOVER THIS? DO YOUR PARENTS KNOW?
LAST NIGHT AND, NO, YOU'RE THE ONLY ONE WHO KNOWS.
front foot
back foot
B.B. SOCIETY
TED, HAVE YOU THOUGHT ABOUT THE POSSIBILITIES?
MARKERS
POSSIBILITIES?
CAN YOU LIFT THINGS?
SCRIBBLE SCRIBBLE

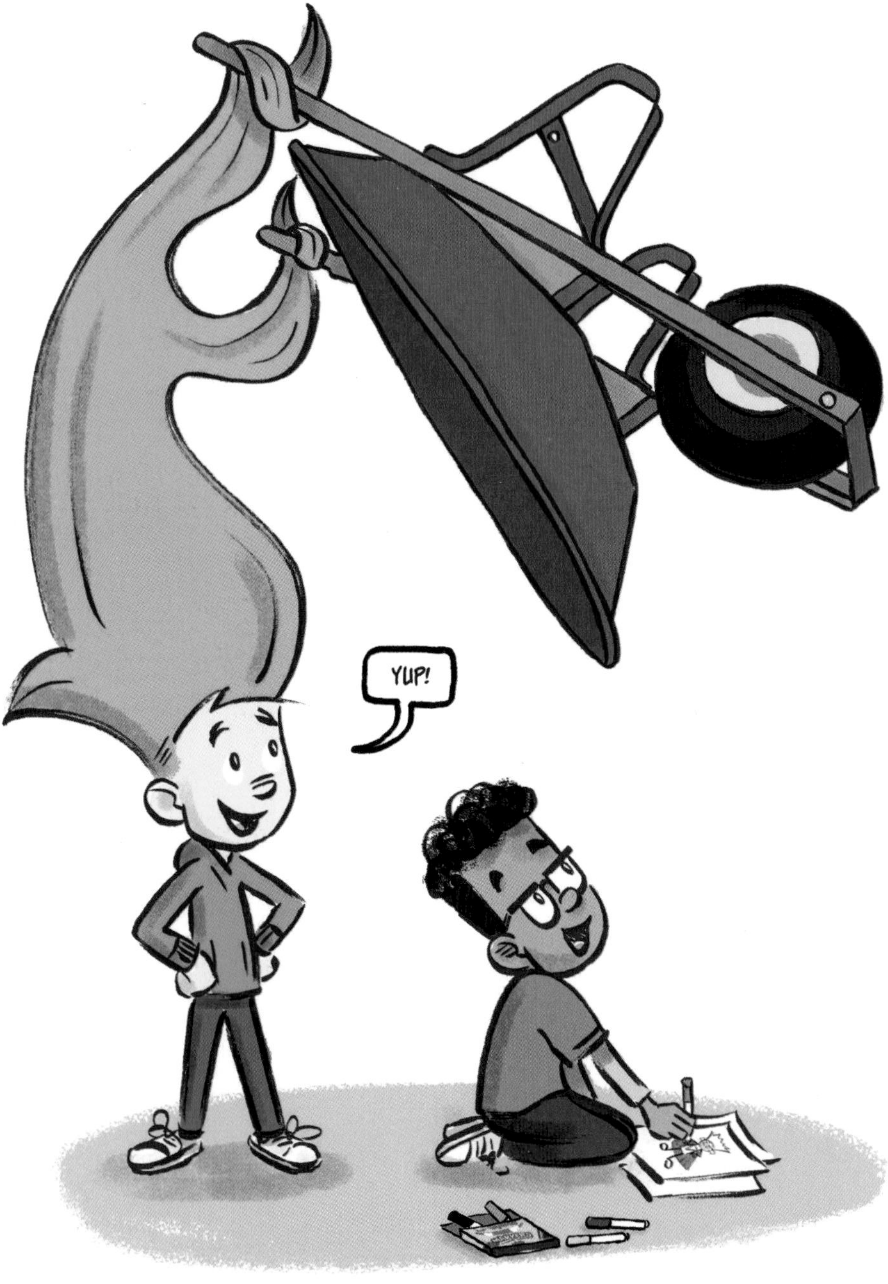
YUP!

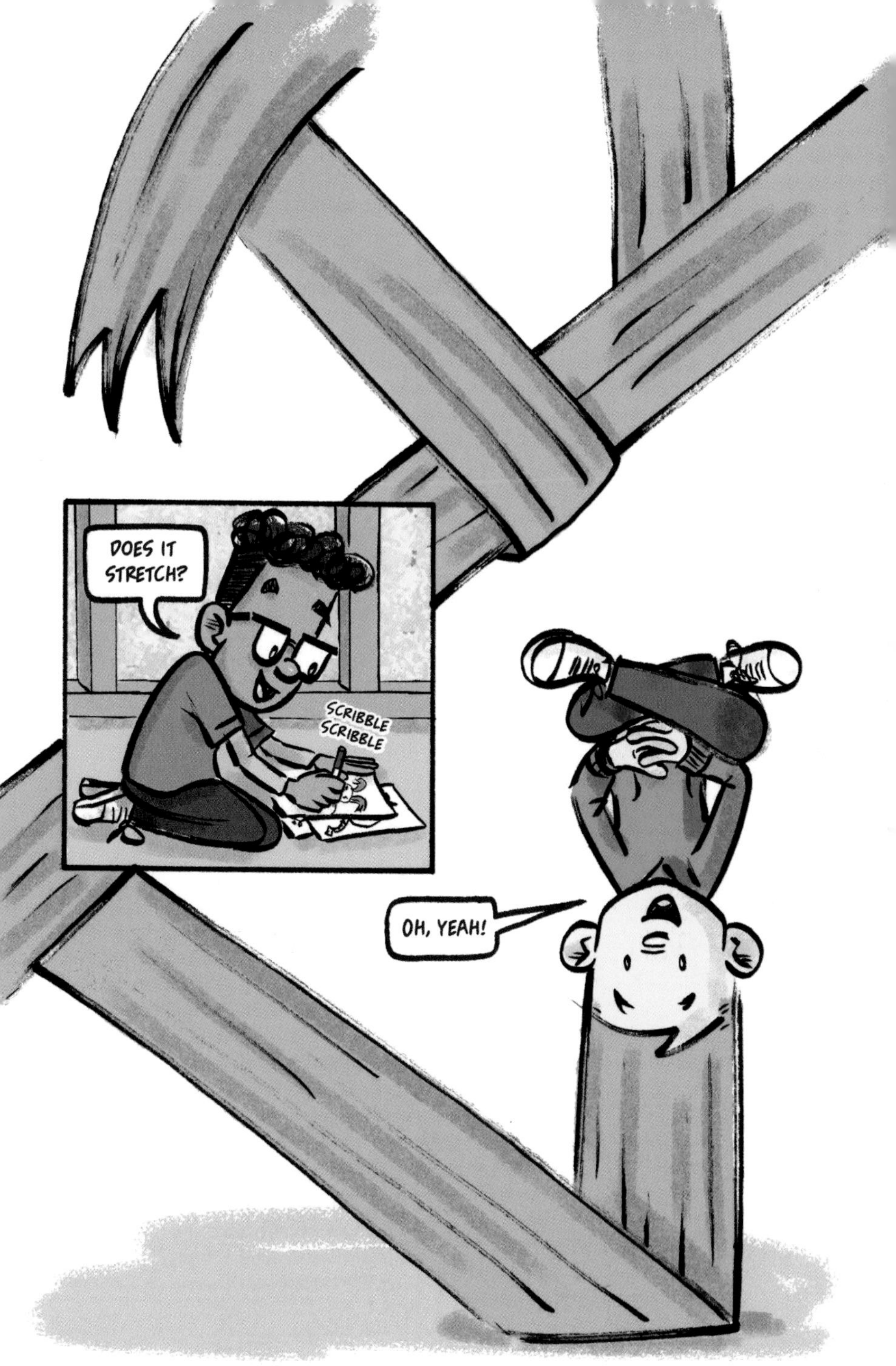
DOES IT STRETCH?
SCRIBBLE SCRIBBLE
OH, YEAH!

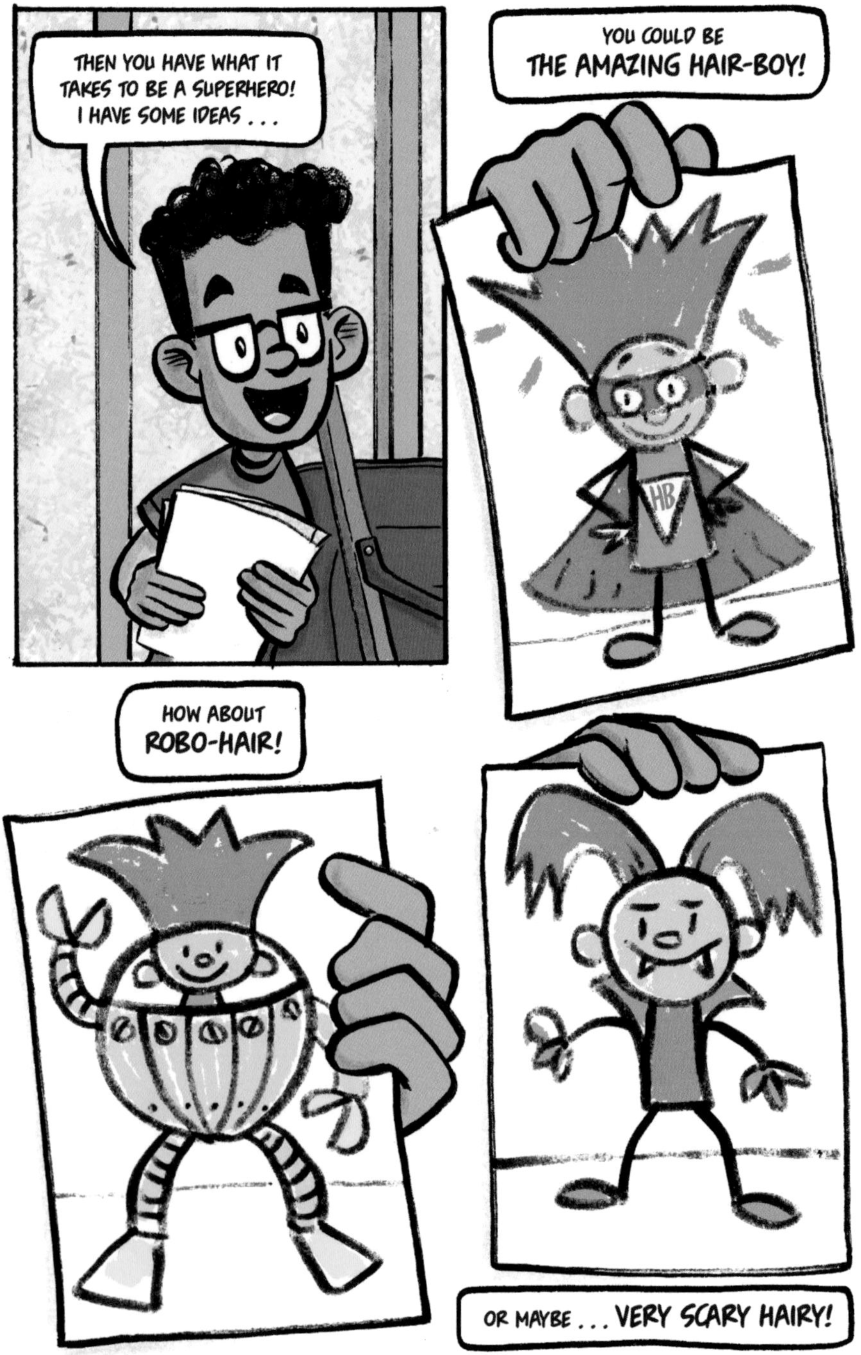
THEN YOU HAVE WHAT IT TAKES TO BE A SUPERHERO! I HAVE SOME IDEAS . . .
YOU COULD BE THE AMAZING HAIR-BOY!
HB
HOW ABOUT ROBO-HAIR!
OR MAYBE . . . VERY SCARY HAIRY!

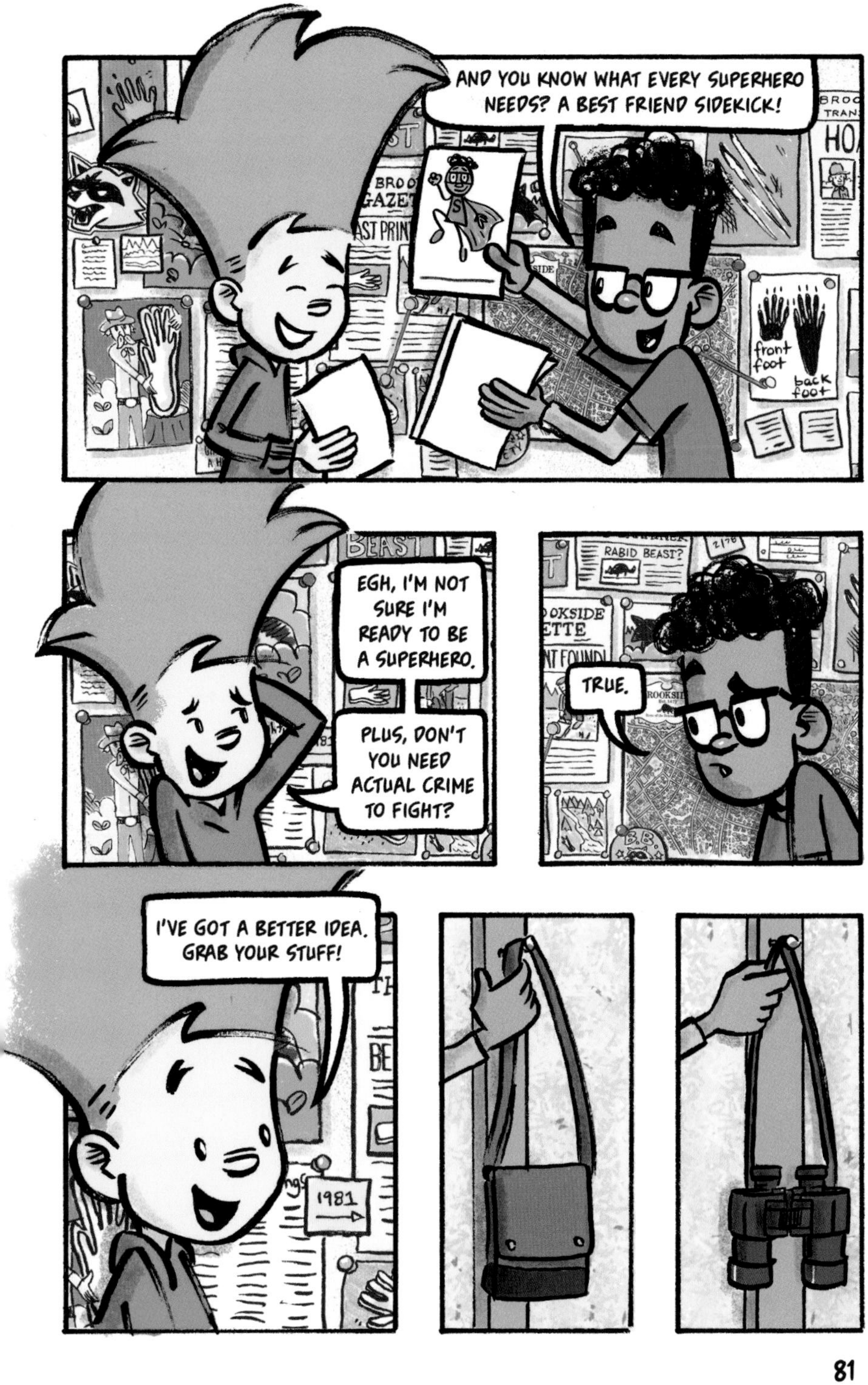
AND YOU KNOW WHAT EVERY SUPERHERO NEEDS? A BEST FRIEND SIDEKICK!
front foot
back foot
EGH, I'M NOT SURE I'M READY TO BE A SUPERHERO.
PLUS, DON'T YOU NEED ACTUAL CRIME TO FIGHT?
RABID BEAST?
TRUE.
I'VE GOT A BETTER IDEA. GRAB YOUR STUFF!
1981

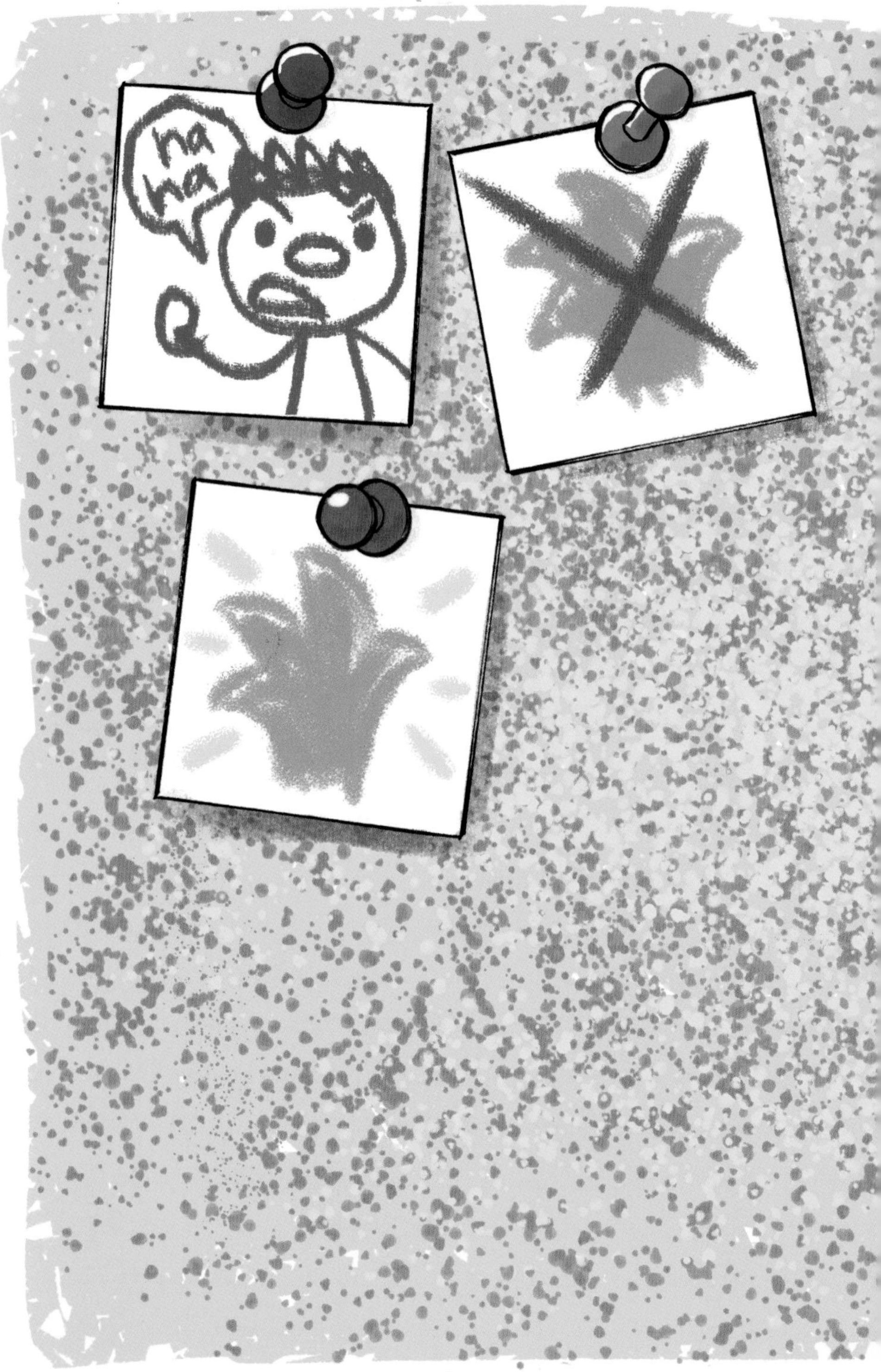
ha ha

CHAPTER 4:

IN SEARCH OF

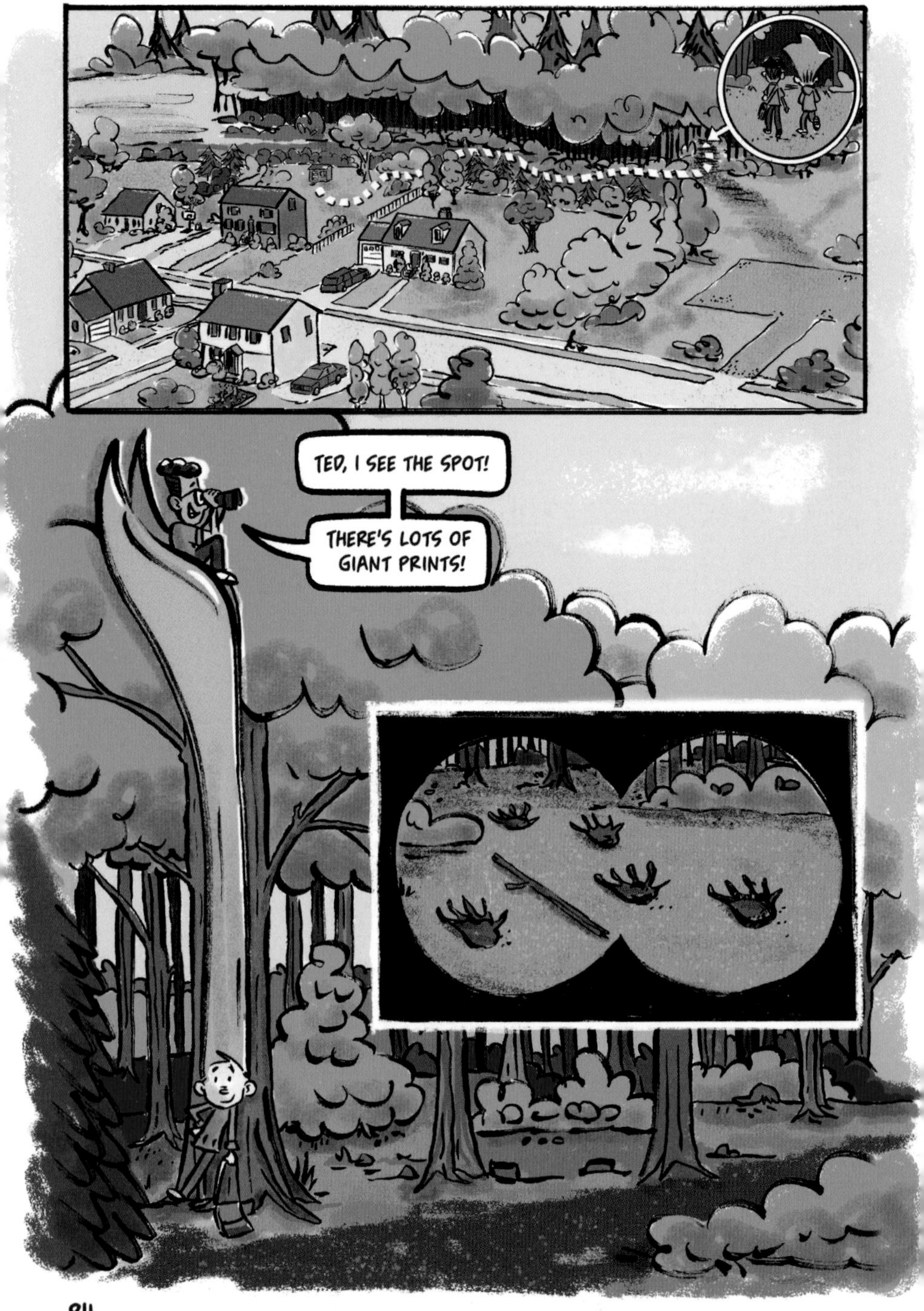
TED, I SEE THE SPOT!
THERE'S LOTS OF GIANT PRINTS!

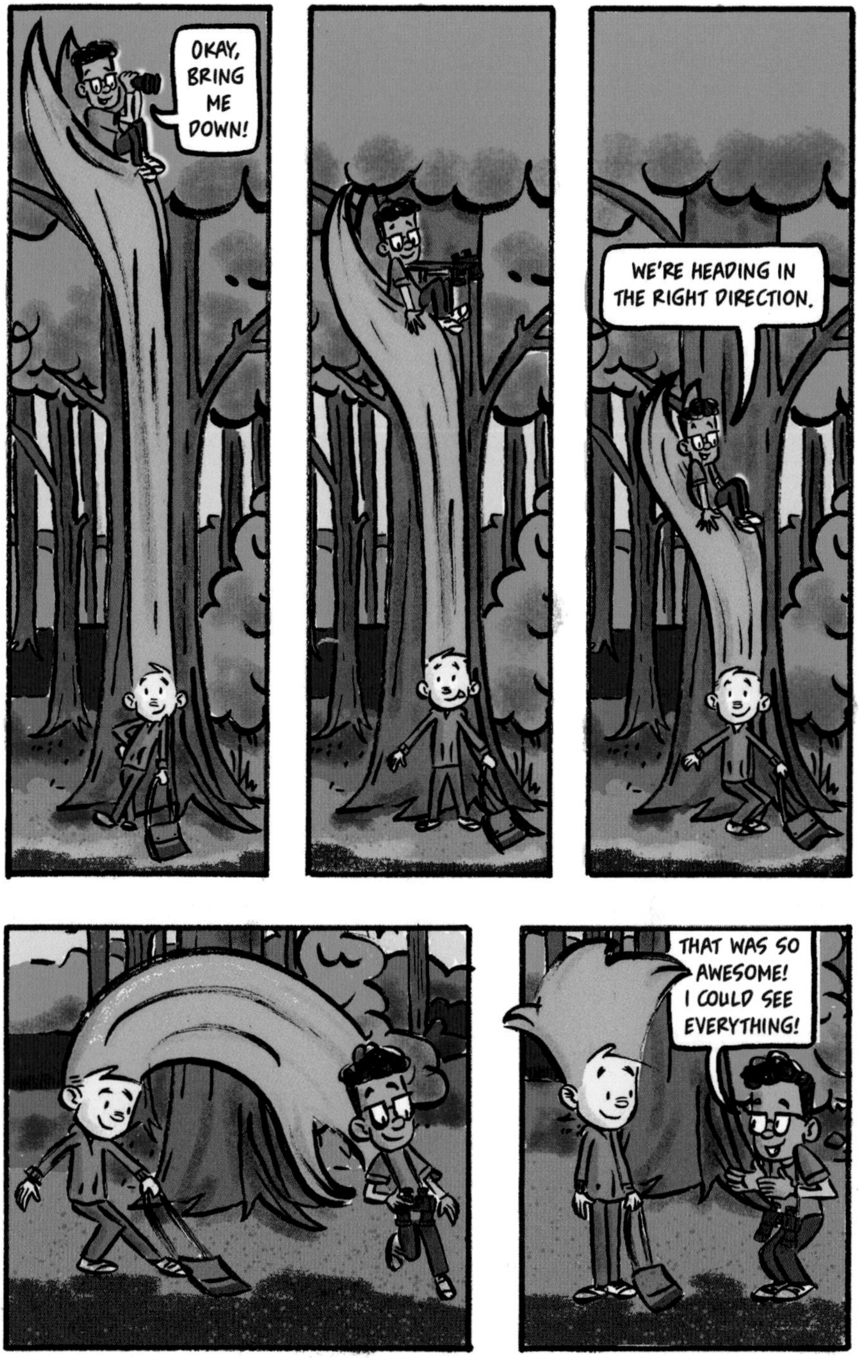
OKAY, BRING ME DOWN!
WE'RE HEADING IN THE RIGHT DIRECTION.
THAT WAS SO AWESOME! I COULD SEE EVERYTHING!

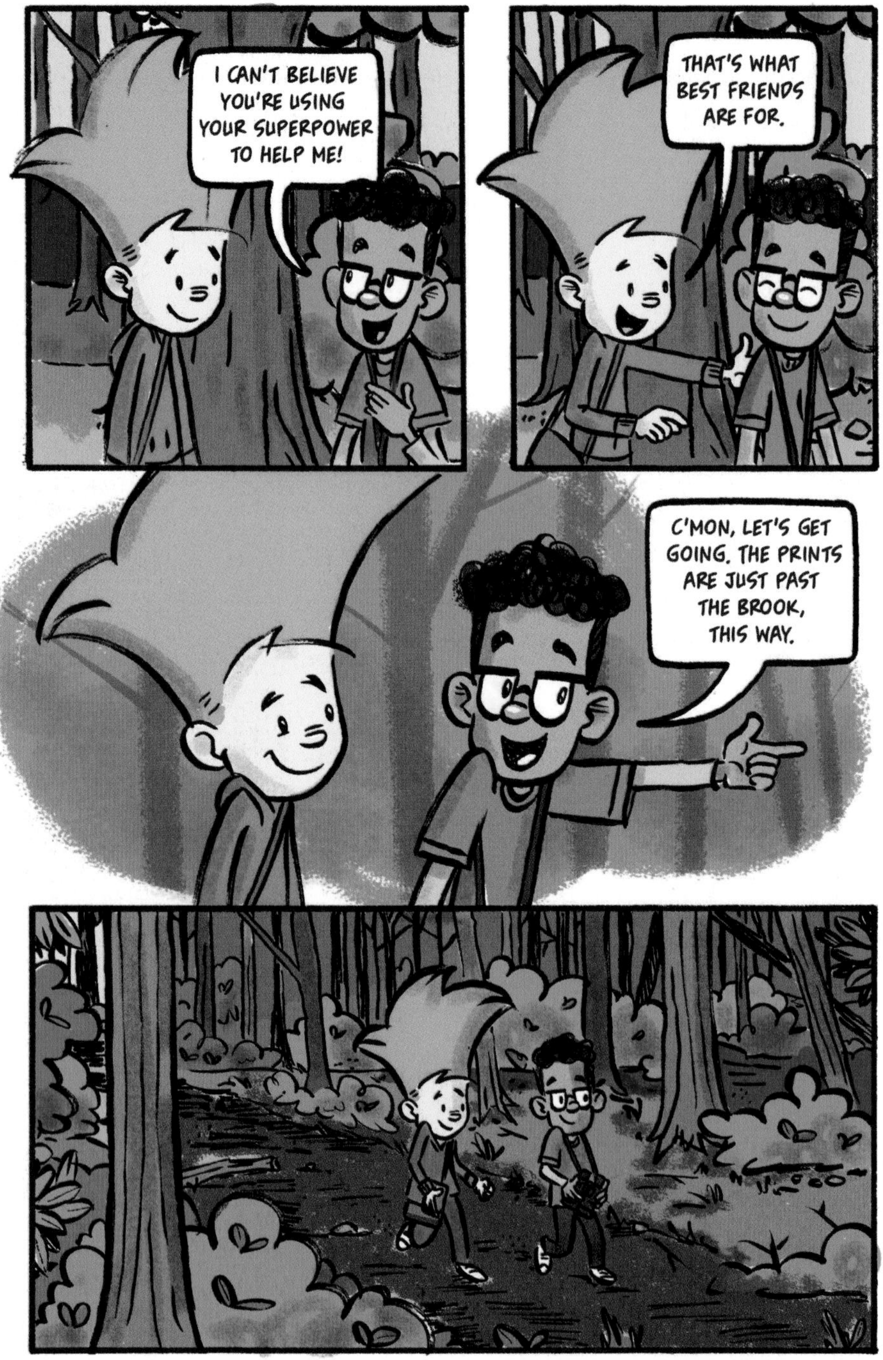
I CAN'T BELIEVE YOU'RE USING YOUR SUPERPOWER TO HELP ME!
THAT'S WHAT BEST FRIENDS ARE FOR.
C'MON, LET'S GET GOING. THE PRINTS ARE JUST PAST THE BROOK, THIS WAY.

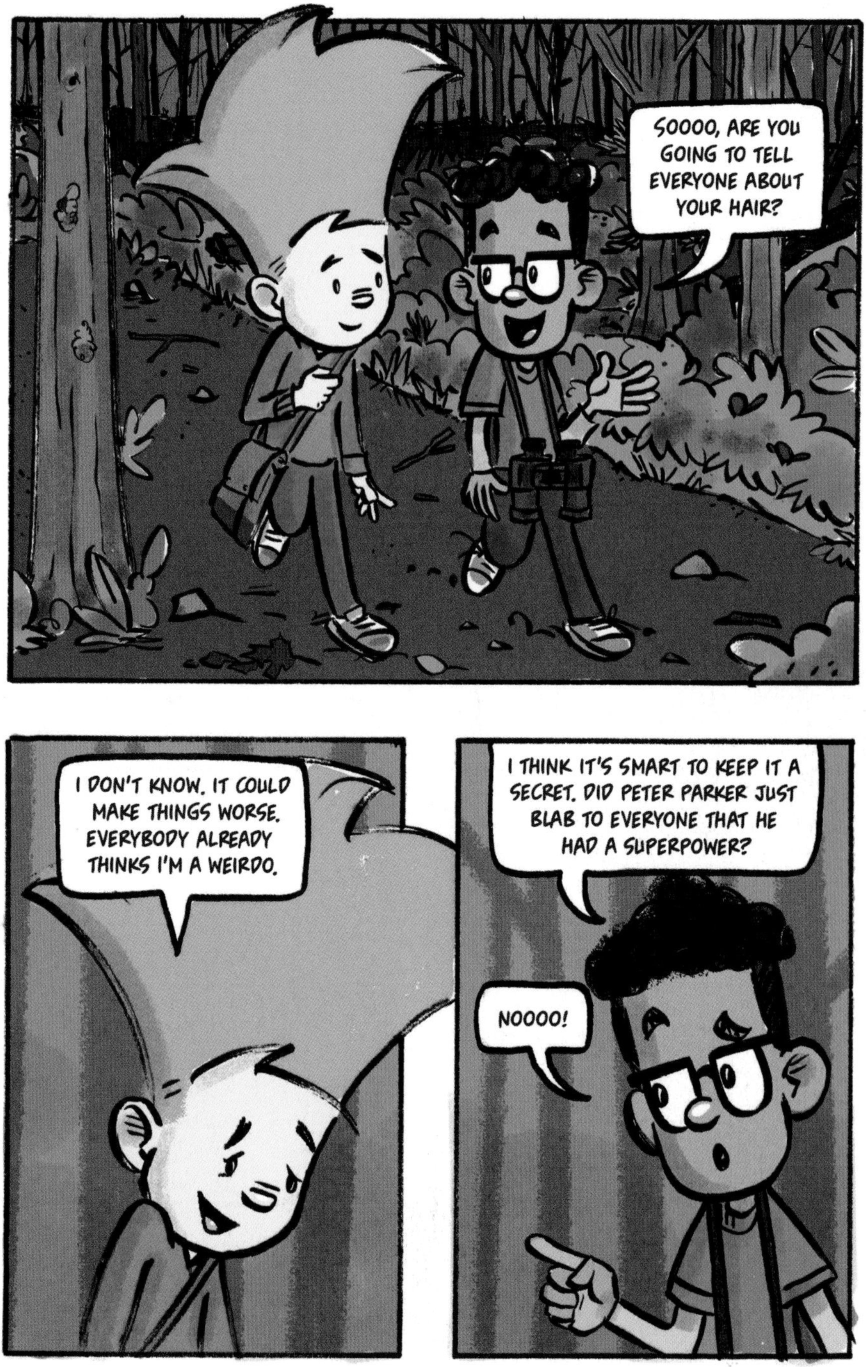
SOOOO, ARE YOU GOING TO TELL EVERYONE ABOUT YOUR HAIR?
I DON'T KNOW. IT COULD MAKE THINGS WORSE. EVERYBODY ALREADY THINKS I'M A WEIRDO.
I THINK IT'S SMART TO KEEP IT A SECRET. DID PETER PARKER JUST BLAB TO EVERYONE THAT HE HAD A SUPERPOWER?
NOOOO!

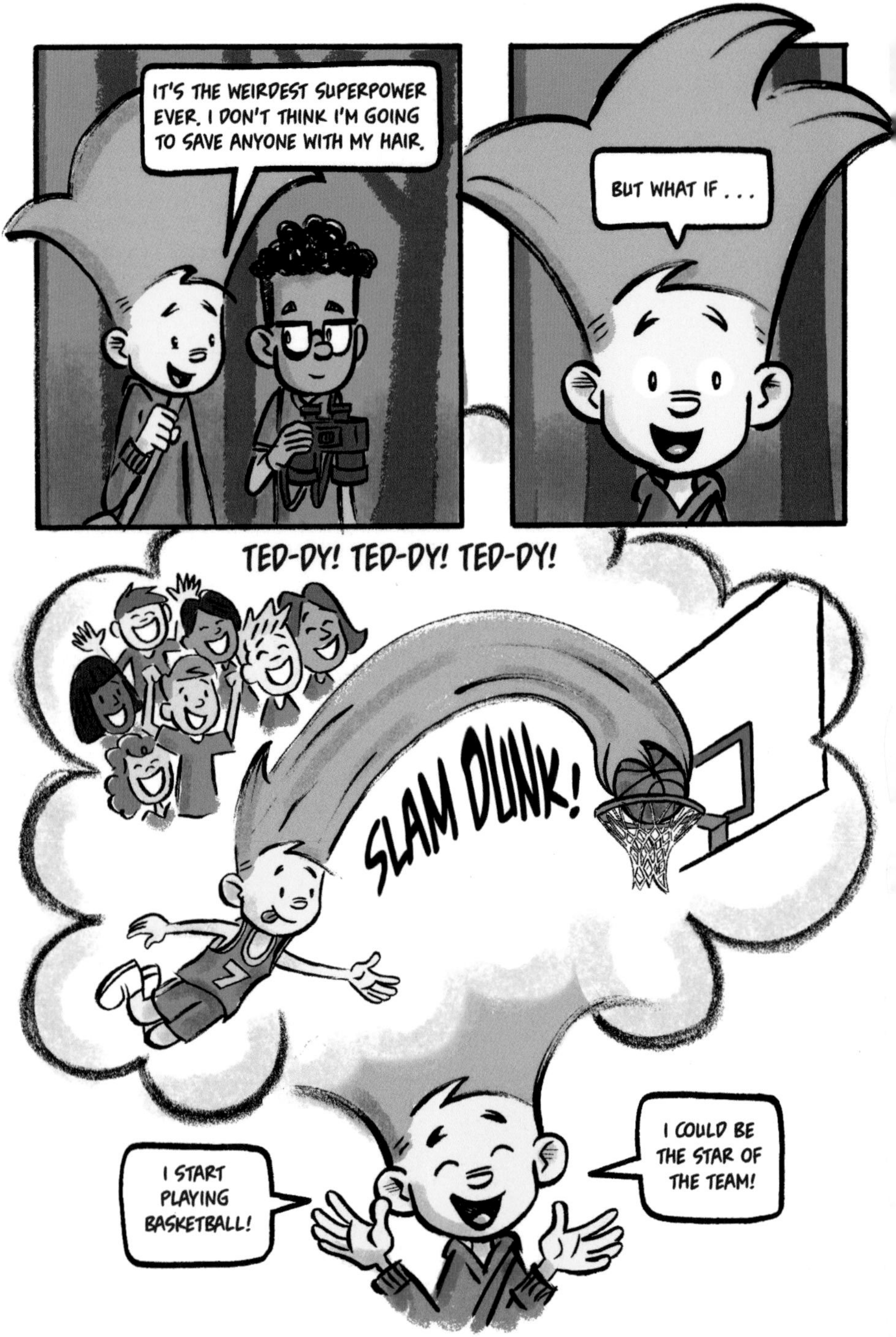
IT'S THE WEIRDEST SUPERPOWER EVER. I DON'T THINK I'M GOING TO SAVE ANYONE WITH MY HAIR.
BUT WHAT IF . . .
TED-DY! TED-DY! TED-DY!
SLAM DUNK!
I START PLAYING BASKETBALL!
I COULD BE THE STAR OF THE TEAM!

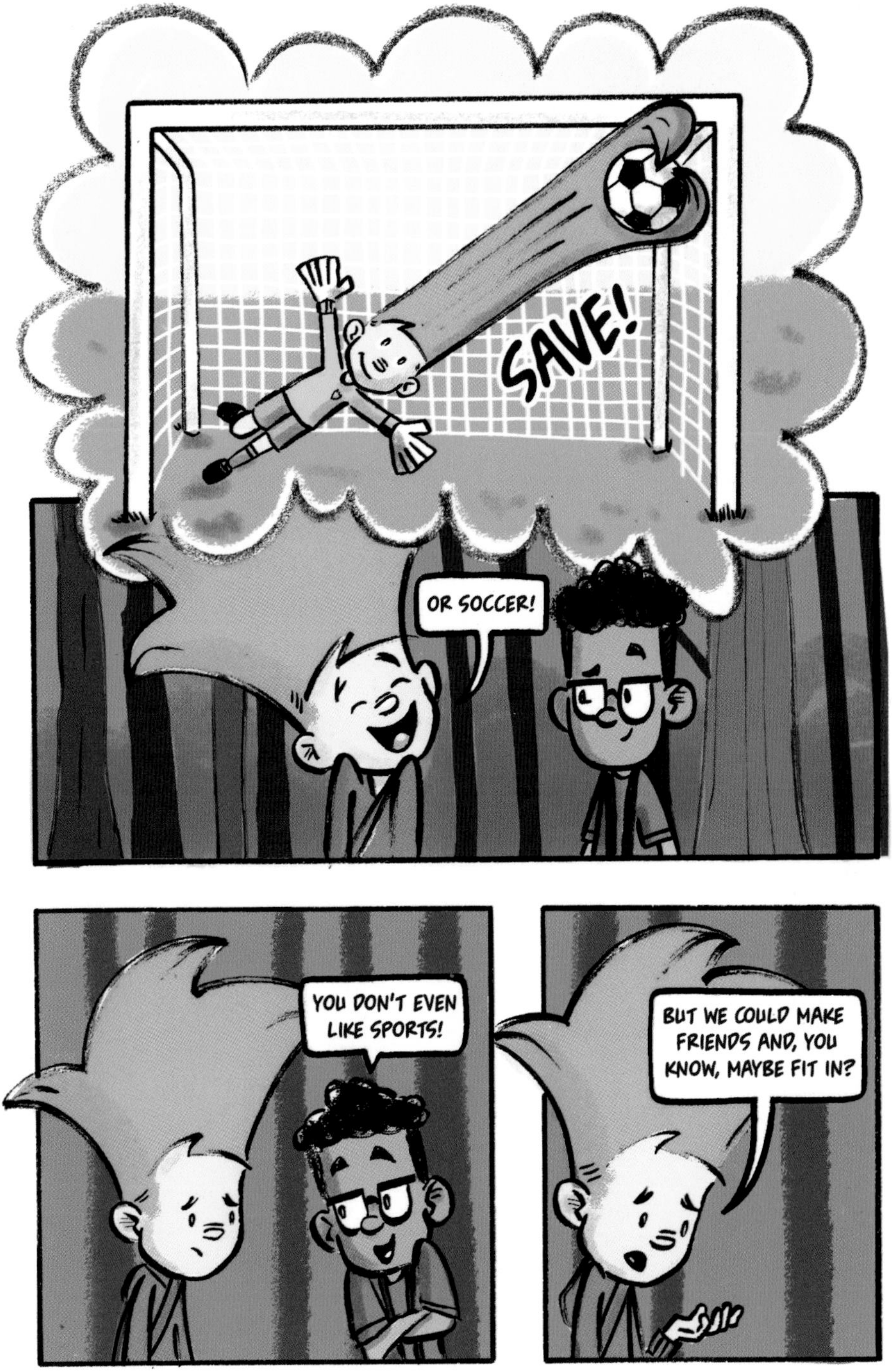
SAVE!
OR SOCCER!
YOU DON'T EVEN LIKE SPORTS!
BUT WE COULD MAKE FRIENDS AND, YOU KNOW, MAYBE FIT IN?

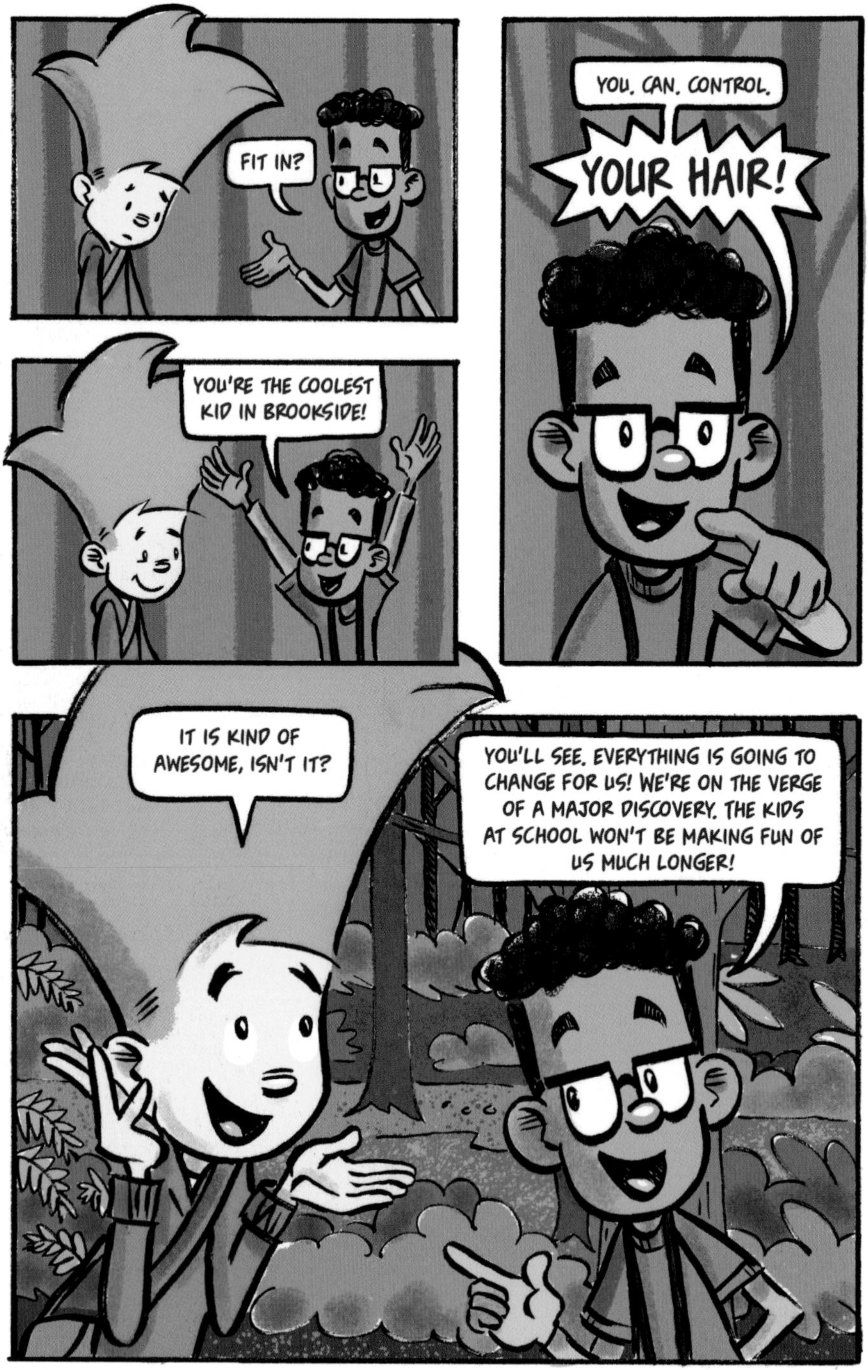
FIT IN?
YOU. CAN. CONTROL.
YOUR HAIR!
YOU'RE THE COOLEST KID IN BROOKSIDE!
IT IS KIND OF AWESOME, ISN'T IT?
YOU'LL SEE. EVERYTHING IS GOING TO CHANGE FOR US! WE'RE ON THE VERGE OF A MAJOR DISCOVERY. THE KIDS AT SCHOOL WON'T BE MAKING FUN OF US MUCH LONGER!

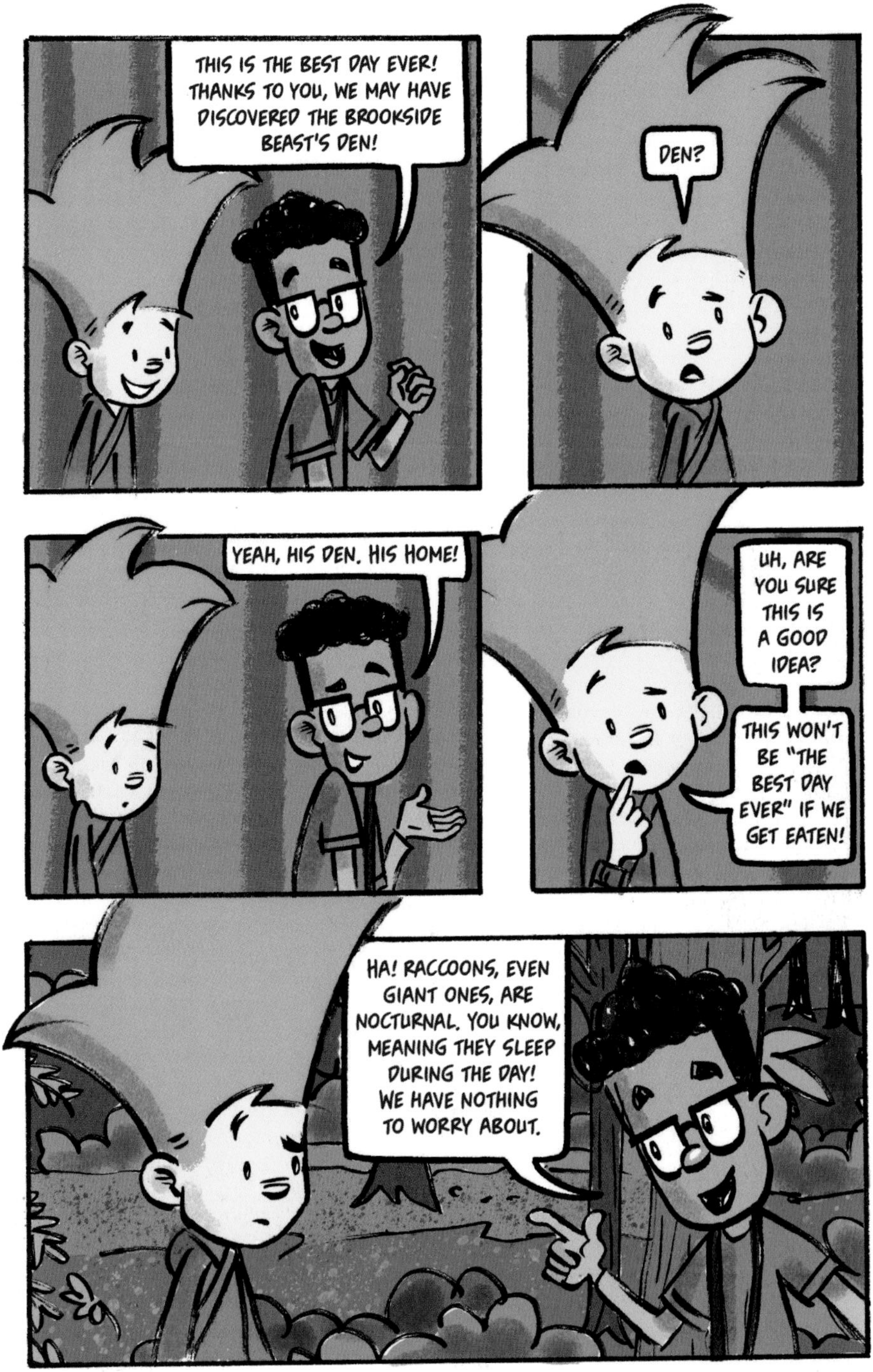
THIS IS THE BEST DAY EVER! THANKS TO YOU, WE MAY HAVE DISCOVERED THE BROOKSIDE BEAST'S DEN!
DEN?
YEAH, HIS DEN. HIS HOME!
UH, ARE YOU SURE THIS IS A GOOD IDEA?
THIS WON'T BE "THE BEST DAY EVER" IF WE GET EATEN!
HA! RACCOONS, EVEN GIANT ONES, ARE NOCTURNAL. YOU KNOW, MEANING THEY SLEEP DURING THE DAY! WE HAVE NOTHING TO WORRY ABOUT.

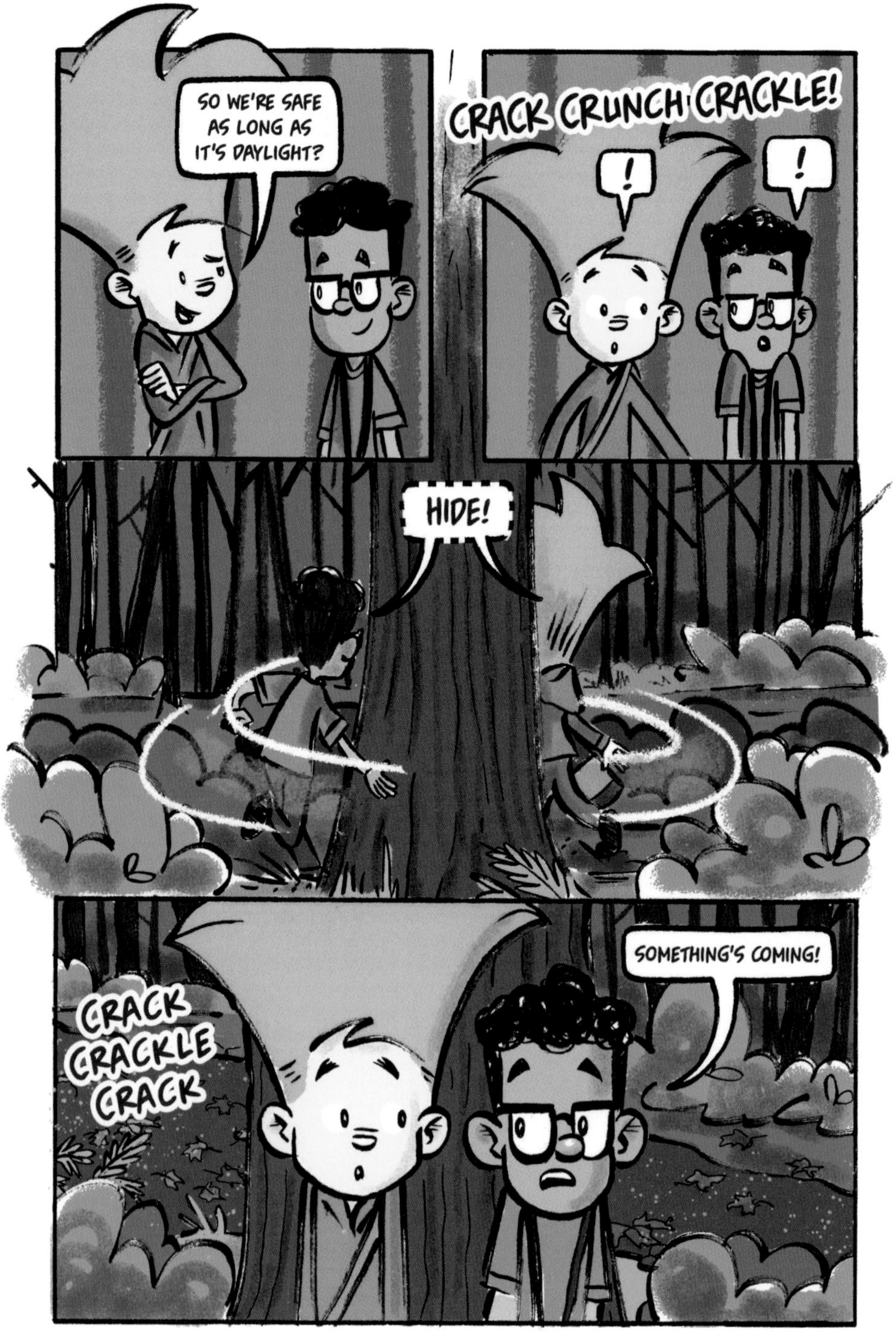
SO WE'RE SAFE AS LONG AS IT'S DAYLIGHT?
CRACK CRUNCH CRACKLE!
!
!
HIDE!
SOMETHING'S COMING!
CRACK CRACKLE CRACK

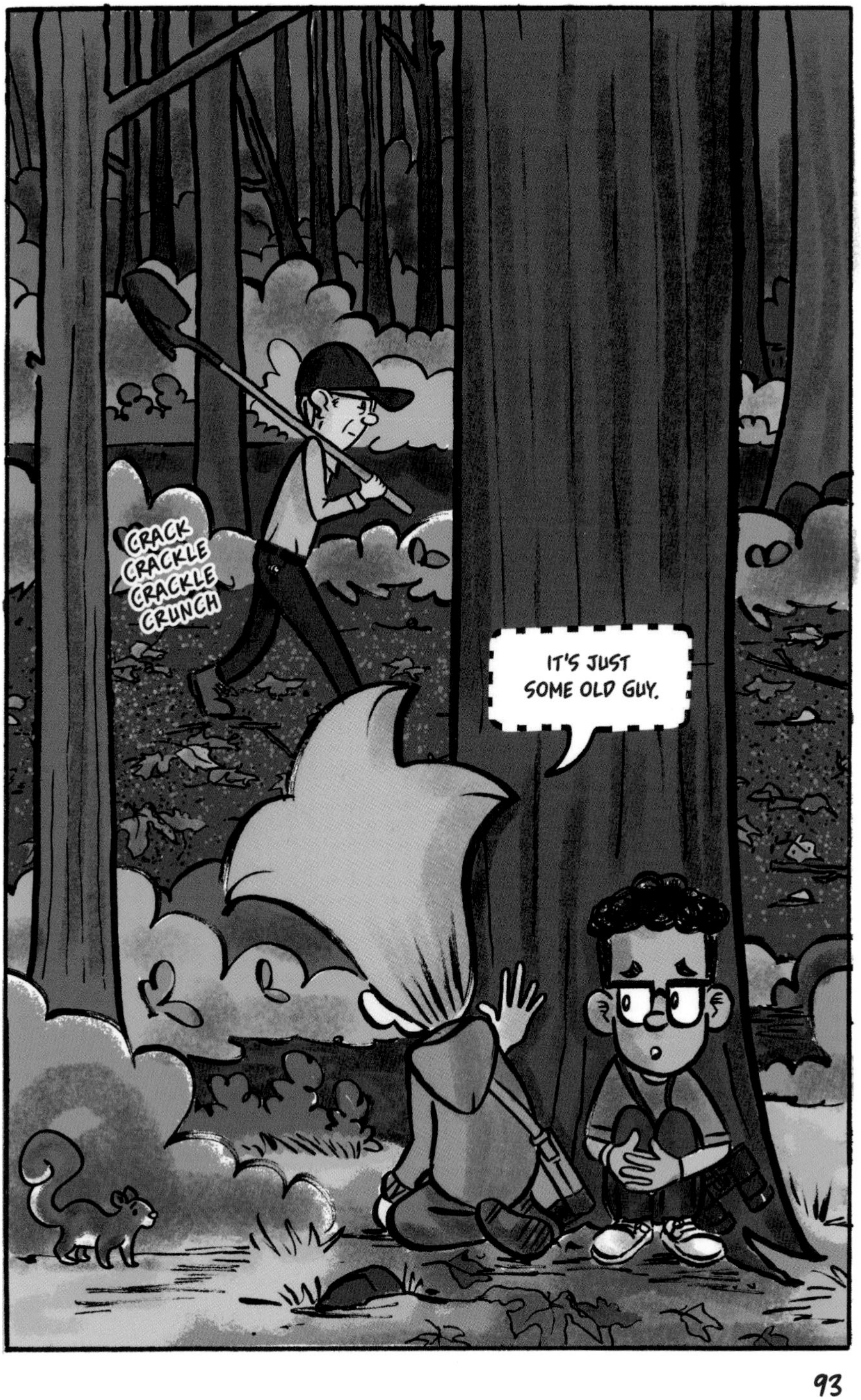
CRACK
CRACKLE
CRACKLE
CRUNCH
IT'S JUST SOME OLD GUY.

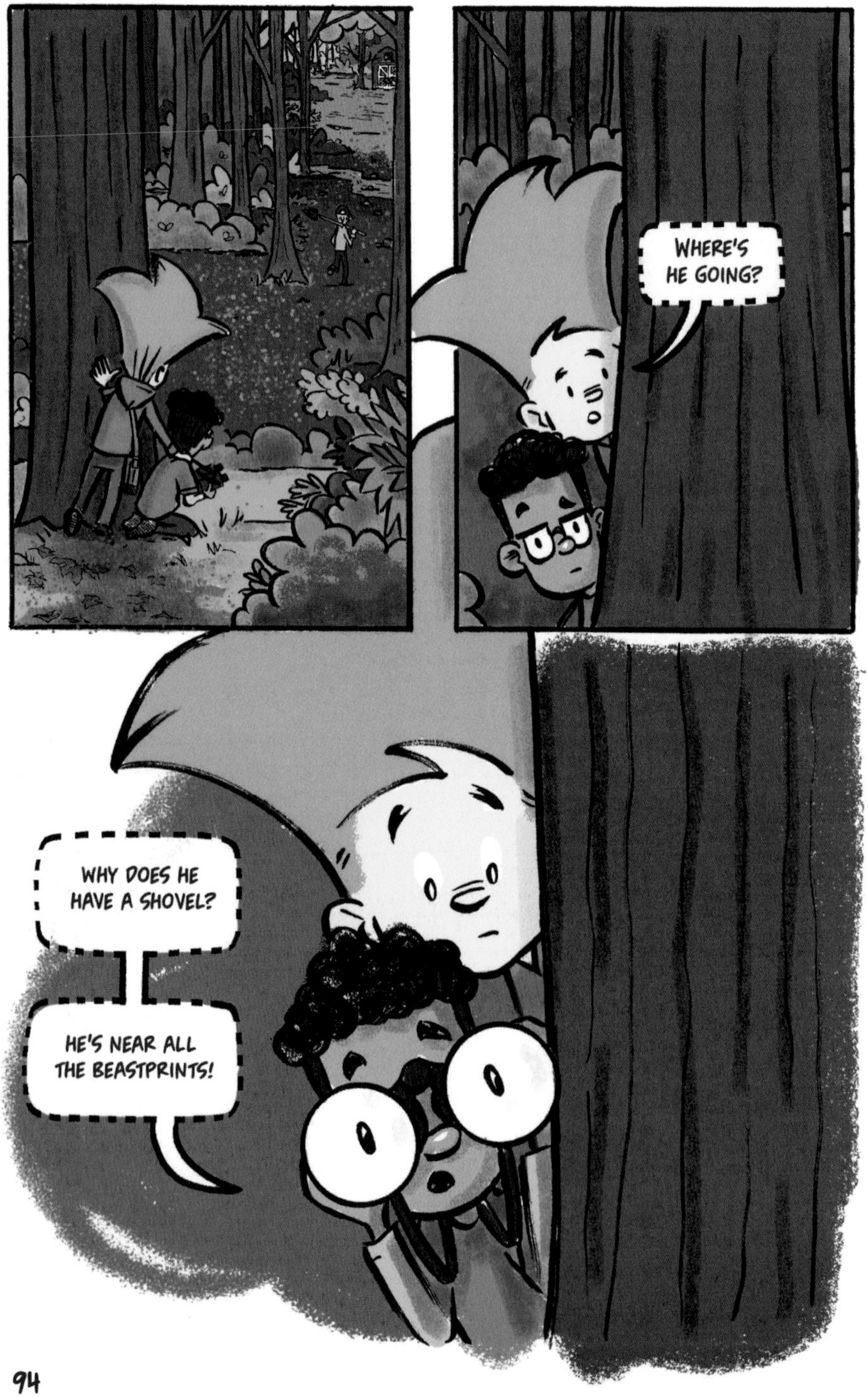
WHERE'S HE GOING?
WHY DOES HE HAVE A SHOVEL?
HE'S NEAR ALL THE BEASTPRINTS!

HE'S WALKING TOWARD AN OLD BARN!

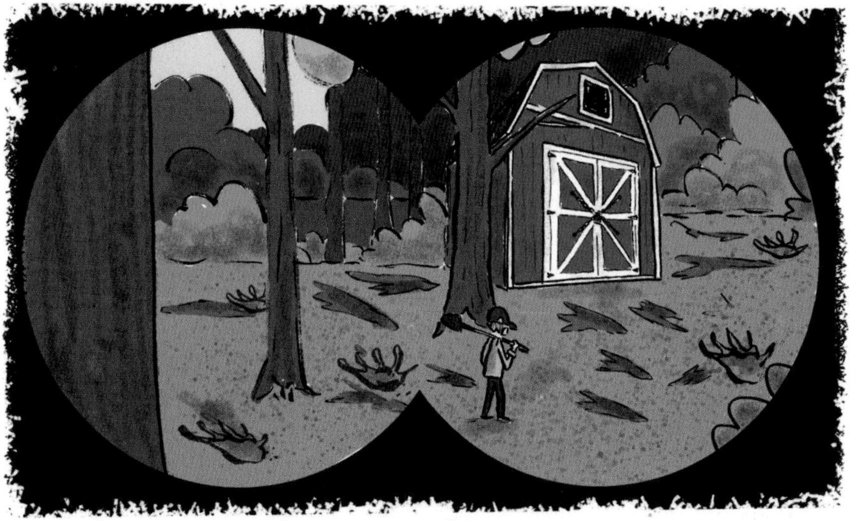

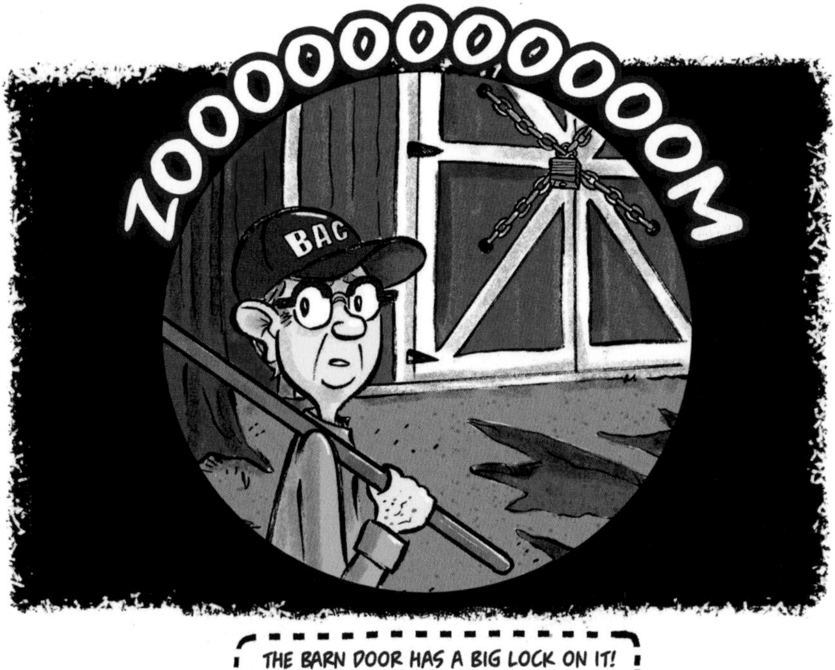
ZOOOOOOOOOOOM
BAC

THE BARN DOOR HAS A BIG LOCK ON IT!

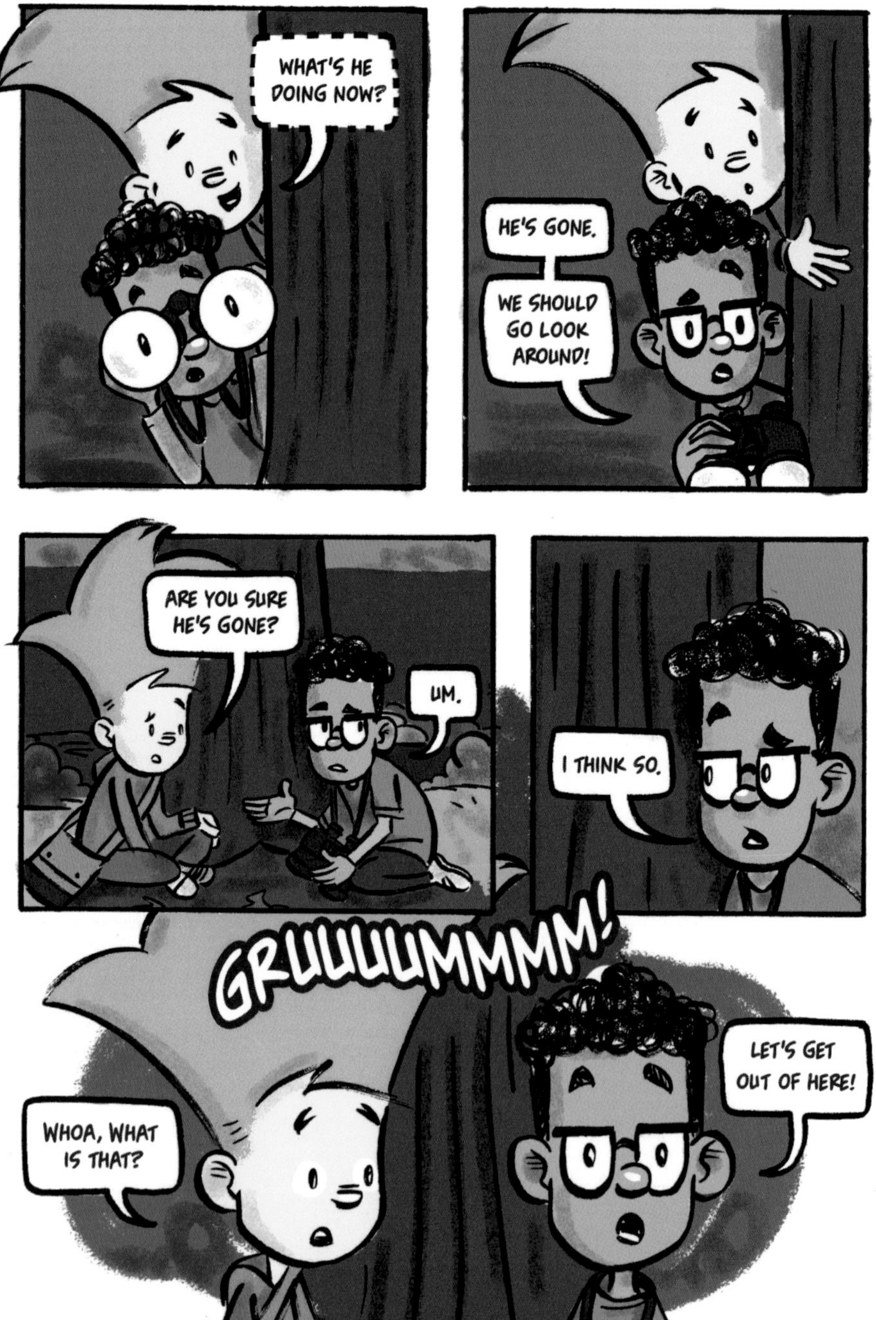
WHAT'S HE DOING NOW?
HE'S GONE.
WE SHOULD GO LOOK AROUND!
ARE YOU SURE HE'S GONE?
UM.
I THINK SO.
GRUUUUMMMM!
WHOA, WHAT IS THAT?
LET'S GET OUT OF HERE!

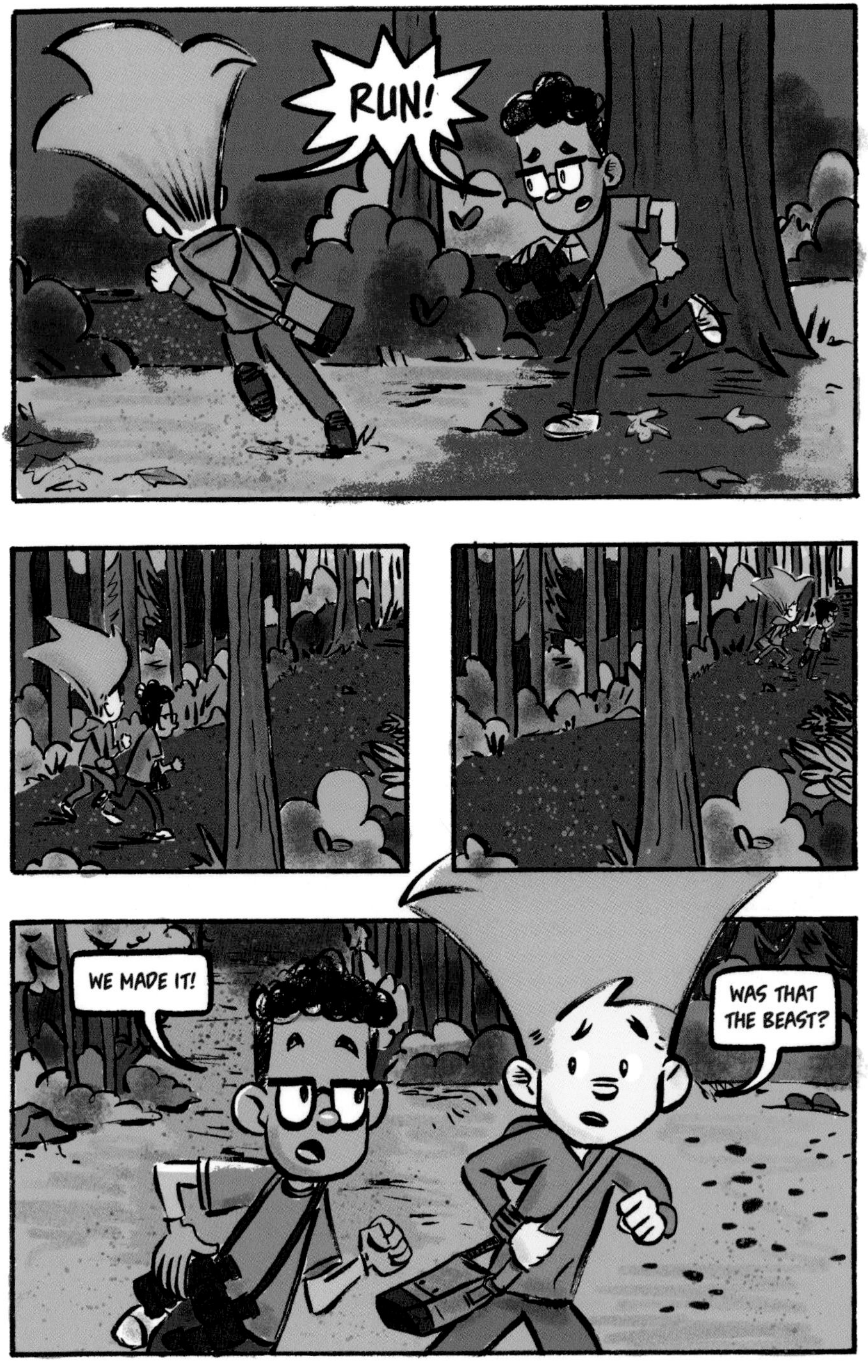
RUN!
WE MADE IT!
WAS THAT
THE BEAST?

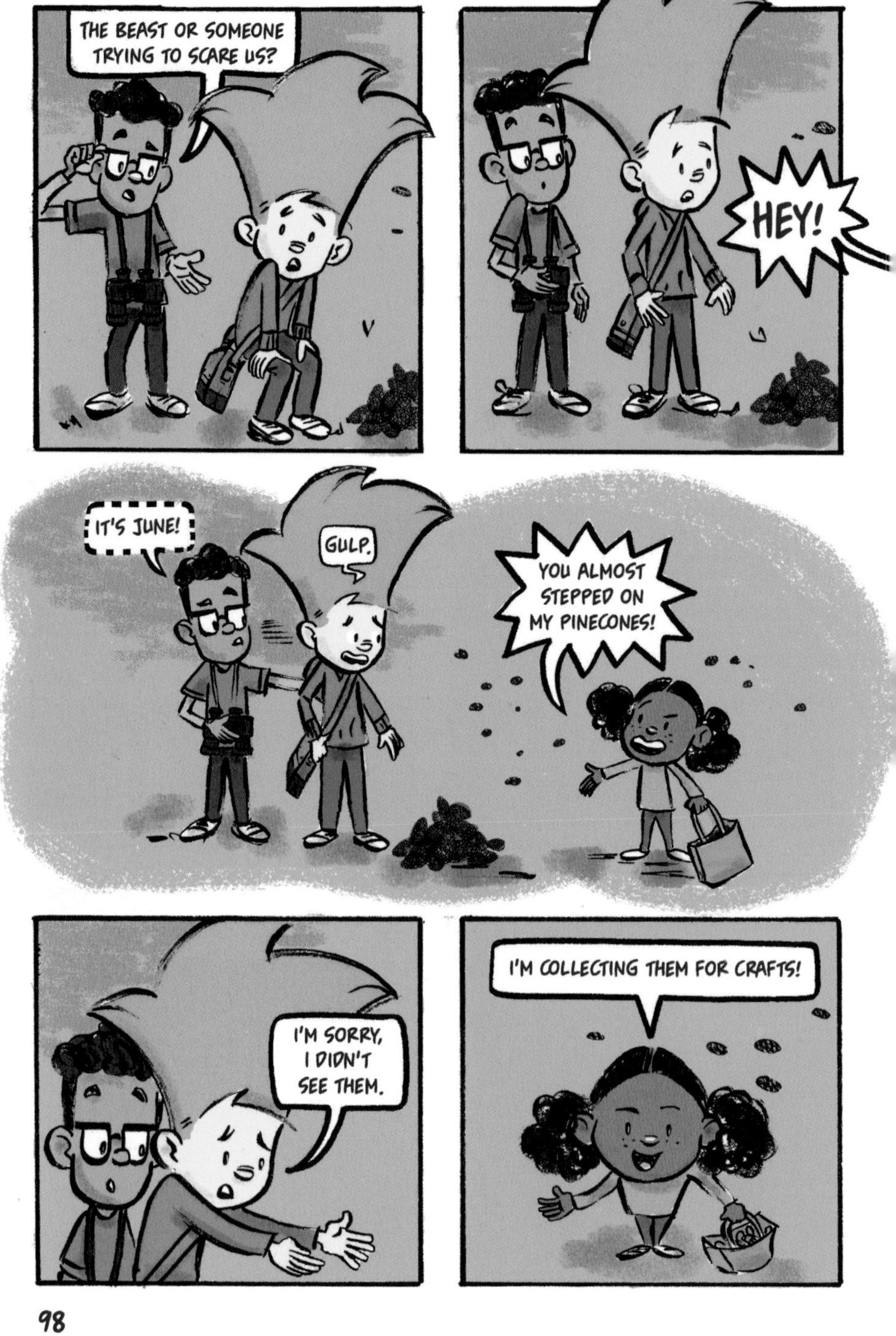
THE BEAST OR SOMEONE TRYING TO SCARE US?
HEY!
IT'S JUNE!
GULP.
YOU ALMOST STEPPED ON MY PINECONES!
I'M SORRY, I DIDN'T SEE THEM.
I'M COLLECTING THEM FOR CRAFTS!

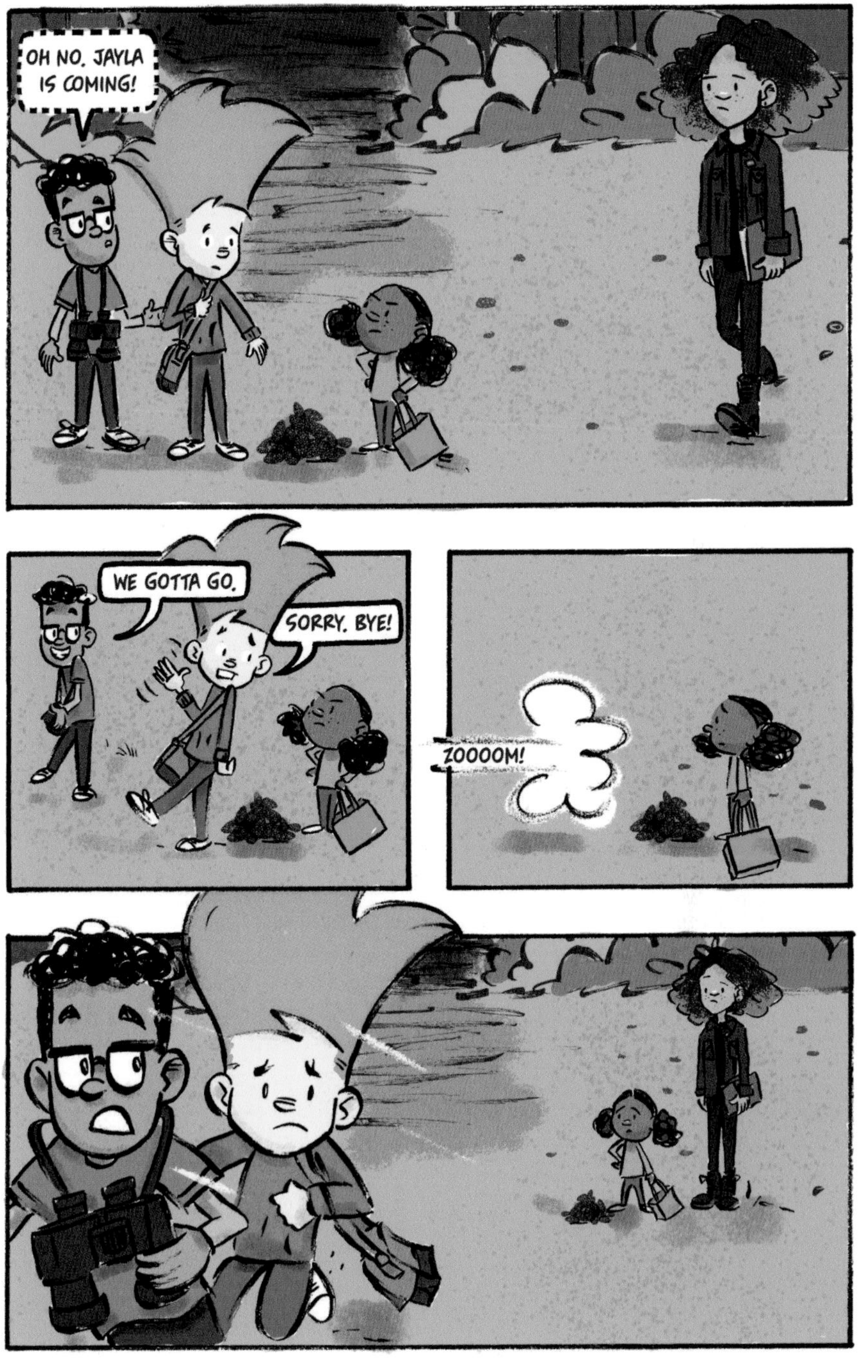
OH NO. JAYLA IS COMING!
WE GOTTA GO.
SORRY. BYE!
ZOOOOM!

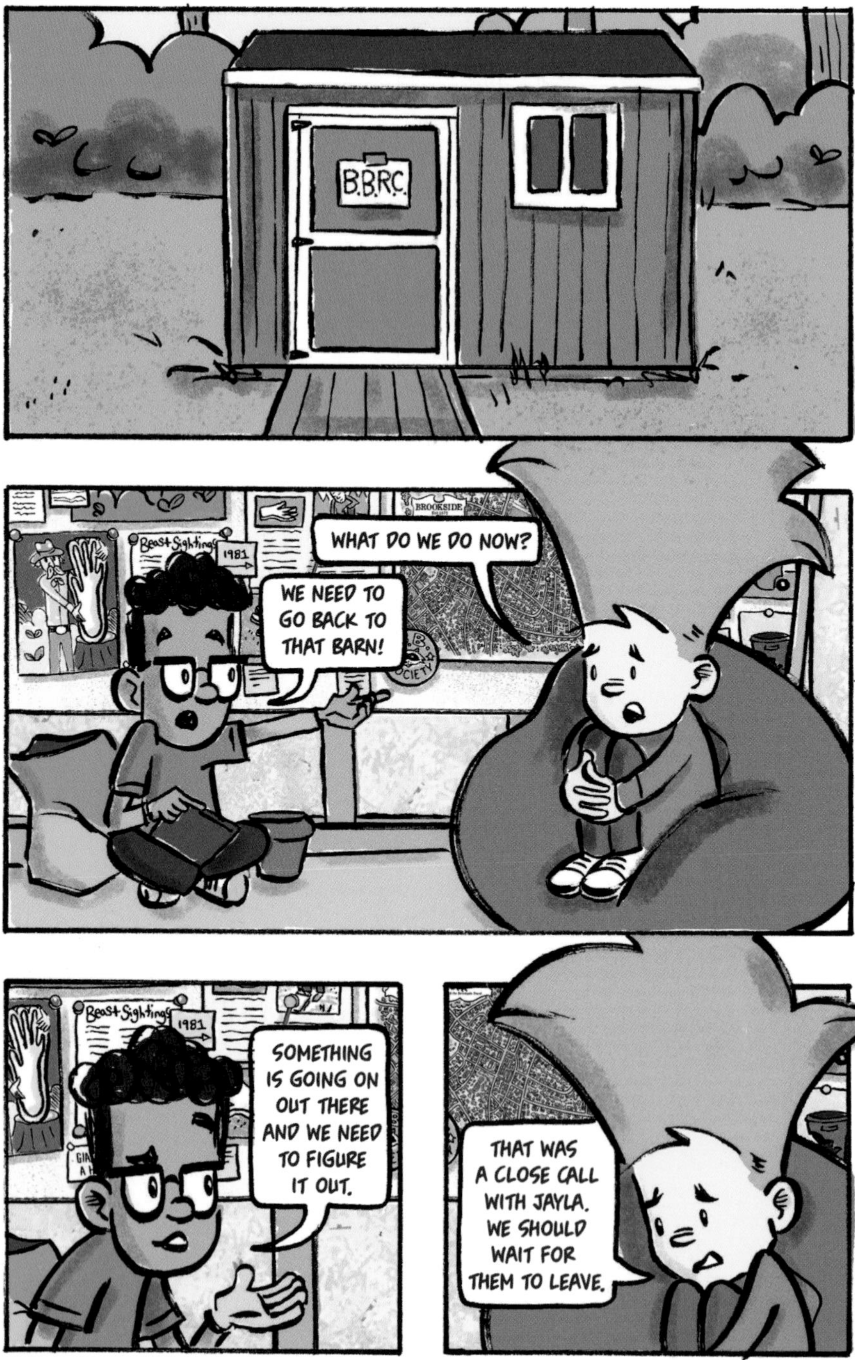
B.B.R.C.
BROOKSIDE
Beast Sightings
1981
WHAT DO WE DO NOW?
WE NEED TO GO BACK TO THAT BARN!
Beast Sightings
1981
SOMETHING IS GOING ON OUT THERE AND WE NEED TO FIGURE IT OUT.
THAT WAS A CLOSE CALL WITH JAYLA. WE SHOULD WAIT FOR THEM TO LEAVE.

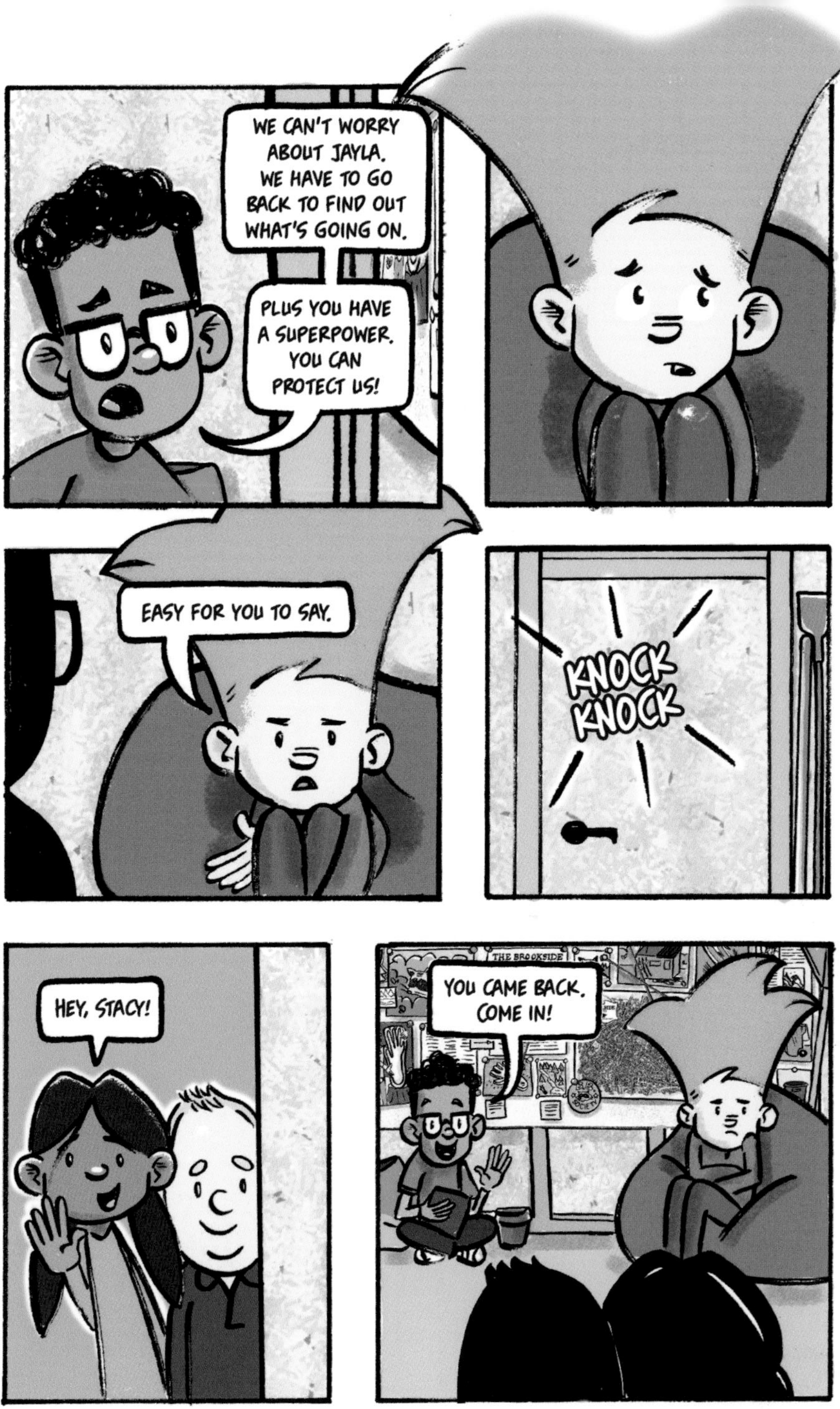
WE CAN'T WORRY ABOUT JAYLA. WE HAVE TO GO BACK TO FIND OUT WHAT'S GOING ON.
PLUS YOU HAVE A SUPERPOWER. YOU CAN PROTECT US!
EASY FOR YOU TO SAY.
KNOCK KNOCK
HEY, STACY!
THE BROOKSIDE
YOU CAME BACK. COME IN!

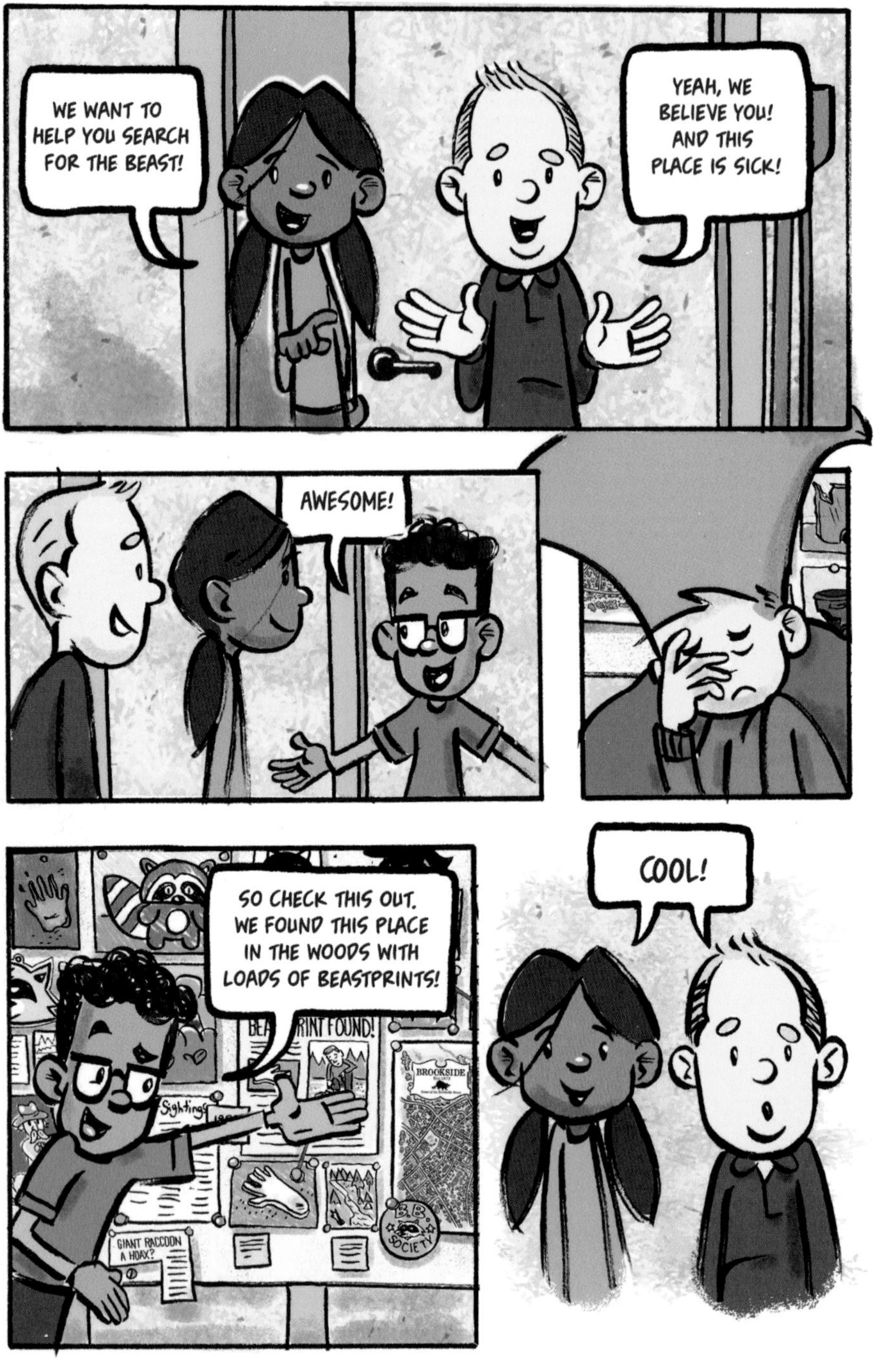
WE WANT TO HELP YOU SEARCH FOR THE BEAST!
YEAH, WE BELIEVE YOU! AND THIS PLACE IS SICK!
AWESOME!
SO CHECK THIS OUT. WE FOUND THIS PLACE IN THE WOODS WITH LOADS OF BEASTPRINTS!
Sightings
BROOKSIDE
GIANT RACCOON A HOAX?
B.B. SOCIETY
COOL!

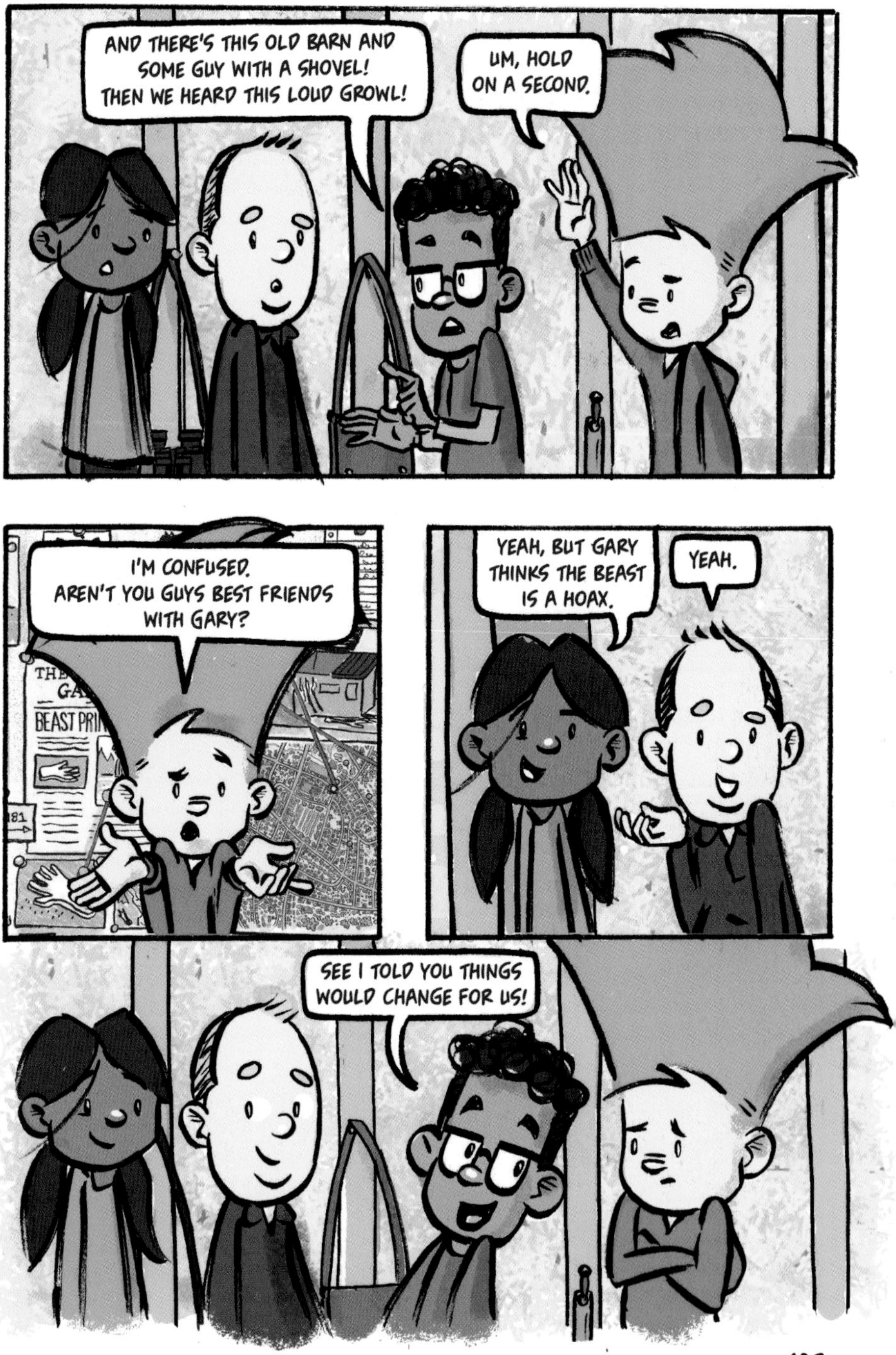
AND THERE'S THIS OLD BARN AND SOME GUY WITH A SHOVEL! THEN WE HEARD THIS LOUD GROWL!
UM, HOLD ON A SECOND.
I'M CONFUSED. AREN'T YOU GUYS BEST FRIENDS WITH GARY?
THE
GA
BEAST PRI
181
YEAH, BUT GARY THINKS THE BEAST IS A HOAX.
YEAH.
SEE I TOLD YOU THINGS WOULD CHANGE FOR US!

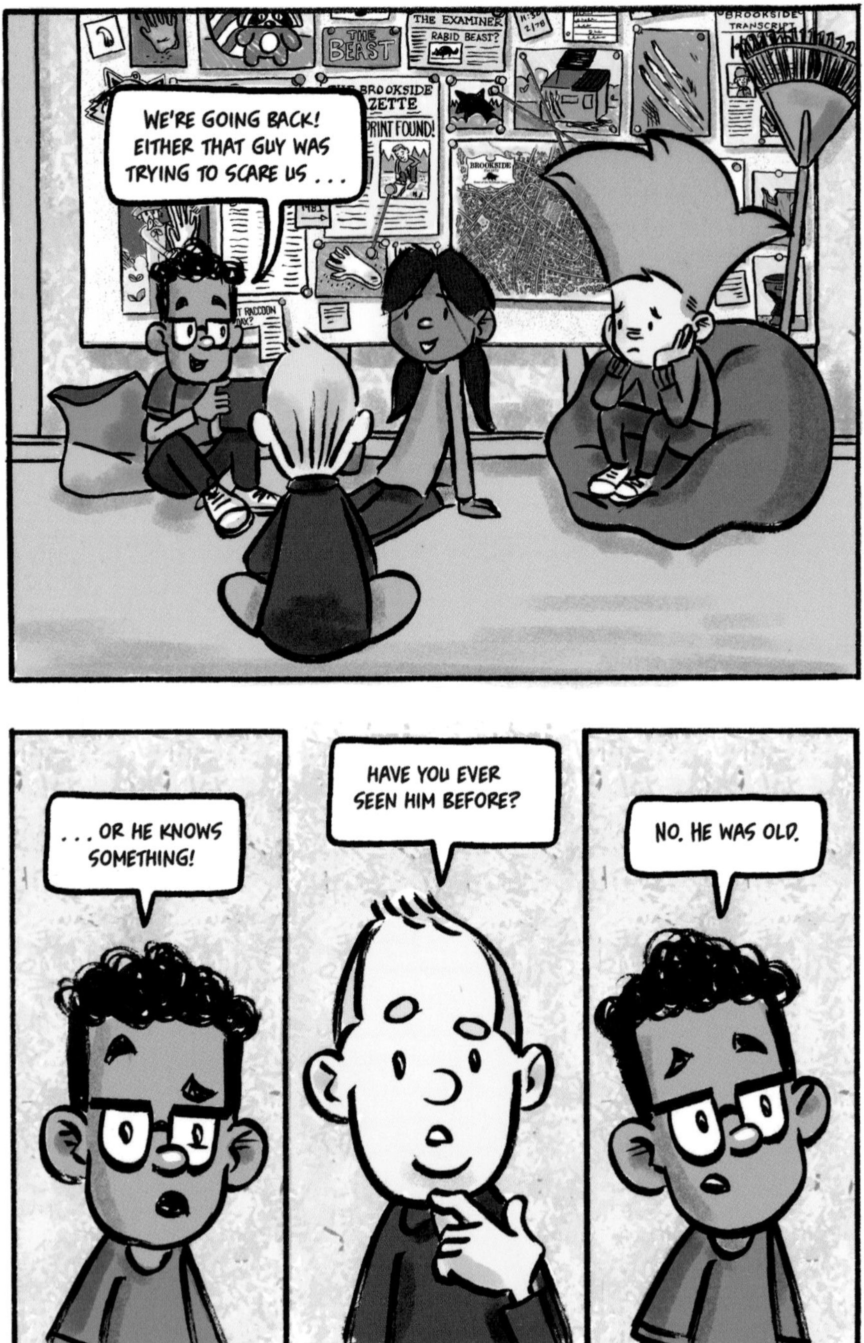
THE EXAMINER
RABID BEAST?
THE BEAST
PRINT FOUND!
BROOKSIDE TRANSCRIPT
WE'RE GOING BACK! EITHER THAT GUY WAS TRYING TO SCARE US . . .
. . . OR HE KNOWS SOMETHING!
HAVE YOU EVER SEEN HIM BEFORE?
NO. HE WAS OLD.

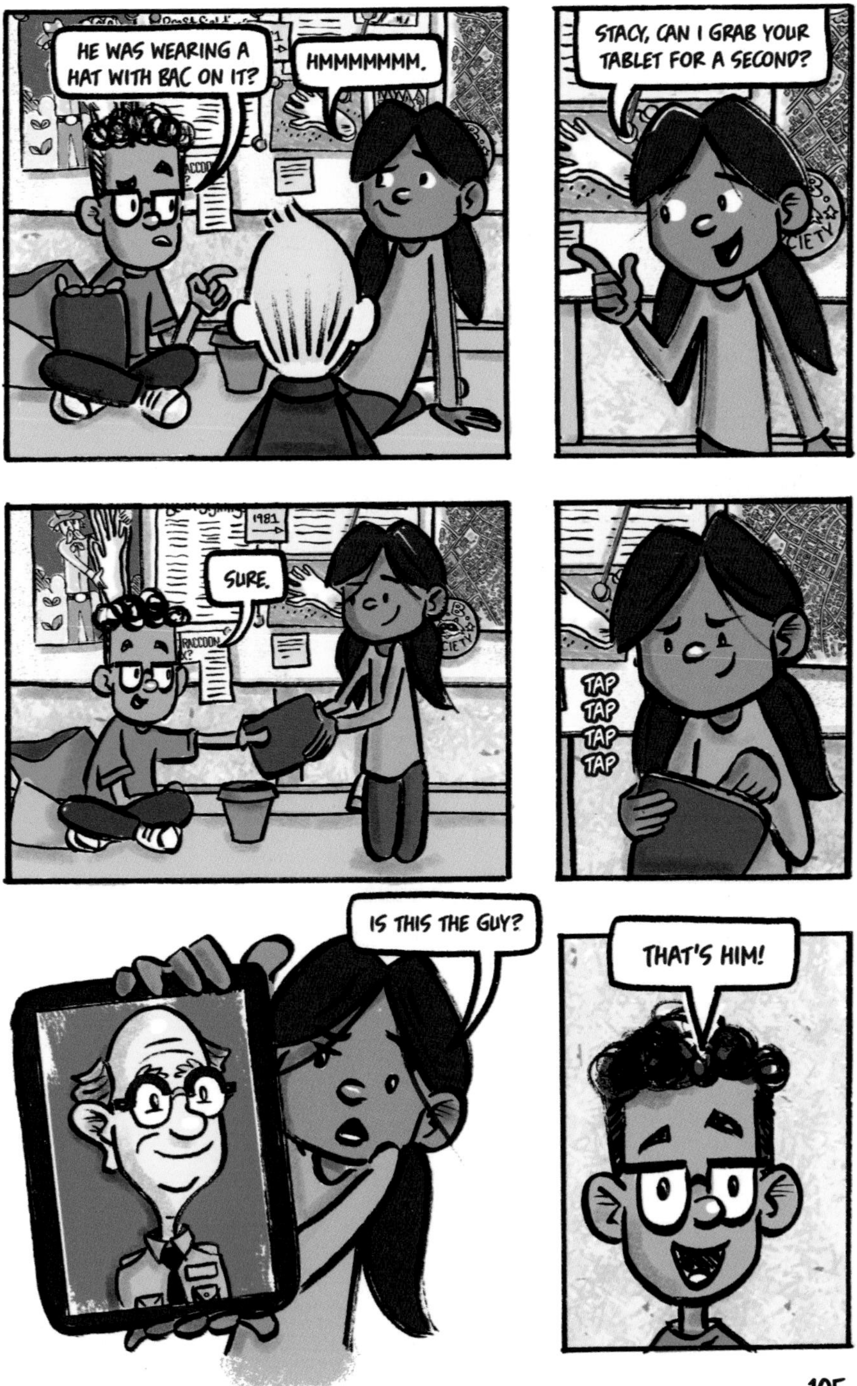
HE WAS WEARING A HAT WITH BAC ON IT?
HMMMMMMM.
STACY, CAN I GRAB YOUR TABLET FOR A SECOND?
SURE.
TAP TAP TAP TAP
IS THIS THE GUY?
THAT'S HIM!

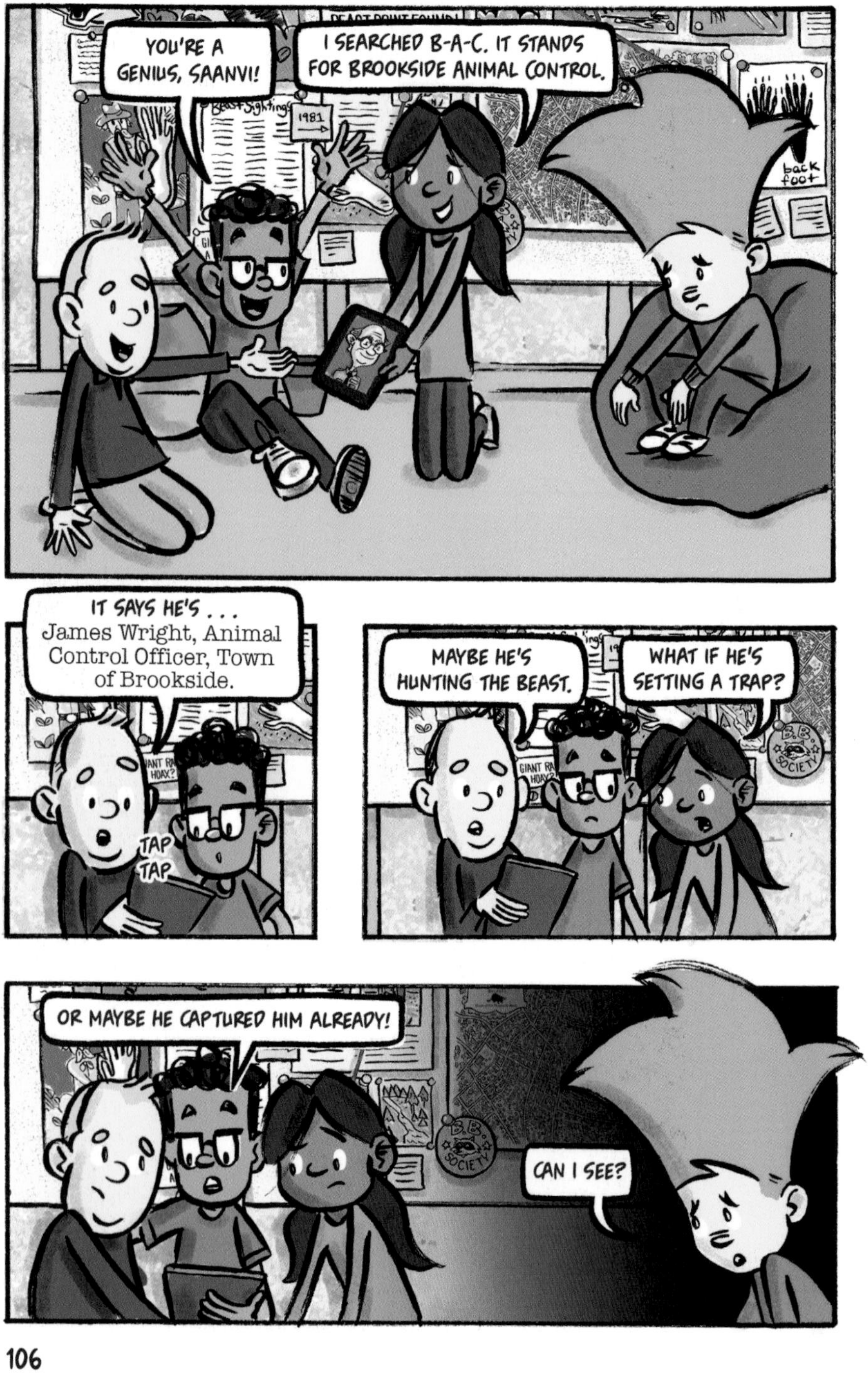
YOU'RE A GENIUS, SAANVI!
I SEARCHED B-A-C. IT STANDS FOR BROOKSIDE ANIMAL CONTROL.
1981
back foot
IT SAYS HE'S . . . James Wright, Animal Control Officer, Town of Brookside.
GIANT RA HOAX?
TAP TAP
MAYBE HE'S HUNTING THE BEAST.
WHAT IF HE'S SETTING A TRAP?
GIANT RA HOAX?
B.B. SOCIETY
OR MAYBE HE CAPTURED HIM ALREADY!
B.B. SOCIETY
CAN I SEE?

WHISPER, WHISPER, WHISPER, WHISPER, WHISPER, WHISPER, WHISPER, WHISPER, WHISPER, WHISPER, WHISPER, WHISPER, WHISPER, WHISPER, WHISPER, WHISPER.

I WAS FEELING LEFT OUT. I HAD TO DO SOMETHING.

HEY, GUYS!

YEAH?

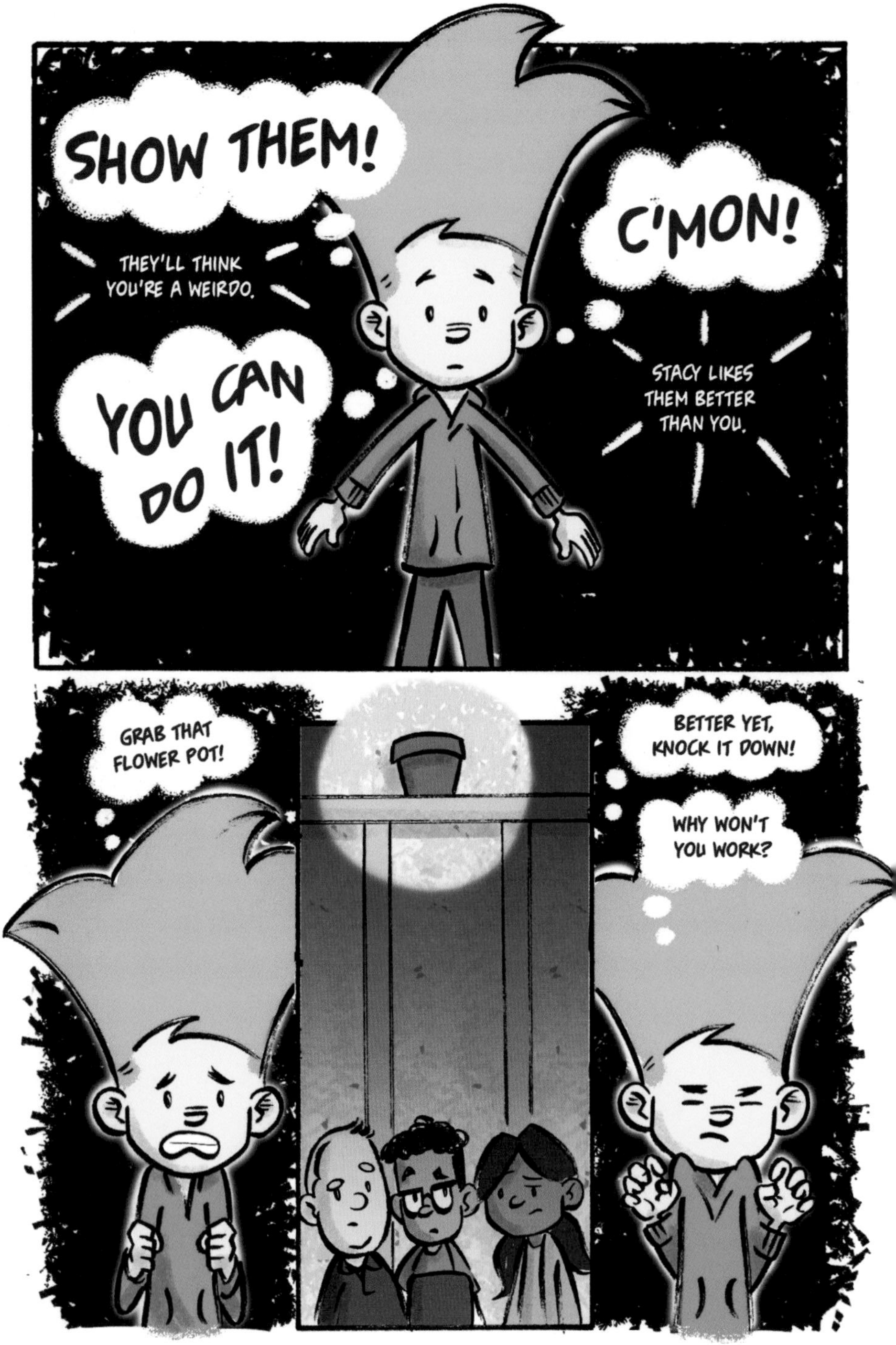
SHOW THEM!
THEY'LL THINK YOU'RE A WEIRDO.
C'MON!
YOU CAN DO IT!
STACY LIKES THEM BETTER THAN YOU.
GRAB THAT FLOWER POT!
BETTER YET, KNOCK IT DOWN!
WHY WON'T YOU WORK?

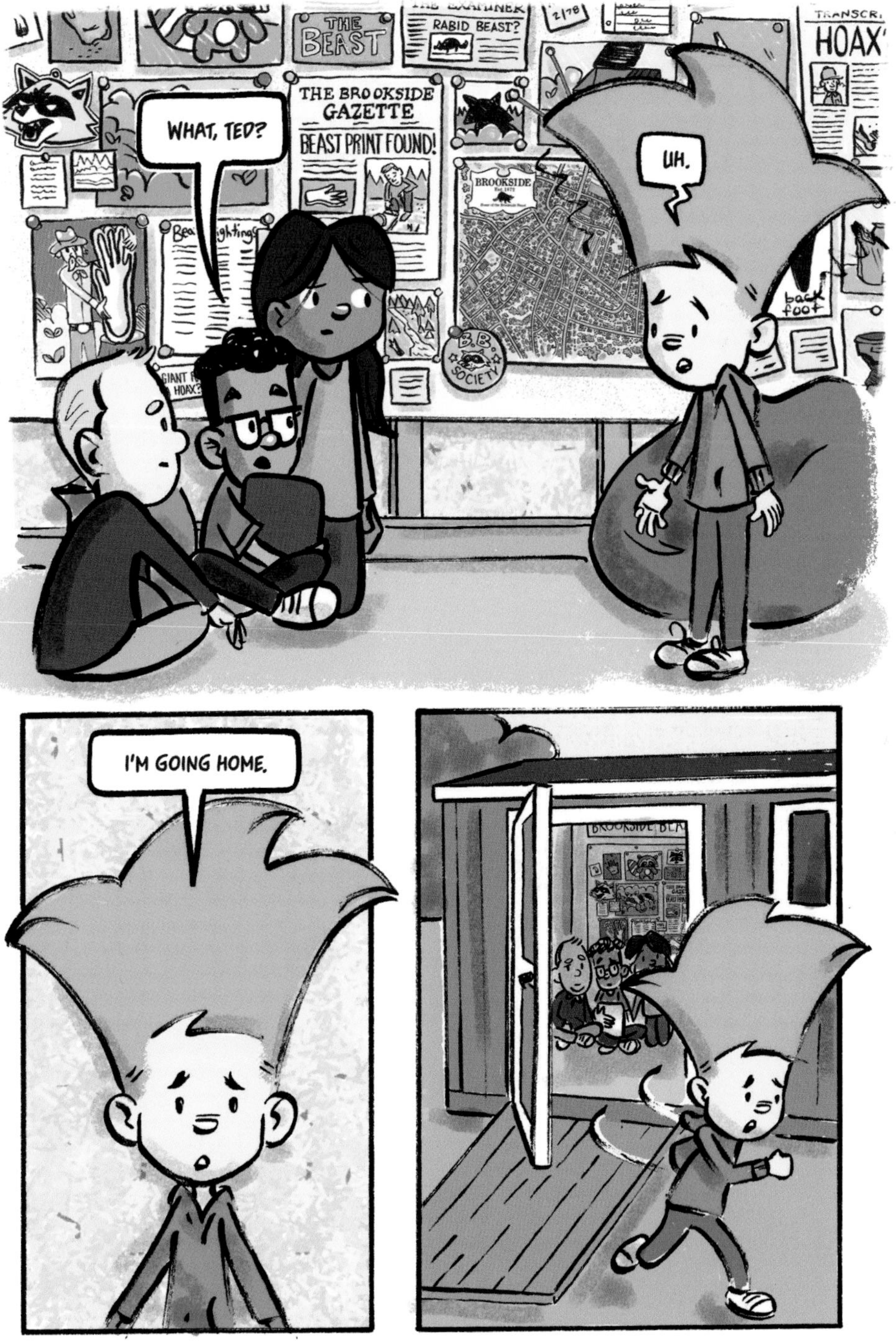
THE BEAST
RABID BEAST?
THE BROOKSIDE GAZETTE
BEAST PRINT FOUND!
HOAX
BROOKSIDE
B.B. SOCIETY
back foot
WHAT, TED?
UH.
I'M GOING HOME.

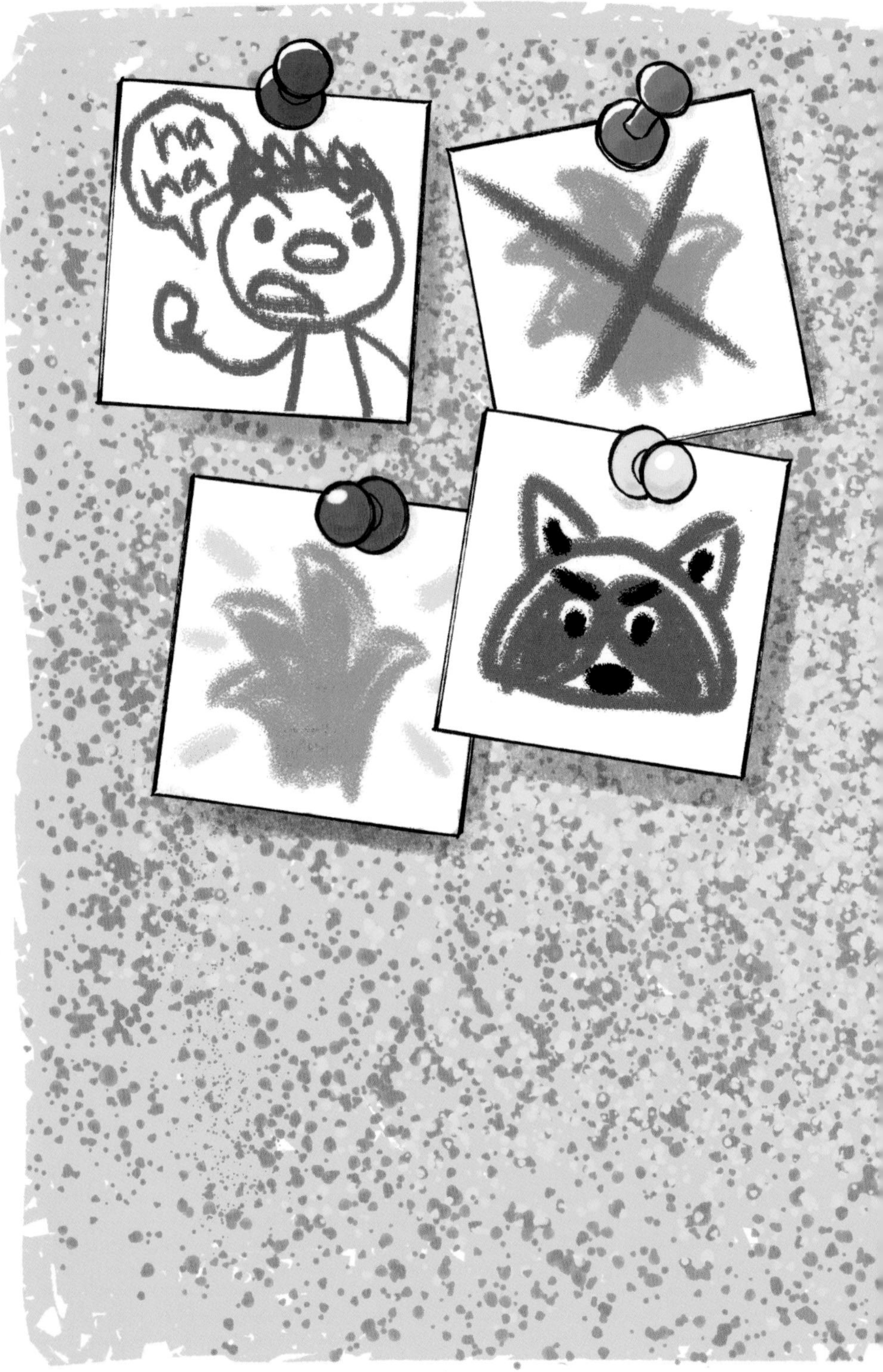
ha ha

CHAPTER 5:

FAMILY SECRET

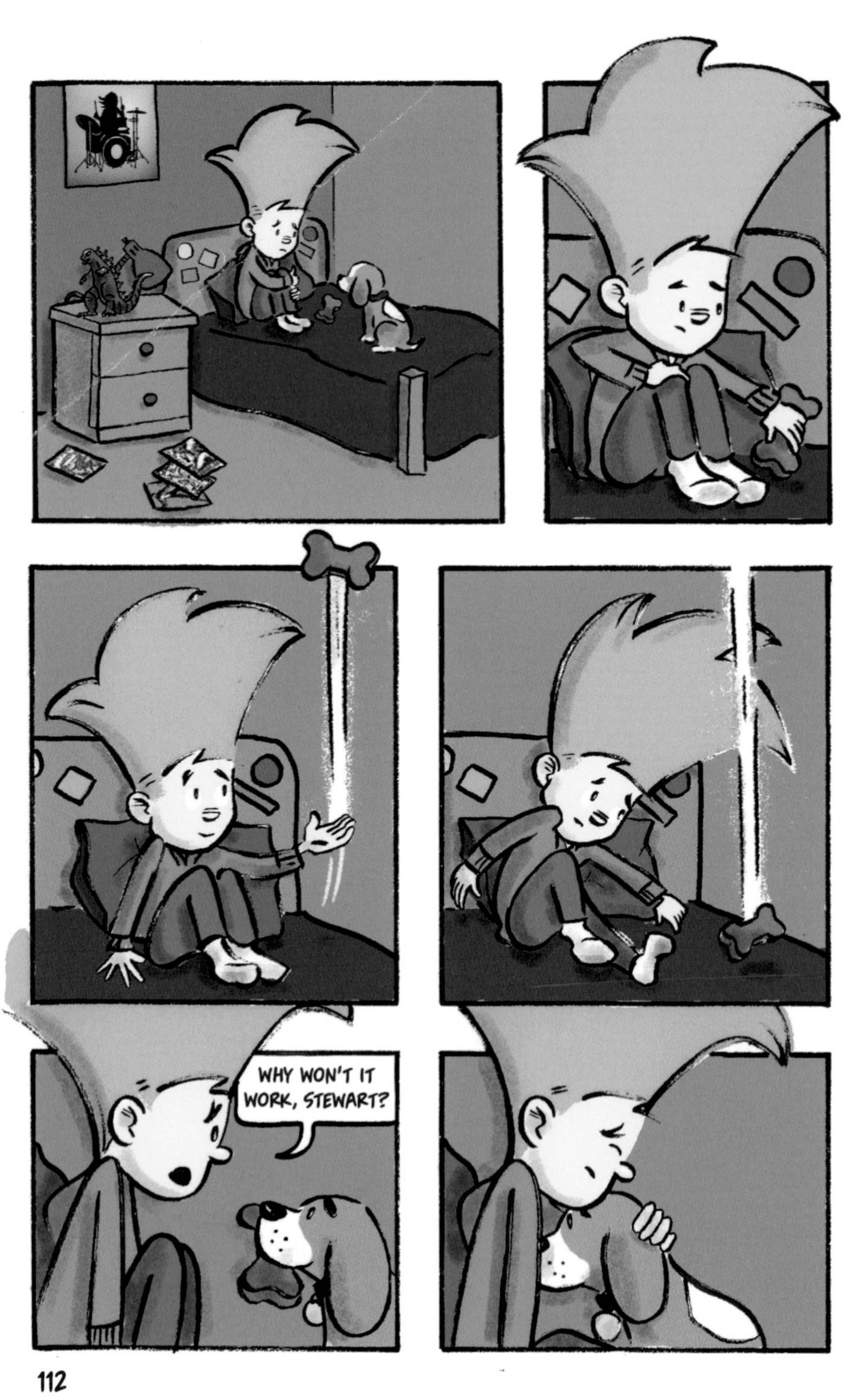
WHY WON'T IT WORK, STEWART?

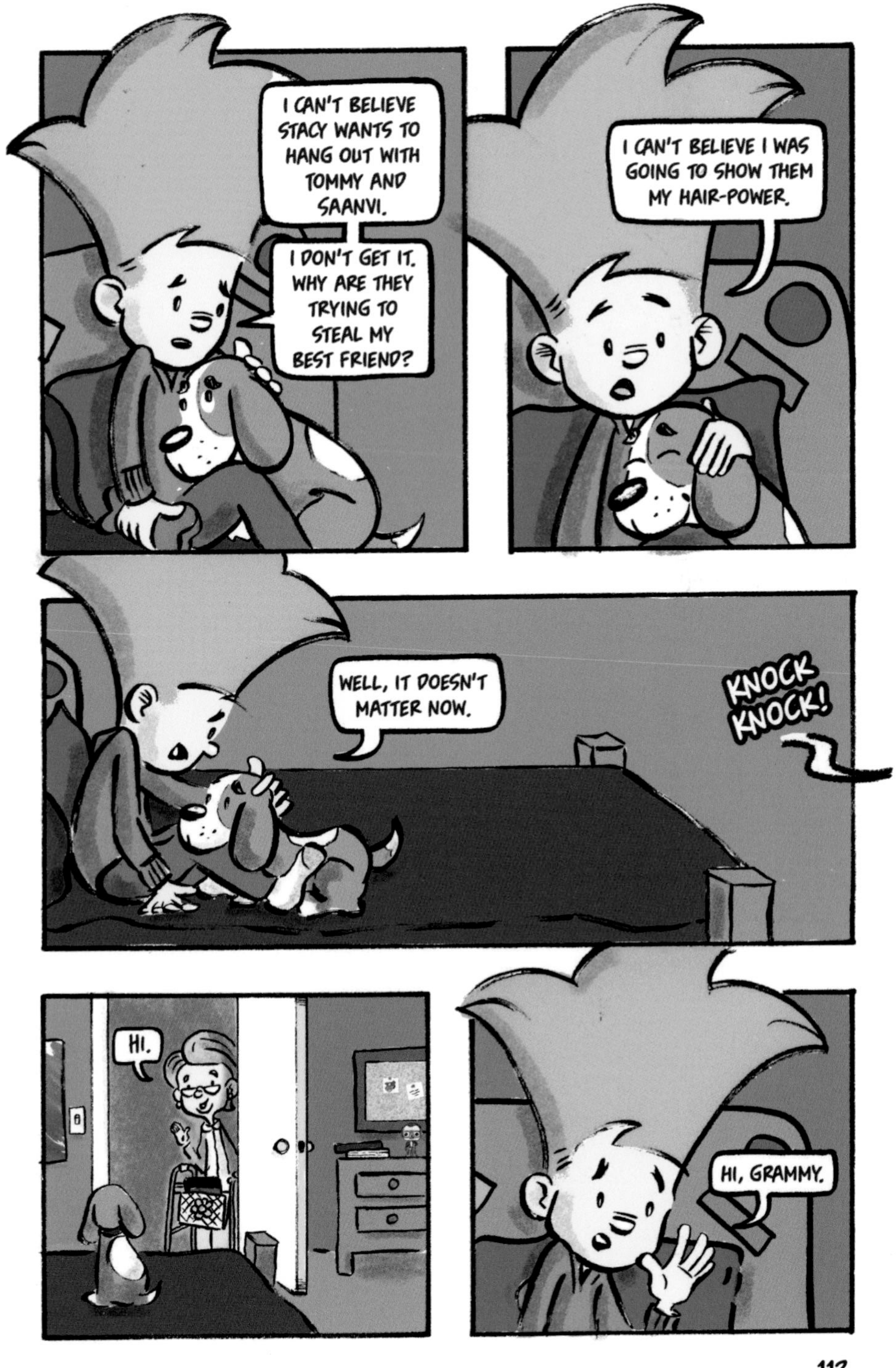
I CAN'T BELIEVE STACY WANTS TO HANG OUT WITH TOMMY AND SAANVI.
I DON'T GET IT. WHY ARE THEY TRYING TO STEAL MY BEST FRIEND?
I CAN'T BELIEVE I WAS GOING TO SHOW THEM MY HAIR-POWER.
WELL, IT DOESN'T MATTER NOW.
KNOCK KNOCK!
HI.
HI, GRAMMY.

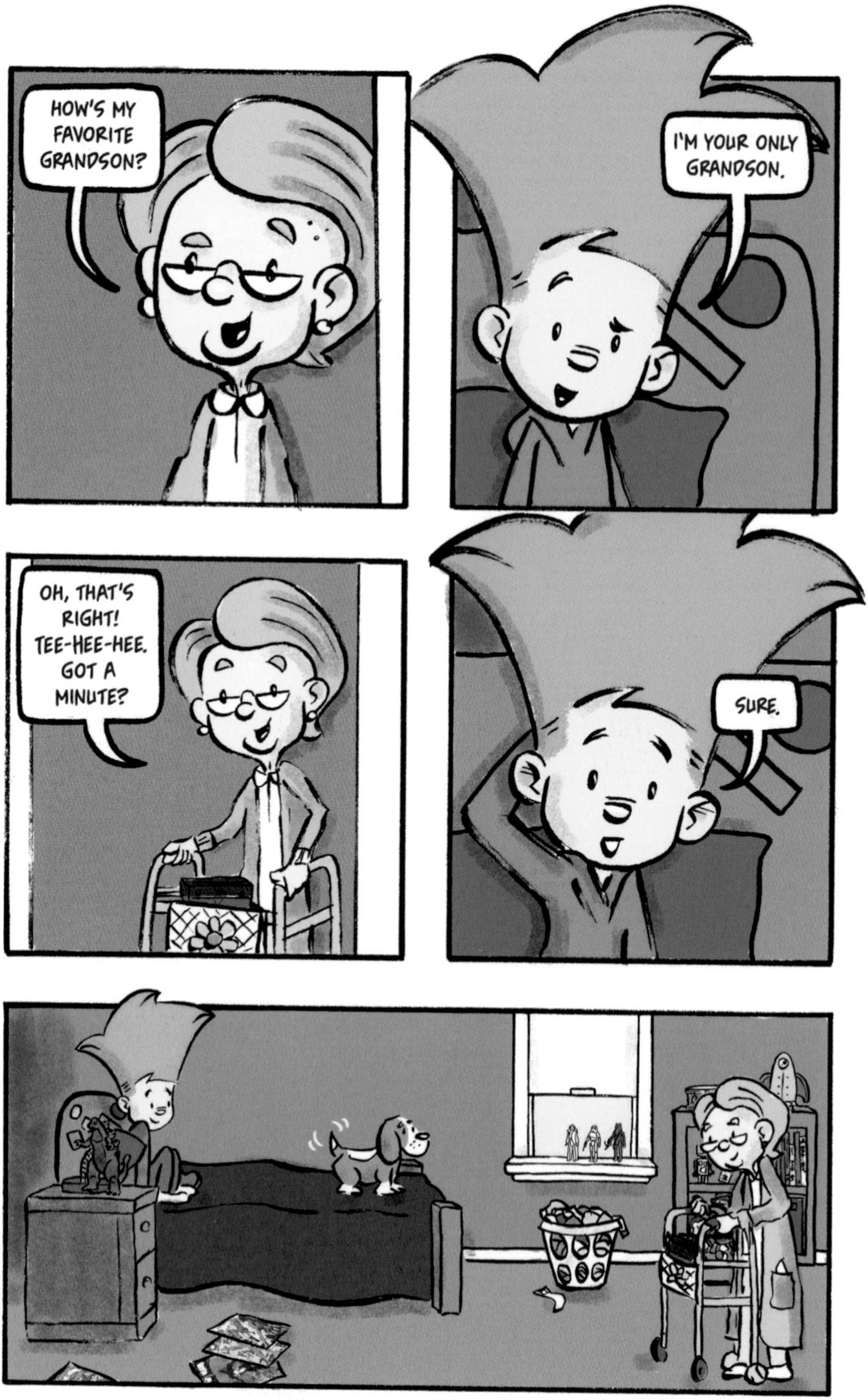
HOW'S MY FAVORITE GRANDSON?
I'M YOUR ONLY GRANDSON.
OH, THAT'S RIGHT! TEE-HEE-HEE. GOT A MINUTE?
SURE.

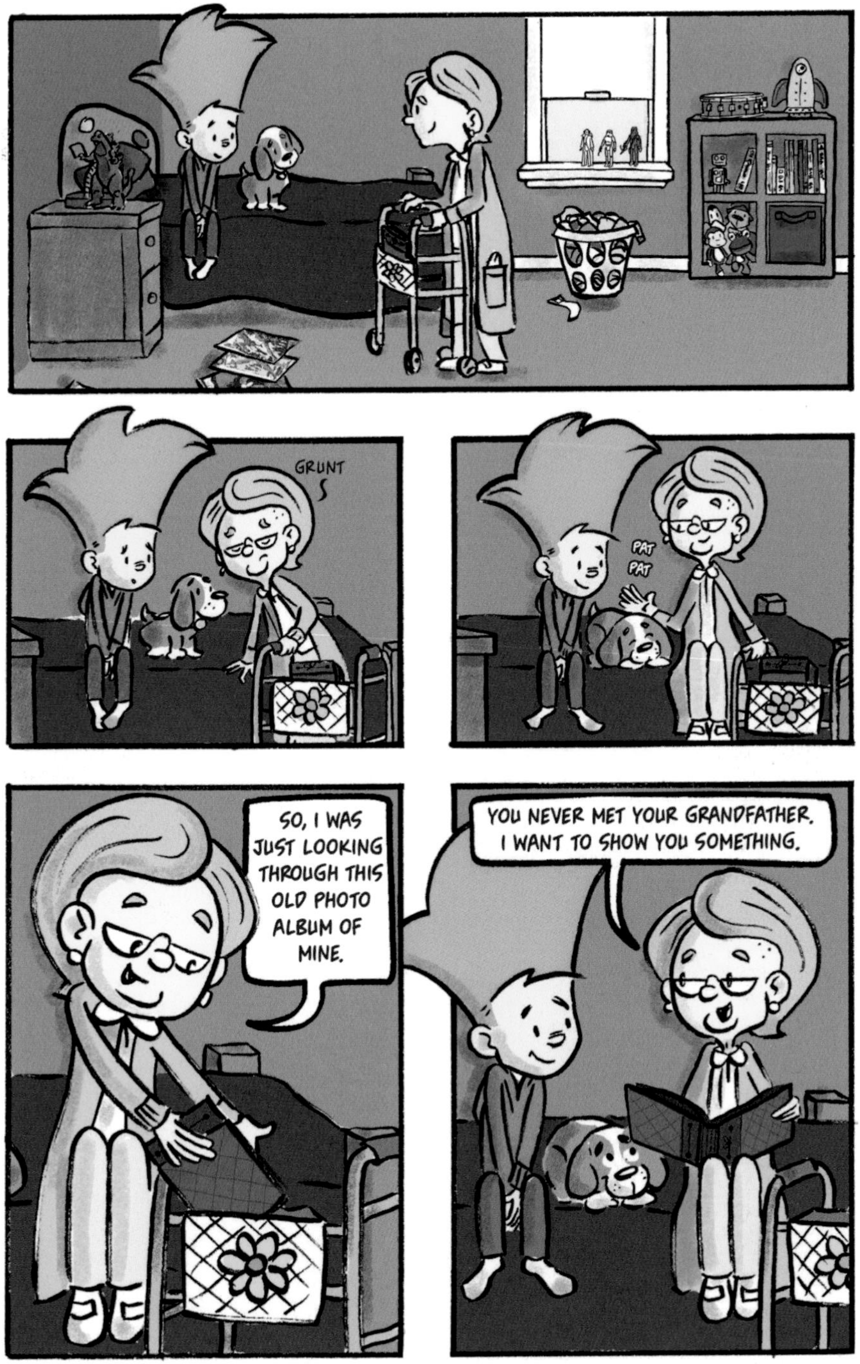
GRUNT
PAT
PAT
SO, I WAS JUST LOOKING THROUGH THIS OLD PHOTO ALBUM OF MINE.
YOU NEVER MET YOUR GRANDFATHER. I WANT TO SHOW YOU SOMETHING.

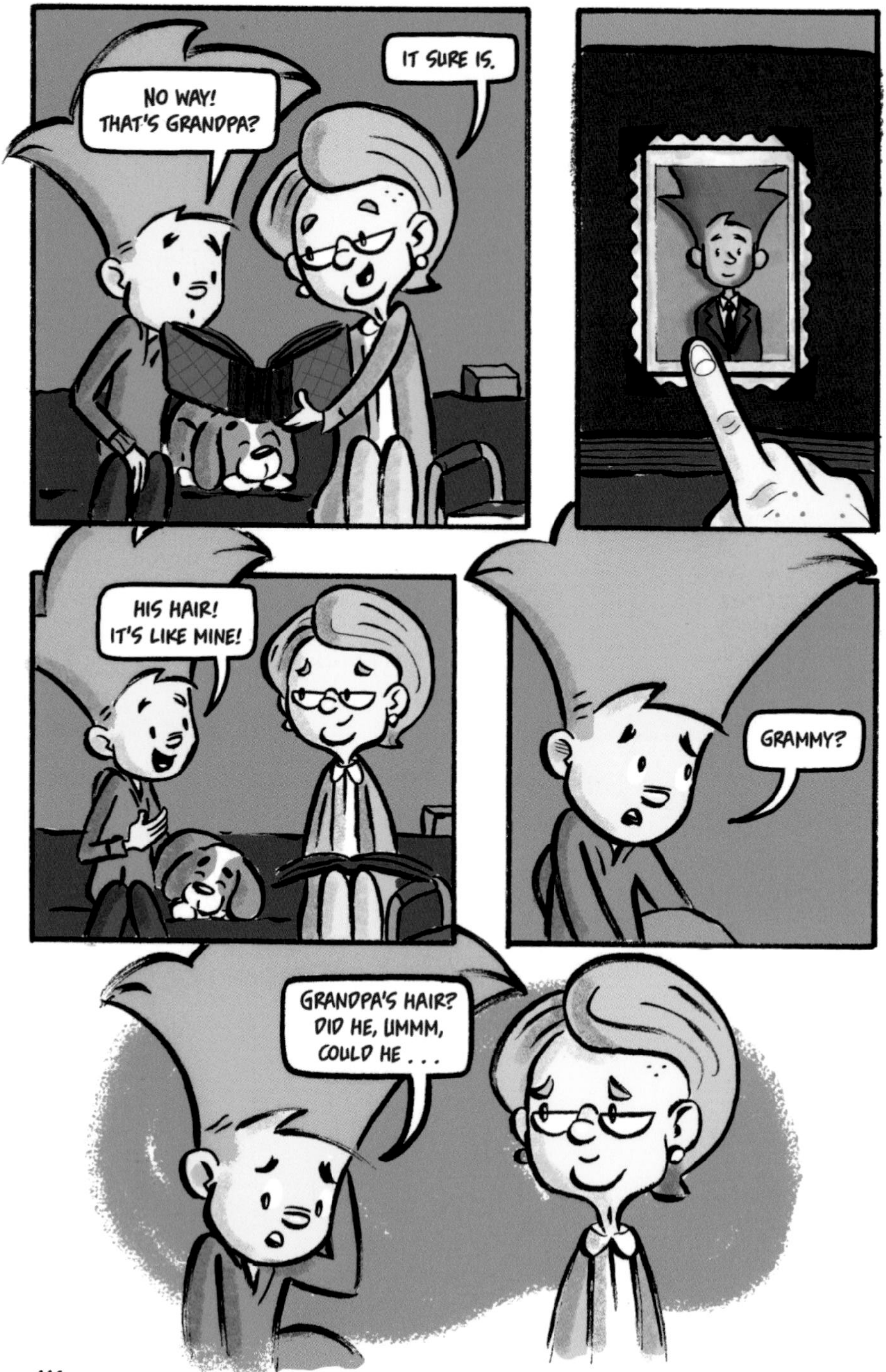
NO WAY! THAT'S GRANDPA?
IT SURE IS.
HIS HAIR! IT'S LIKE MINE!
GRAMMY?
GRANDPA'S HAIR? DID HE, UMMM, COULD HE . . .

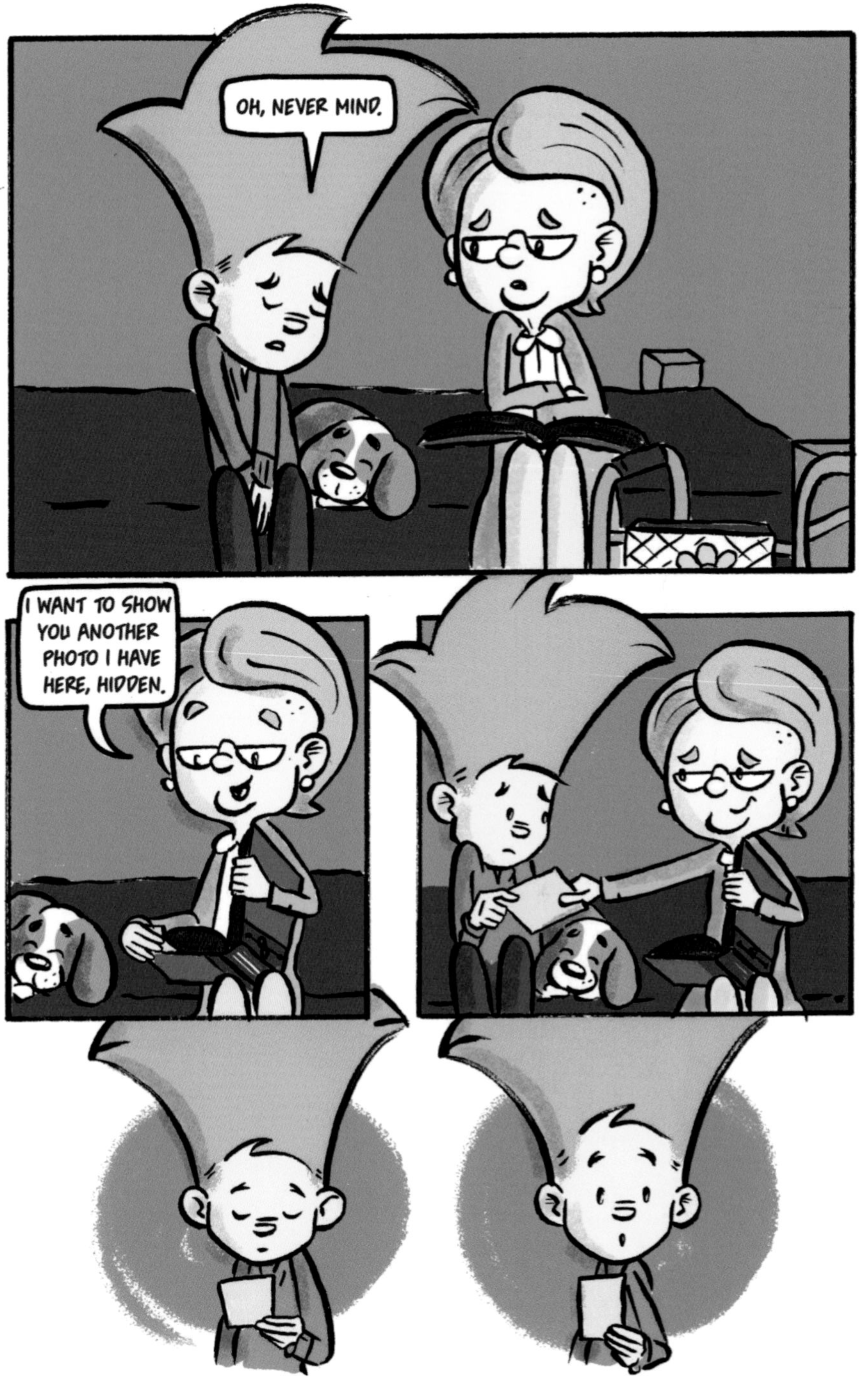
OH, NEVER MIND.
I WANT TO SHOW YOU ANOTHER PHOTO I HAVE HERE, HIDDEN.

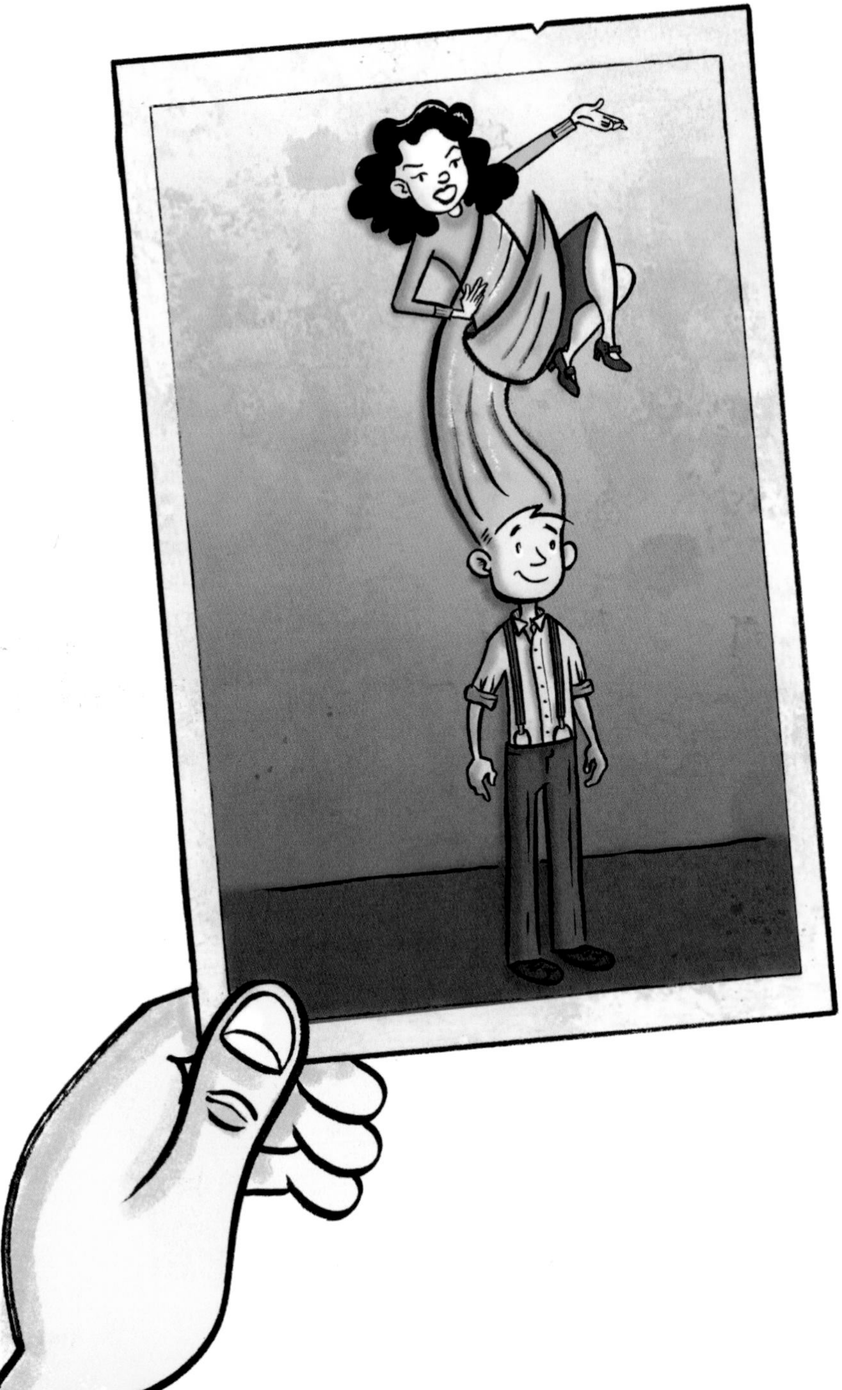

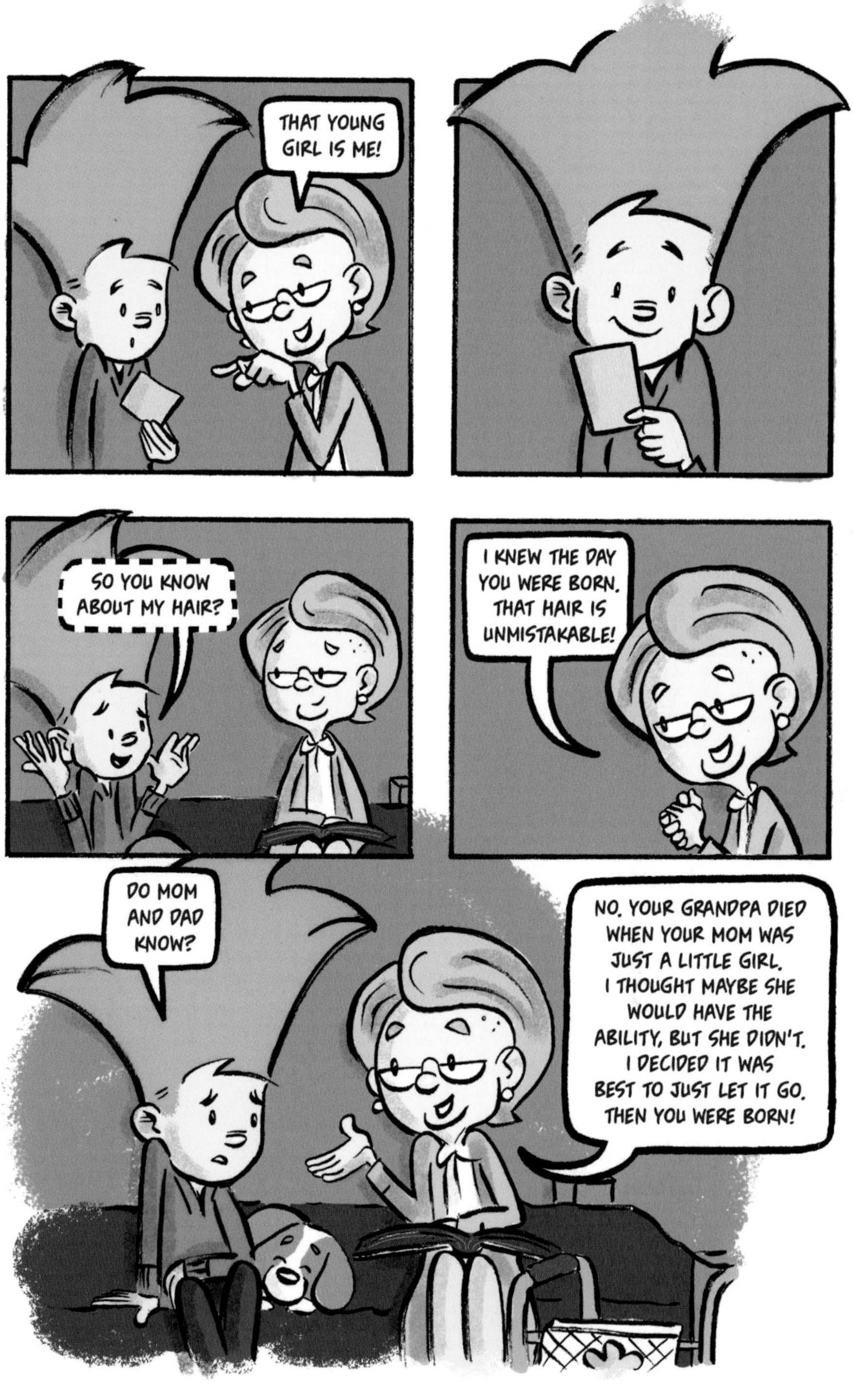
THAT YOUNG GIRL IS ME!
SO YOU KNOW ABOUT MY HAIR?
I KNEW THE DAY YOU WERE BORN. THAT HAIR IS UNMISTAKABLE!
DO MOM AND DAD KNOW?
NO. YOUR GRANDPA DIED WHEN YOUR MOM WAS JUST A LITTLE GIRL. I THOUGHT MAYBE SHE WOULD HAVE THE ABILITY, BUT SHE DIDN'T. I DECIDED IT WAS BEST TO JUST LET IT GO. THEN YOU WERE BORN!

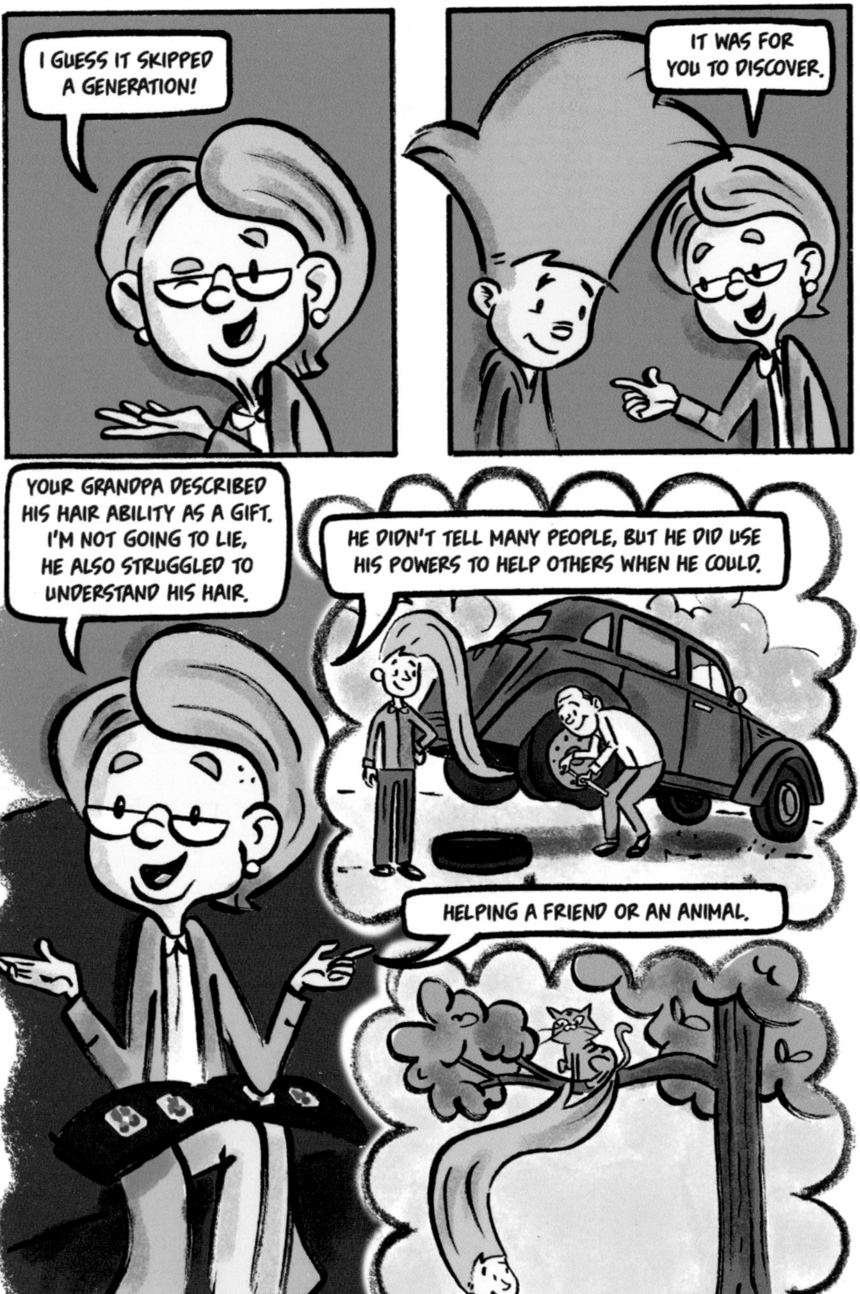
I GUESS IT SKIPPED A GENERATION!
IT WAS FOR YOU TO DISCOVER.
YOUR GRANDPA DESCRIBED HIS HAIR ABILITY AS A GIFT. I'M NOT GOING TO LIE, HE ALSO STRUGGLED TO UNDERSTAND HIS HAIR.
HE DIDN'T TELL MANY PEOPLE, BUT HE DID USE HIS POWERS TO HELP OTHERS WHEN HE COULD.
HELPING A FRIEND OR AN ANIMAL.

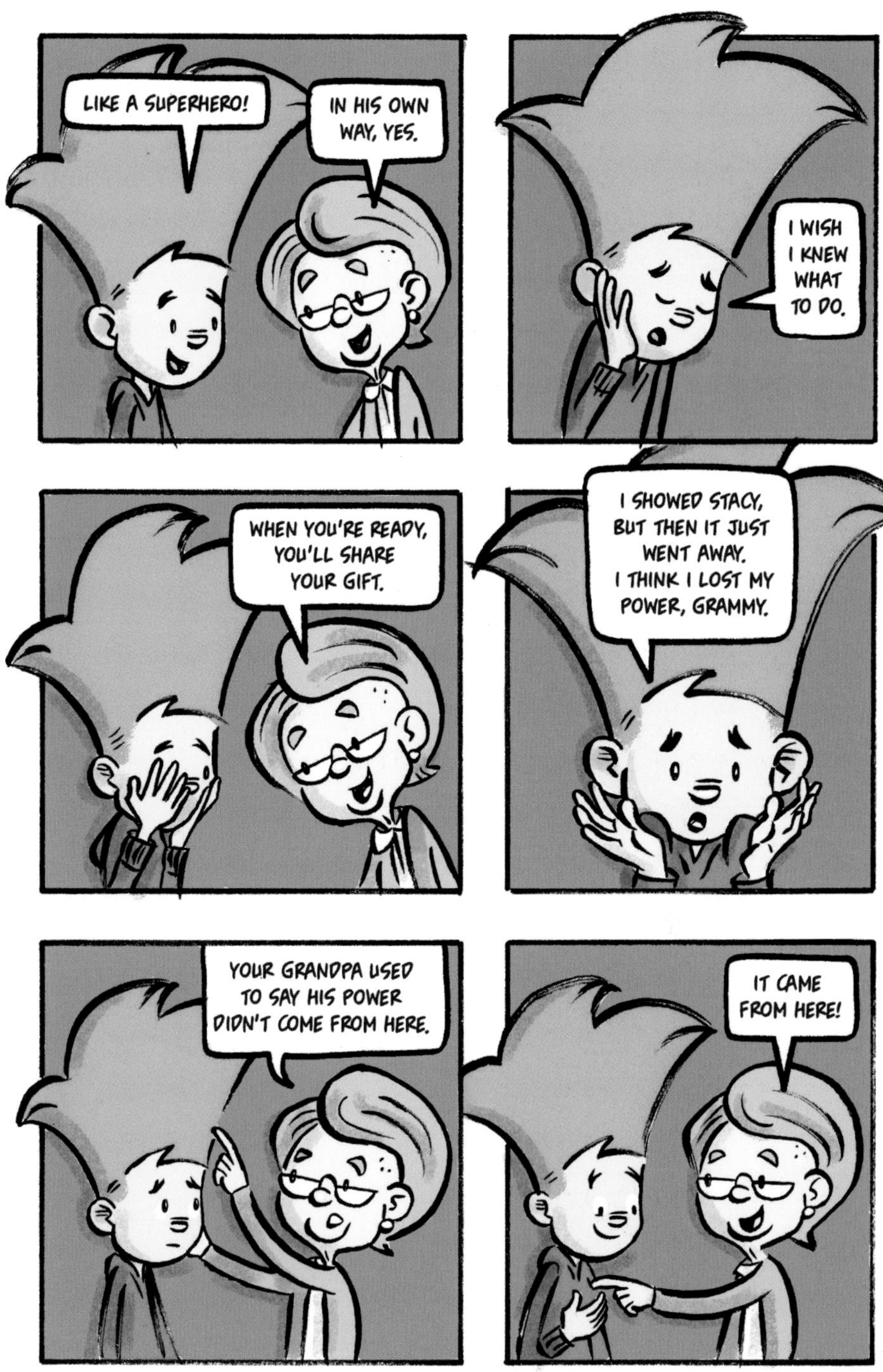
LIKE A SUPERHERO!
IN HIS OWN WAY, YES.
I WISH I KNEW WHAT TO DO.
WHEN YOU'RE READY, YOU'LL SHARE YOUR GIFT.
I SHOWED STACY, BUT THEN IT JUST WENT AWAY. I THINK I LOST MY POWER, GRAMMY.
YOUR GRANDPA USED TO SAY HIS POWER DIDN'T COME FROM HERE.
IT CAME FROM HERE!

SMOOCH

YOU KEEP THESE.

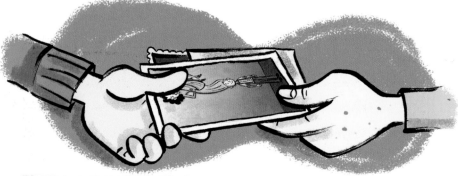

IT WASN'T UNTIL SHE LEFT THE ROOM THAT I NOTICED THE ENVELOPE BETWEEN THE PHOTOS.

MY HAIR!

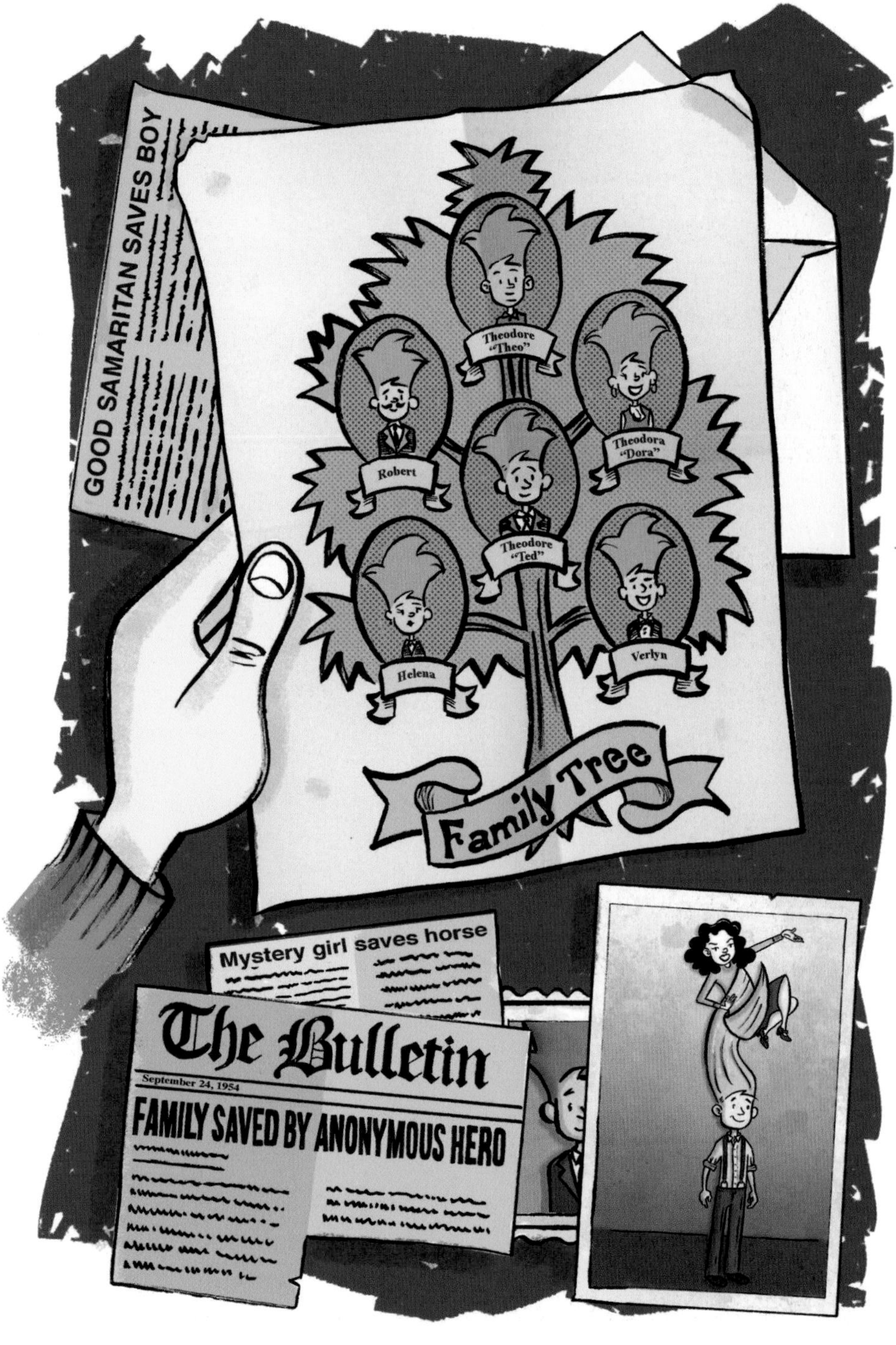
GOOD SAMARITAN SAVES BOY
Theodore "Theo"
Robert
Theodora "Dora"
Theodore "Ted"
Helena
Verlyn
Family Tree
Mystery girl saves horse
The Bulletin
September 24, 1954
FAMILY SAVED BY ANONYMOUS HERO

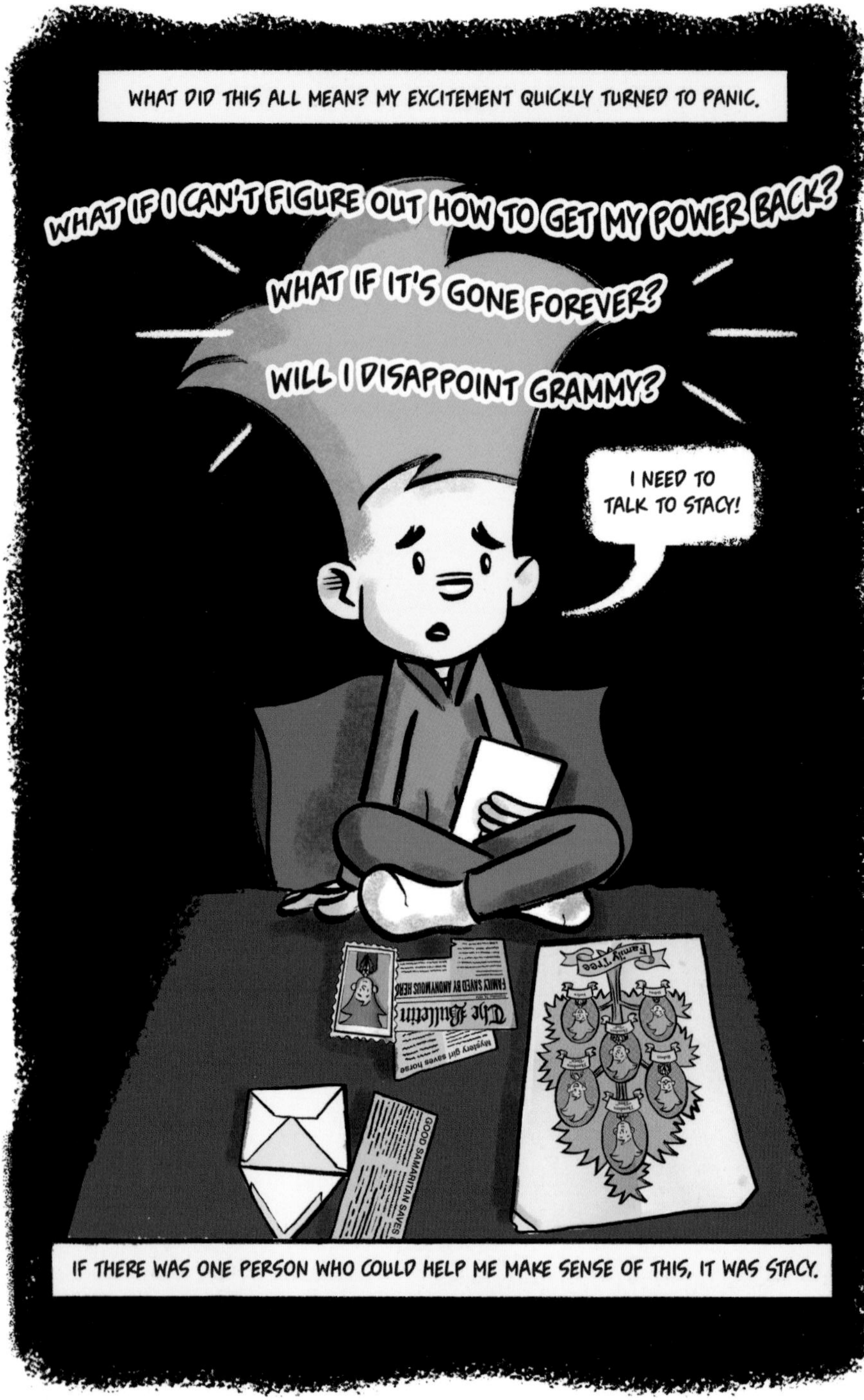
WHAT DID THIS ALL MEAN? MY EXCITEMENT QUICKLY TURNED TO PANIC.
WHAT IF I CAN'T FIGURE OUT HOW TO GET MY POWER BACK?
WHAT IF IT'S GONE FOREVER?
WILL I DISAPPOINT GRAMMY?
I NEED TO TALK TO STACY!
Family Tree
The Bulletin
FAMILY SAVED BY ANONYMOUS HERO
Mystery girl saves horse
GOOD SAMARITAN SAVES
IF THERE WAS ONE PERSON WHO COULD HELP ME MAKE SENSE OF THIS, IT WAS STACY.

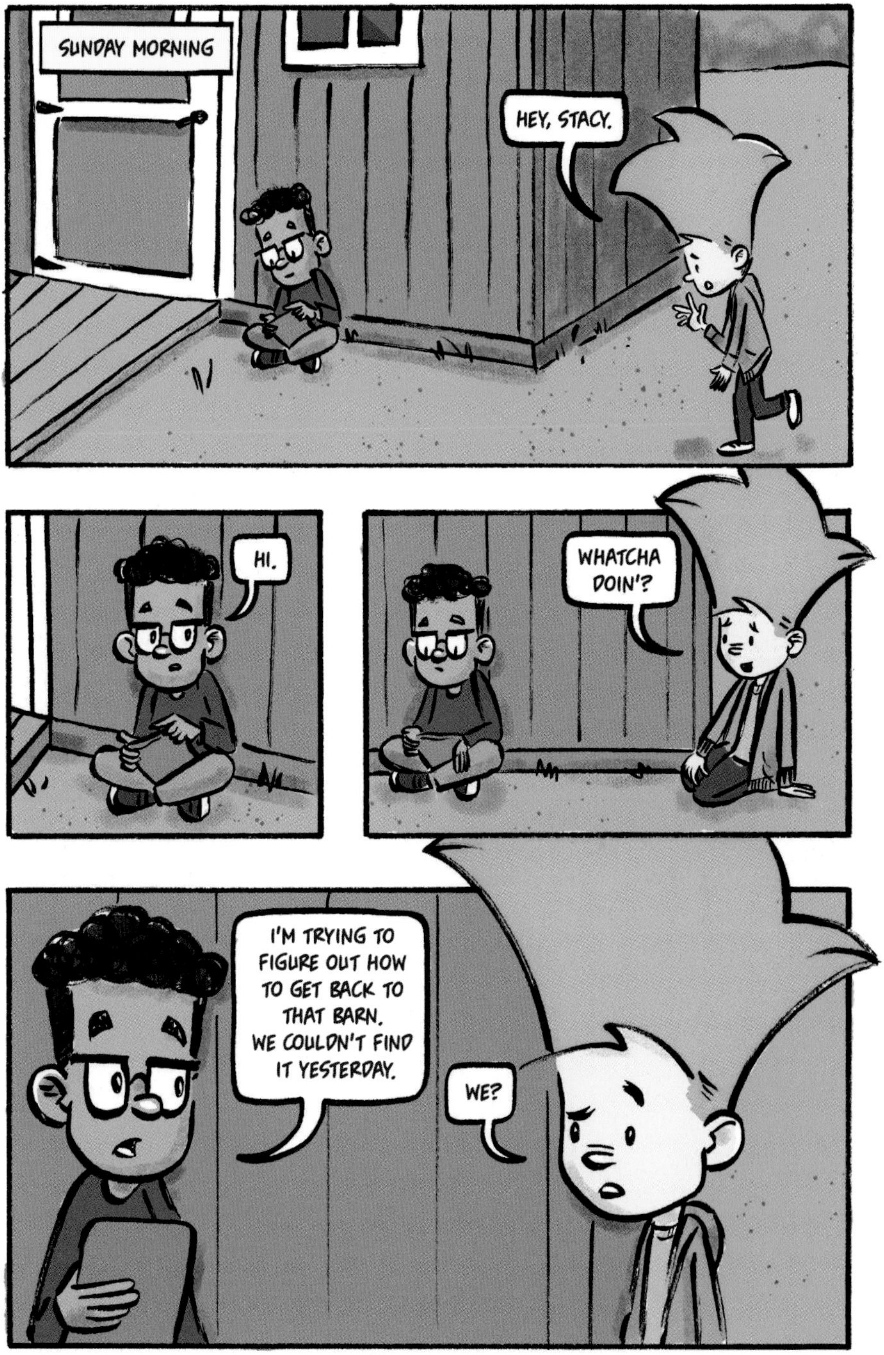
SUNDAY MORNING
HEY, STACY.
HI.
WHATCHA DOIN'?
I'M TRYING TO FIGURE OUT HOW TO GET BACK TO THAT BARN. WE COULDN'T FIND IT YESTERDAY.
WE?

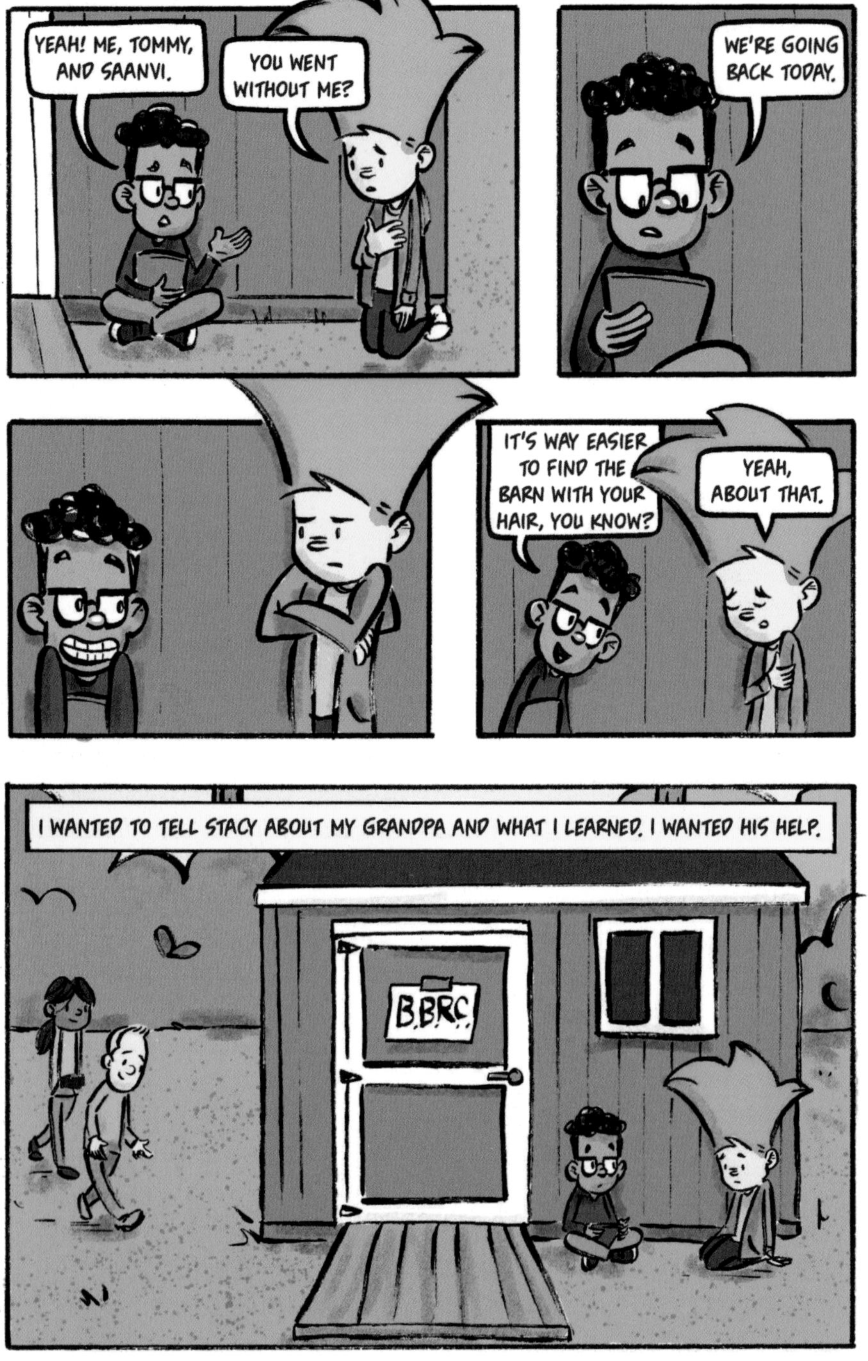
YEAH! ME, TOMMY, AND SAANVI.
YOU WENT WITHOUT ME?
WE'RE GOING BACK TODAY.
IT'S WAY EASIER TO FIND THE BARN WITH YOUR HAIR, YOU KNOW?
YEAH, ABOUT THAT.
I WANTED TO TELL STACY ABOUT MY GRANDPA AND WHAT I LEARNED. I WANTED HIS HELP.
B.B.R.C.

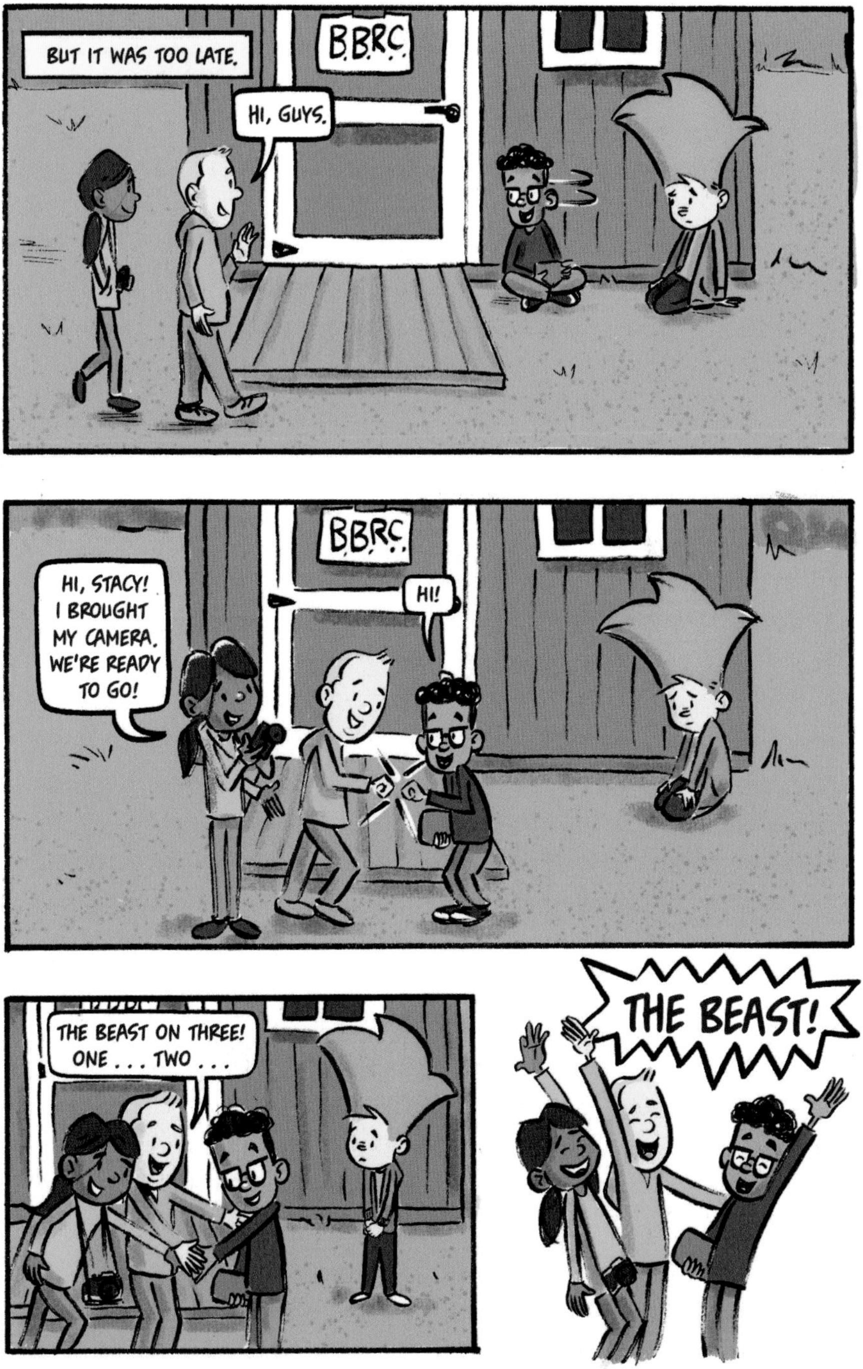
BUT IT WAS TOO LATE.
B.B.R.C.
HI, GUYS.
B.B.R.C.
HI, STACY! I BROUGHT MY CAMERA. WE'RE READY TO GO!
HI!
THE BEAST ON THREE! ONE . . . TWO . . .
THE BEAST!

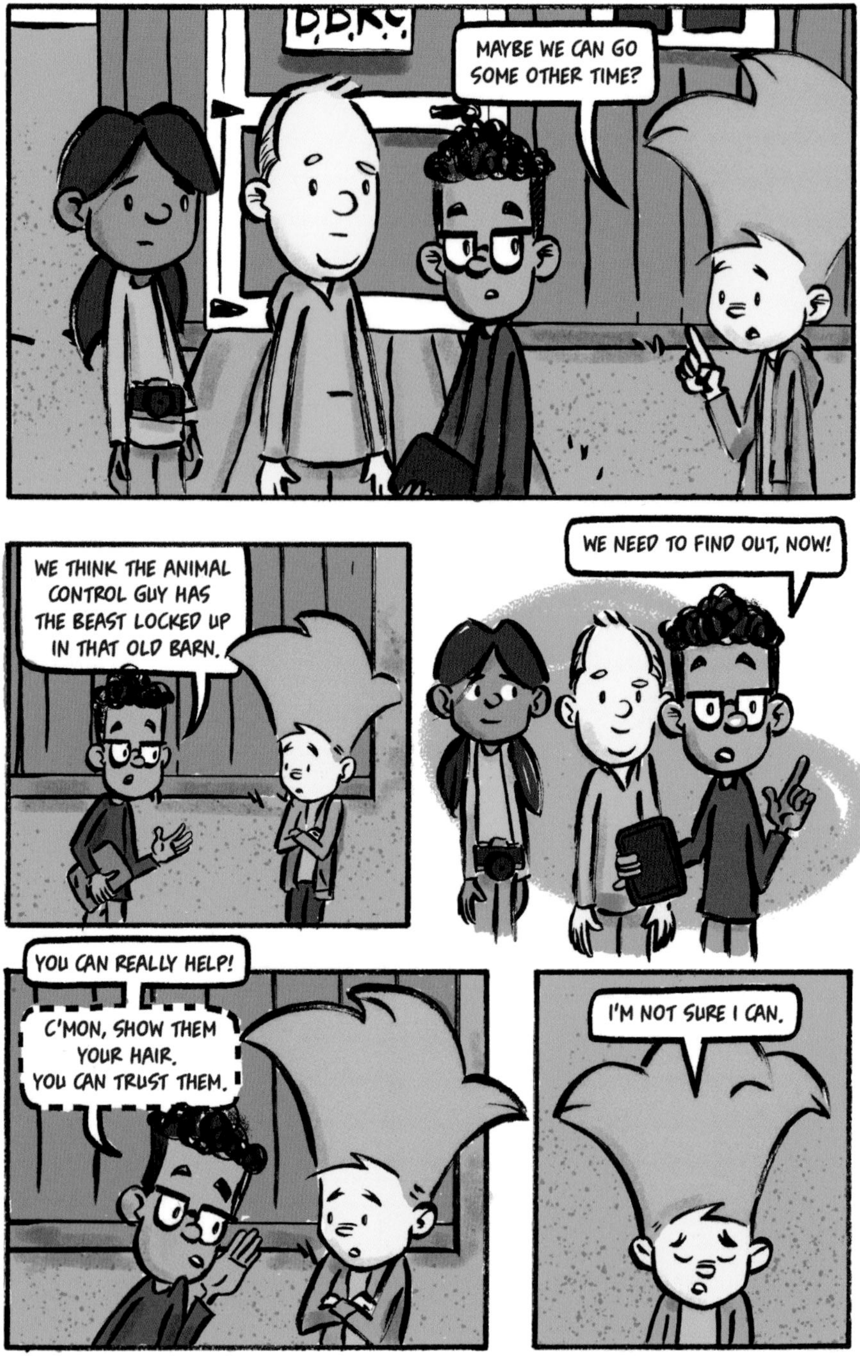
D.D.K.C.
MAYBE WE CAN GO SOME OTHER TIME?
WE THINK THE ANIMAL CONTROL GUY HAS THE BEAST LOCKED UP IN THAT OLD BARN.
WE NEED TO FIND OUT, NOW!
YOU CAN REALLY HELP!
C'MON, SHOW THEM YOUR HAIR. YOU CAN TRUST THEM.
I'M NOT SURE I CAN.

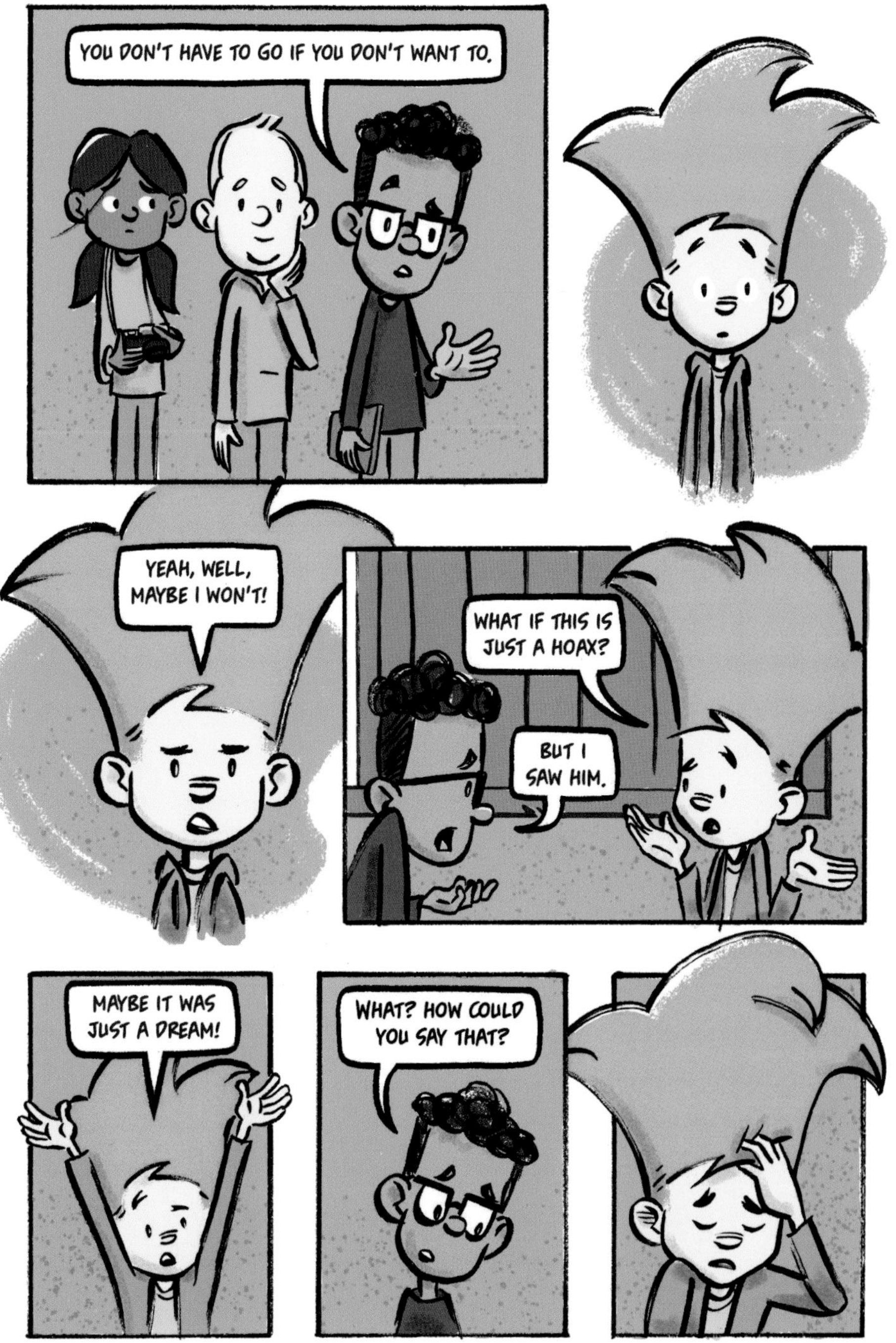
YOU DON'T HAVE TO GO IF YOU DON'T WANT TO.
YEAH, WELL, MAYBE I WON'T!
WHAT IF THIS IS JUST A HOAX?
BUT I SAW HIM.
MAYBE IT WAS JUST A DREAM!
WHAT? HOW COULD YOU SAY THAT?

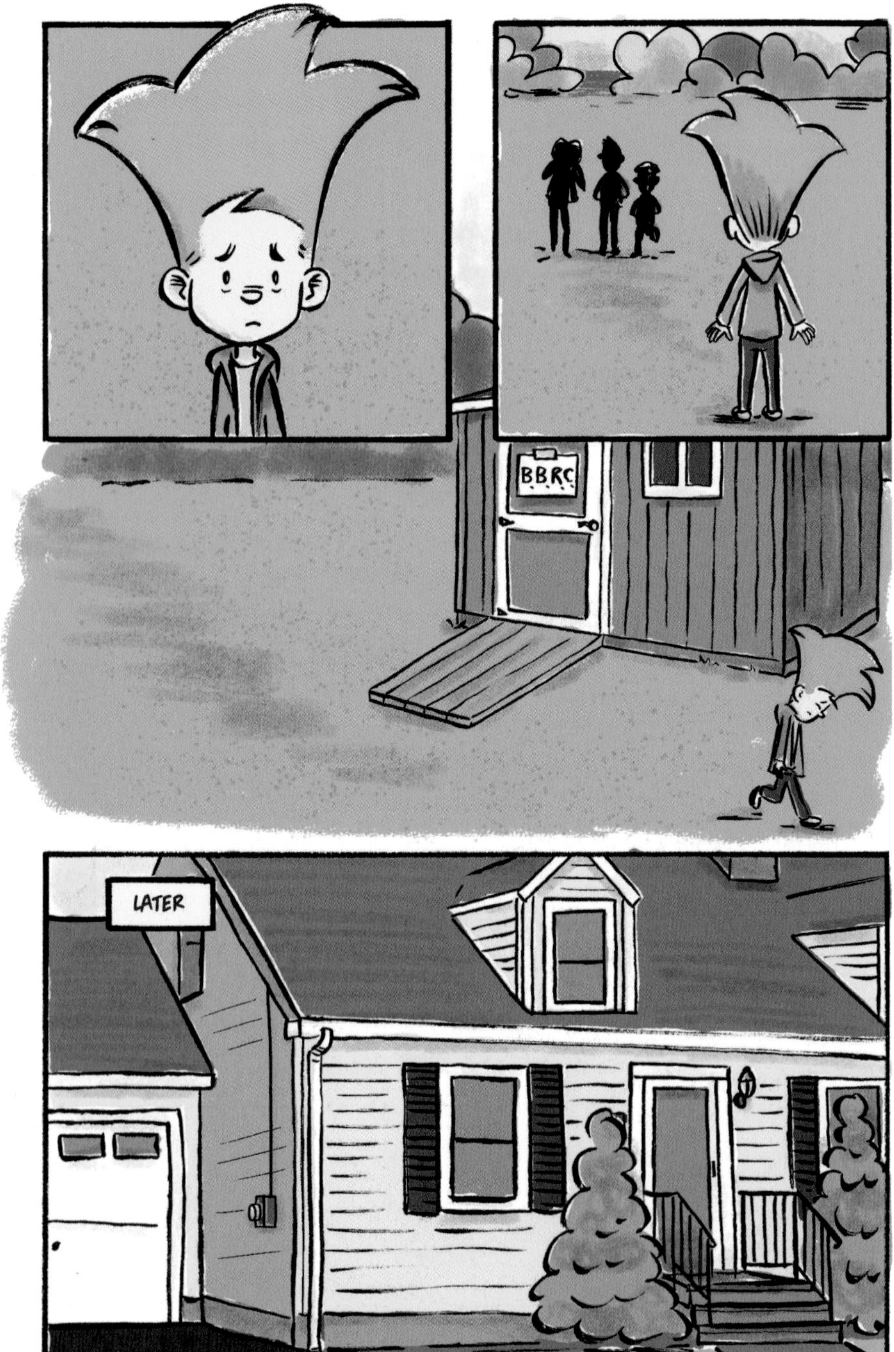
BBRC
LATER

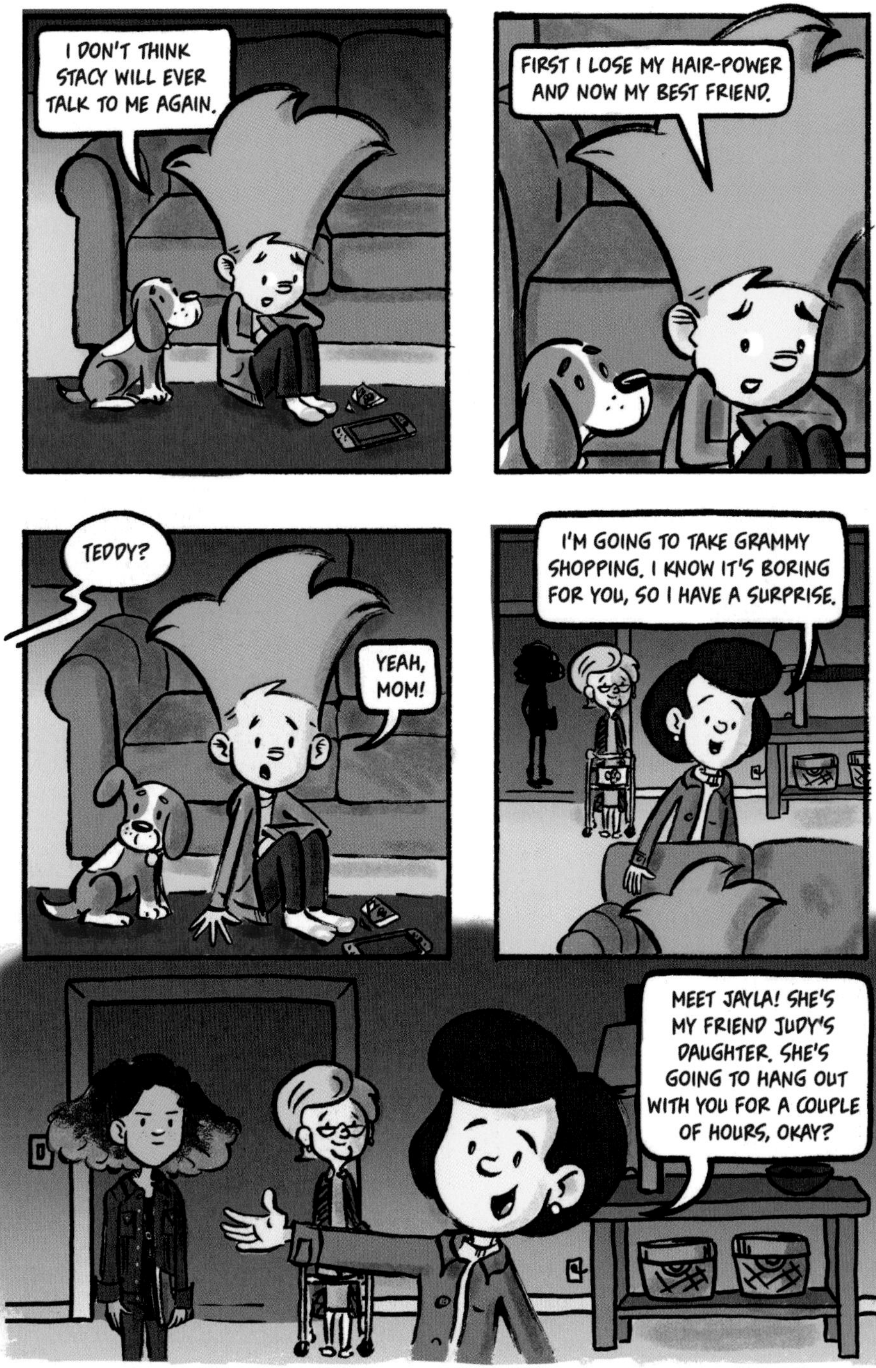
I DON'T THINK STACY WILL EVER TALK TO ME AGAIN.
FIRST I LOSE MY HAIR-POWER AND NOW MY BEST FRIEND.
TEDDY?
YEAH, MOM!
I'M GOING TO TAKE GRAMMY SHOPPING. I KNOW IT'S BORING FOR YOU, SO I HAVE A SURPRISE.
MEET JAYLA! SHE'S MY FRIEND JUDY'S DAUGHTER. SHE'S GOING TO HANG OUT WITH YOU FOR A COUPLE OF HOURS, OKAY?

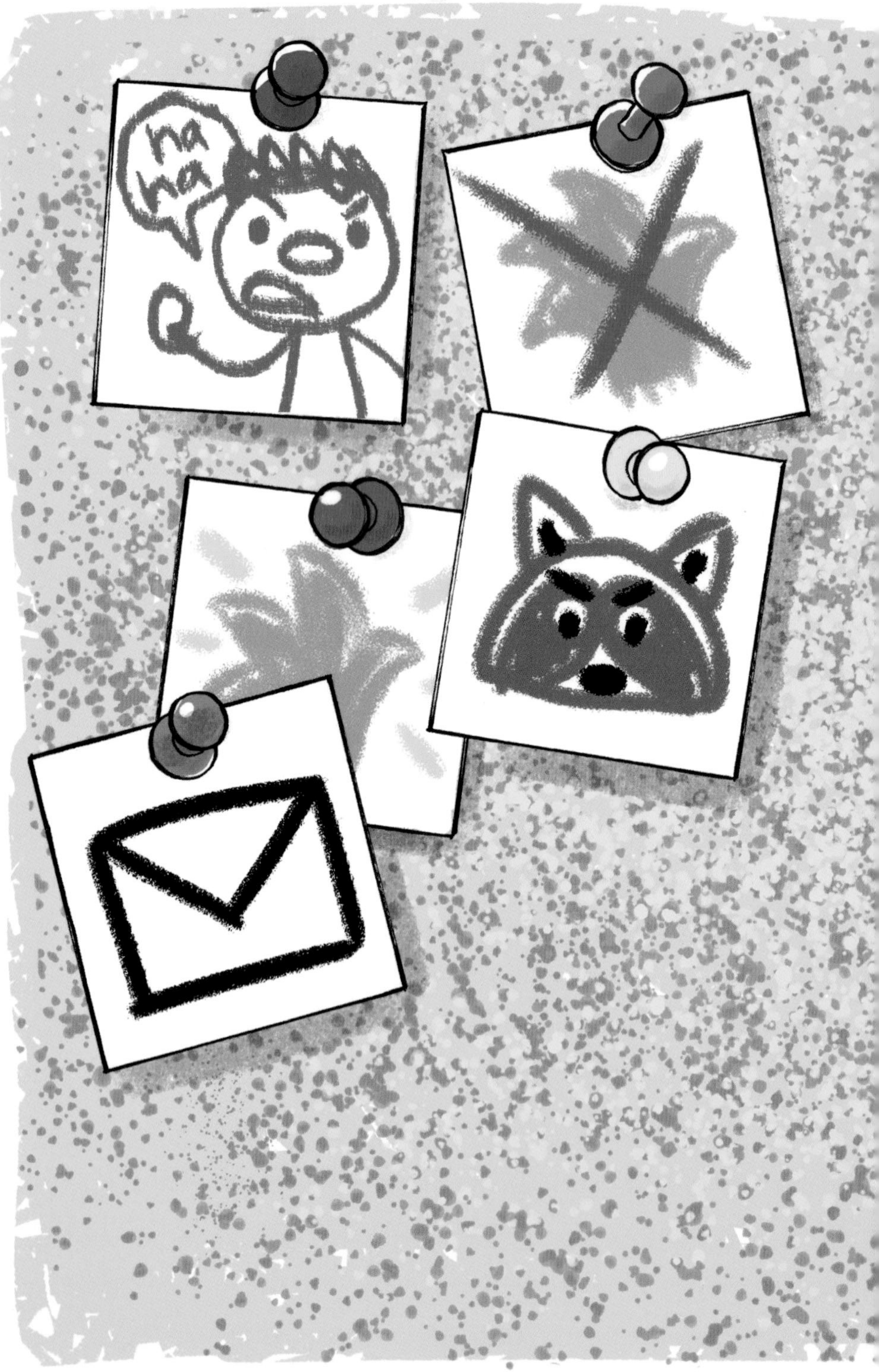
ha ha

CHAPTER 6:

THE BABYSITTER

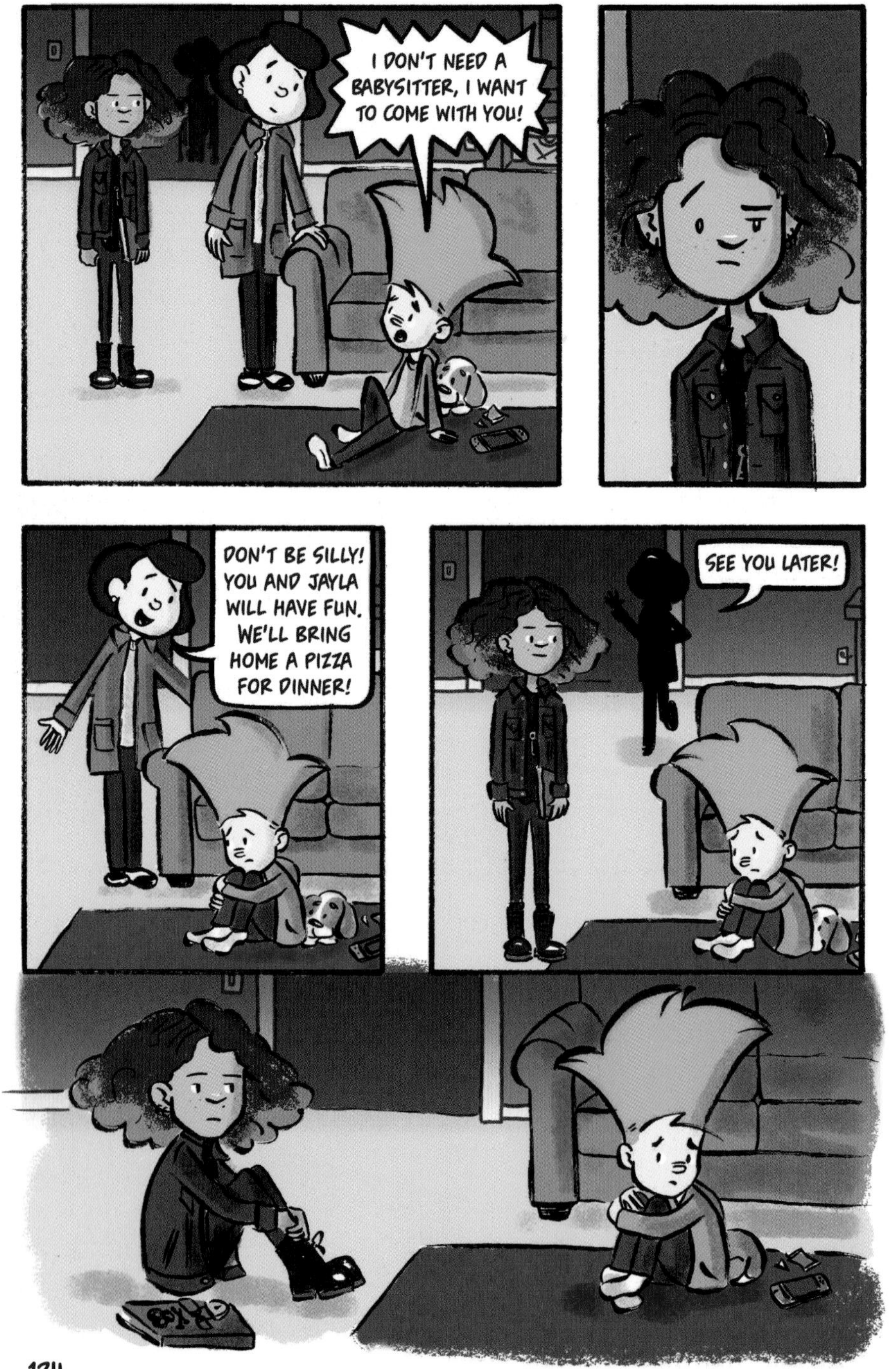
I DON'T NEED A BABYSITTER, I WANT TO COME WITH YOU!
DON'T BE SILLY! YOU AND JAYLA WILL HAVE FUN. WE'LL BRING HOME A PIZZA FOR DINNER!
SEE YOU LATER!

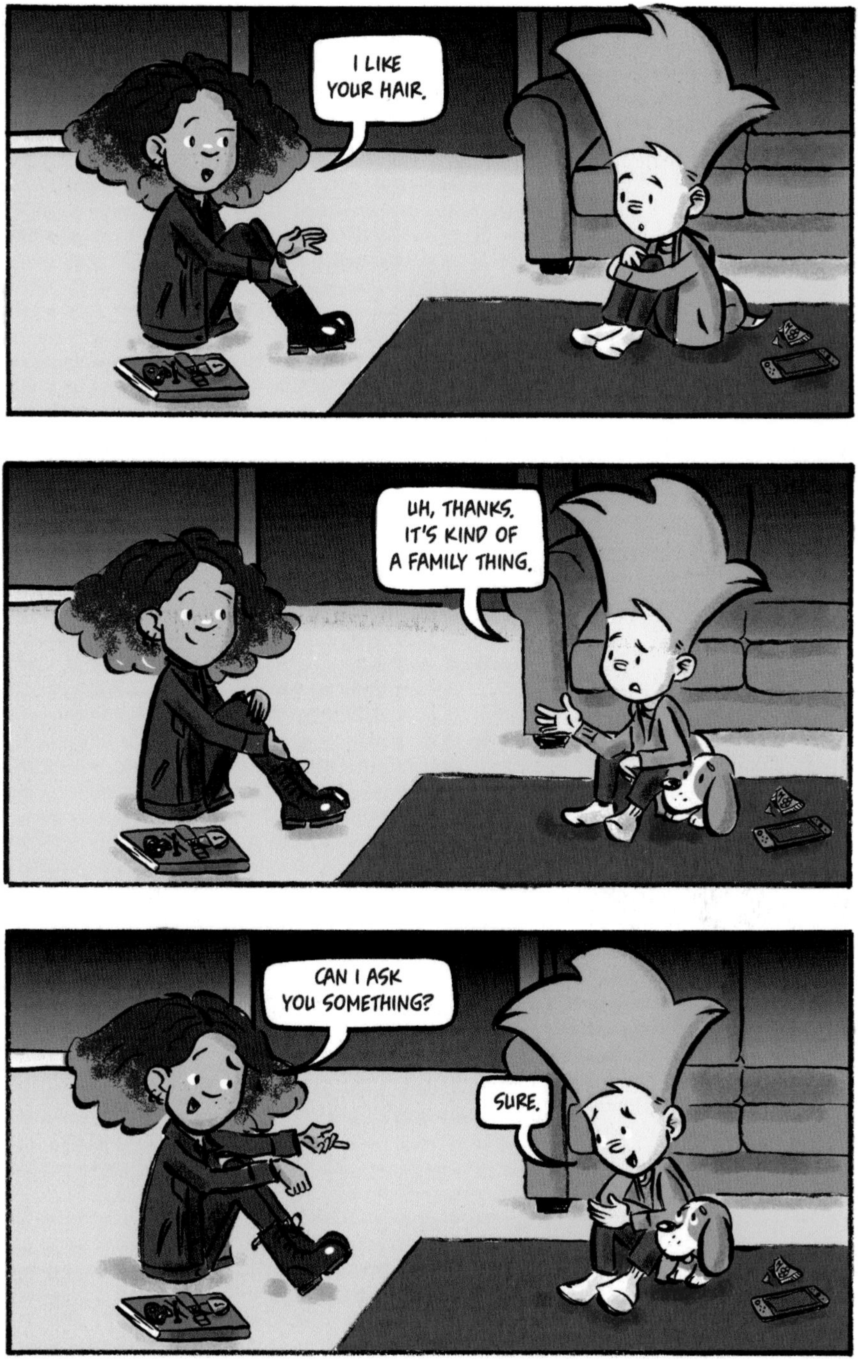
I LIKE YOUR HAIR.
UH, THANKS. IT'S KIND OF A FAMILY THING.
CAN I ASK YOU SOMETHING?
SURE.

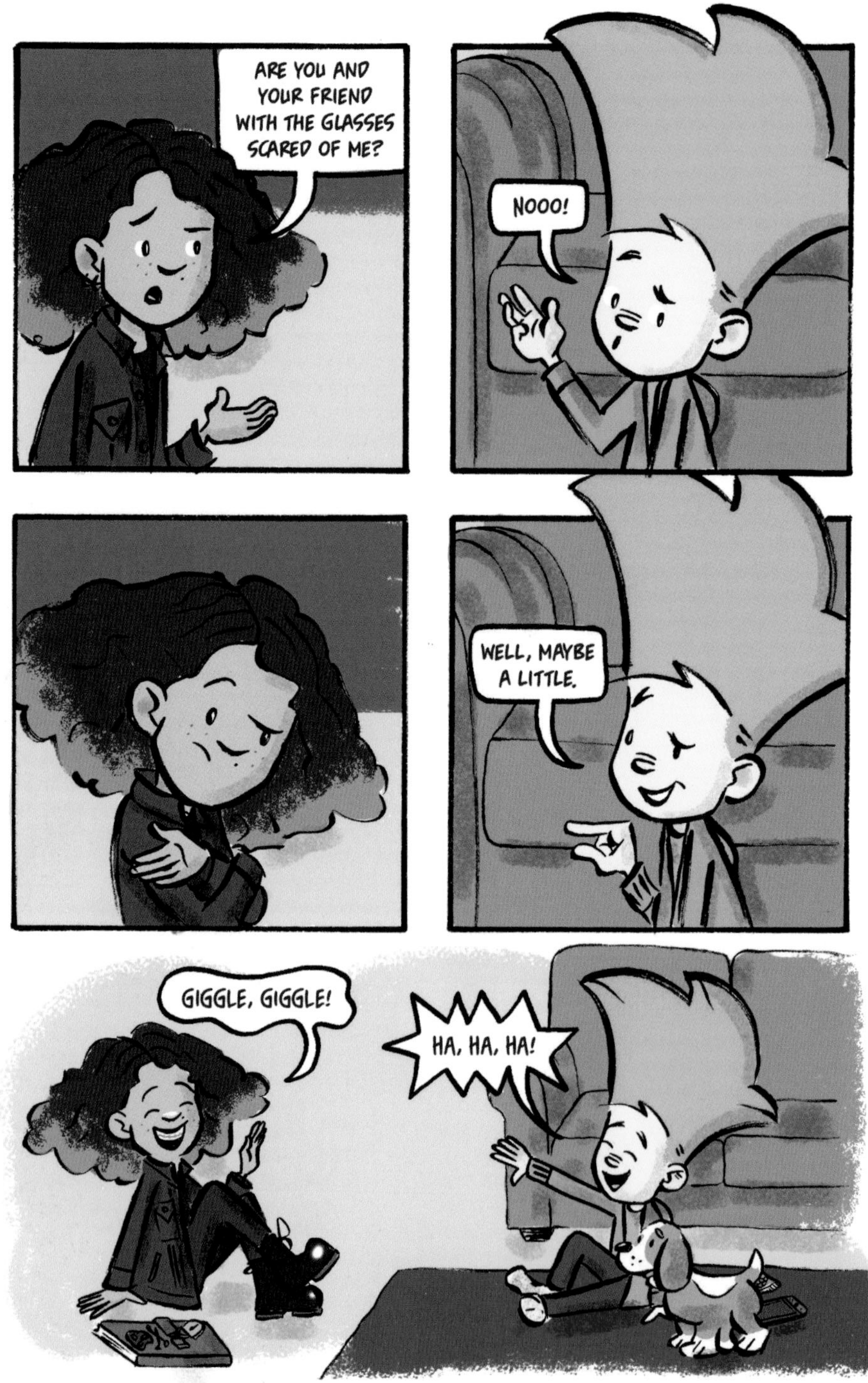
ARE YOU AND YOUR FRIEND WITH THE GLASSES SCARED OF ME?
NOOO!
WELL, MAYBE A LITTLE.
GIGGLE, GIGGLE!
HA, HA, HA!

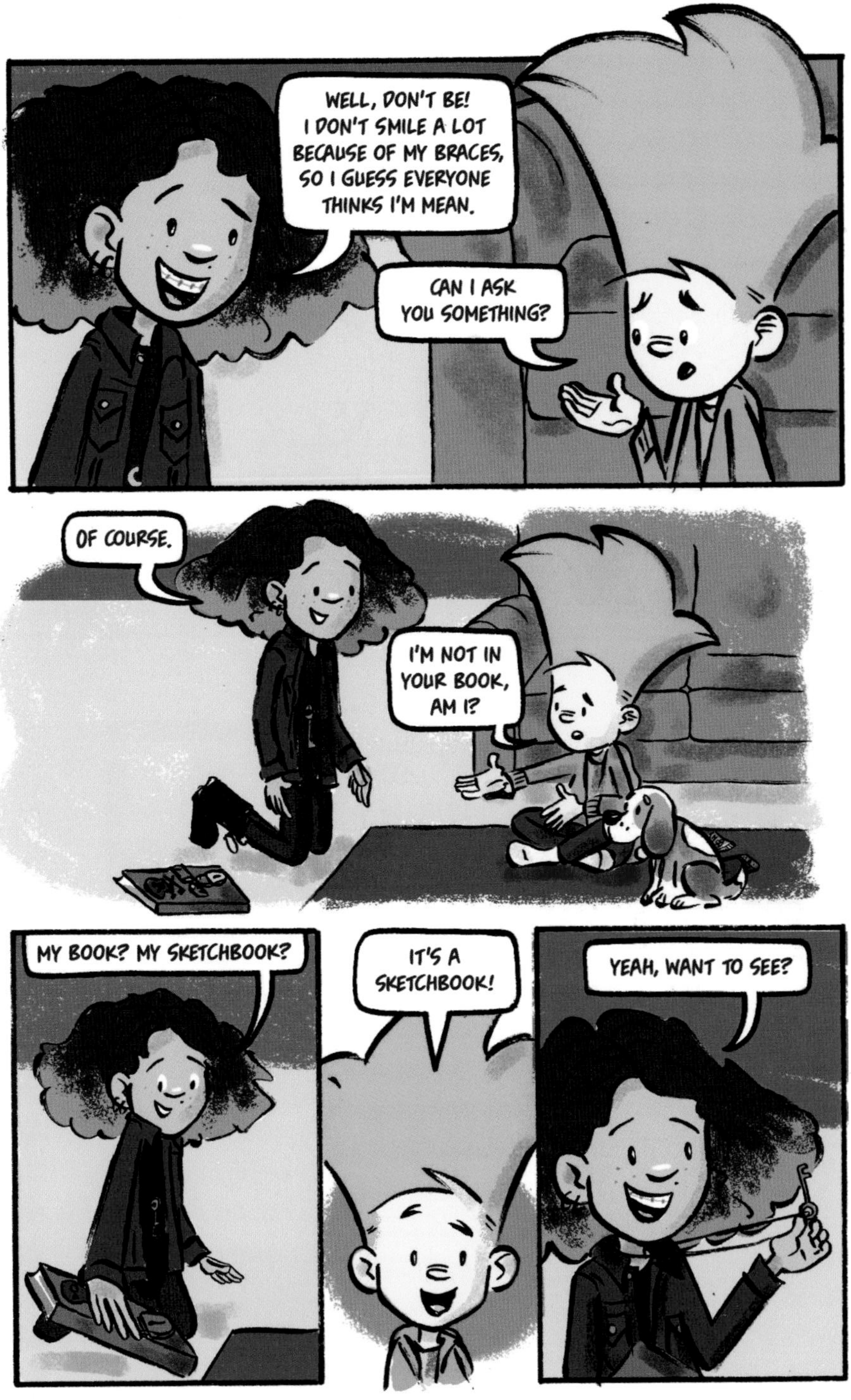
WELL, DON'T BE! I DON'T SMILE A LOT BECAUSE OF MY BRACES, SO I GUESS EVERYONE THINKS I'M MEAN.
CAN I ASK YOU SOMETHING?
OF COURSE.
I'M NOT IN YOUR BOOK, AM I?
MY BOOK? MY SKETCHBOOK?
IT'S A SKETCHBOOK!
YEAH, WANT TO SEE?

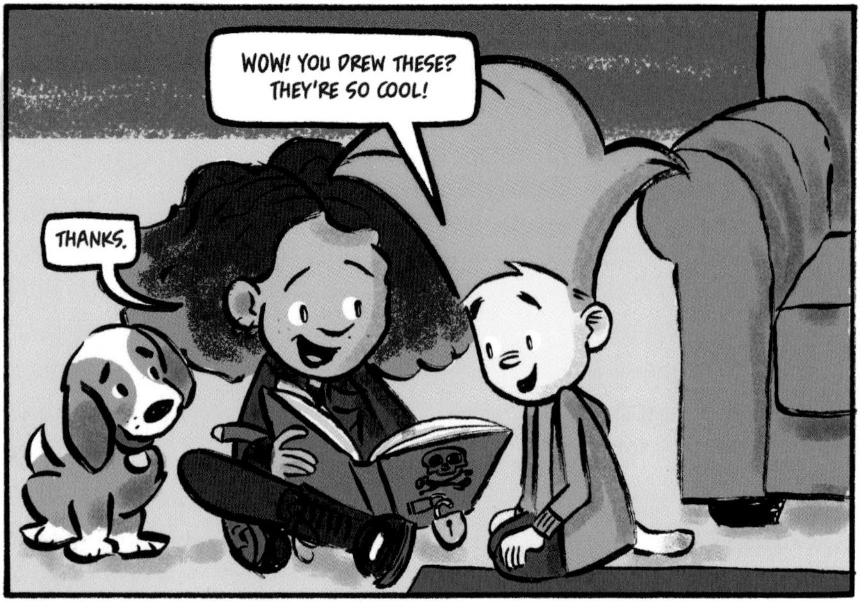
WOW! YOU DREW THESE? THEY'RE SO COOL!
THANKS.

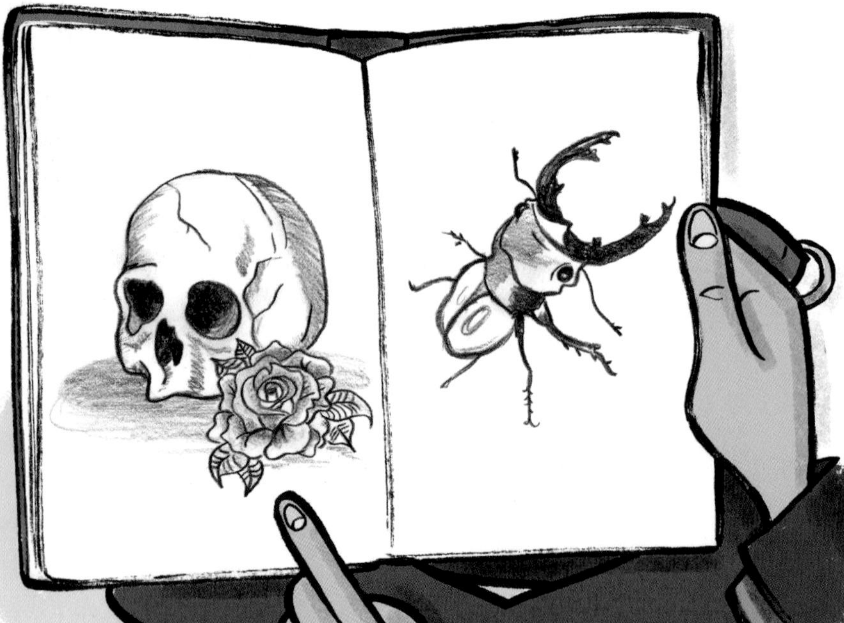

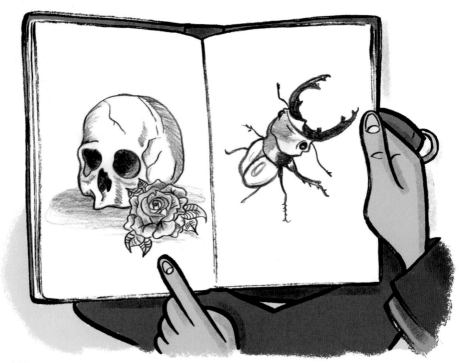

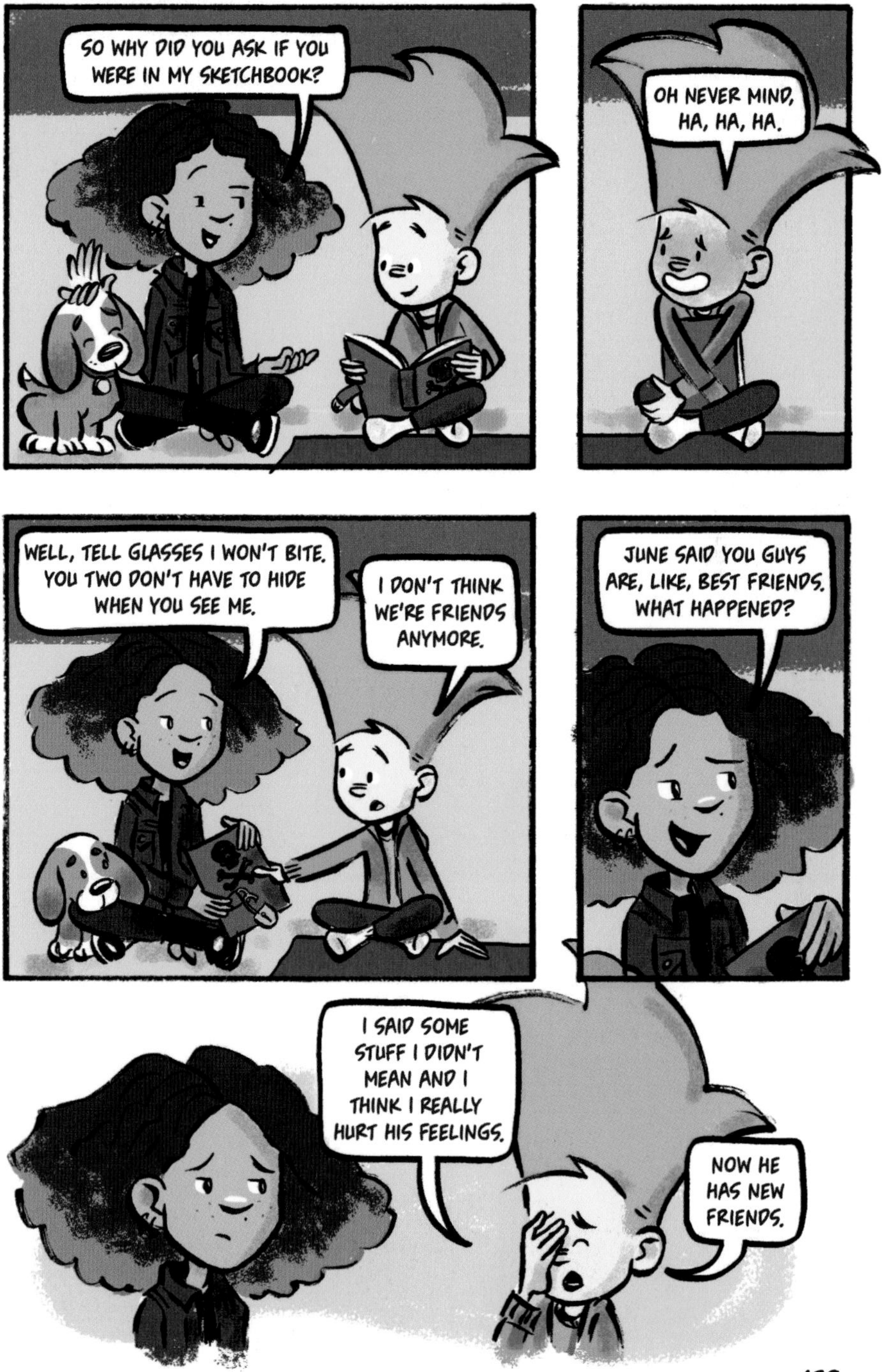
SO WHY DID YOU ASK IF YOU WERE IN MY SKETCHBOOK?
OH NEVER MIND, HA, HA, HA.
WELL, TELL GLASSES I WON'T BITE. YOU TWO DON'T HAVE TO HIDE WHEN YOU SEE ME.
I DON'T THINK WE'RE FRIENDS ANYMORE.
JUNE SAID YOU GUYS ARE, LIKE, BEST FRIENDS. WHAT HAPPENED?
I SAID SOME STUFF I DIDN'T MEAN AND I THINK I REALLY HURT HIS FEELINGS.
NOW HE HAS NEW FRIENDS.

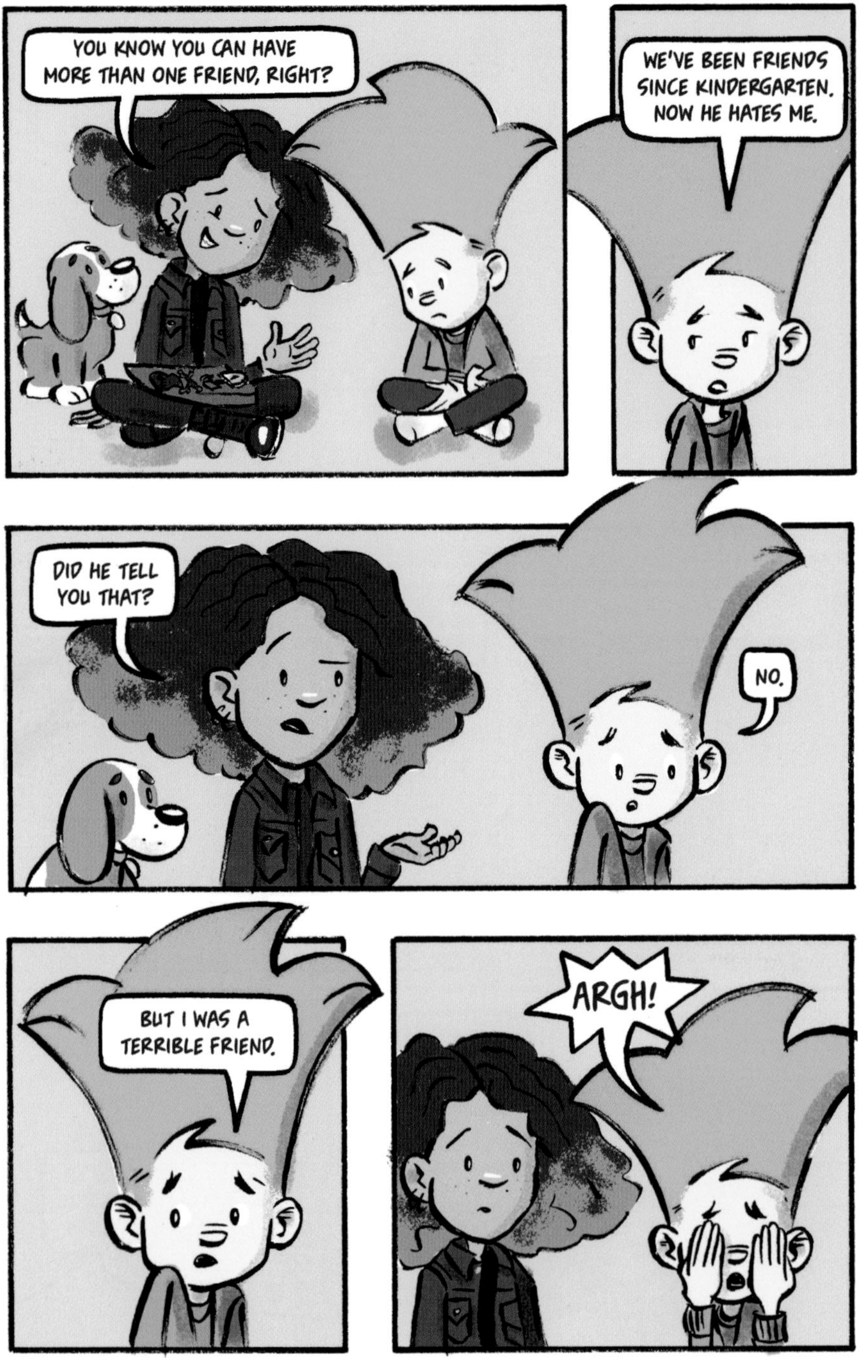
YOU KNOW YOU CAN HAVE MORE THAN ONE FRIEND, RIGHT?
WE'VE BEEN FRIENDS SINCE KINDERGARTEN. NOW HE HATES ME.
DID HE TELL YOU THAT?
NO.
BUT I WAS A TERRIBLE FRIEND.
ARGH!

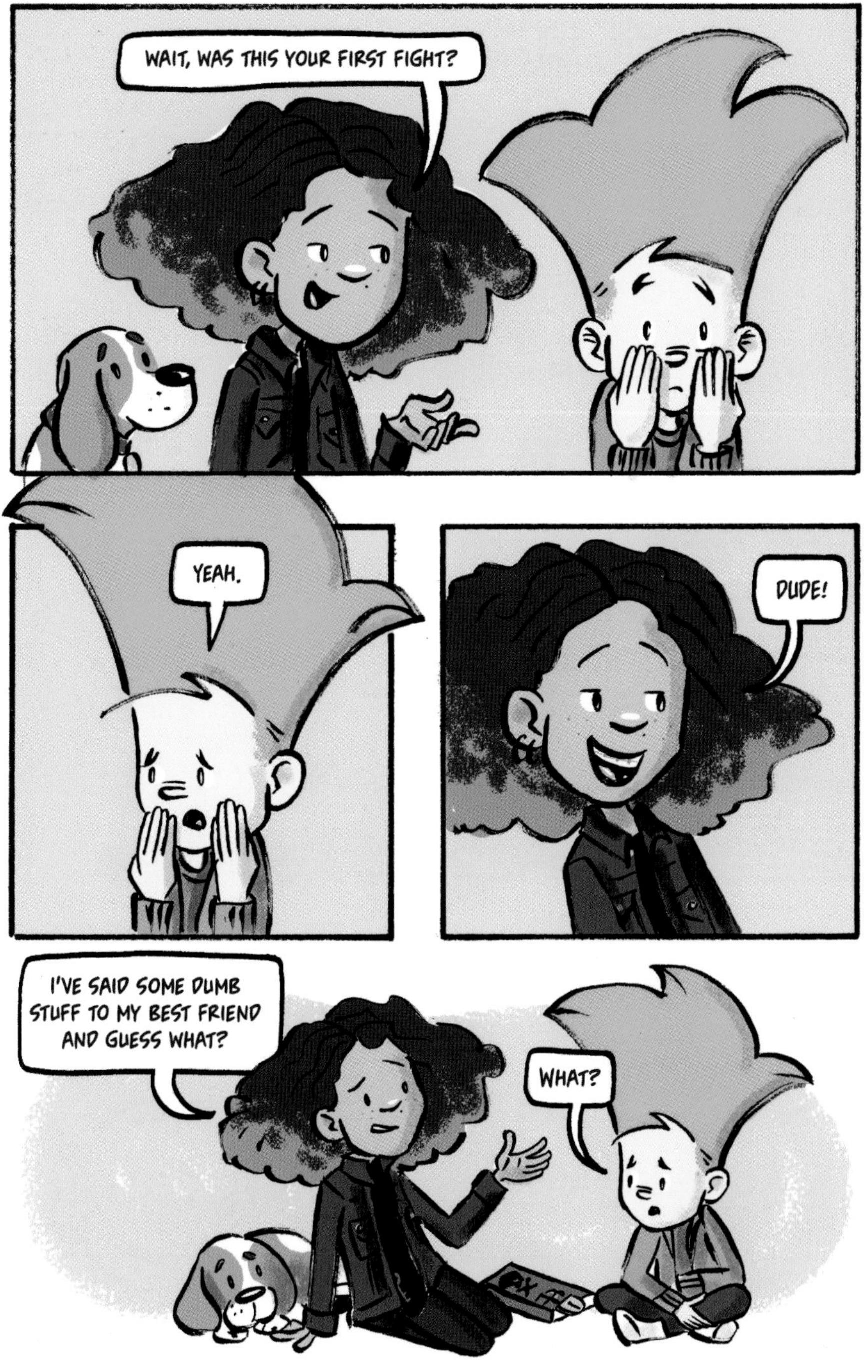
WAIT, WAS THIS YOUR FIRST FIGHT?
YEAH.
DUDE!
I'VE SAID SOME DUMB STUFF TO MY BEST FRIEND AND GUESS WHAT?
WHAT?

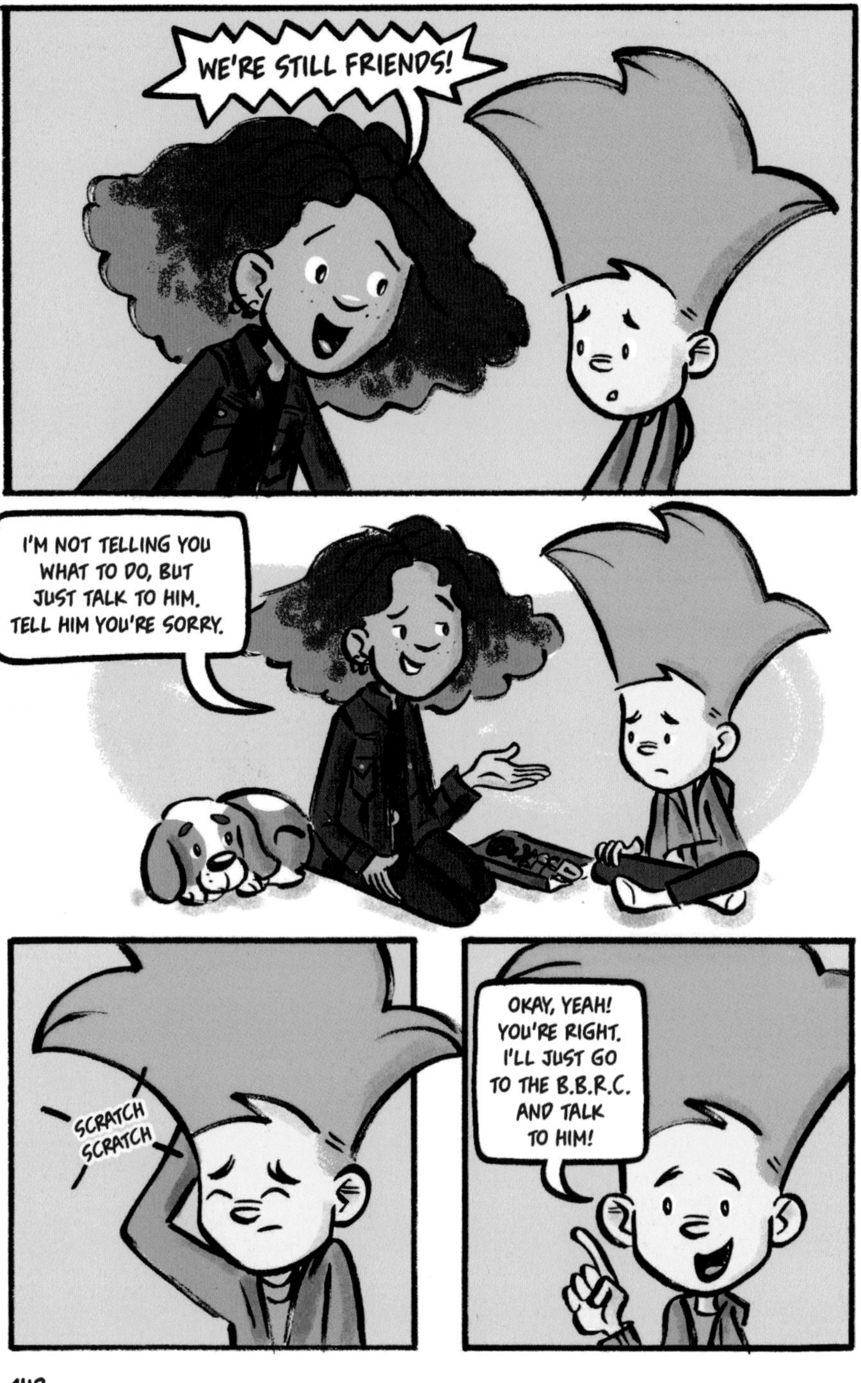
WE'RE STILL FRIENDS!
I'M NOT TELLING YOU WHAT TO DO, BUT JUST TALK TO HIM. TELL HIM YOU'RE SORRY.
SCRATCH SCRATCH
OKAY, YEAH! YOU'RE RIGHT. I'LL JUST GO TO THE B.B.R.C. AND TALK TO HIM!

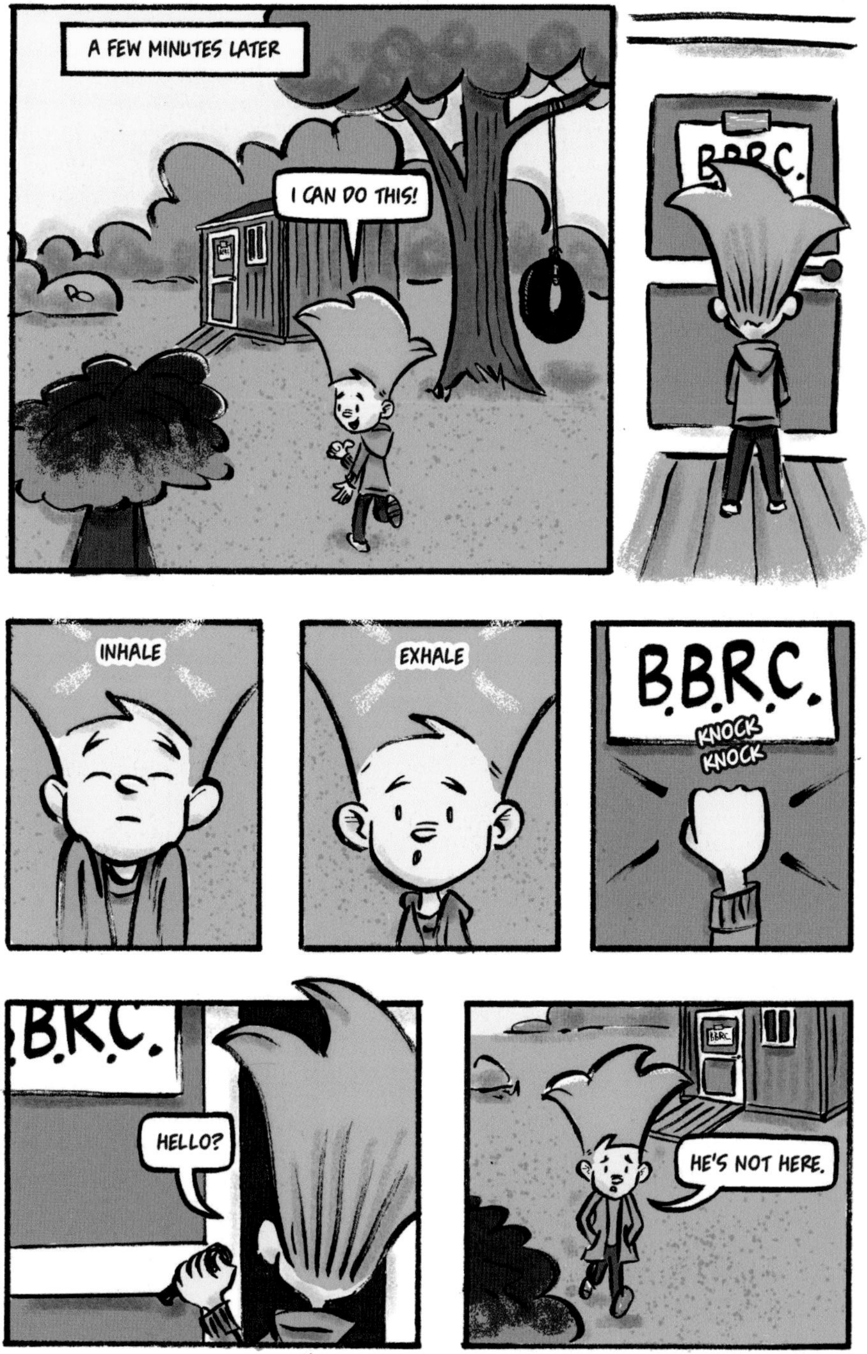
A FEW MINUTES LATER
I CAN DO THIS!
B.B.R.C.
INHALE
EXHALE
B.B.R.C.
KNOCK
KNOCK
B.R.C.
HELLO?
HE'S NOT HERE.

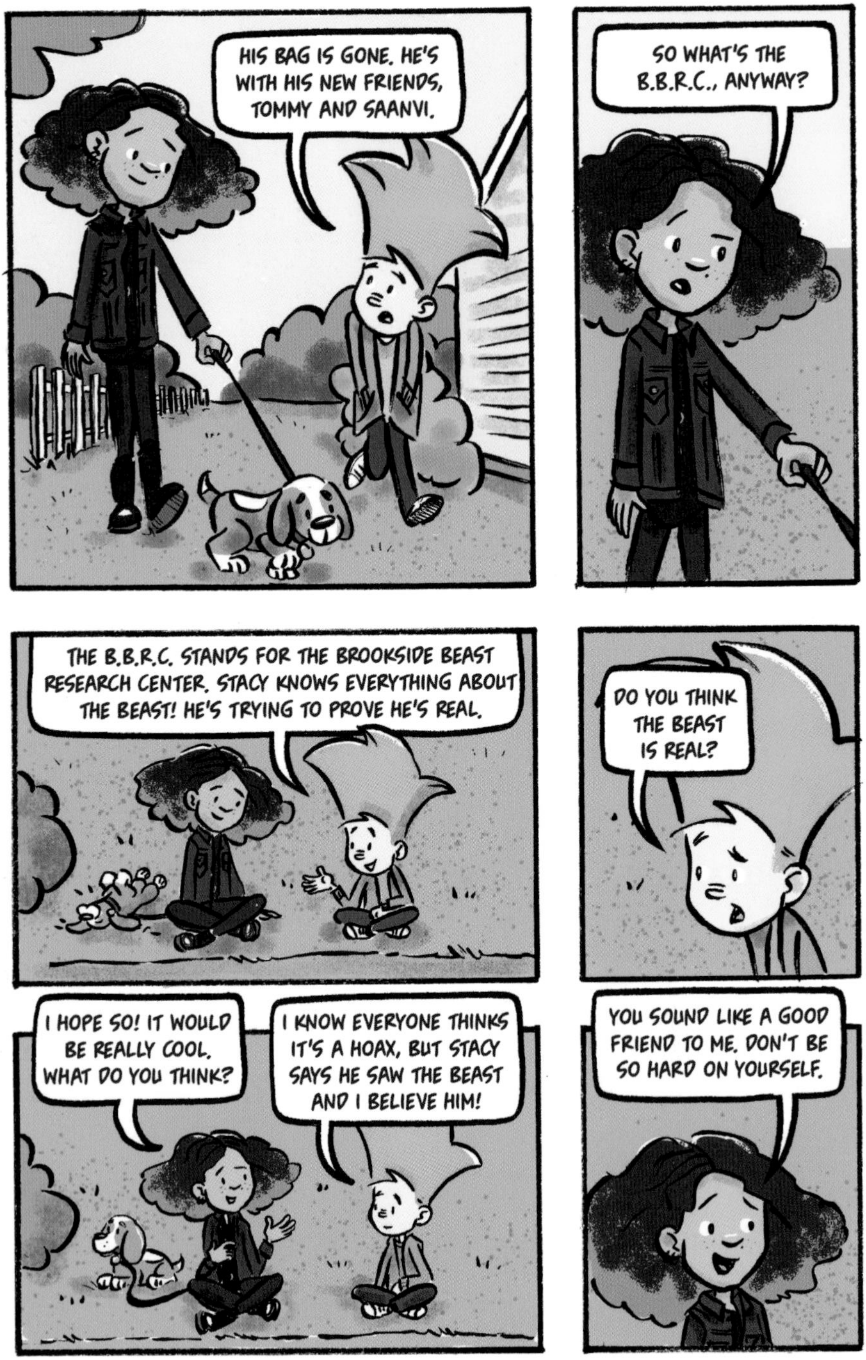
HIS BAG IS GONE. HE'S WITH HIS NEW FRIENDS, TOMMY AND SAANVI.
SO WHAT'S THE B.B.R.C., ANYWAY?
THE B.B.R.C. STANDS FOR THE BROOKSIDE BEAST RESEARCH CENTER. STACY KNOWS EVERYTHING ABOUT THE BEAST! HE'S TRYING TO PROVE HE'S REAL.
DO YOU THINK THE BEAST IS REAL?
I HOPE SO! IT WOULD BE REALLY COOL. WHAT DO YOU THINK?
I KNOW EVERYONE THINKS IT'S A HOAX, BUT STACY SAYS HE SAW THE BEAST AND I BELIEVE HIM!
YOU SOUND LIKE A GOOD FRIEND TO ME. DON'T BE SO HARD ON YOURSELF.

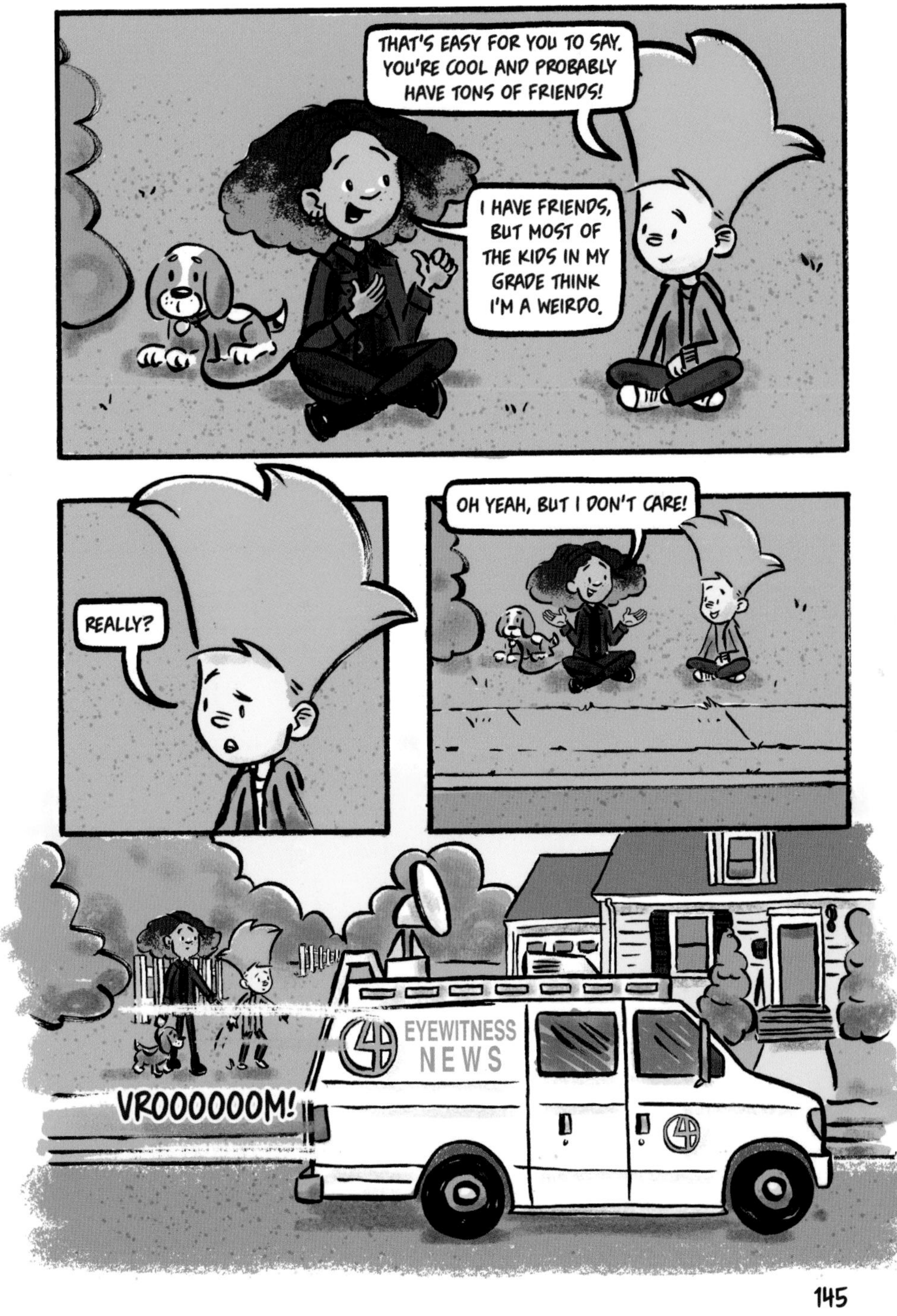
THAT'S EASY FOR YOU TO SAY. YOU'RE COOL AND PROBABLY HAVE TONS OF FRIENDS!
I HAVE FRIENDS, BUT MOST OF THE KIDS IN MY GRADE THINK I'M A WEIRDO.
REALLY?
OH YEAH, BUT I DON'T CARE!
EYEWITNESS NEWS
VROOOOOOM!

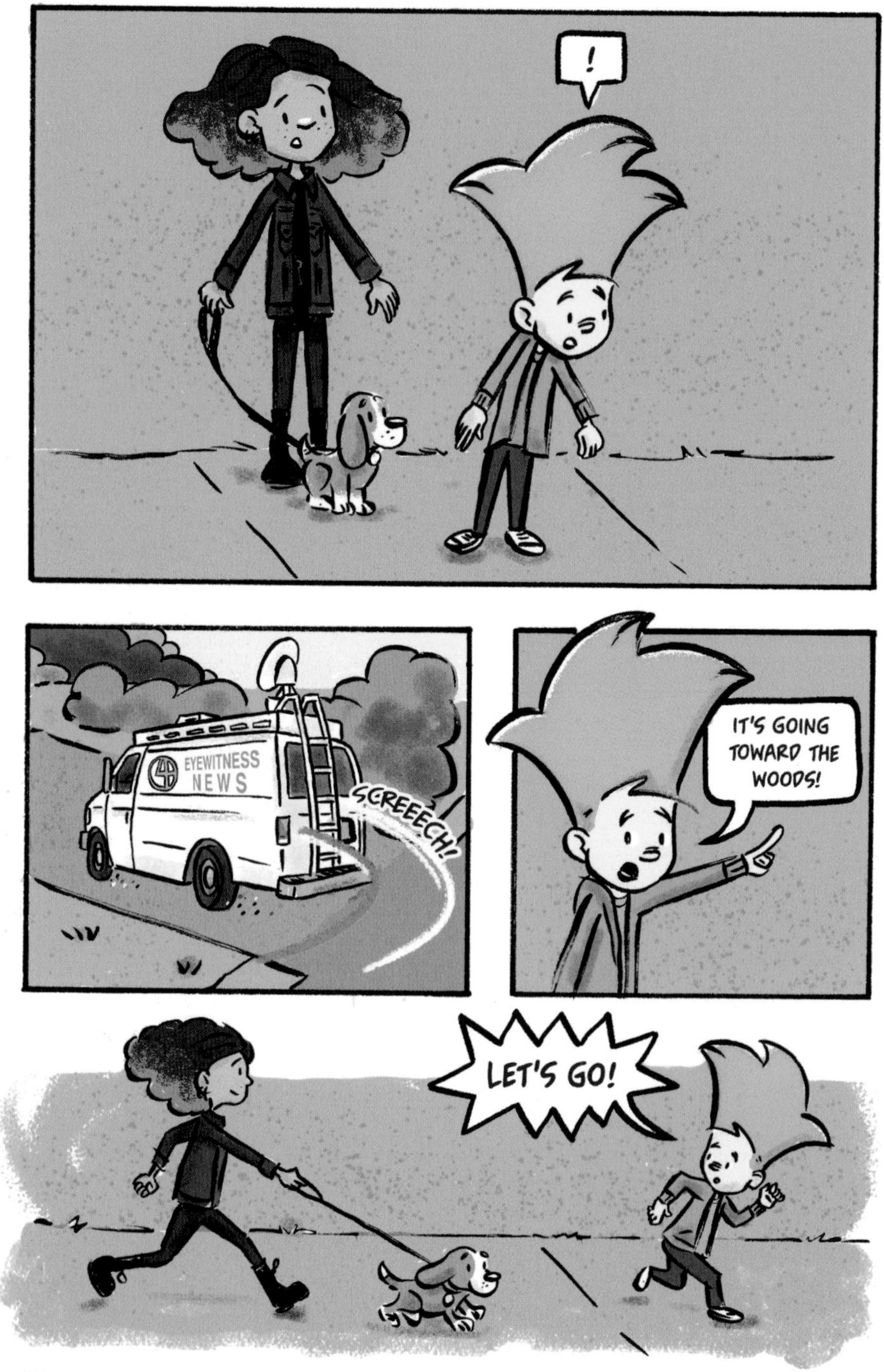
!
EYEWITNESS NEWS
SCREEECH!
IT'S GOING TOWARD THE WOODS!
LET'S GO!

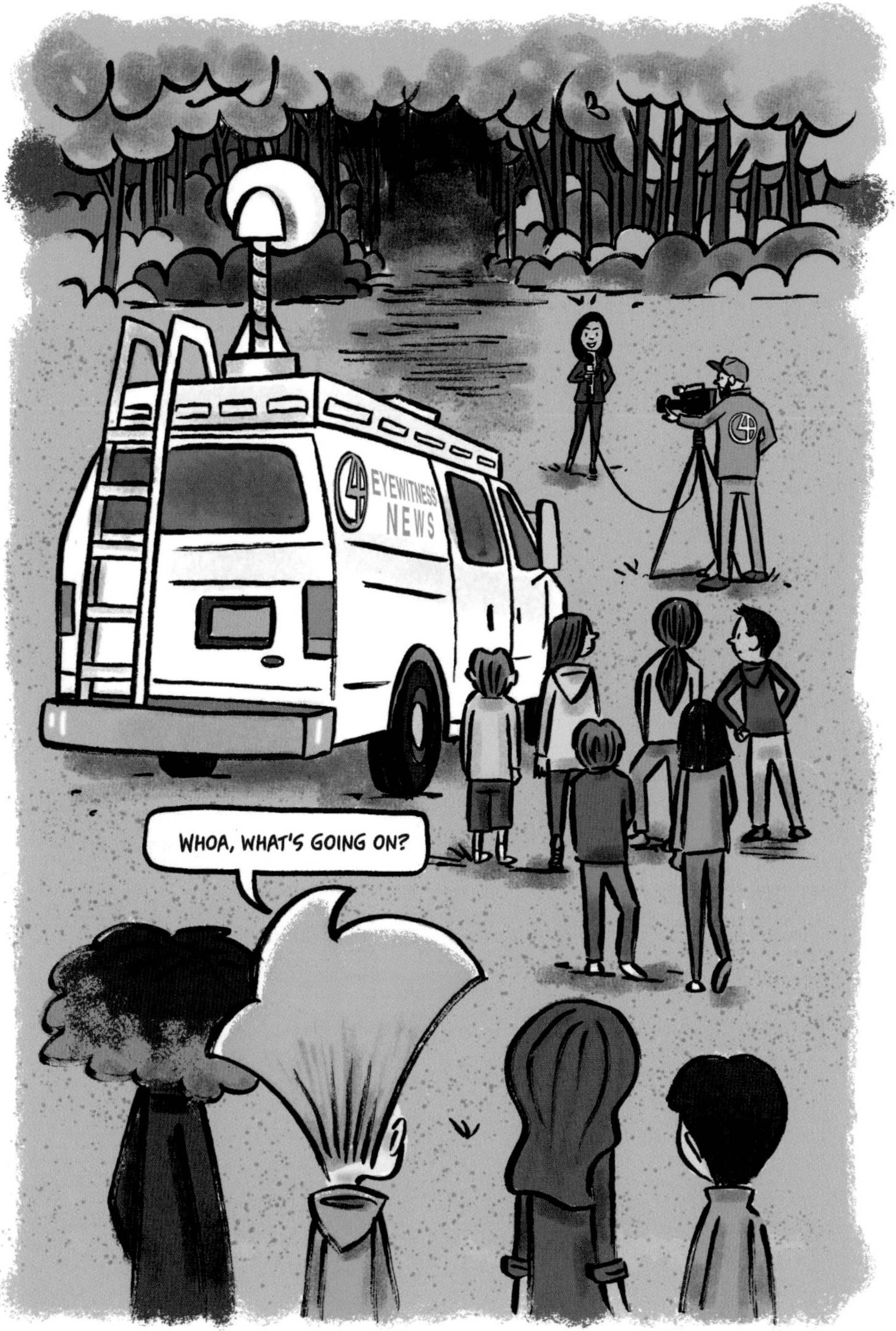
EYEWITNESS
NEWS
WHOA, WHAT'S GOING ON?

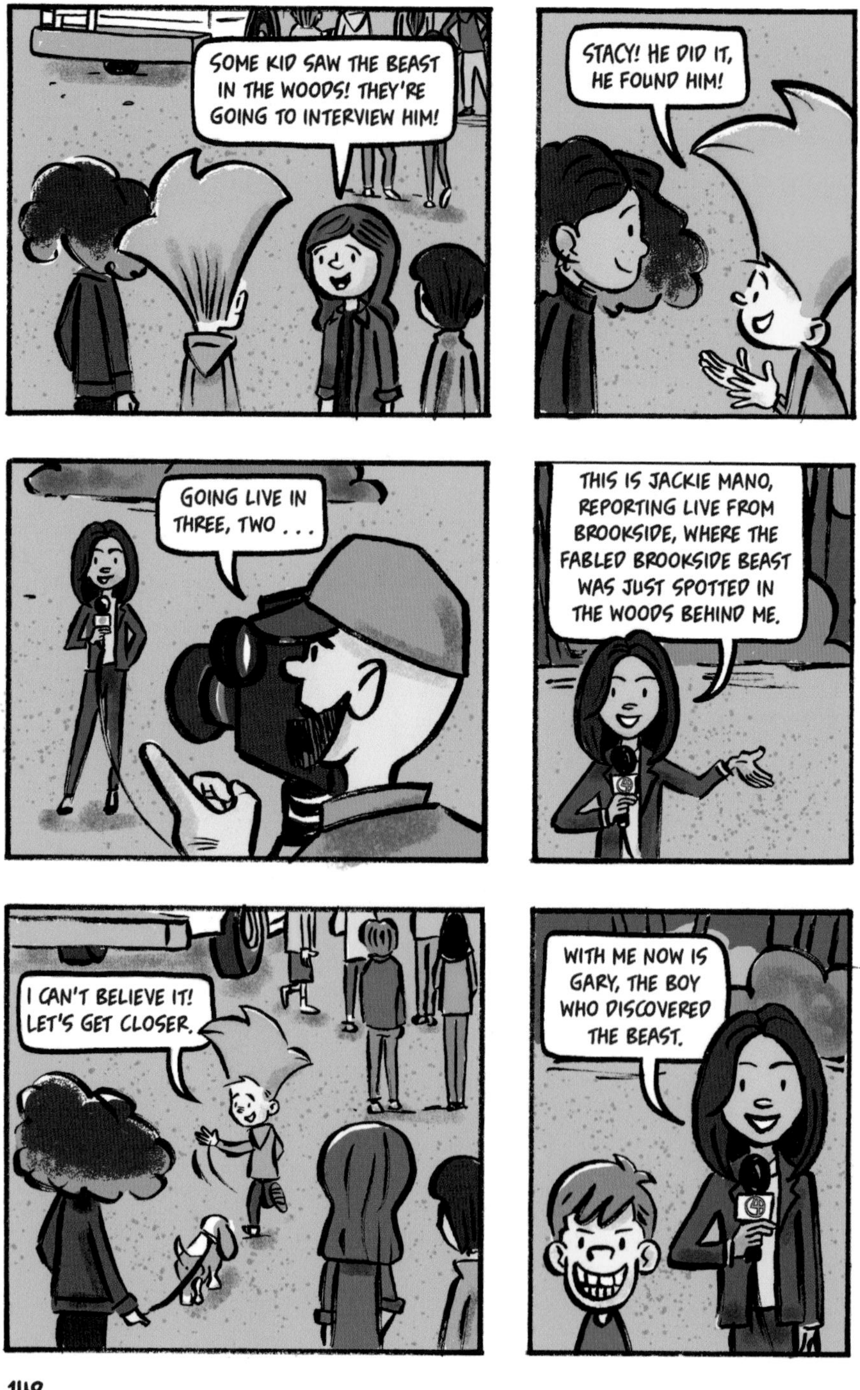
SOME KID SAW THE BEAST IN THE WOODS! THEY'RE GOING TO INTERVIEW HIM!
STACY! HE DID IT, HE FOUND HIM!
GOING LIVE IN THREE, TWO . . .
THIS IS JACKIE MANO, REPORTING LIVE FROM BROOKSIDE, WHERE THE FABLED BROOKSIDE BEAST WAS JUST SPOTTED IN THE WOODS BEHIND ME.
I CAN'T BELIEVE IT! LET'S GET CLOSER.
WITH ME NOW IS GARY, THE BOY WHO DISCOVERED THE BEAST.

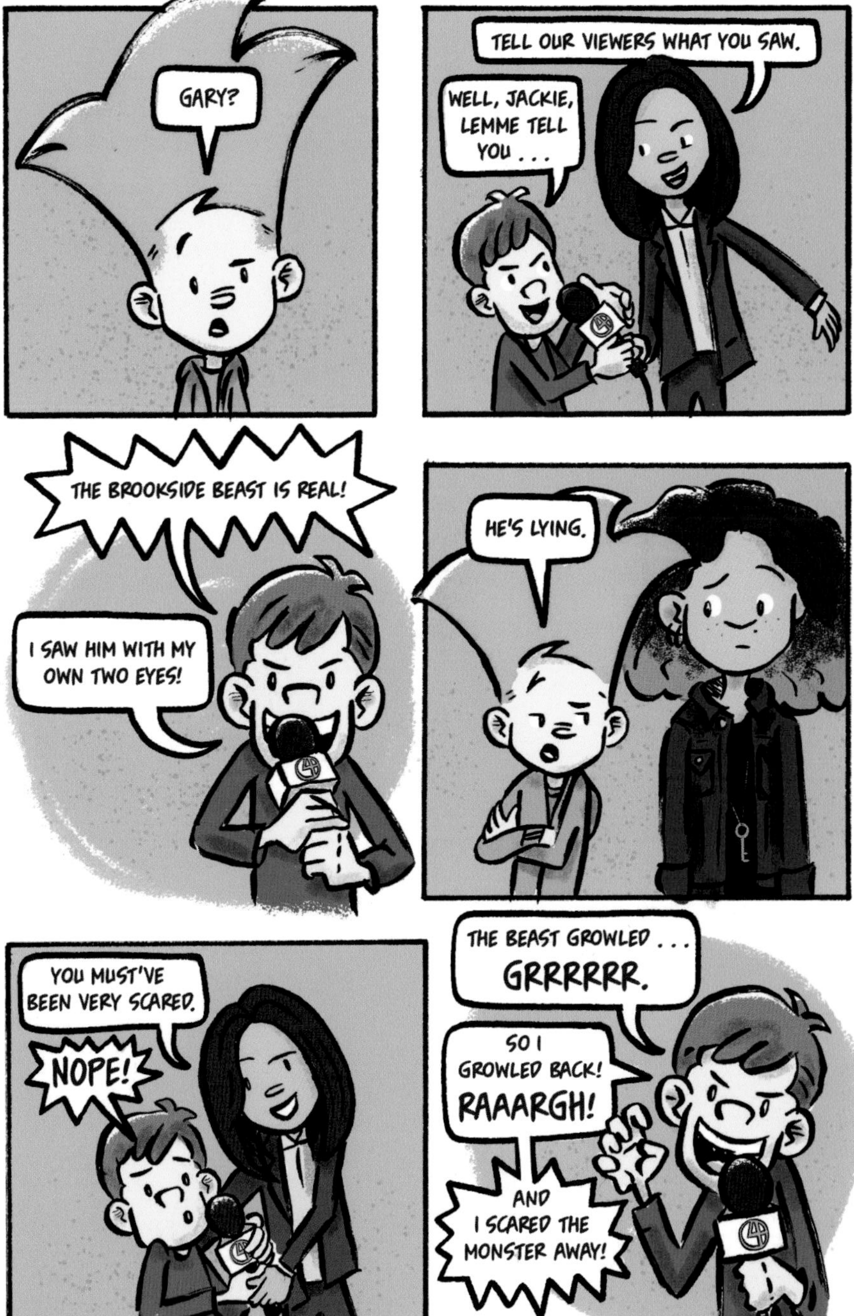
GARY?
TELL OUR VIEWERS WHAT YOU SAW.
WELL, JACKIE, LEMME TELL YOU . . .
THE BROOKSIDE BEAST IS REAL!
I SAW HIM WITH MY OWN TWO EYES!
HE'S LYING.
YOU MUST'VE BEEN VERY SCARED.
NOPE!
THE BEAST GROWLED . . . GRRRRRR.
SO I GROWLED BACK! RAAARGH!
AND I SCARED THE MONSTER AWAY!

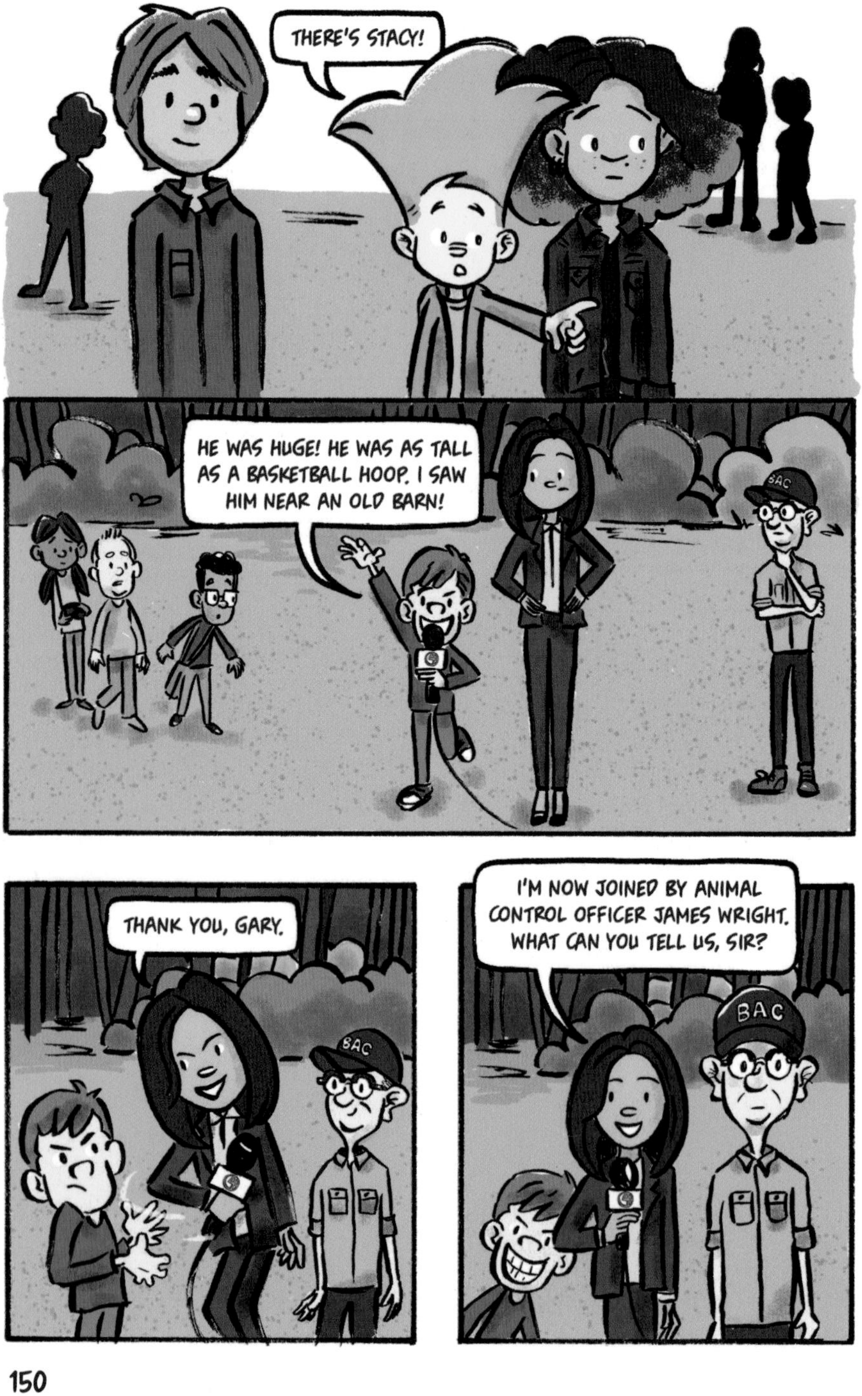
THERE'S STACY!
HE WAS HUGE! HE WAS AS TALL AS A BASKETBALL HOOP. I SAW HIM NEAR AN OLD BARN!
BAC
THANK YOU, GARY.
BAC
I'M NOW JOINED BY ANIMAL CONTROL OFFICER JAMES WRIGHT. WHAT CAN YOU TELL US, SIR?
BAC

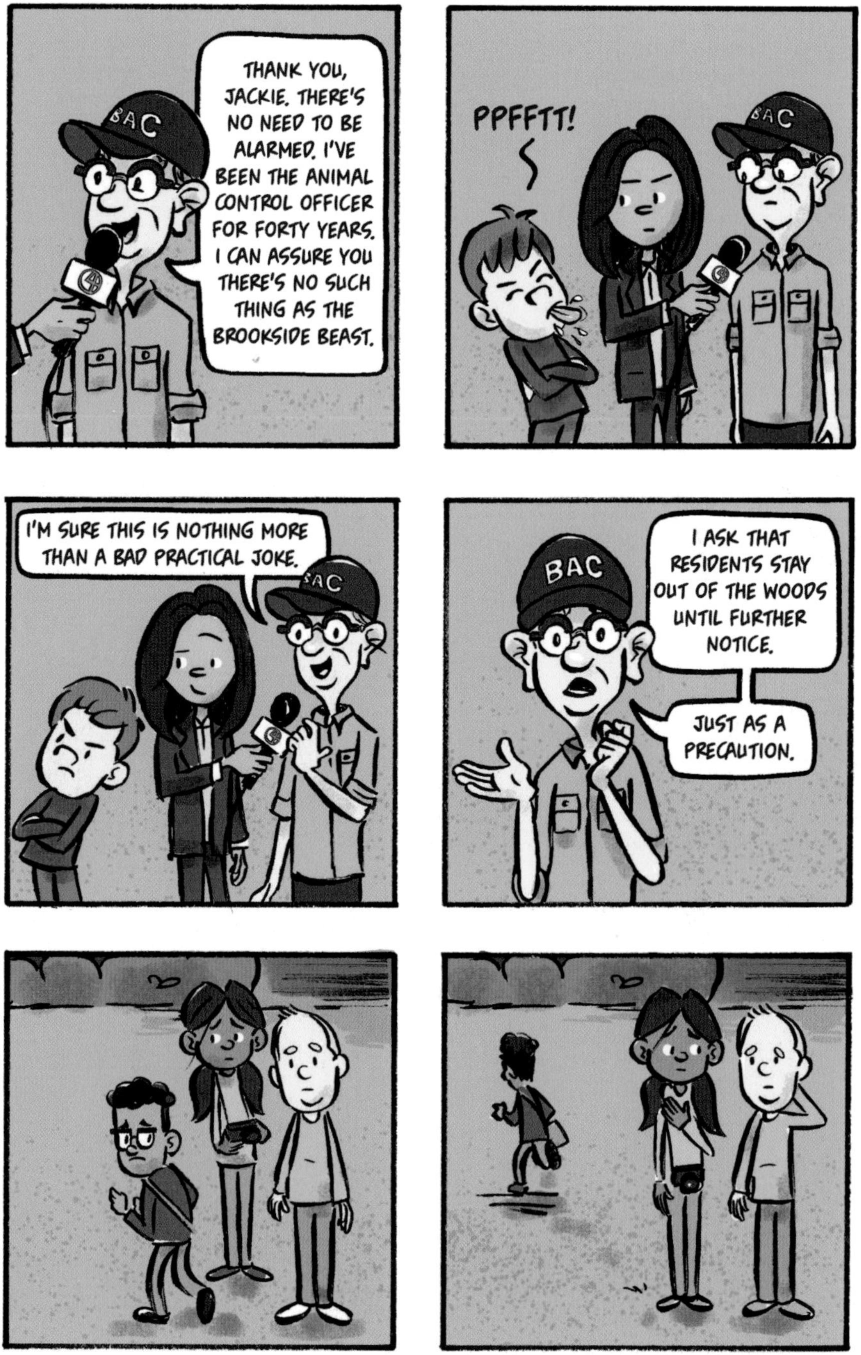
THANK YOU, JACKIE. THERE'S NO NEED TO BE ALARMED. I'VE BEEN THE ANIMAL CONTROL OFFICER FOR FORTY YEARS. I CAN ASSURE YOU THERE'S NO SUCH THING AS THE BROOKSIDE BEAST.
BAC
PPFFTT!
BAC
I'M SURE THIS IS NOTHING MORE THAN A BAD PRACTICAL JOKE.
BAC
BAC
I ASK THAT RESIDENTS STAY OUT OF THE WOODS UNTIL FURTHER NOTICE.
JUST AS A PRECAUTION.

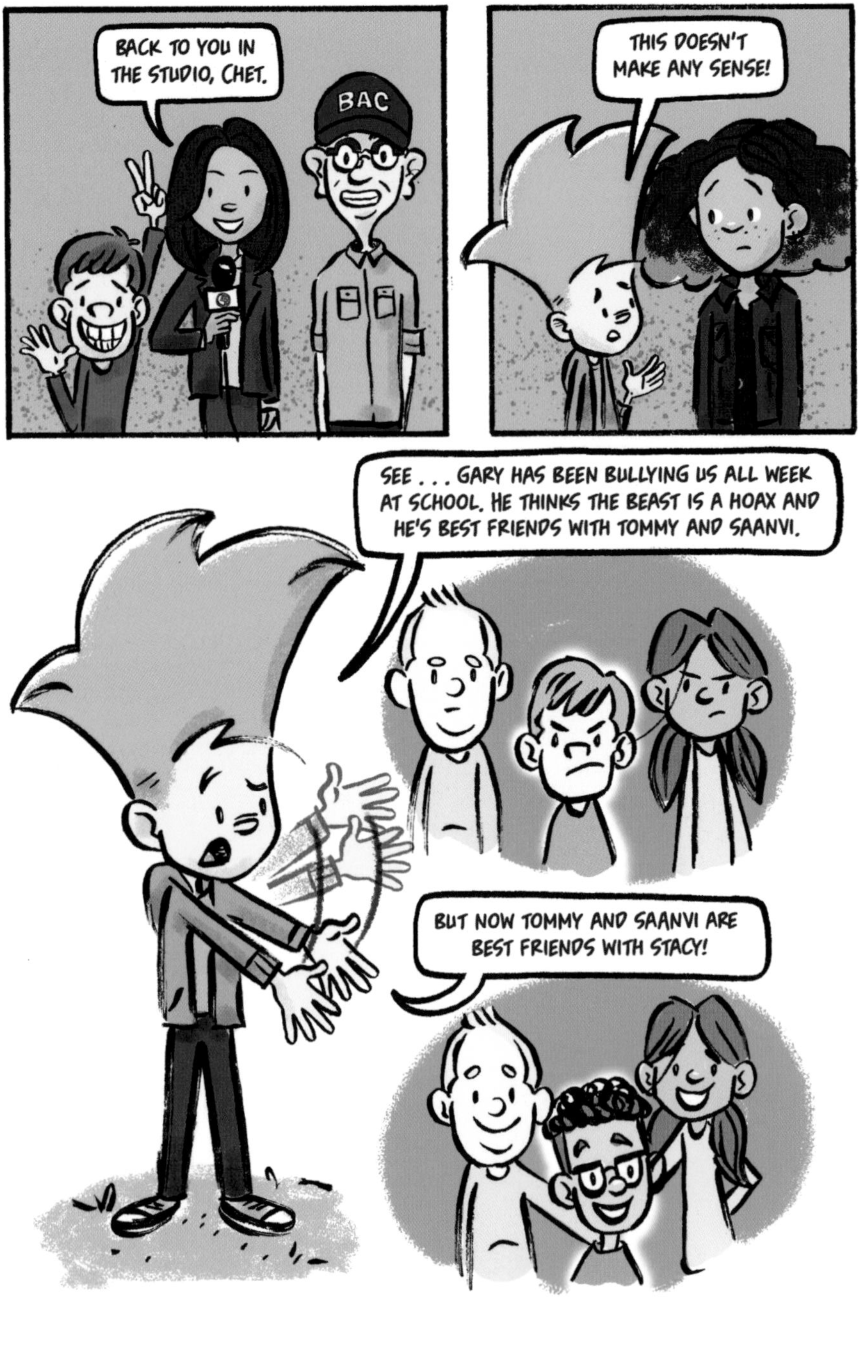
BACK TO YOU IN THE STUDIO, CHET.
BAC
THIS DOESN'T MAKE ANY SENSE!
SEE . . . GARY HAS BEEN BULLYING US ALL WEEK AT SCHOOL. HE THINKS THE BEAST IS A HOAX AND HE'S BEST FRIENDS WITH TOMMY AND SAANVI.
BUT NOW TOMMY AND SAANVI ARE BEST FRIENDS WITH STACY!

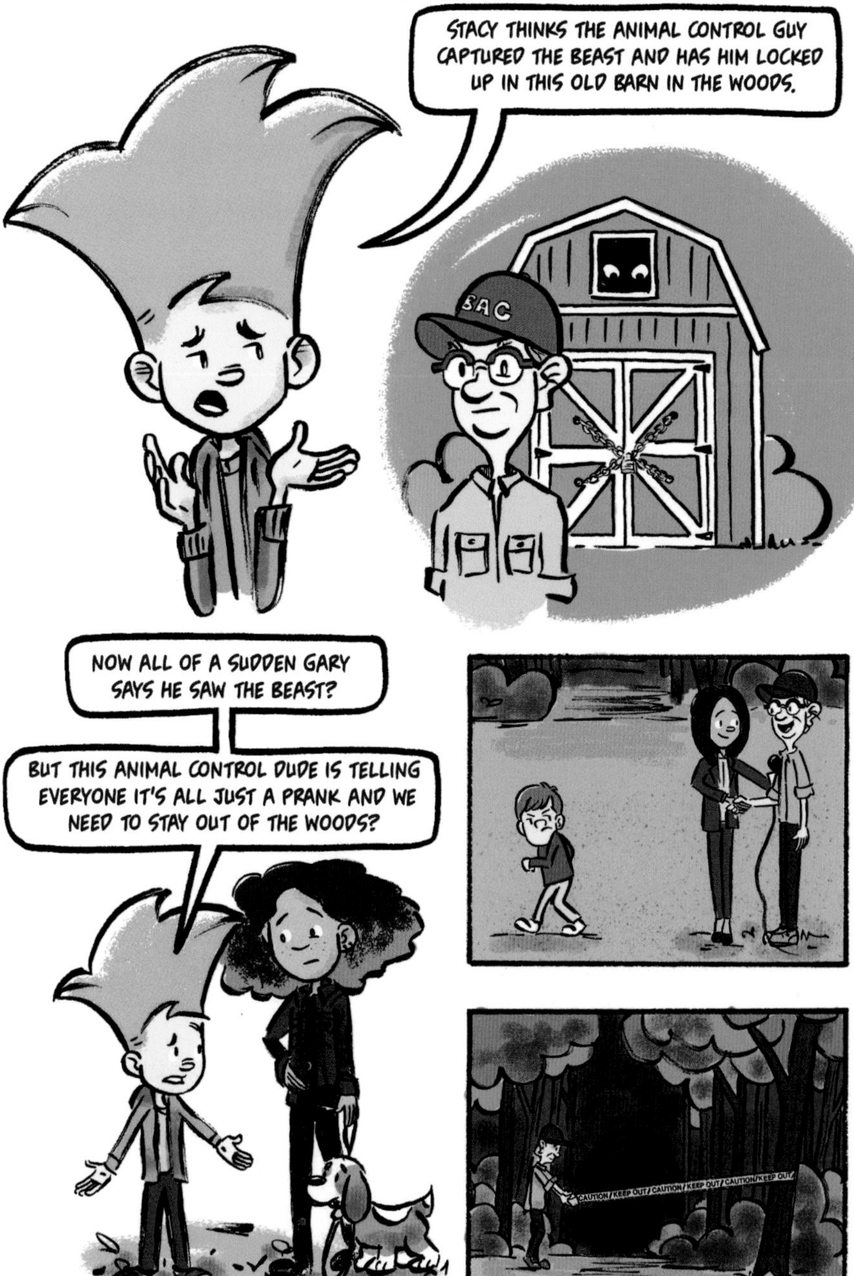
STACY THINKS THE ANIMAL CONTROL GUY CAPTURED THE BEAST AND HAS HIM LOCKED UP IN THIS OLD BARN IN THE WOODS.
SAC
NOW ALL OF A SUDDEN GARY SAYS HE SAW THE BEAST?
BUT THIS ANIMAL CONTROL DUDE IS TELLING EVERYONE IT'S ALL JUST A PRANK AND WE NEED TO STAY OUT OF THE WOODS?
CAUTION / KEEP OUT / CAUTION / KEEP OUT / CAUTION / KEEP OUT

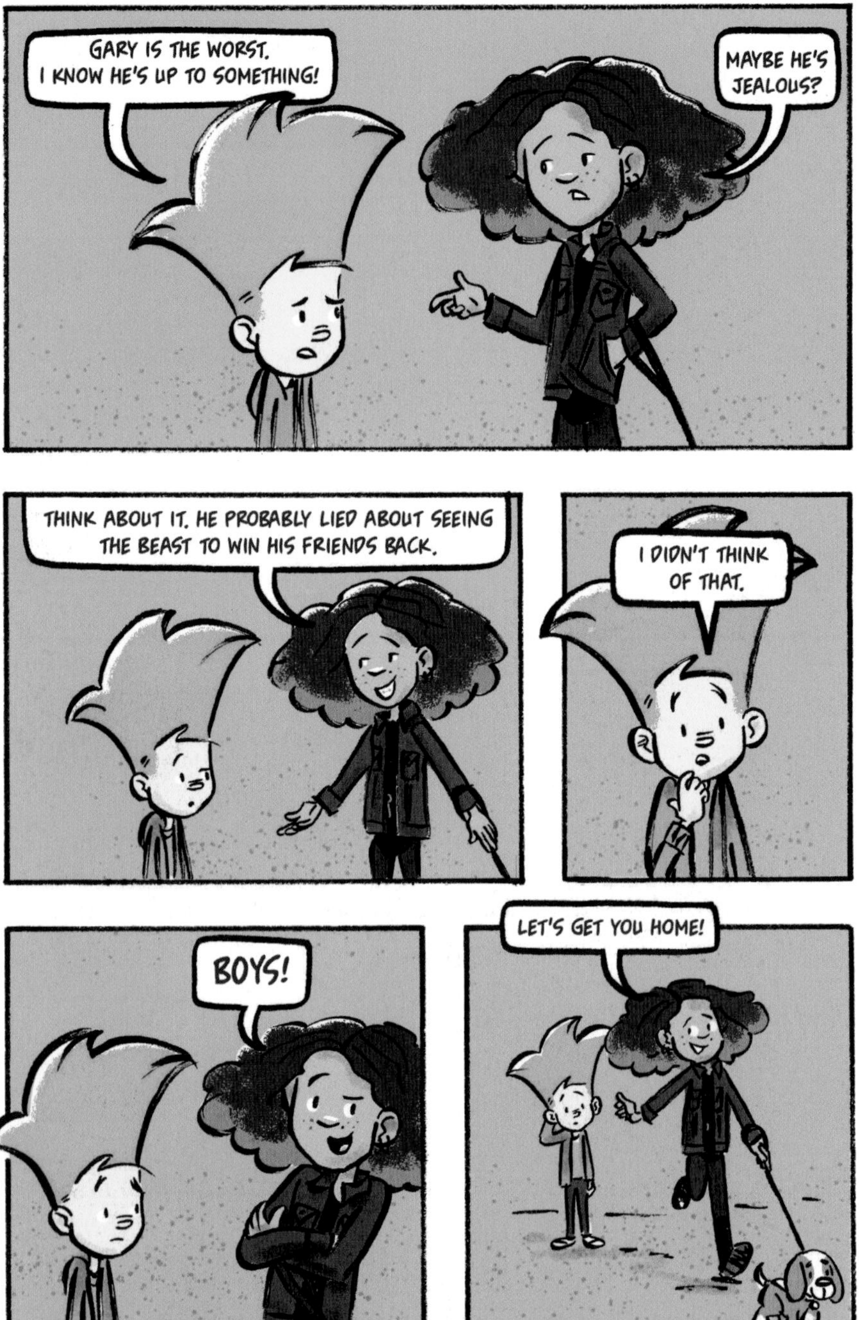
GARY IS THE WORST. I KNOW HE'S UP TO SOMETHING!
MAYBE HE'S JEALOUS?
THINK ABOUT IT. HE PROBABLY LIED ABOUT SEEING THE BEAST TO WIN HIS FRIENDS BACK.
I DIDN'T THINK OF THAT.
BOYS!
LET'S GET YOU HOME!

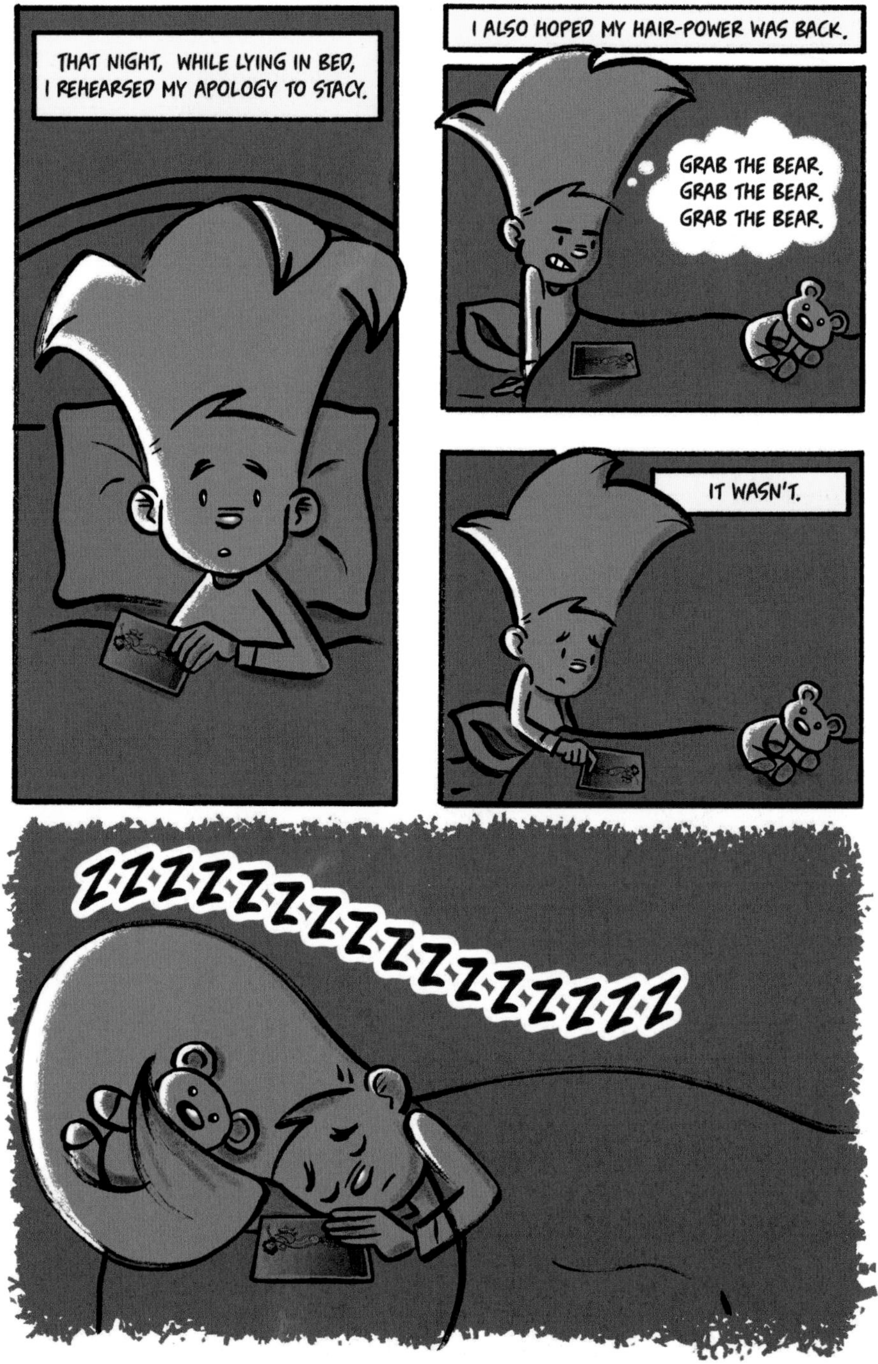
THAT NIGHT, WHILE LYING IN BED, I REHEARSED MY APOLOGY TO STACY.
I ALSO HOPED MY HAIR-POWER WAS BACK.
GRAB THE BEAR. GRAB THE BEAR. GRAB THE BEAR.
IT WASN'T.
ZZZZZZZZZZZZZZZZZ

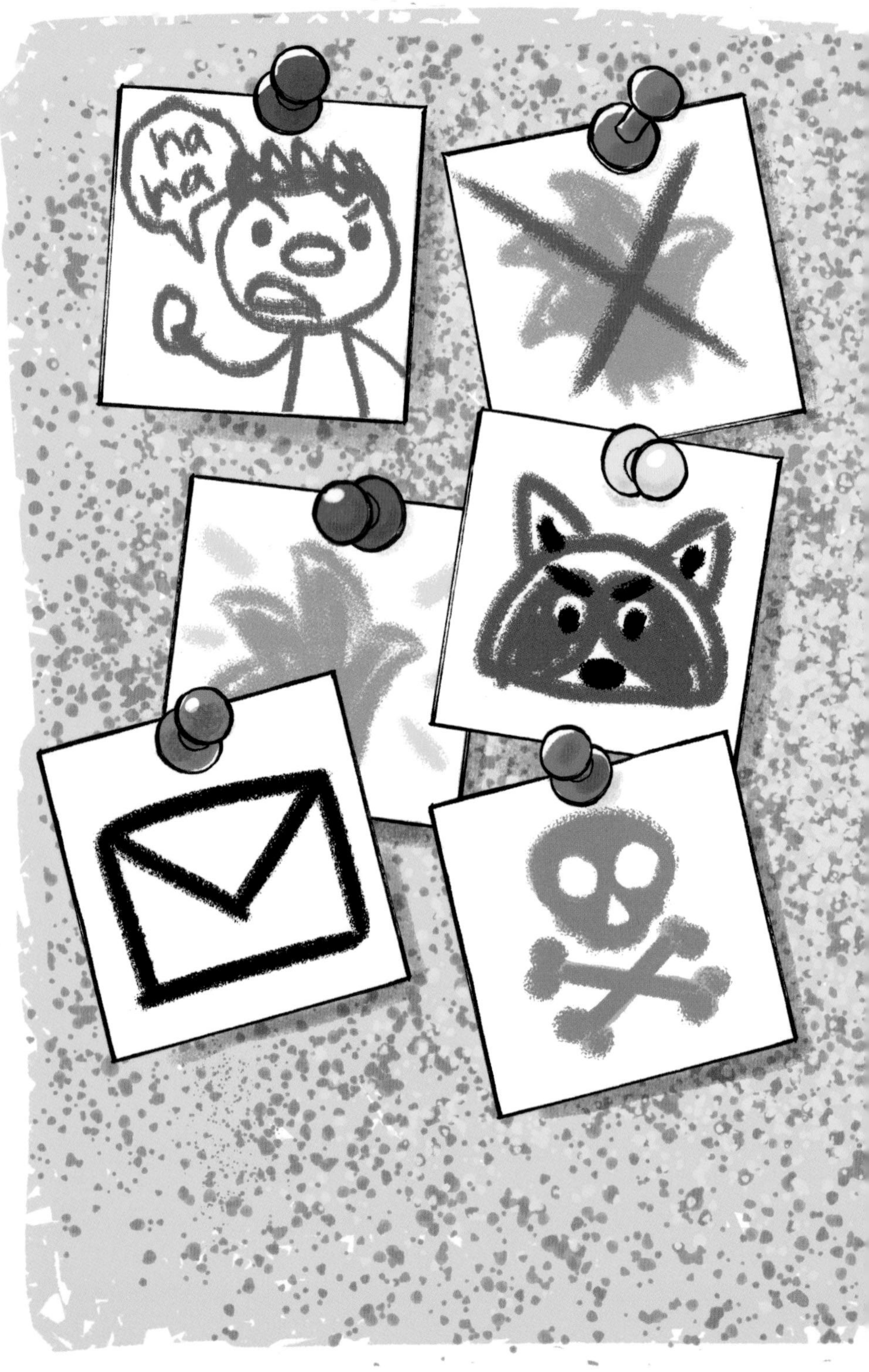
ha ha

CHAPTER 7:

ICE-CREAM
(NOT SO)
SOCIAL

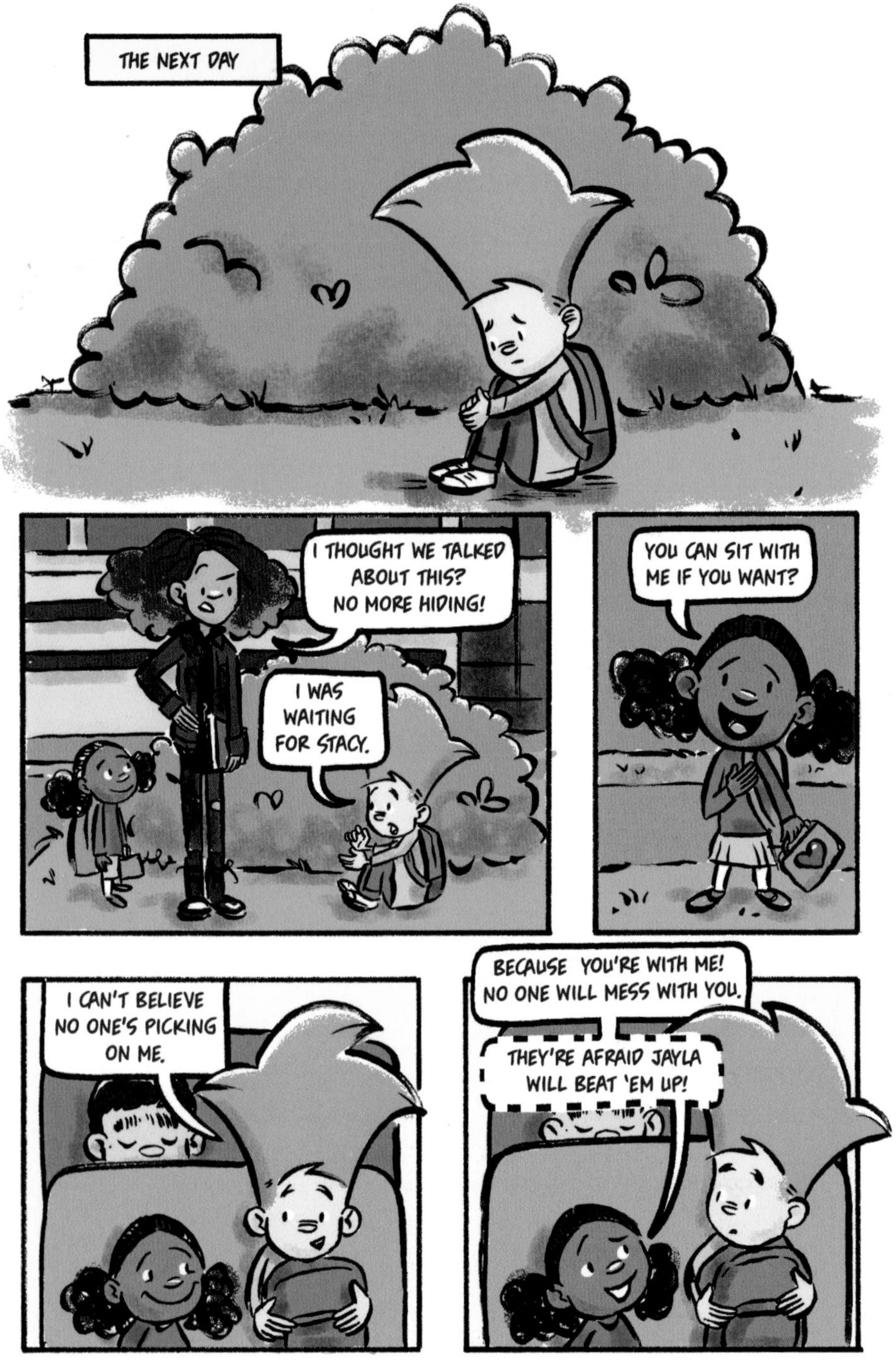
THE NEXT DAY
I THOUGHT WE TALKED ABOUT THIS? NO MORE HIDING!
I WAS WAITING FOR STACY.
YOU CAN SIT WITH ME IF YOU WANT?
I CAN'T BELIEVE NO ONE'S PICKING ON ME.
BECAUSE YOU'RE WITH ME! NO ONE WILL MESS WITH YOU.
THEY'RE AFRAID JAYLA WILL BEAT 'EM UP!

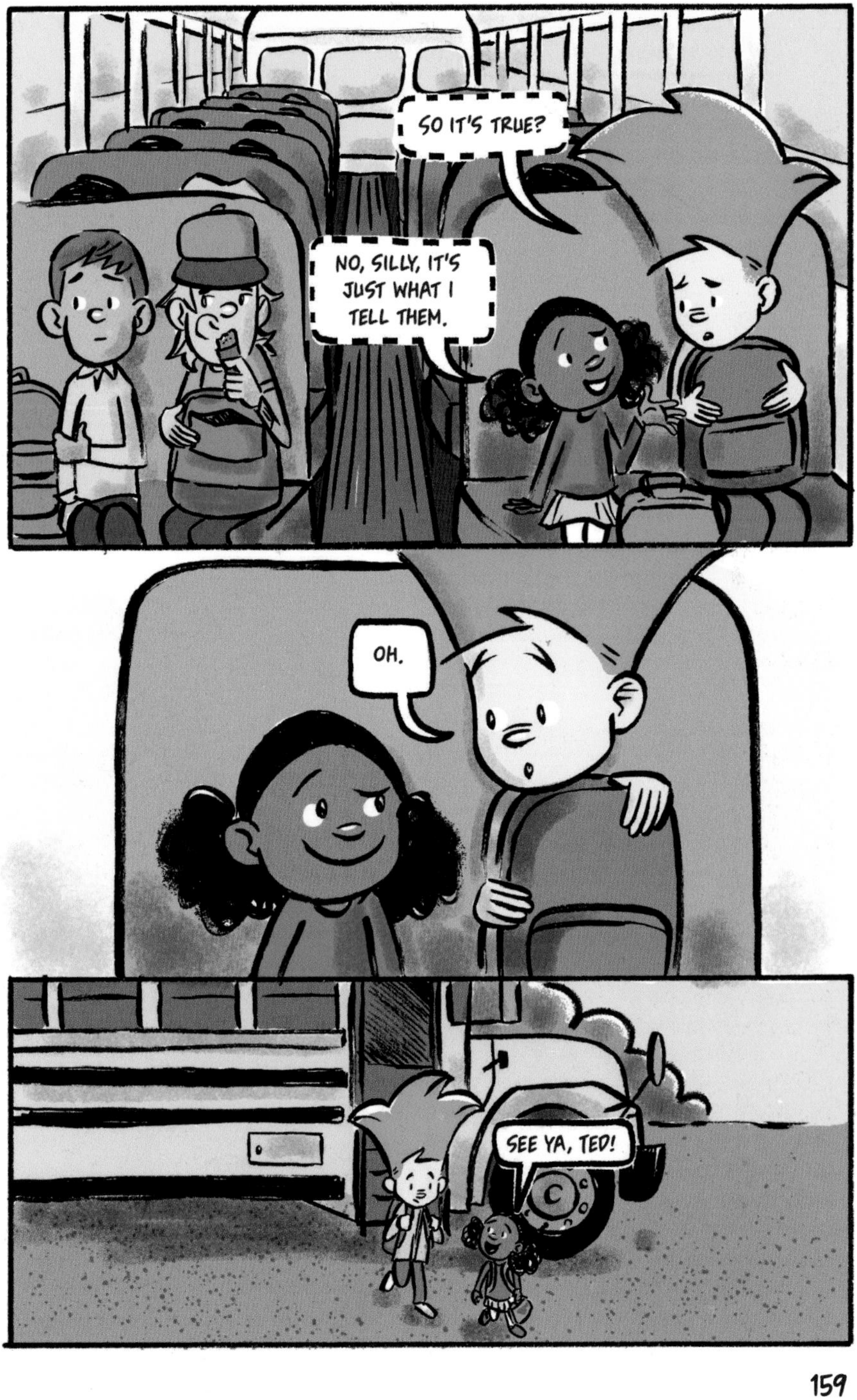
SO IT'S TRUE?
NO, SILLY, IT'S JUST WHAT I TELL THEM.
OH.
SEE YA, TED!

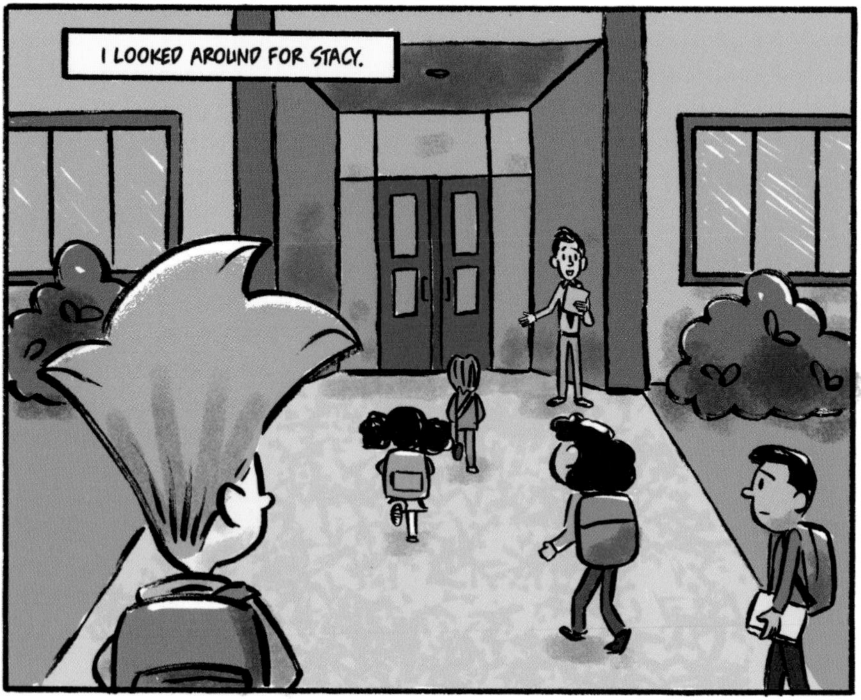
I LOOKED AROUND FOR STACY.

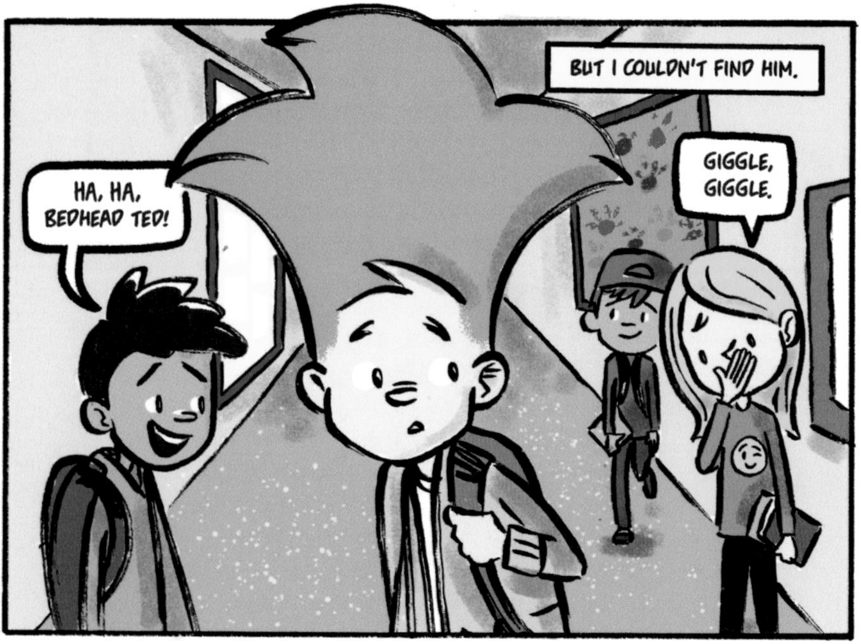
BUT I COULDN'T FIND HIM.
HA, HA, BEDHEAD TED!
GIGGLE, GIGGLE.

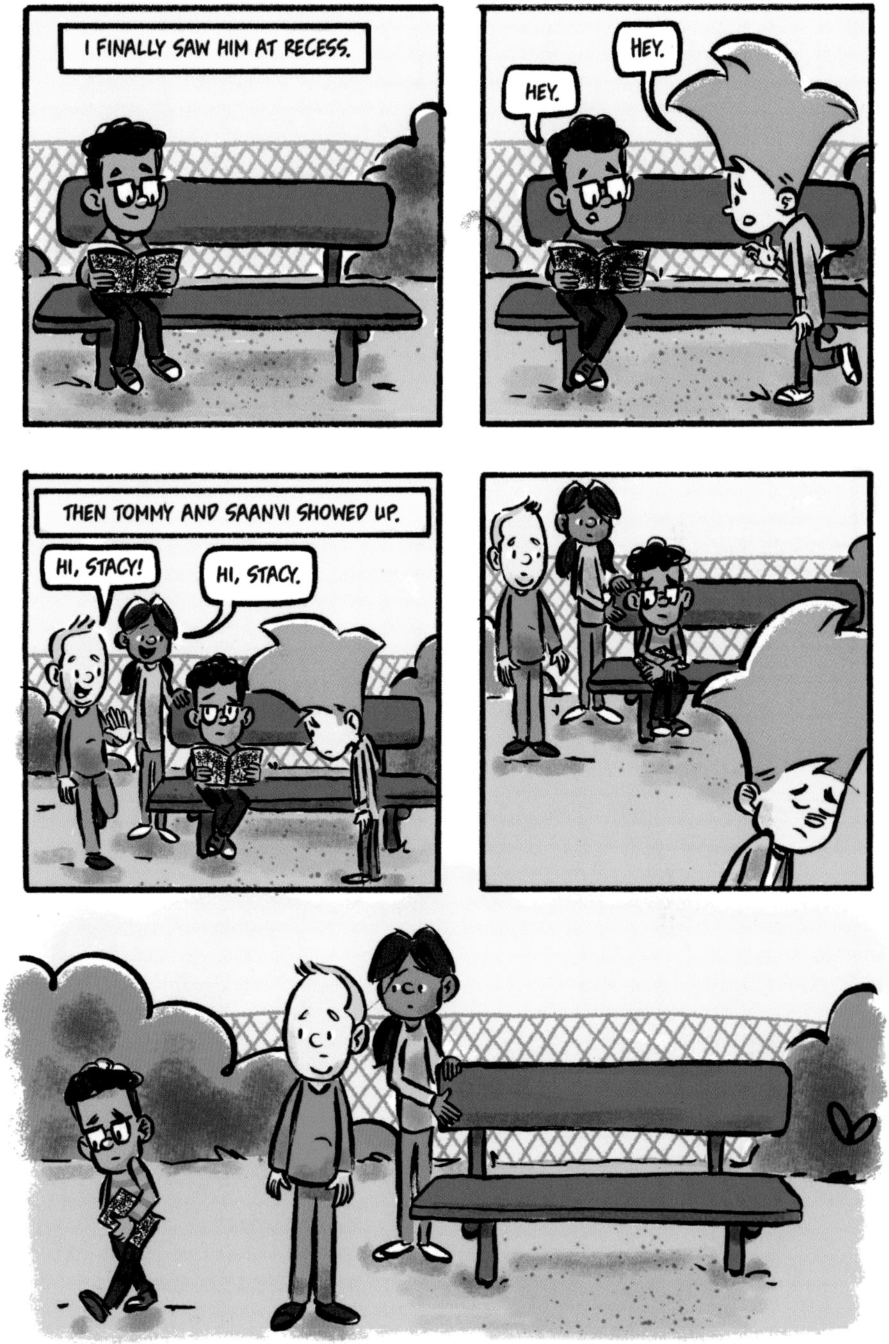
I FINALLY SAW HIM AT RECESS.
HEY.
HEY.
THEN TOMMY AND SAANVI SHOWED UP.
HI, STACY!
HI, STACY.

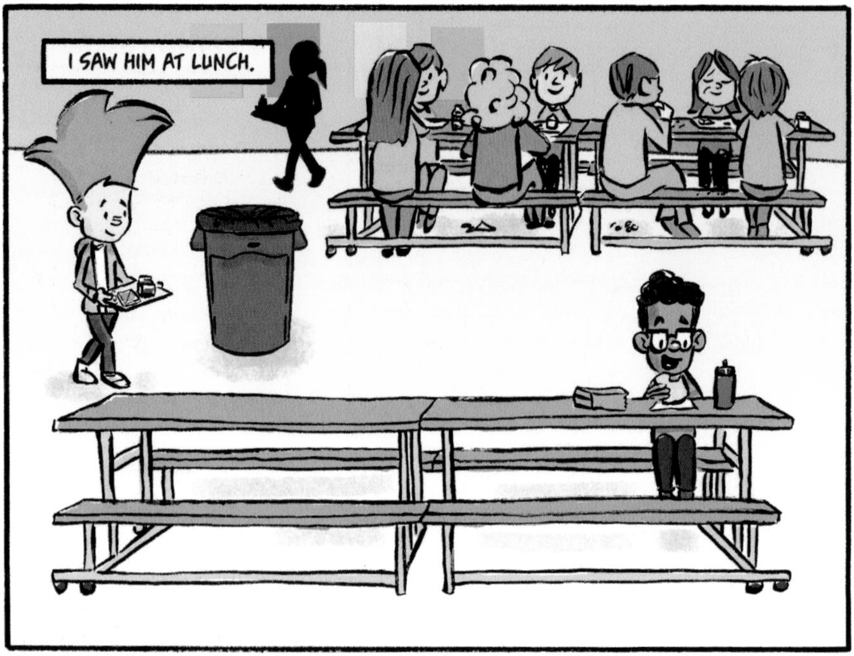
I SAW HIM AT LUNCH.

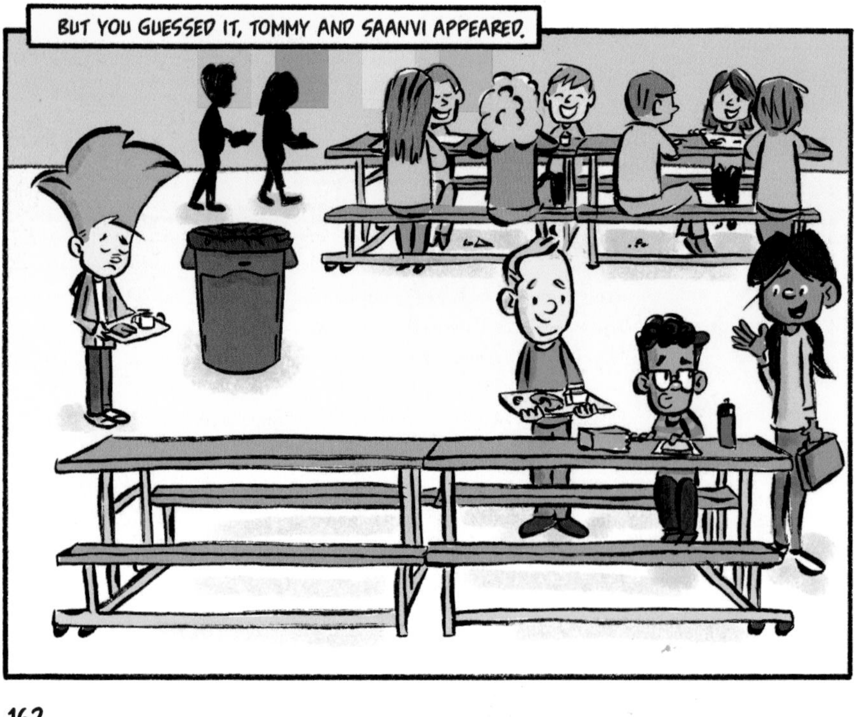
BUT YOU GUESSED IT, TOMMY AND SAANVI APPEARED.

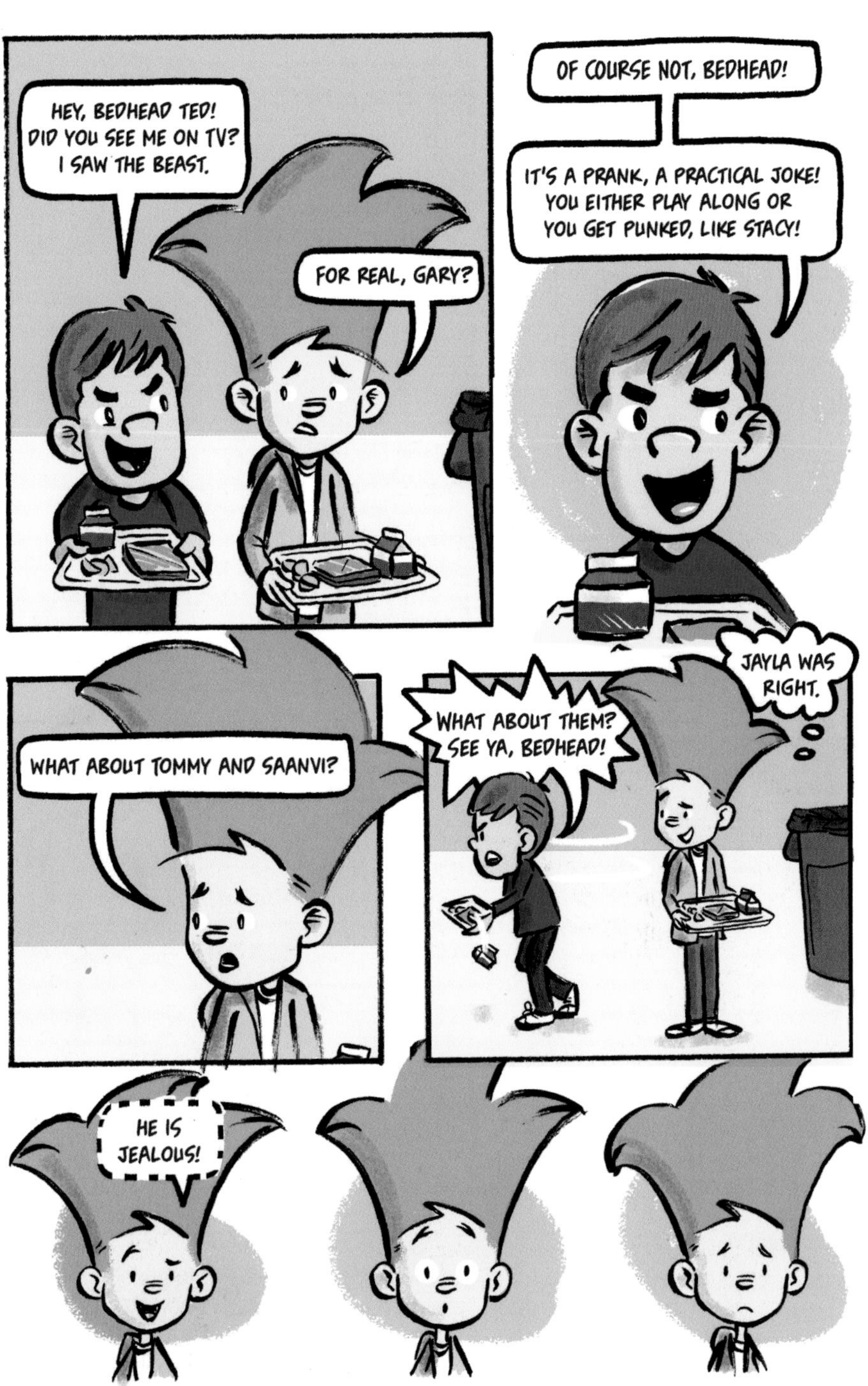
HEY, BEDHEAD TED! DID YOU SEE ME ON TV? I SAW THE BEAST.
FOR REAL, GARY?
OF COURSE NOT, BEDHEAD!
IT'S A PRANK, A PRACTICAL JOKE! YOU EITHER PLAY ALONG OR YOU GET PUNKED, LIKE STACY!
WHAT ABOUT TOMMY AND SAANVI?
WHAT ABOUT THEM? SEE YA, BEDHEAD!
JAYLA WAS RIGHT.
HE IS JEALOUS!

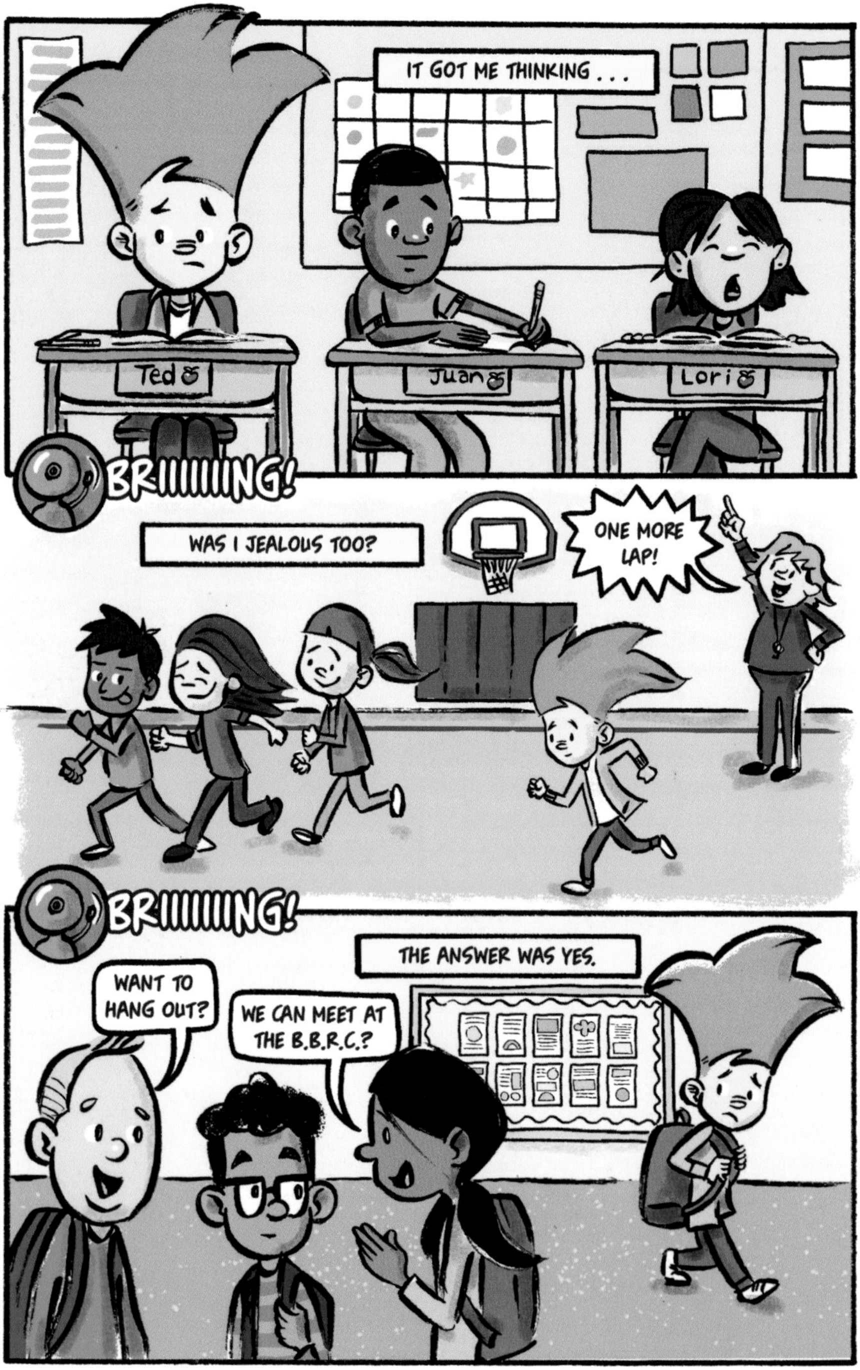
IT GOT ME THINKING . . .
Ted
Juan
Lori
BRIIIIIIING!
WAS I JEALOUS TOO?
ONE MORE LAP!
BRIIIIIIING!
THE ANSWER WAS YES.
WANT TO HANG OUT?
WE CAN MEET AT THE B.B.R.C.?

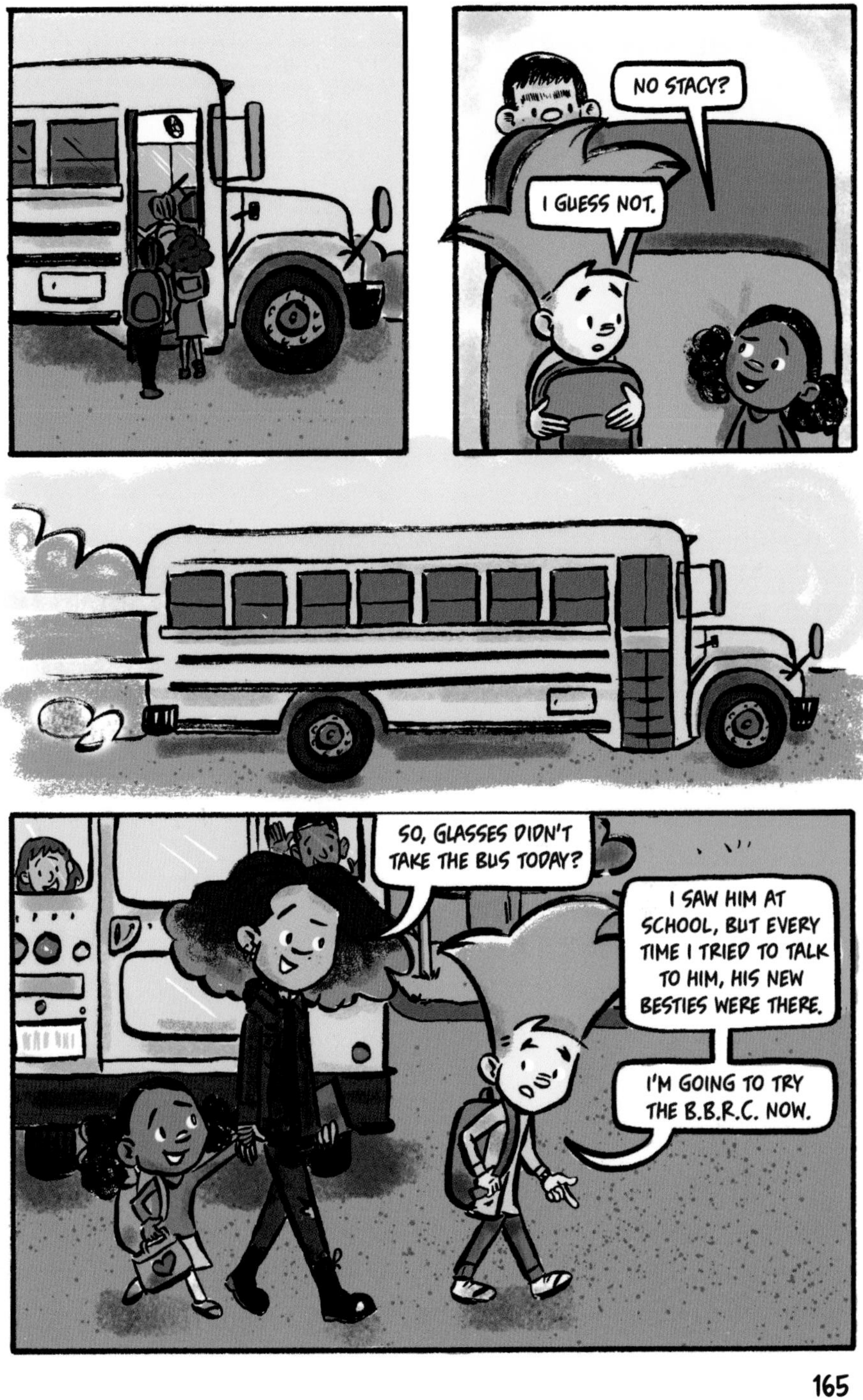
NO STACY?
I GUESS NOT.
SO, GLASSES DIDN'T TAKE THE BUS TODAY?
I SAW HIM AT SCHOOL, BUT EVERY TIME I TRIED TO TALK TO HIM, HIS NEW BESTIES WERE THERE.
I'M GOING TO TRY THE B.B.R.C. NOW.

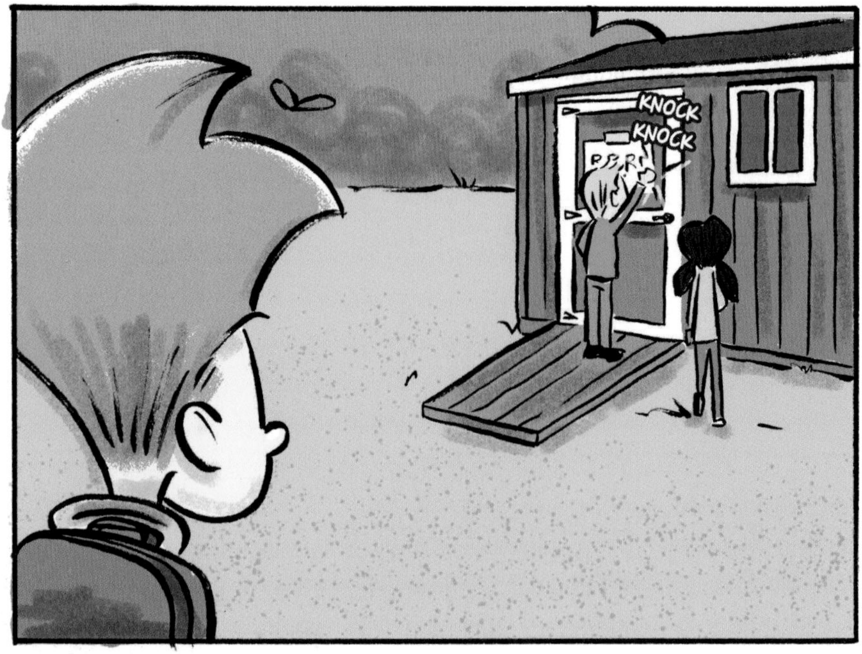
KNOCK
KNOCK

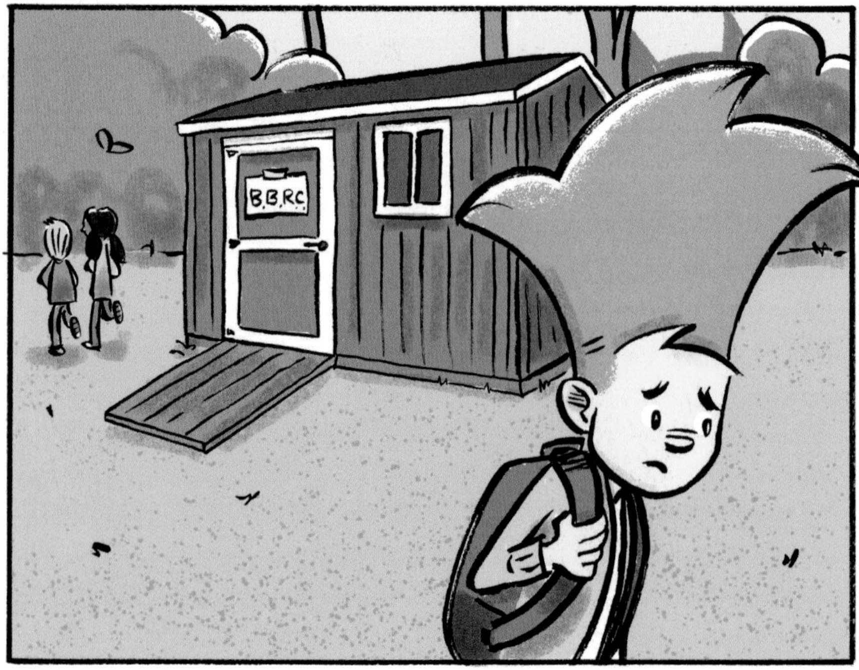
B.B.R.C.

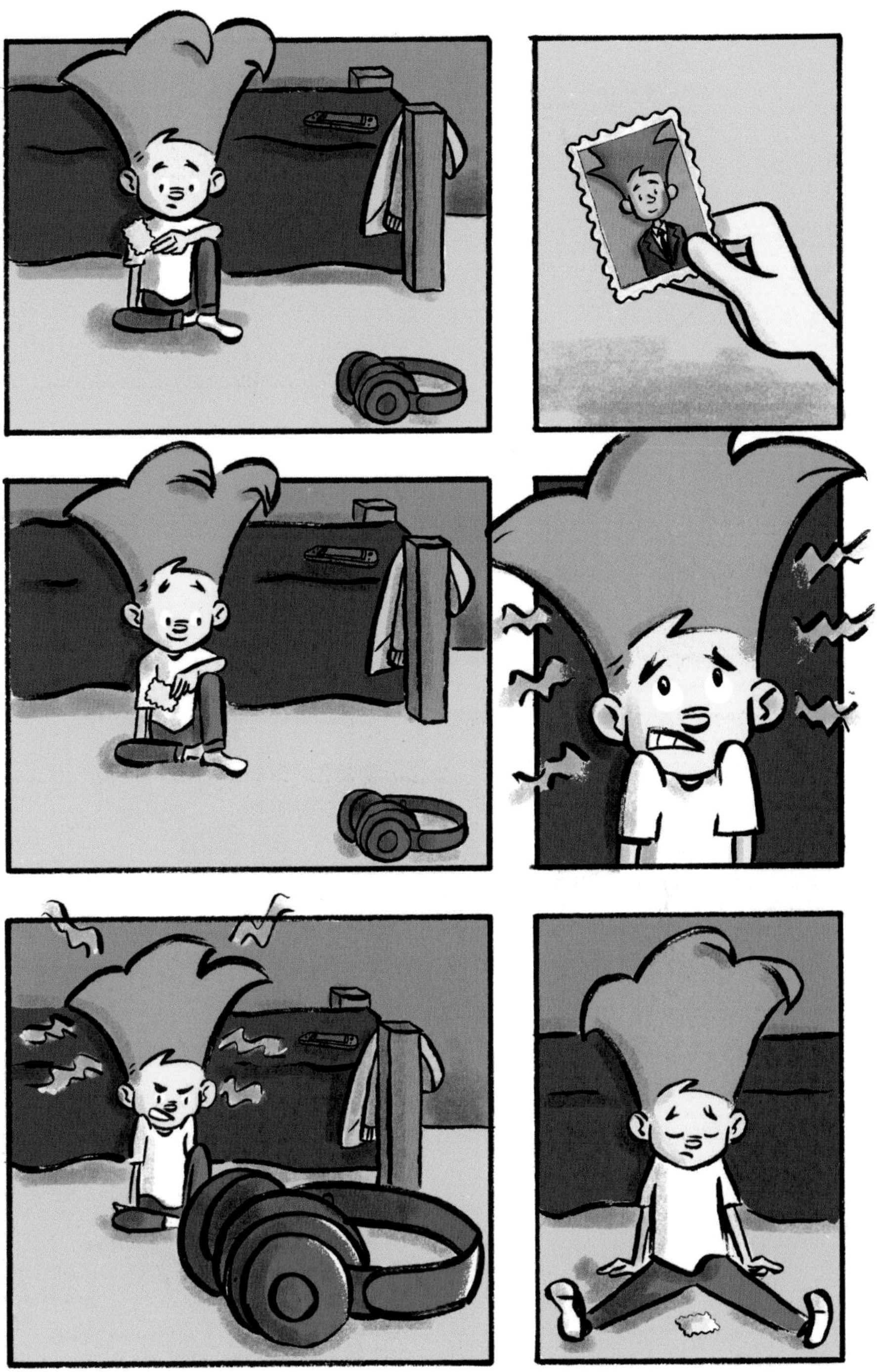

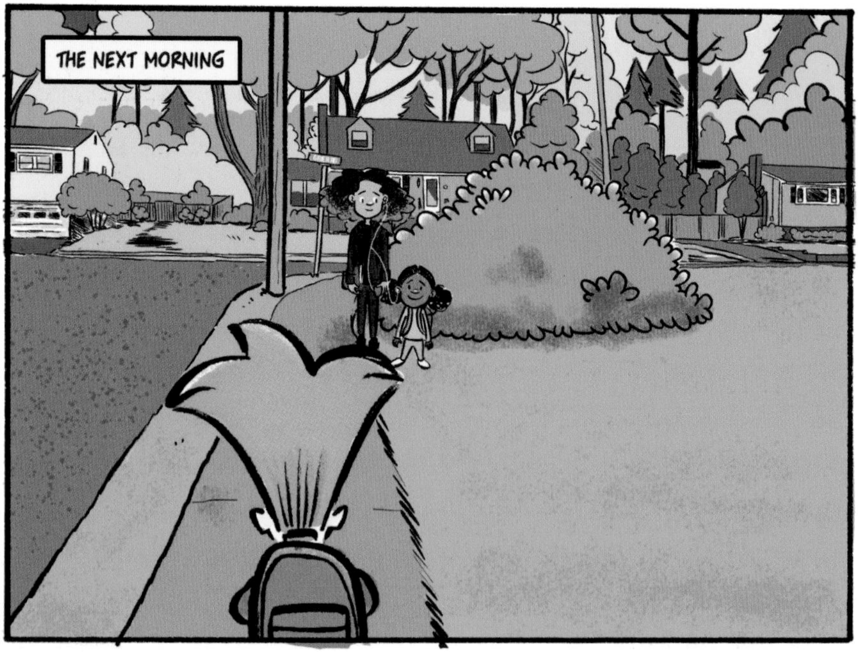
THE NEXT MORNING

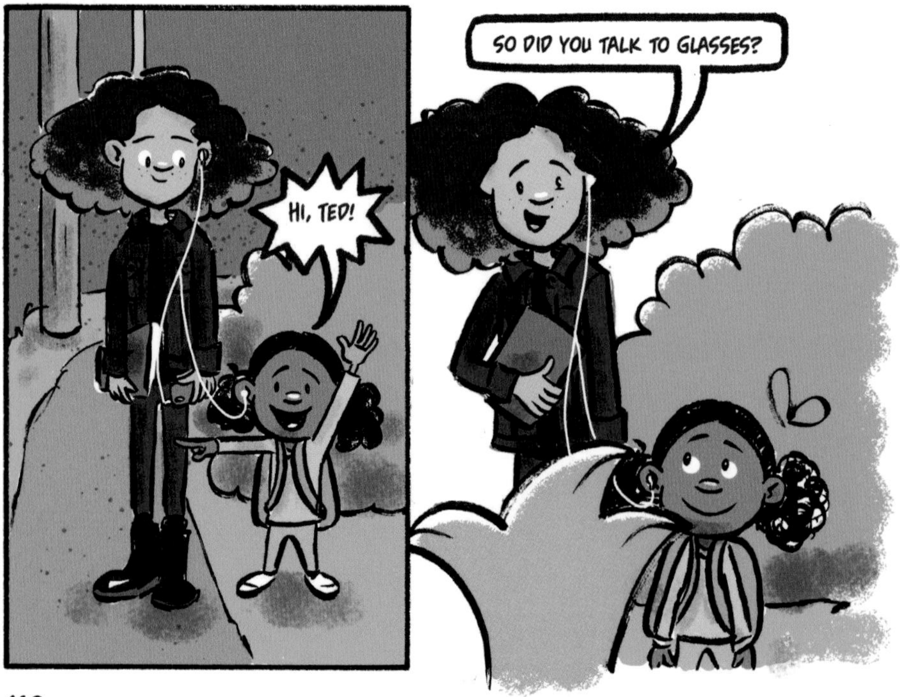
HI, TED!
SO DID YOU TALK TO GLASSES?

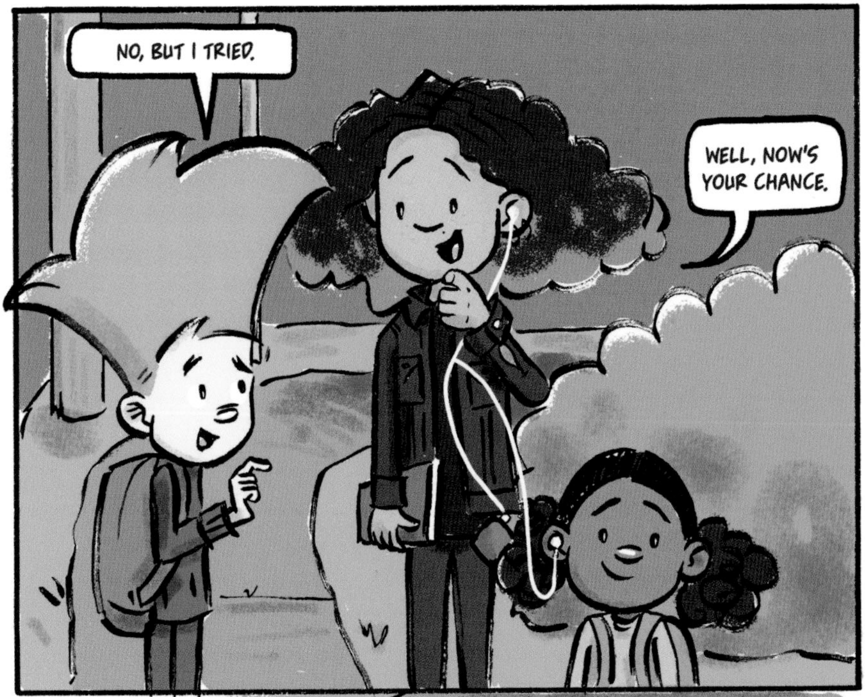
NO, BUT I TRIED.
WELL, NOW'S YOUR CHANCE.
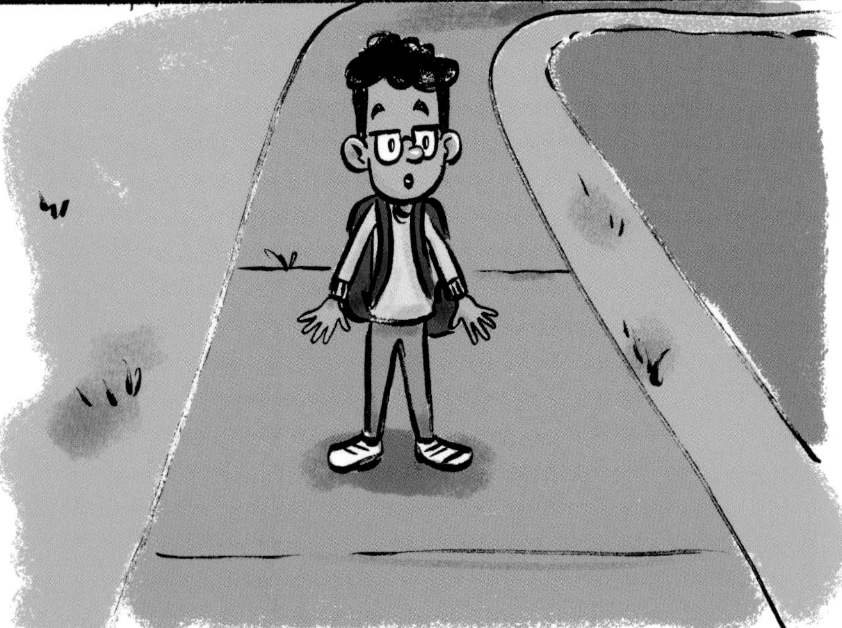

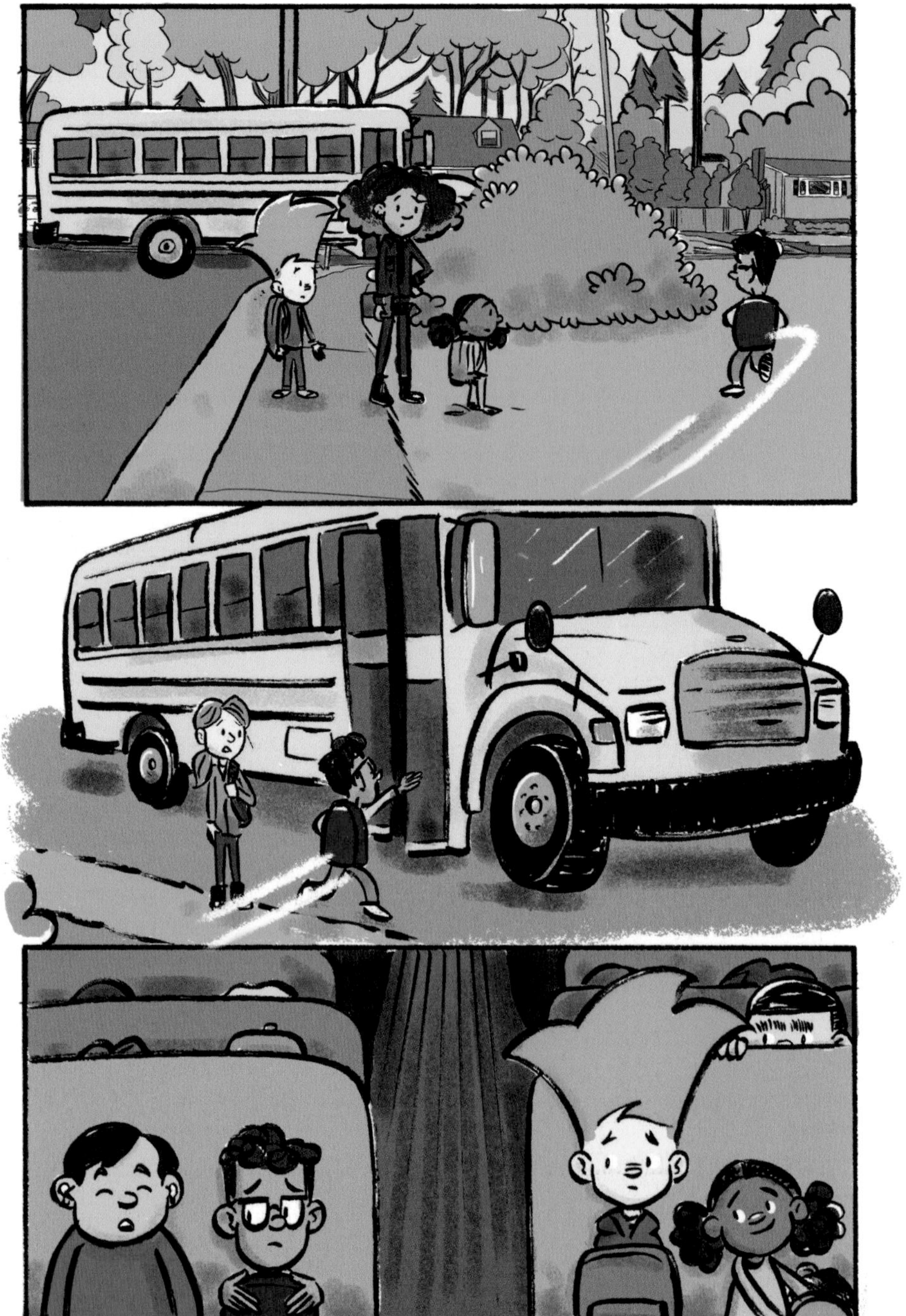

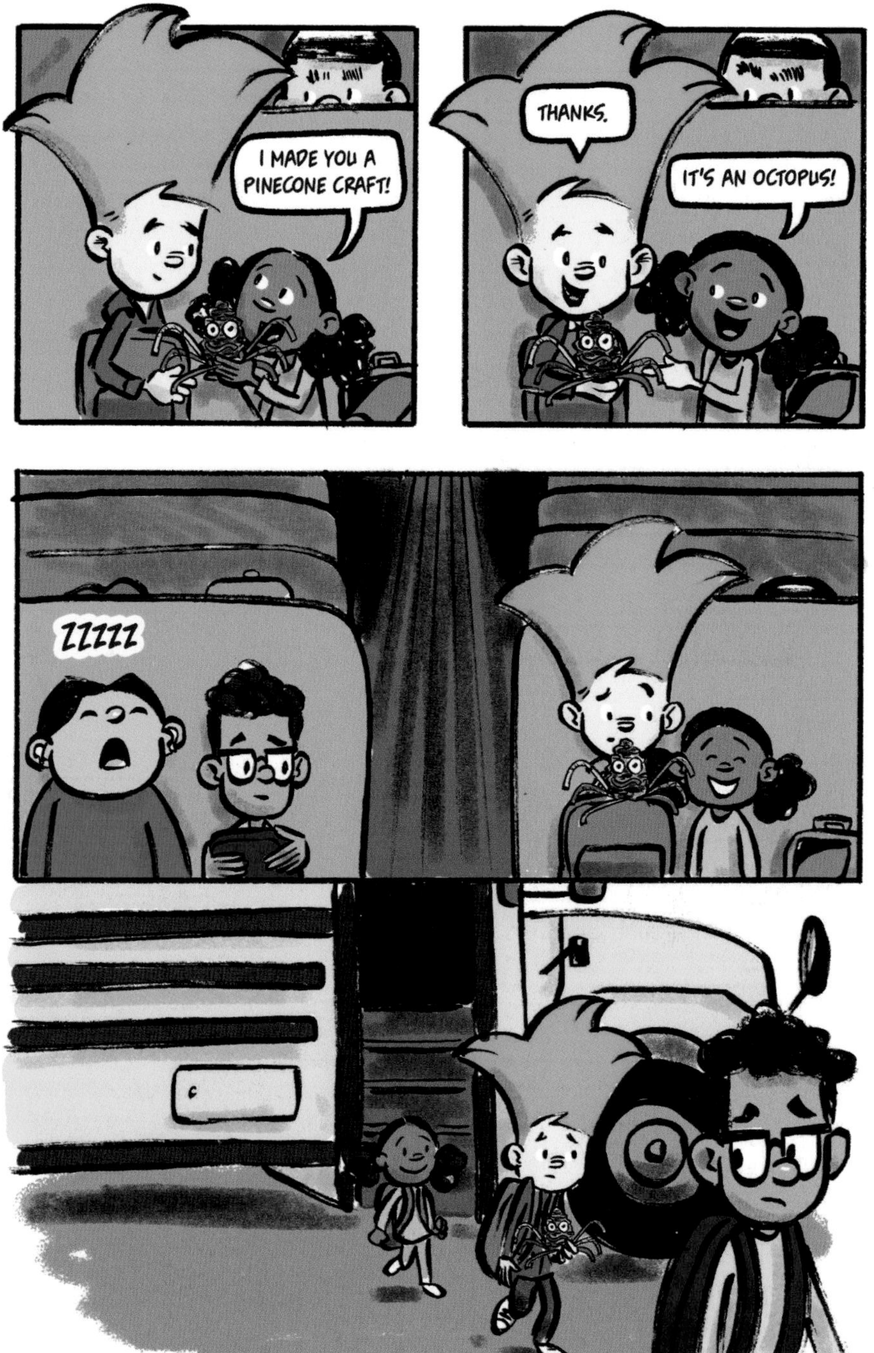
I MADE YOU A PINECONE CRAFT!
THANKS.
IT'S AN OCTOPUS!
ZZZZZ

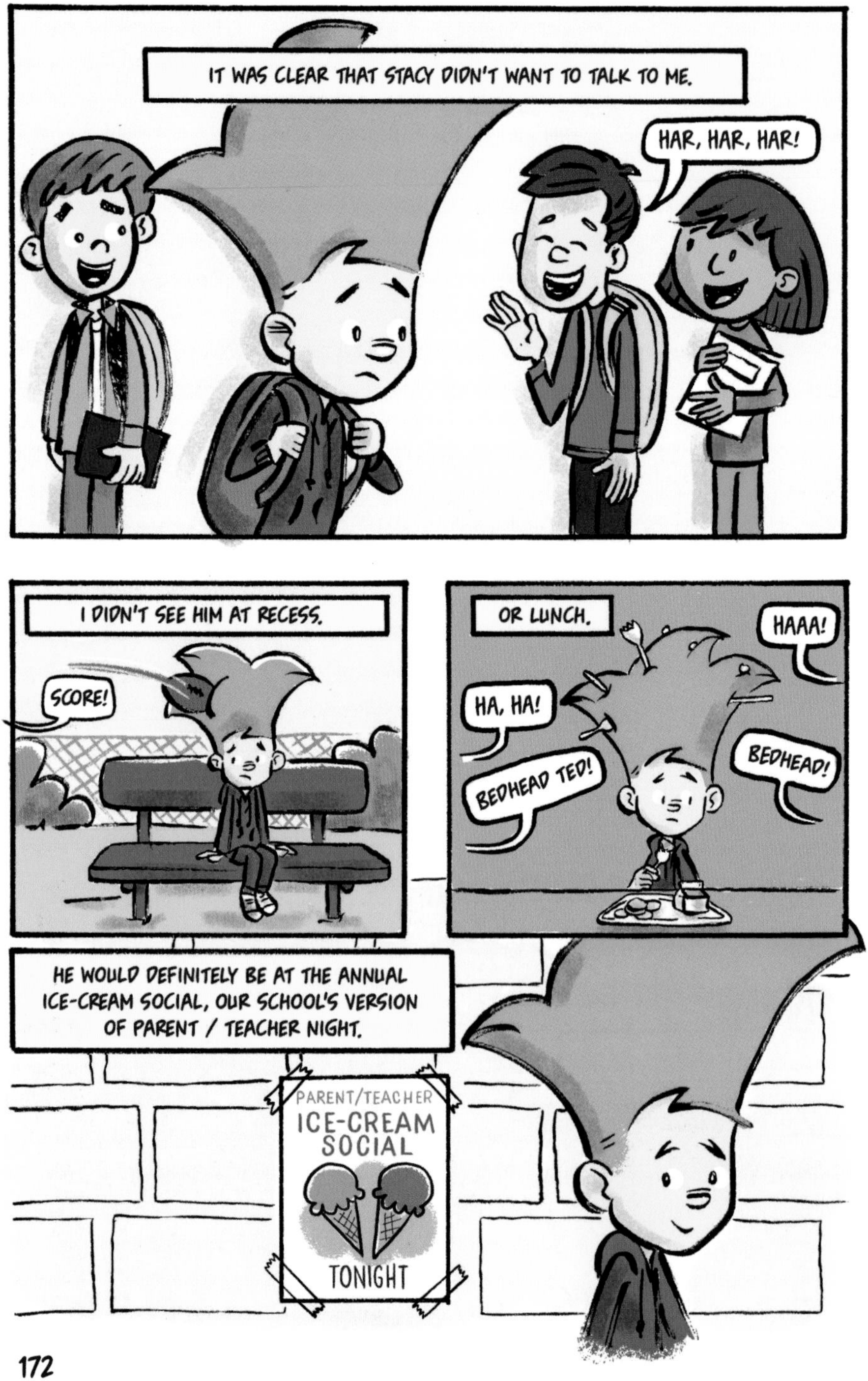
IT WAS CLEAR THAT STACY DIDN'T WANT TO TALK TO ME.
HAR, HAR, HAR!
I DIDN'T SEE HIM AT RECESS.
SCORE!
OR LUNCH.
HAAAA!
HA, HA!
BEDHEAD TED!
BEDHEAD!
HE WOULD DEFINITELY BE AT THE ANNUAL ICE-CREAM SOCIAL, OUR SCHOOL'S VERSION OF PARENT / TEACHER NIGHT.
PARENT/TEACHER
ICE-CREAM SOCIAL
TONIGHT

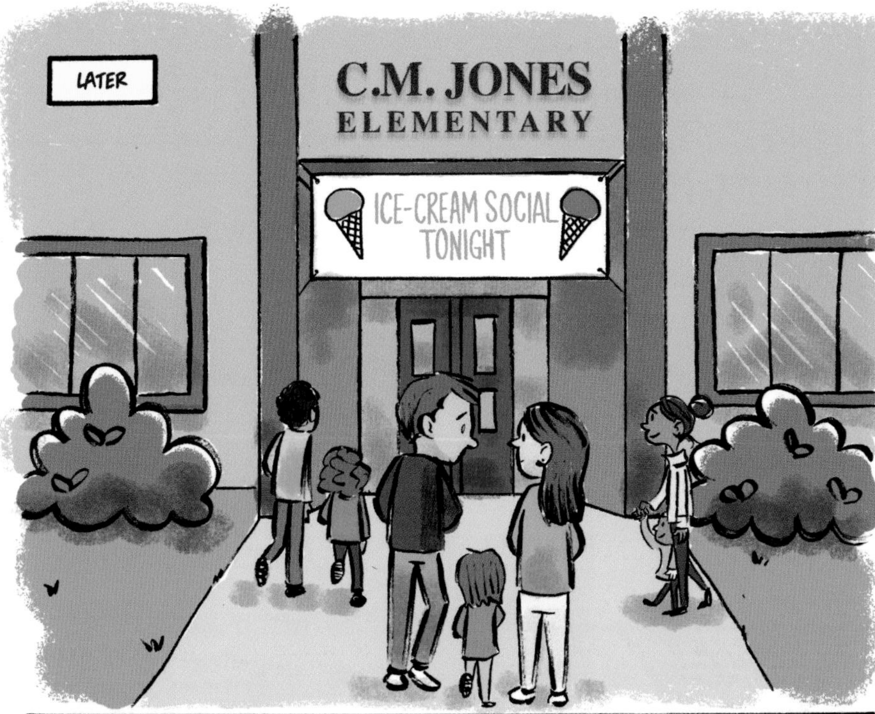
LATER
C.M. JONES
ELEMENTARY
ICE-CREAM SOCIAL
TONIGHT

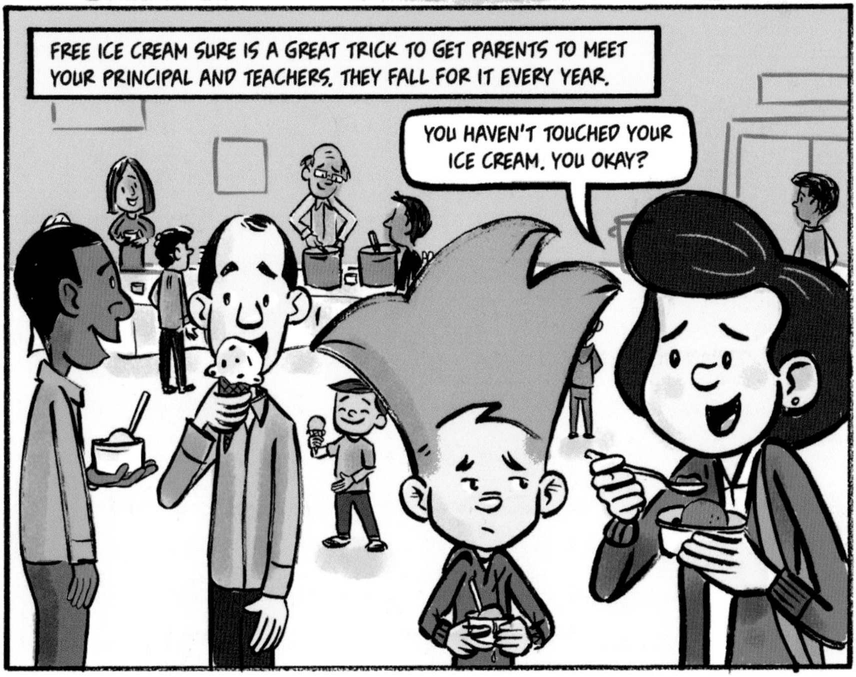
FREE ICE CREAM SURE IS A GREAT TRICK TO GET PARENTS TO MEET YOUR PRINCIPAL AND TEACHERS. THEY FALL FOR IT EVERY YEAR.
YOU HAVEN'T TOUCHED YOUR ICE CREAM. YOU OKAY?

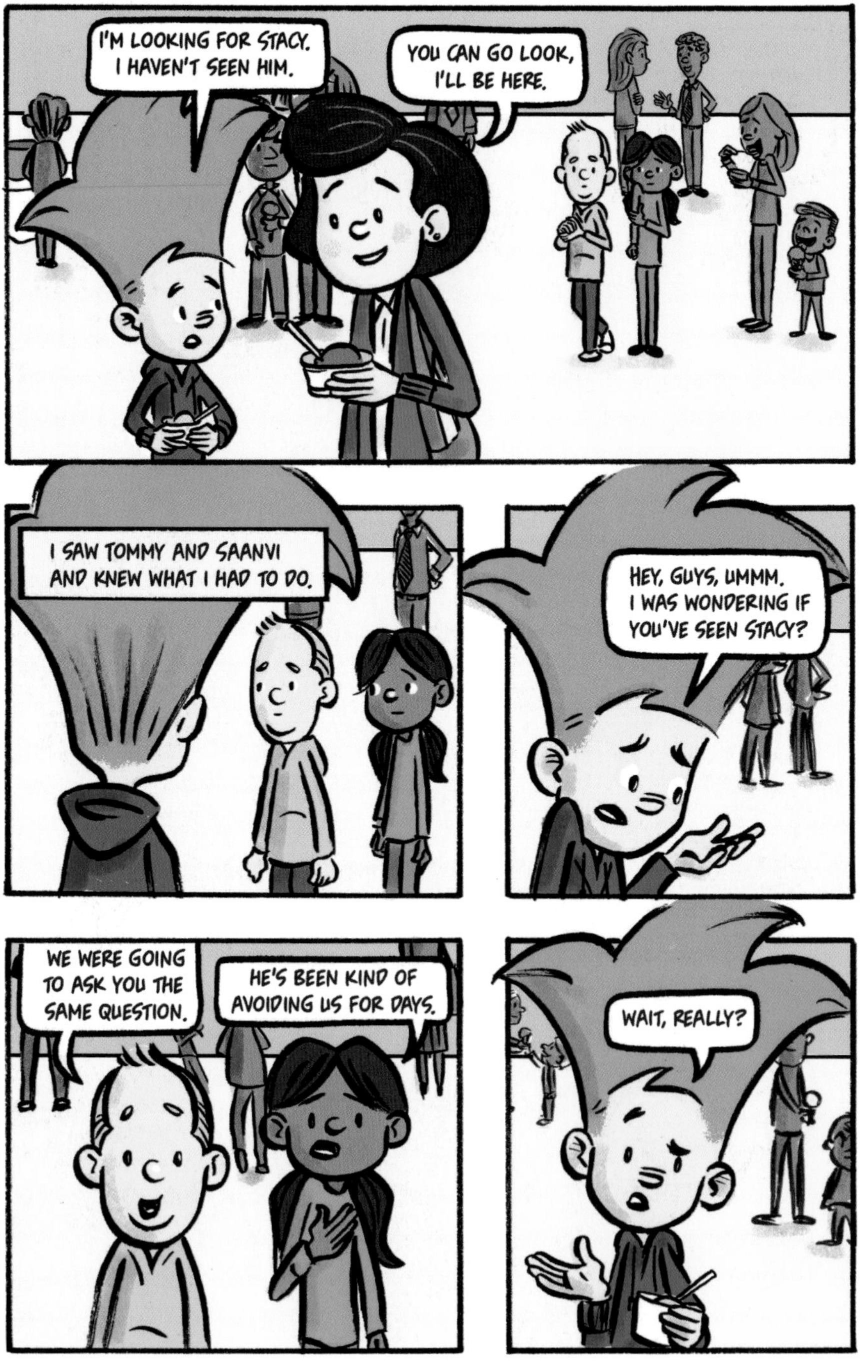
I'M LOOKING FOR STACY. I HAVEN'T SEEN HIM.
YOU CAN GO LOOK, I'LL BE HERE.
I SAW TOMMY AND SAANVI AND KNEW WHAT I HAD TO DO.
HEY, GUYS, UMMM. I WAS WONDERING IF YOU'VE SEEN STACY?
WE WERE GOING TO ASK YOU THE SAME QUESTION.
HE'S BEEN KIND OF AVOIDING US FOR DAYS.
WAIT, REALLY?

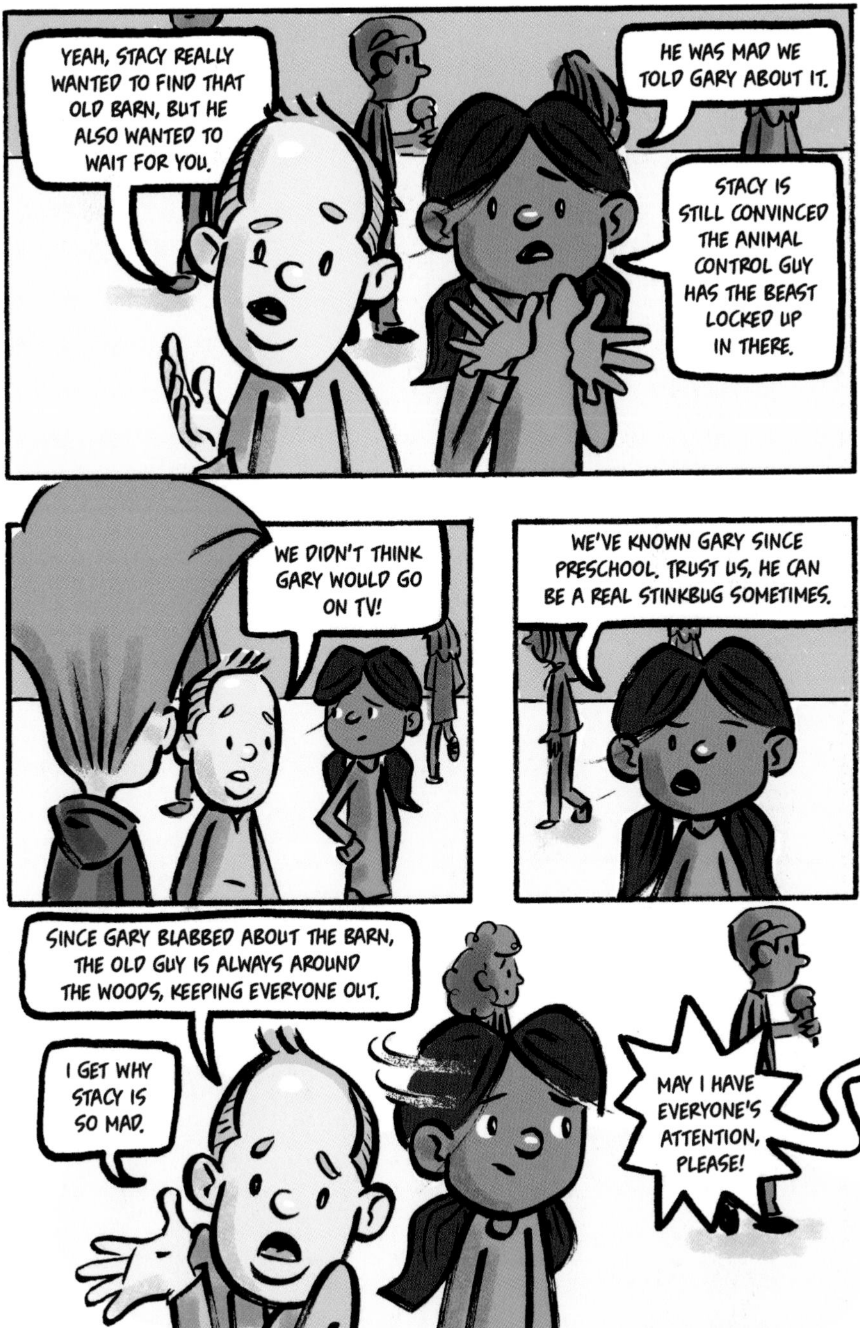
YEAH, STACY REALLY WANTED TO FIND THAT OLD BARN, BUT HE ALSO WANTED TO WAIT FOR YOU.
HE WAS MAD WE TOLD GARY ABOUT IT.
STACY IS STILL CONVINCED THE ANIMAL CONTROL GUY HAS THE BEAST LOCKED UP IN THERE.
WE DIDN'T THINK GARY WOULD GO ON TV!
WE'VE KNOWN GARY SINCE PRESCHOOL. TRUST US, HE CAN BE A REAL STINKBUG SOMETIMES.
SINCE GARY BLABBED ABOUT THE BARN, THE OLD GUY IS ALWAYS AROUND THE WOODS, KEEPING EVERYONE OUT.
I GET WHY STACY IS SO MAD.
MAY I HAVE EVERYONE'S ATTENTION, PLEASE!

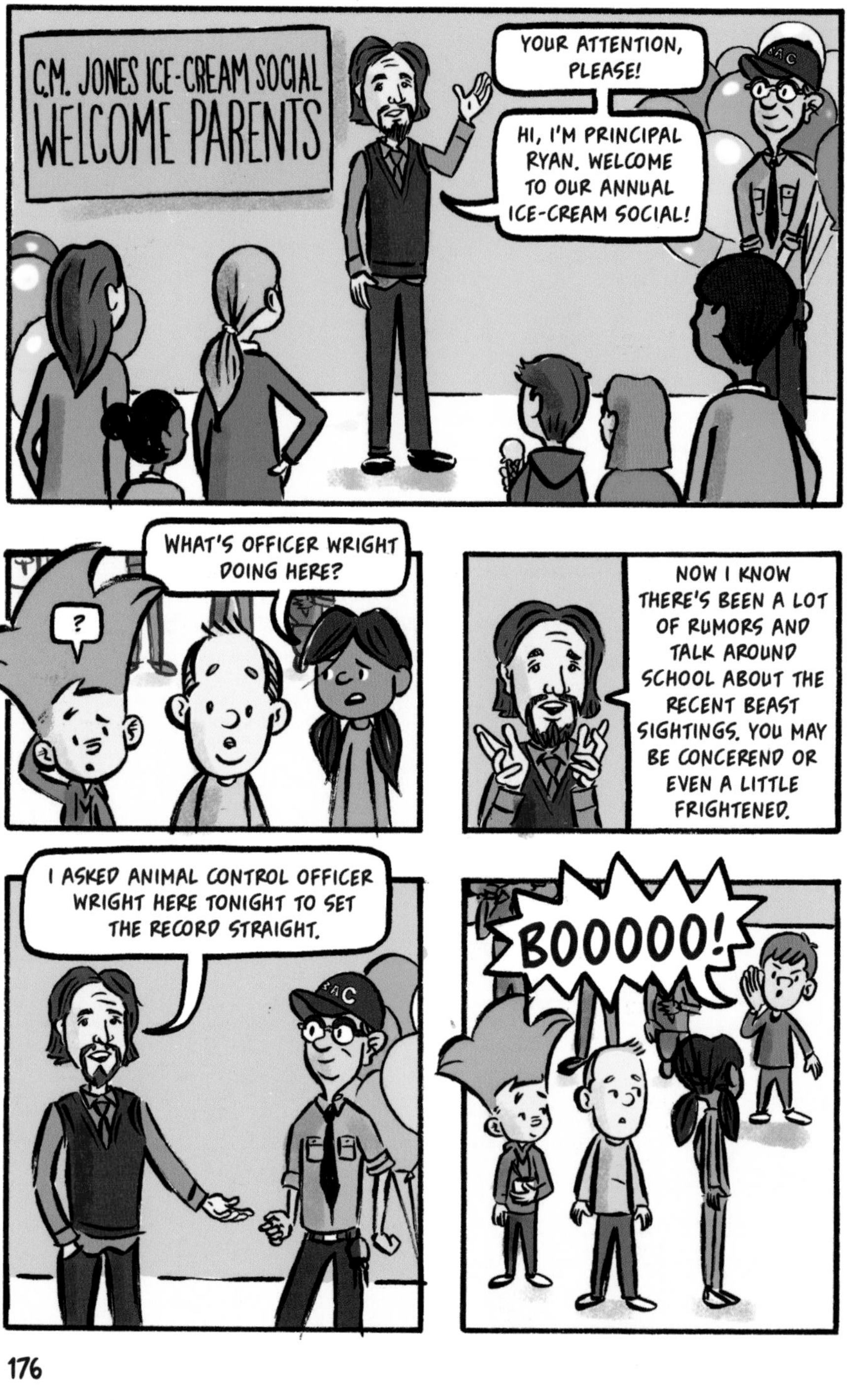
C.M. JONES ICE-CREAM SOCIAL
WELCOME PARENTS
YOUR ATTENTION, PLEASE!
HI, I'M PRINCIPAL RYAN. WELCOME TO OUR ANNUAL ICE-CREAM SOCIAL!
?
WHAT'S OFFICER WRIGHT DOING HERE?
NOW I KNOW THERE'S BEEN A LOT OF RUMORS AND TALK AROUND SCHOOL ABOUT THE RECENT BEAST SIGHTINGS. YOU MAY BE CONCEREND OR EVEN A LITTLE FRIGHTENED.
I ASKED ANIMAL CONTROL OFFICER WRIGHT HERE TONIGHT TO SET THE RECORD STRAIGHT.
BOOOOO!

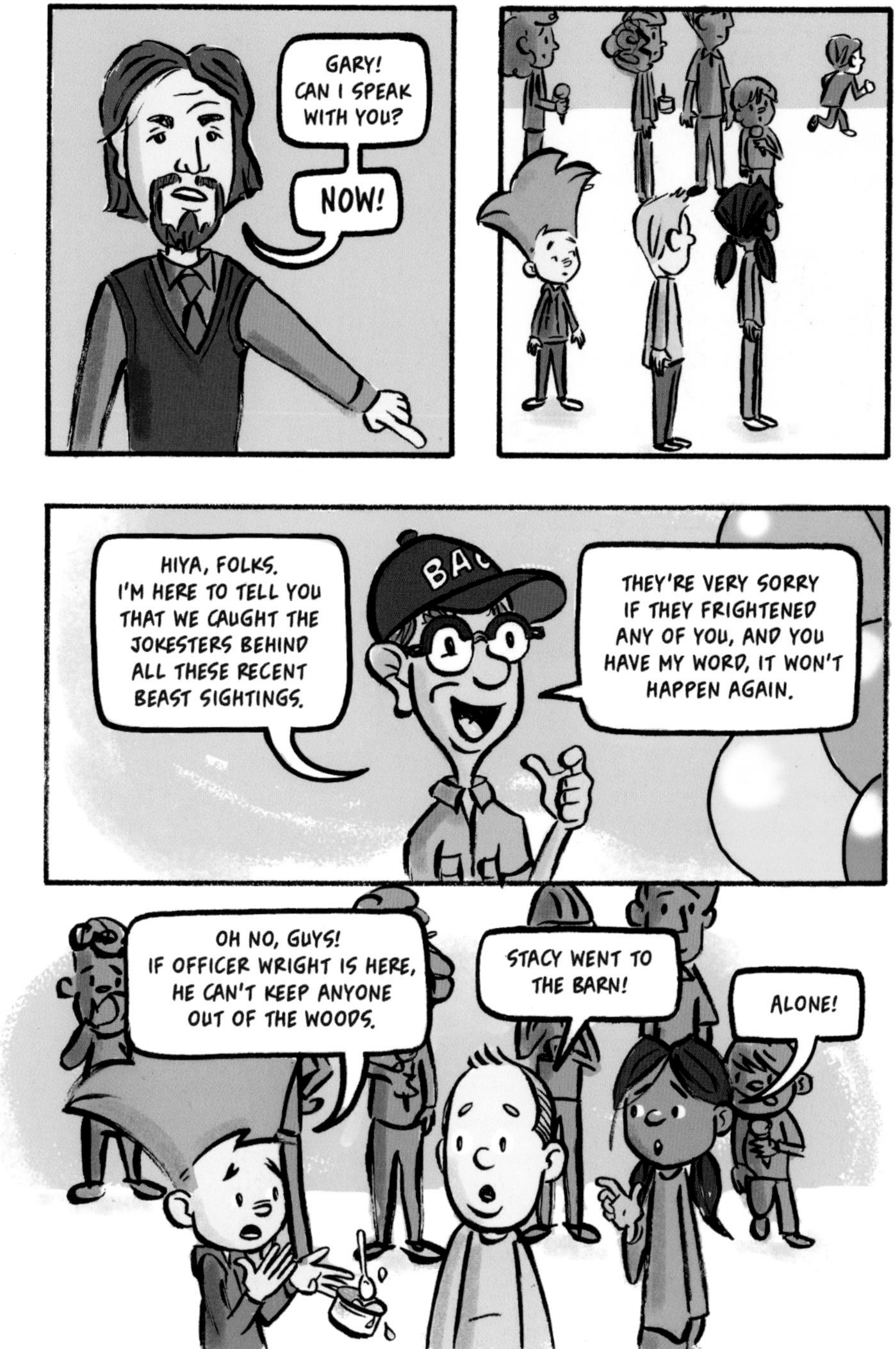
GARY! CAN I SPEAK WITH YOU?
NOW!
BAC
HIYA, FOLKS. I'M HERE TO TELL YOU THAT WE CAUGHT THE JOKESTERS BEHIND ALL THESE RECENT BEAST SIGHTINGS.
THEY'RE VERY SORRY IF THEY FRIGHTENED ANY OF YOU, AND YOU HAVE MY WORD, IT WON'T HAPPEN AGAIN.
OH NO, GUYS! IF OFFICER WRIGHT IS HERE, HE CAN'T KEEP ANYONE OUT OF THE WOODS.
STACY WENT TO THE BARN!
ALONE!

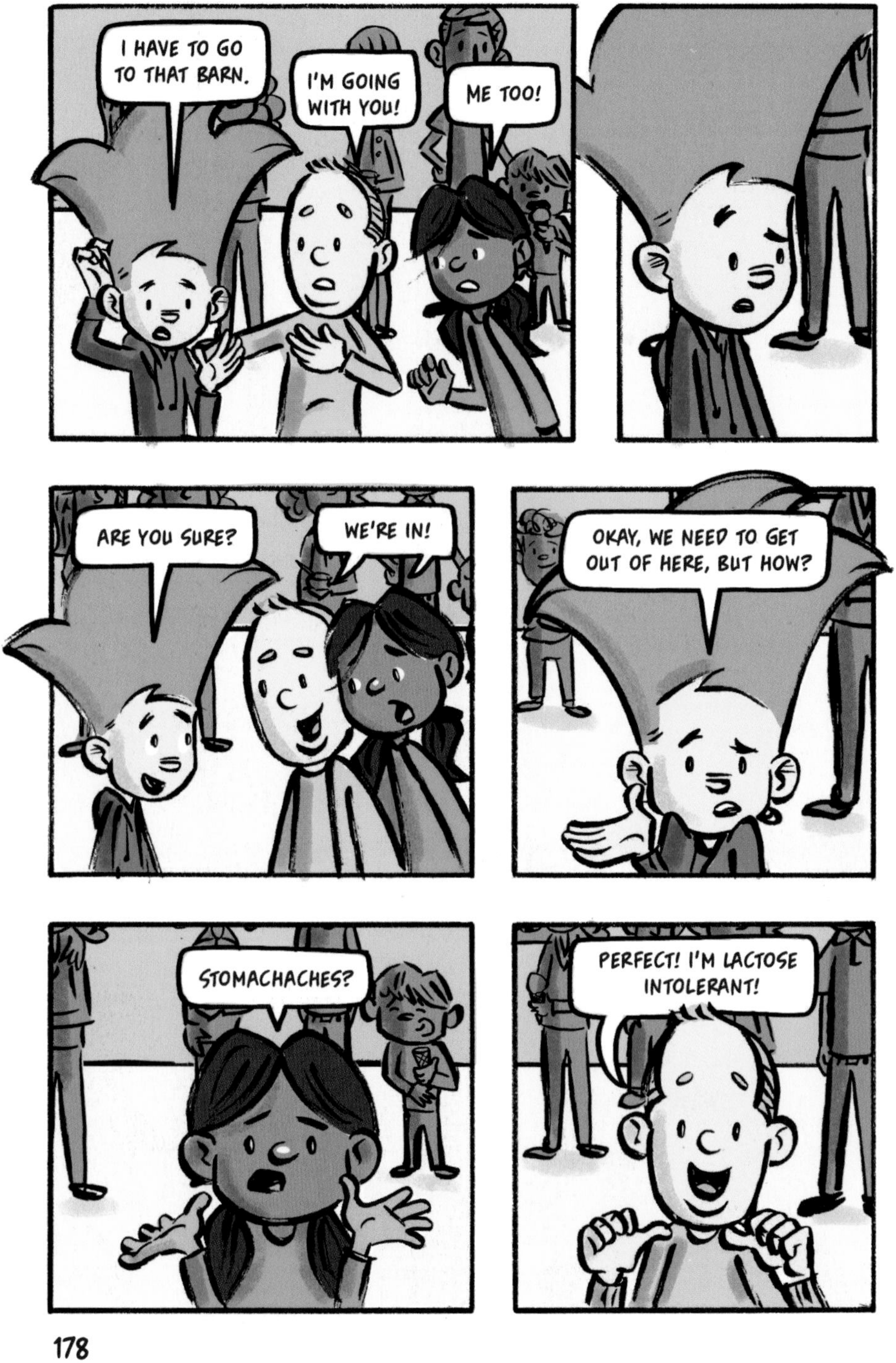
I HAVE TO GO TO THAT BARN.
I'M GOING WITH YOU!
ME TOO!
ARE YOU SURE?
WE'RE IN!
OKAY, WE NEED TO GET OUT OF HERE, BUT HOW?
STOMACHACHES?
PERFECT! I'M LACTOSE INTOLERANT!

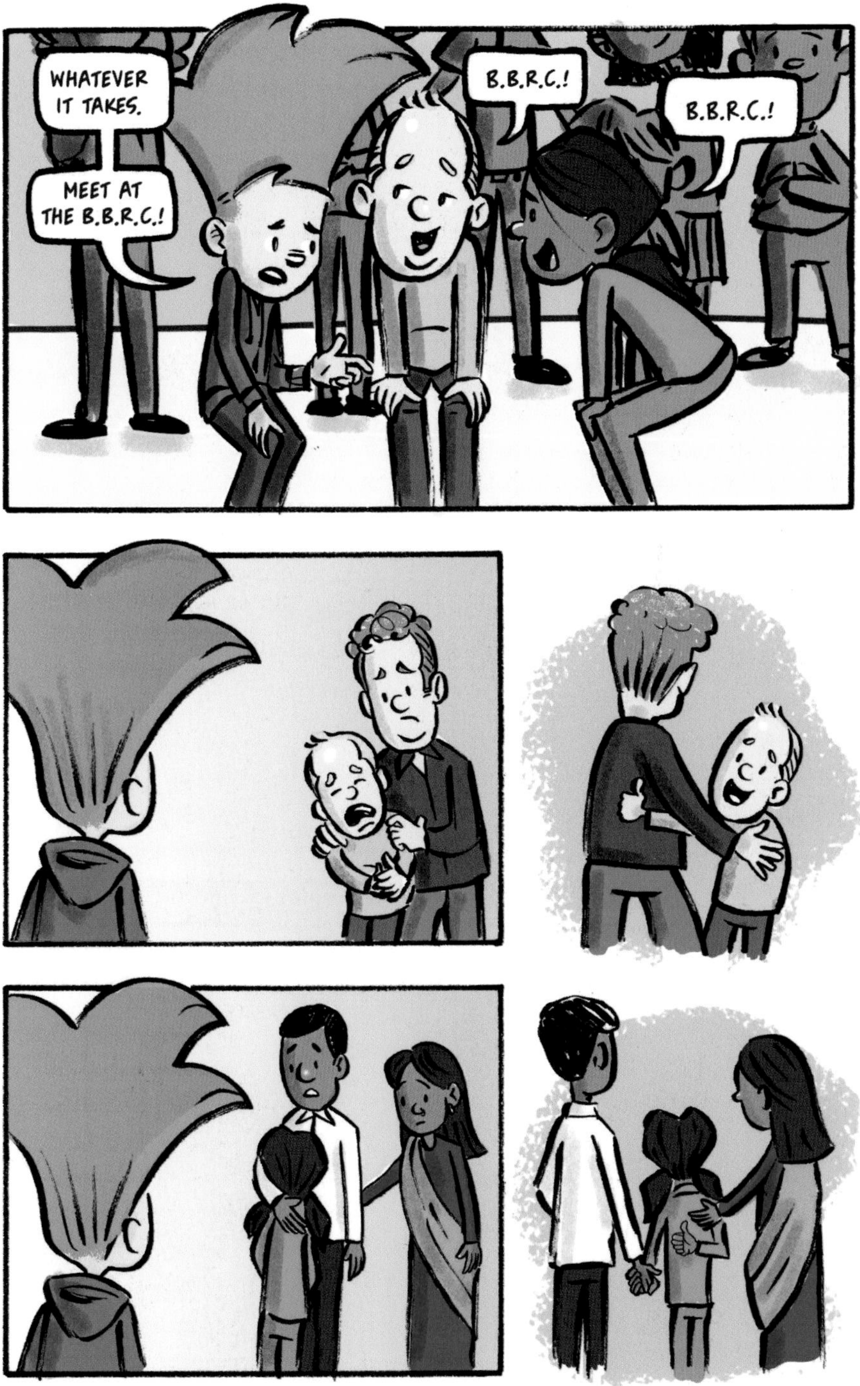
WHATEVER IT TAKES.
MEET AT THE B.B.R.C.!
B.B.R.C.!
B.B.R.C.!

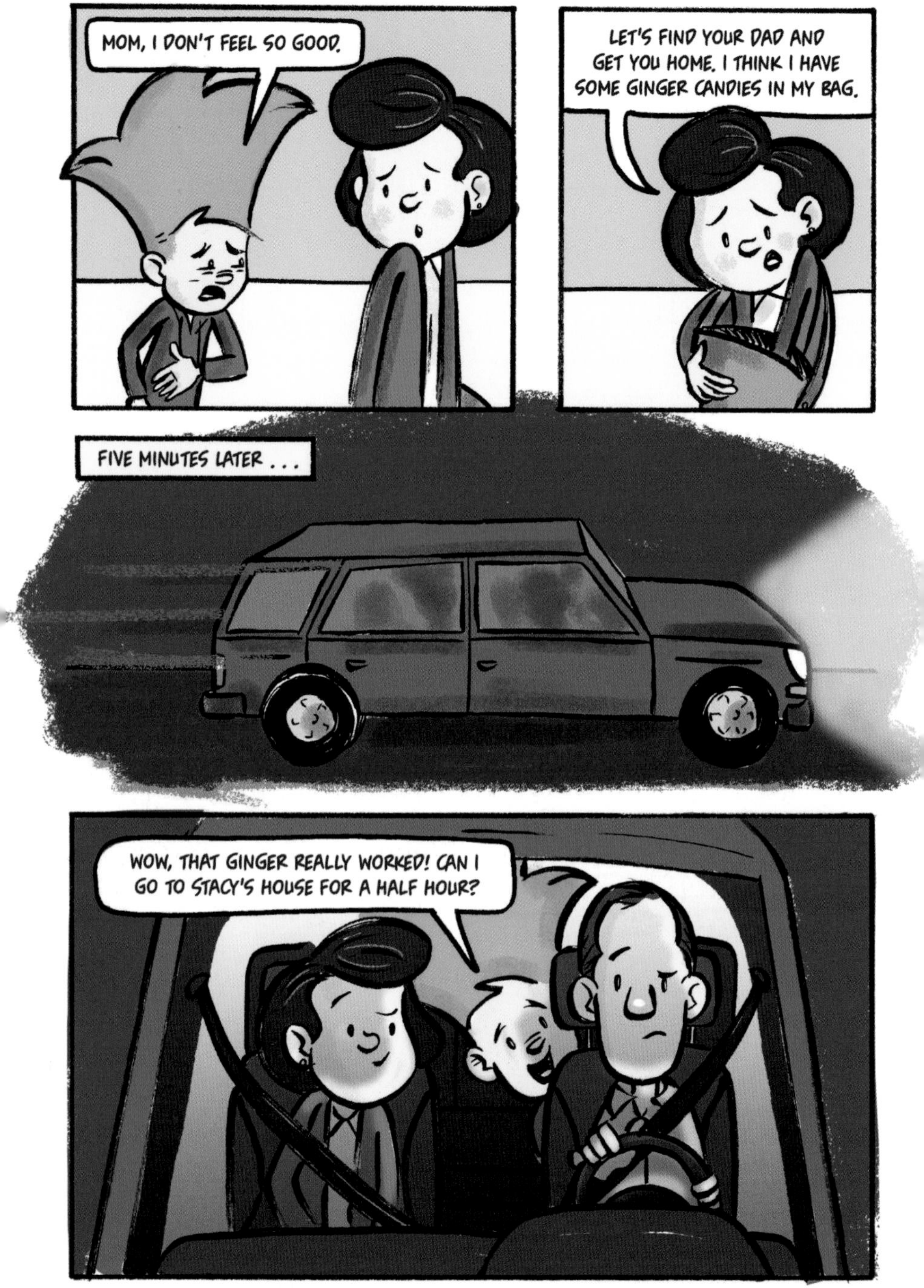
MOM, I DON'T FEEL SO GOOD.
LET'S FIND YOUR DAD AND GET YOU HOME. I THINK I HAVE SOME GINGER CANDIES IN MY BAG.
FIVE MINUTES LATER . . .
WOW, THAT GINGER REALLY WORKED! CAN I GO TO STACY'S HOUSE FOR A HALF HOUR?

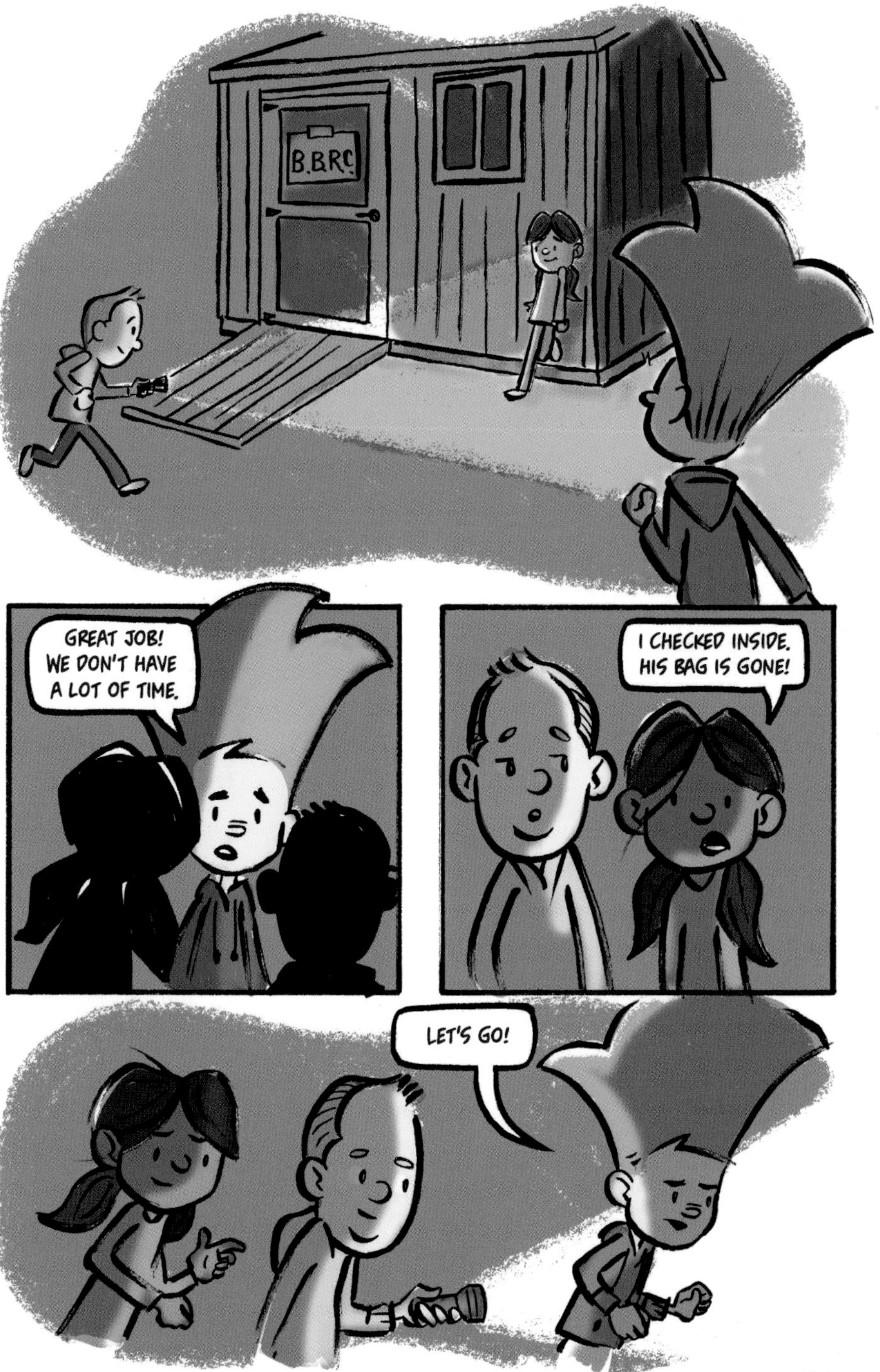
B.B.R.C.
GREAT JOB! WE DON'T HAVE A LOT OF TIME.
I CHECKED INSIDE. HIS BAG IS GONE!
LET'S GO!

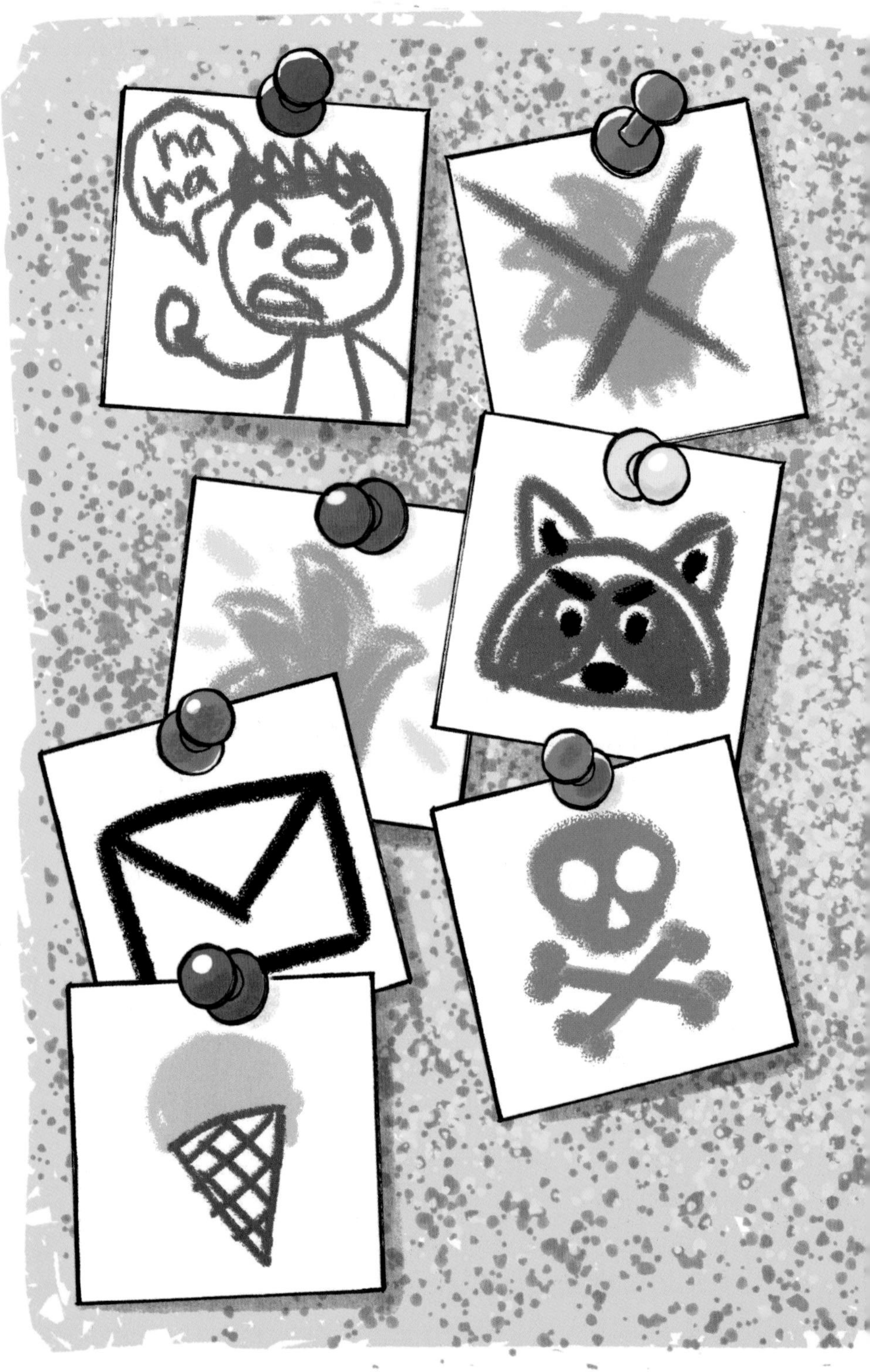
ha ha

CHAPTER 8:

THE WOODS

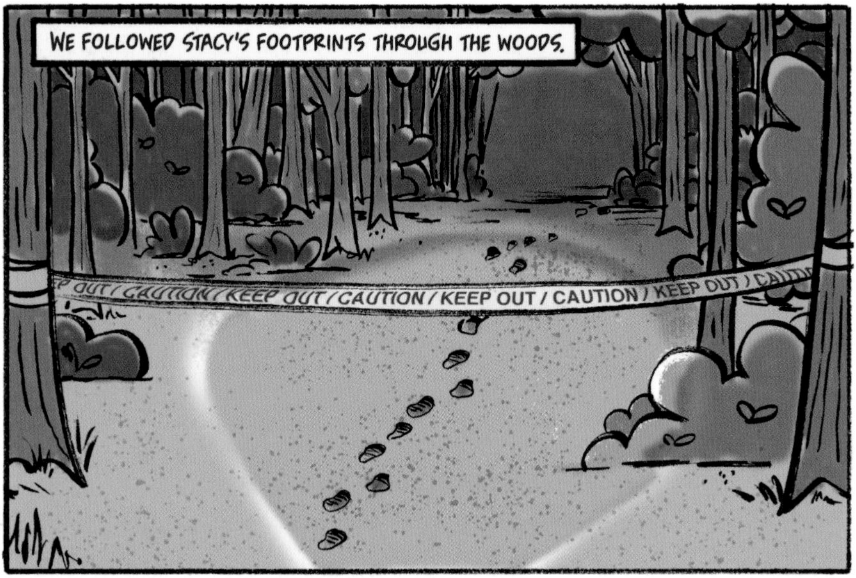
WE FOLLOWED STACY'S FOOTPRINTS THROUGH THE WOODS.
P OUT / CAUTION / KEEP OUT / CAUTION / KEEP OUT / CAUTION / KEEP OUT / CAUTIO

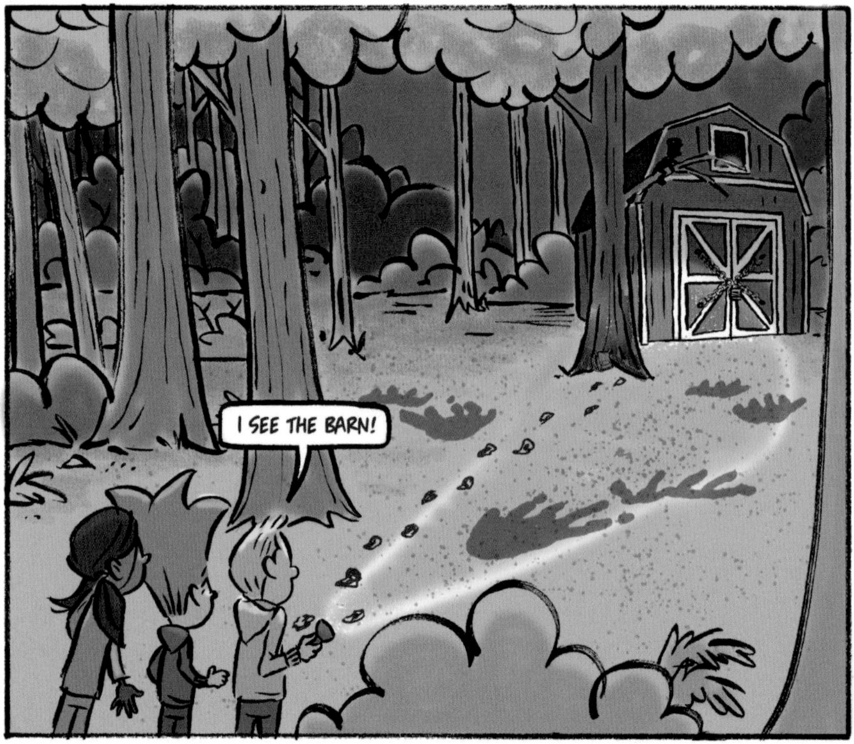
I SEE THE BARN!

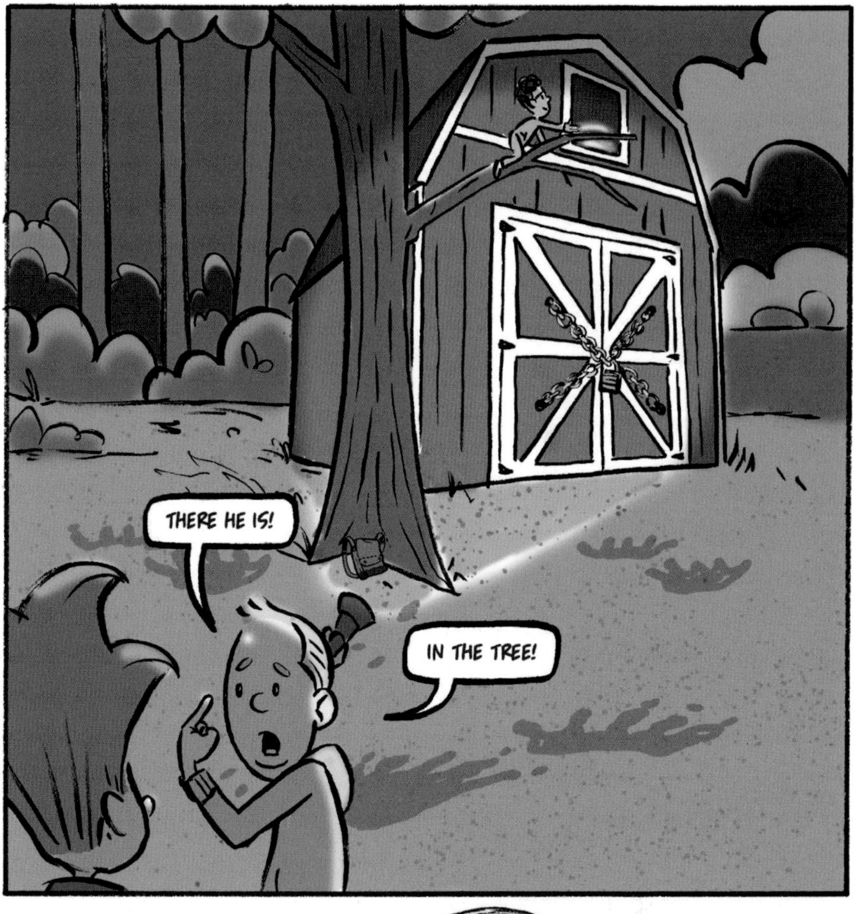
THERE HE IS!
IN THE TREE!

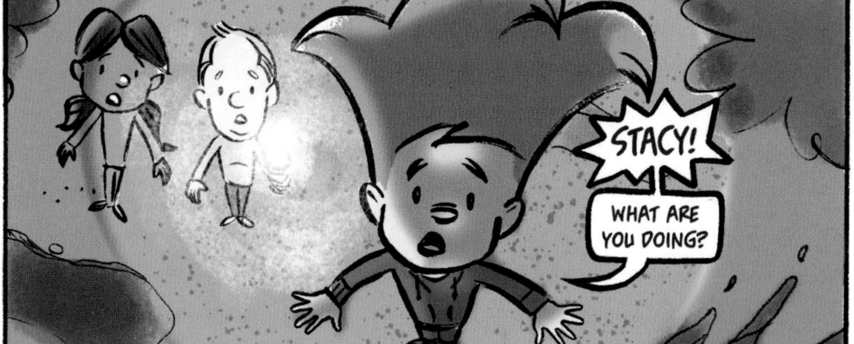
STACY!
WHAT ARE YOU DOING?

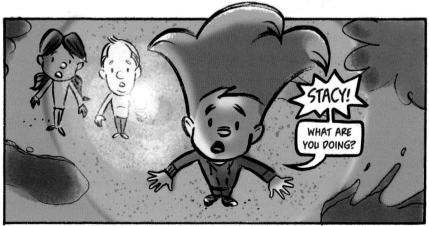

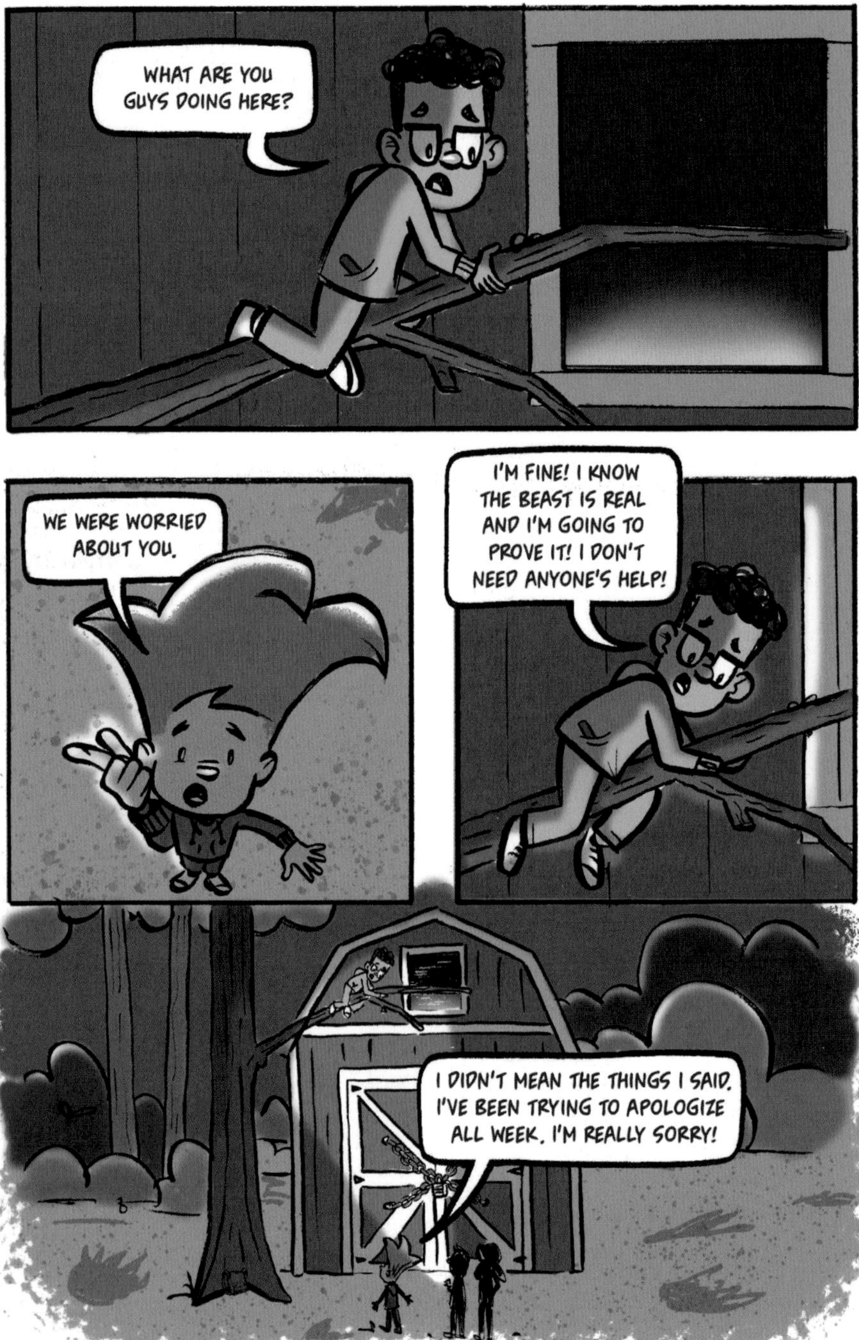
WHAT ARE YOU GUYS DOING HERE?
WE WERE WORRIED ABOUT YOU.
I'M FINE! I KNOW THE BEAST IS REAL AND I'M GOING TO PROVE IT! I DON'T NEED ANYONE'S HELP!
I DIDN'T MEAN THE THINGS I SAID. I'VE BEEN TRYING TO APOLOGIZE ALL WEEK. I'M REALLY SORRY!

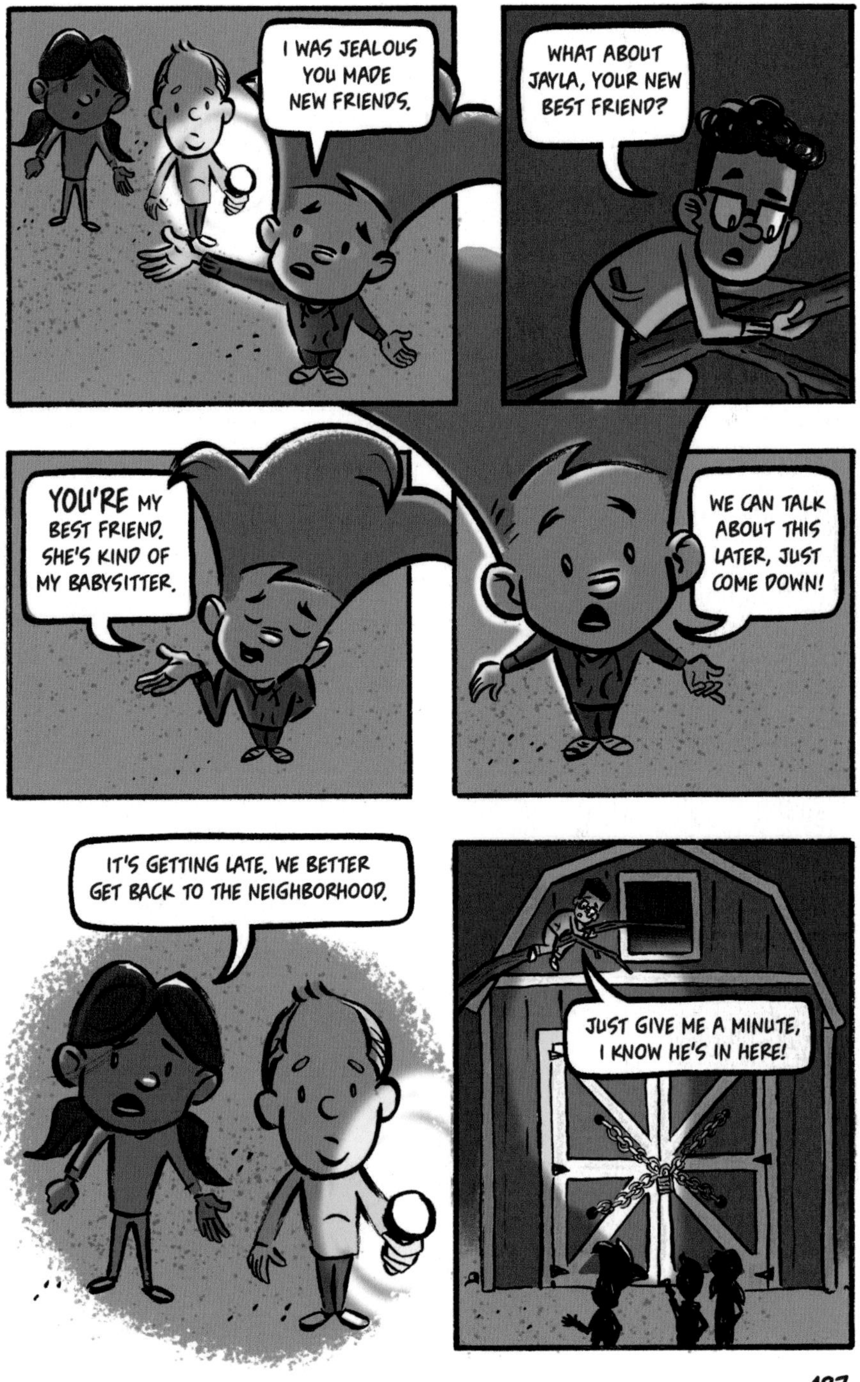
I WAS JEALOUS YOU MADE NEW FRIENDS.
WHAT ABOUT JAYLA, YOUR NEW BEST FRIEND?
YOU'RE MY BEST FRIEND. SHE'S KIND OF MY BABYSITTER.
WE CAN TALK ABOUT THIS LATER, JUST COME DOWN!
IT'S GETTING LATE. WE BETTER GET BACK TO THE NEIGHBORHOOD.
JUST GIVE ME A MINUTE, I KNOW HE'S IN HERE!

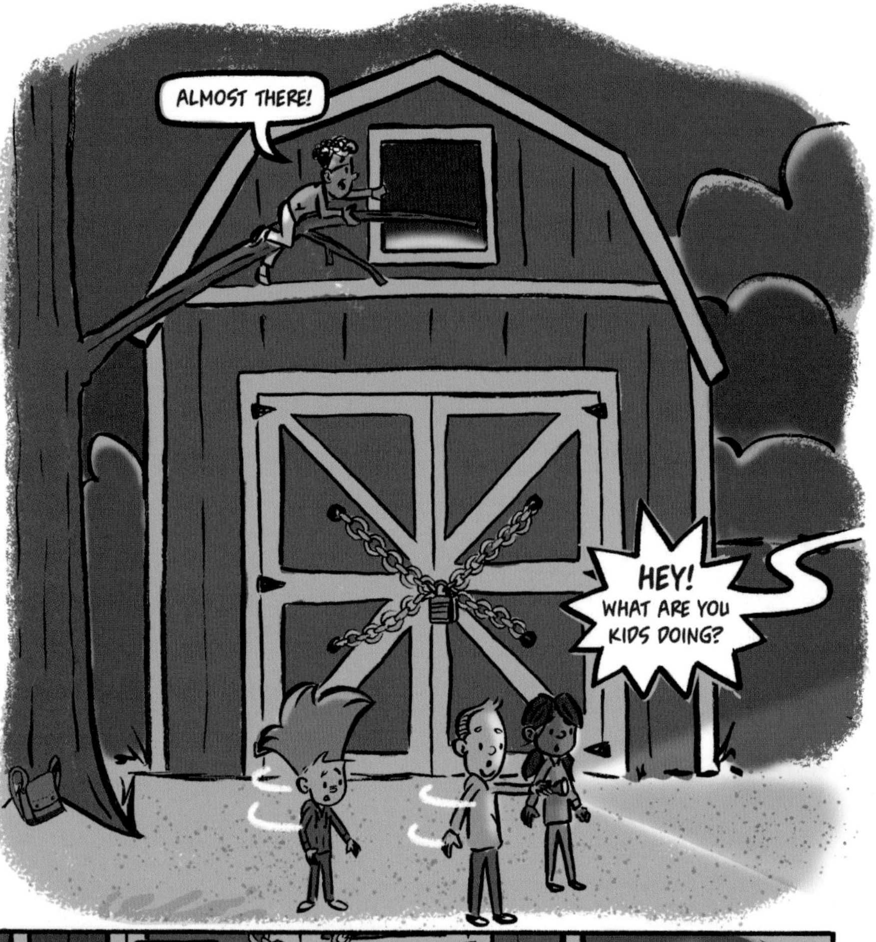
ALMOST THERE!
HEY! WHAT ARE YOU KIDS DOING?

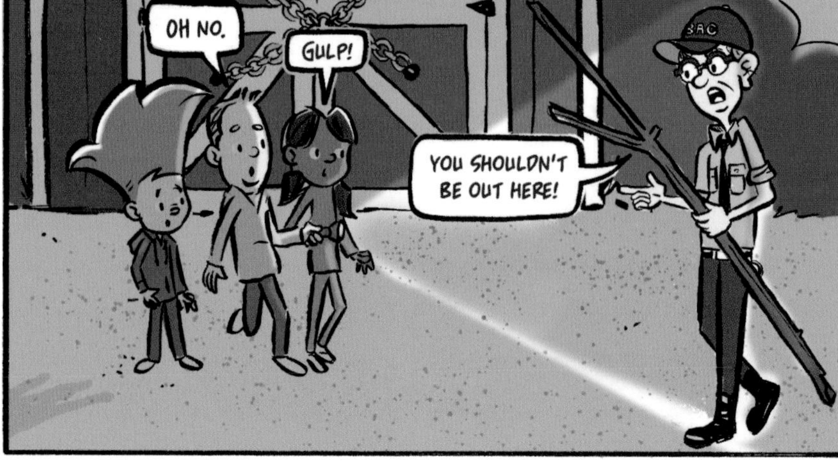
OH NO.
GULP!
YOU SHOULDN'T BE OUT HERE!
BRC

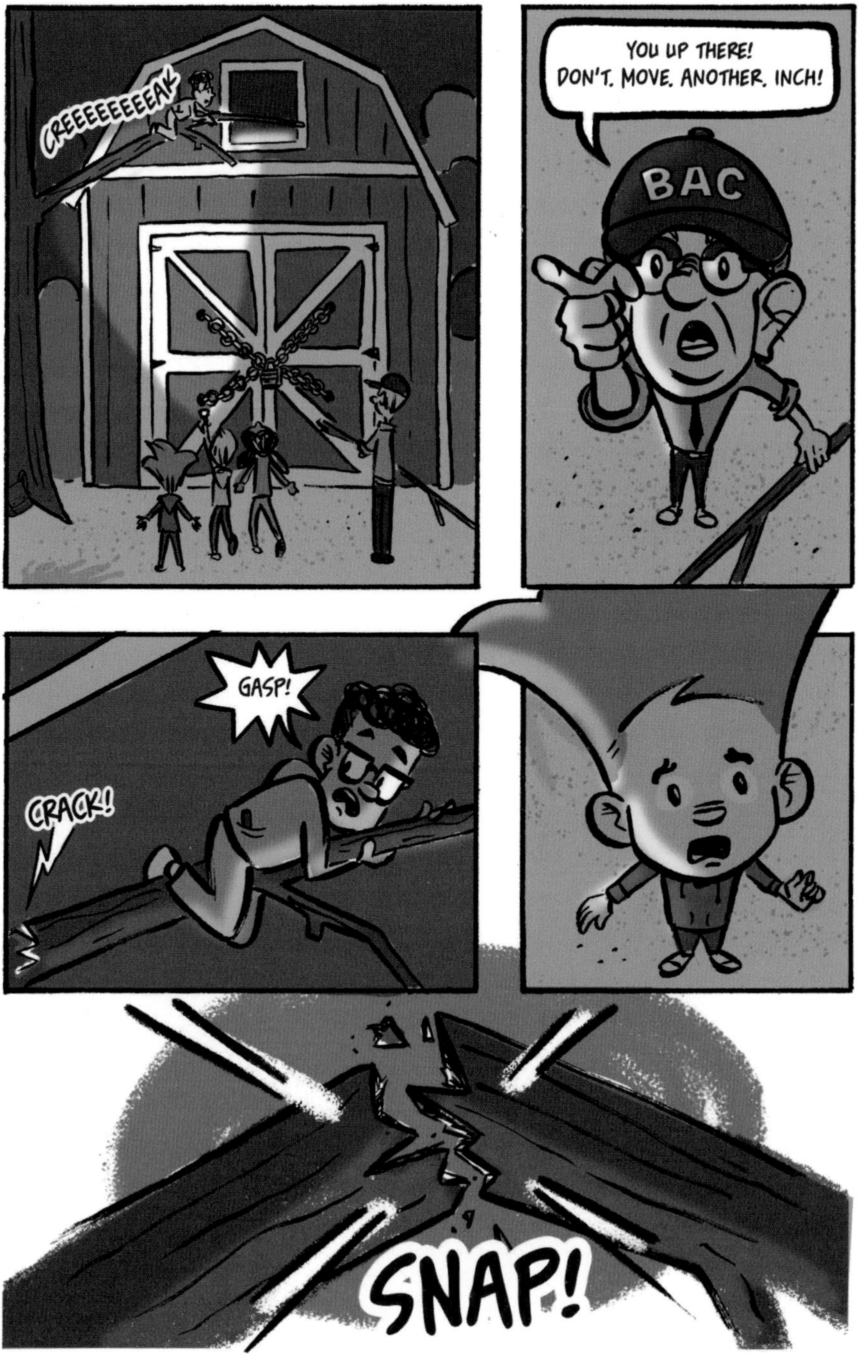
CREEEEEEEEAK
YOU UP THERE!
DON'T. MOVE. ANOTHER. INCH!
BAC
GASP!
CRACK!
SNAP!

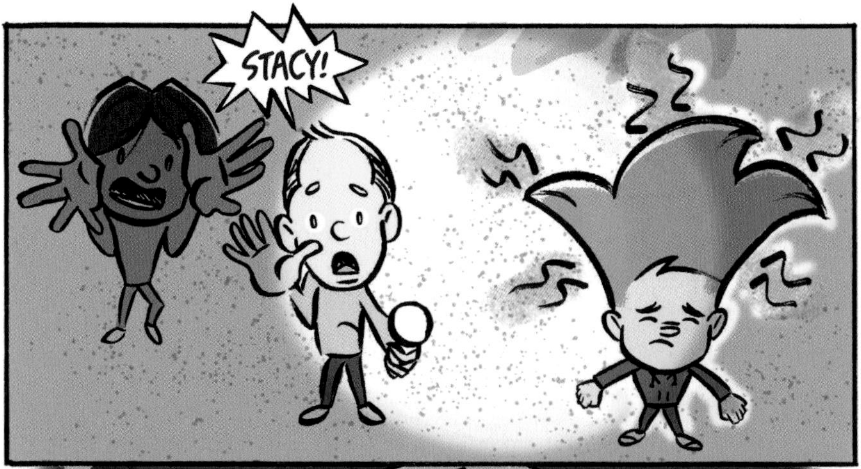
STACY!

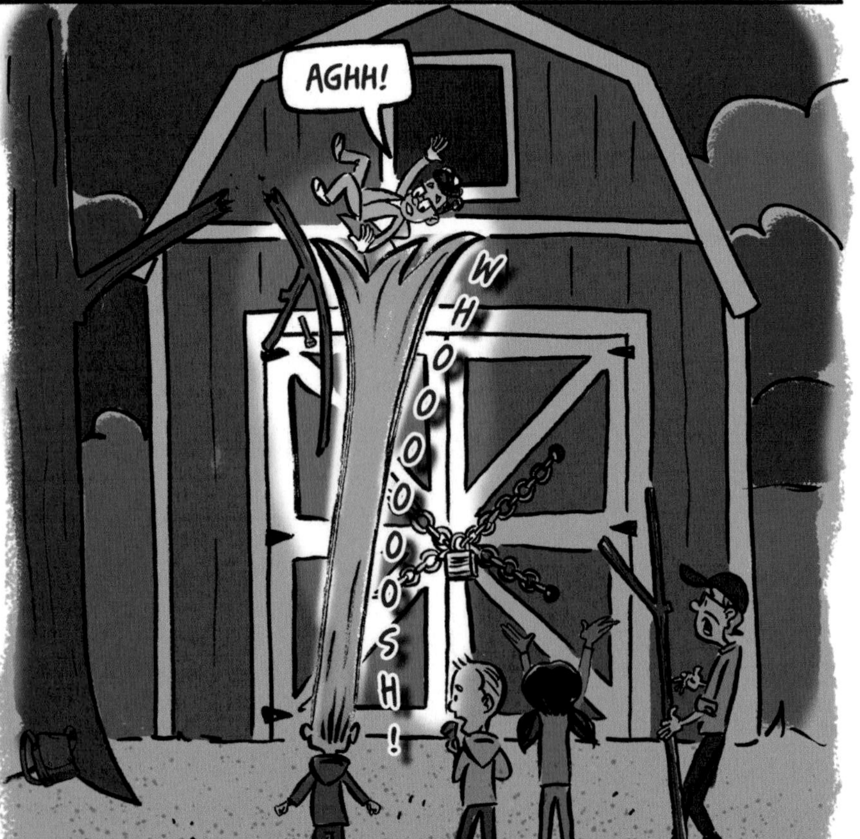
AGHH!
WHOOOOOOOOOSH!

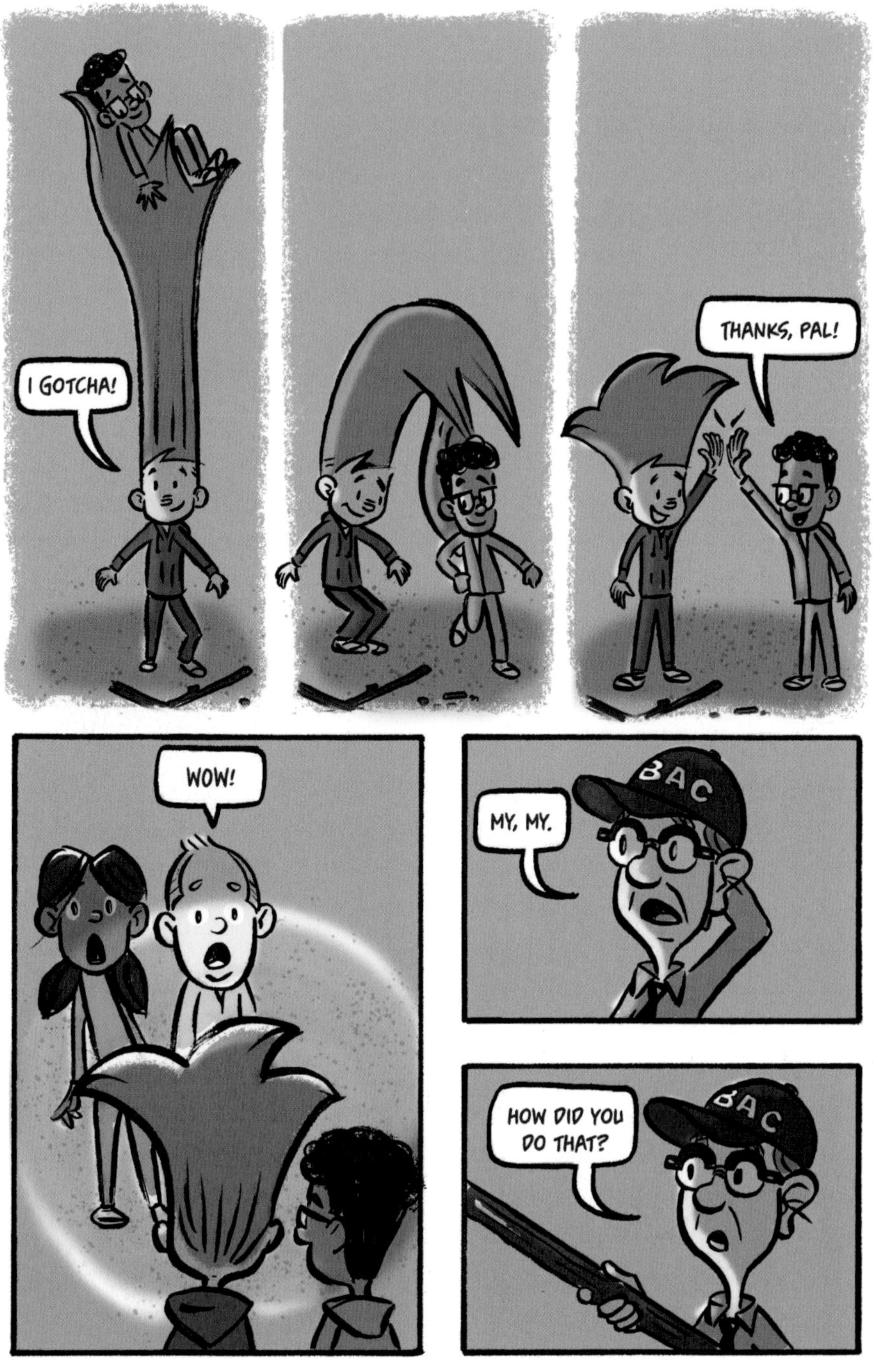
I GOTCHA!
THANKS, PAL!
WOW!
MY, MY.
HOW DID YOU DO THAT?

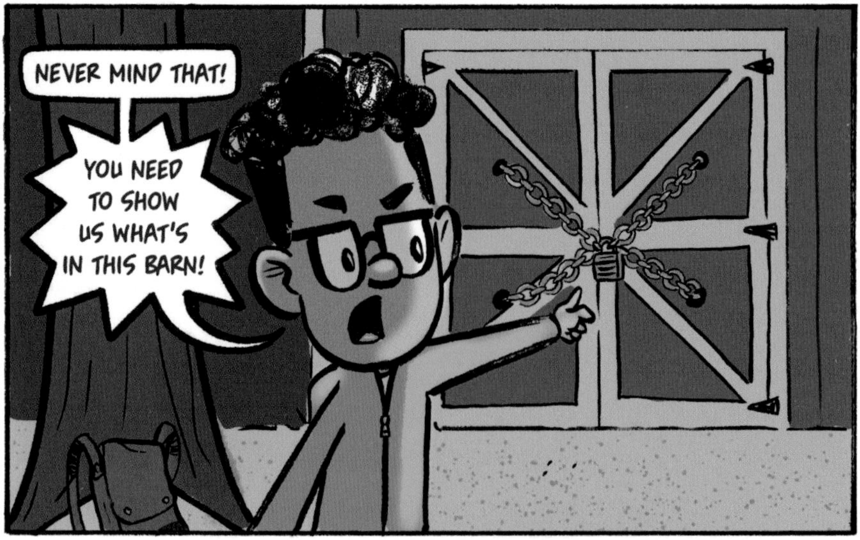
NEVER MIND THAT!
YOU NEED TO SHOW US WHAT'S IN THIS BARN!

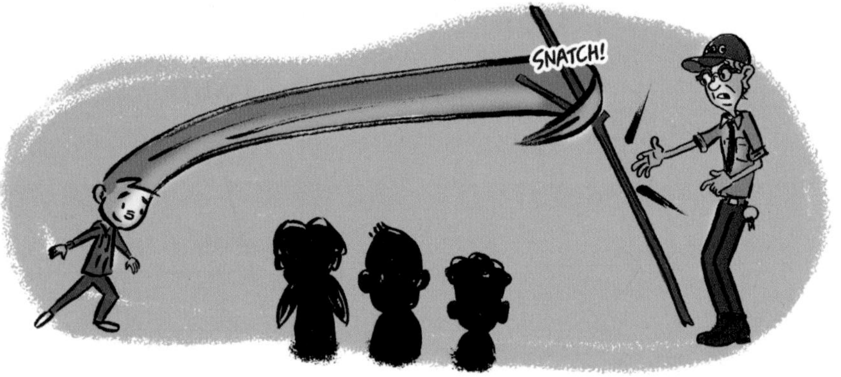
SNATCH!

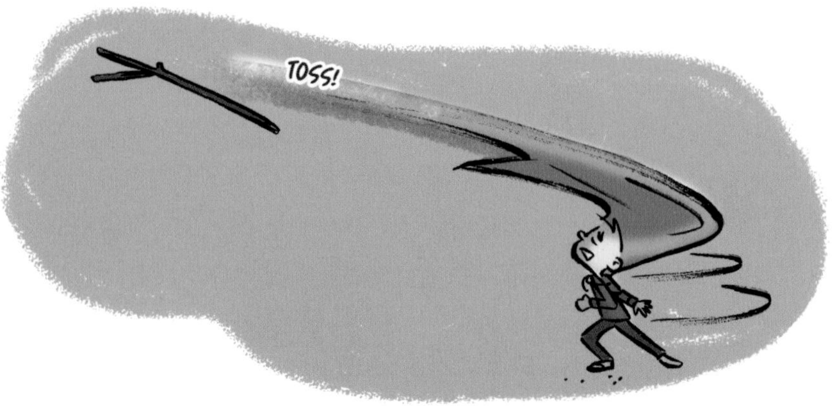
TOSS!

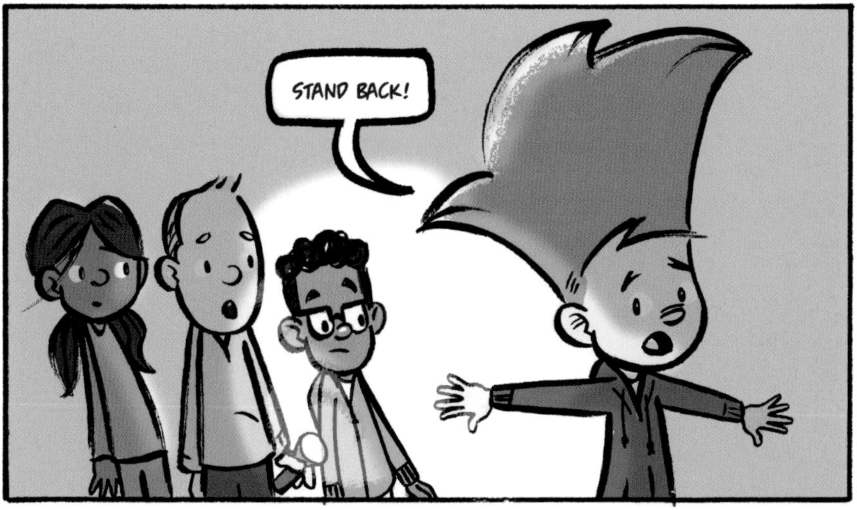
STAND BACK!

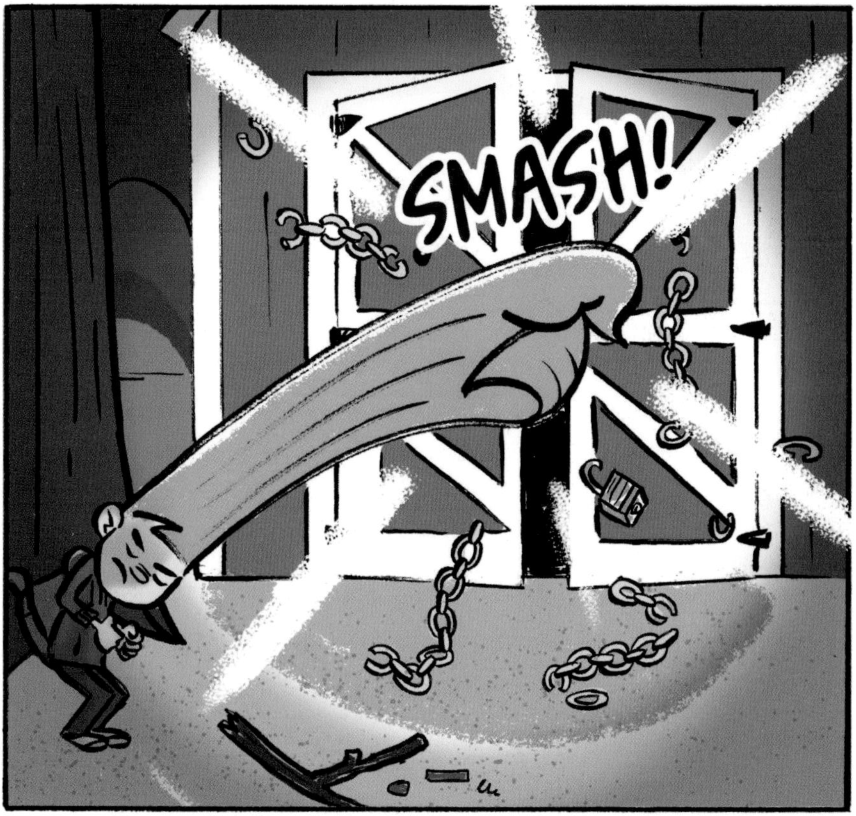
SMASH!

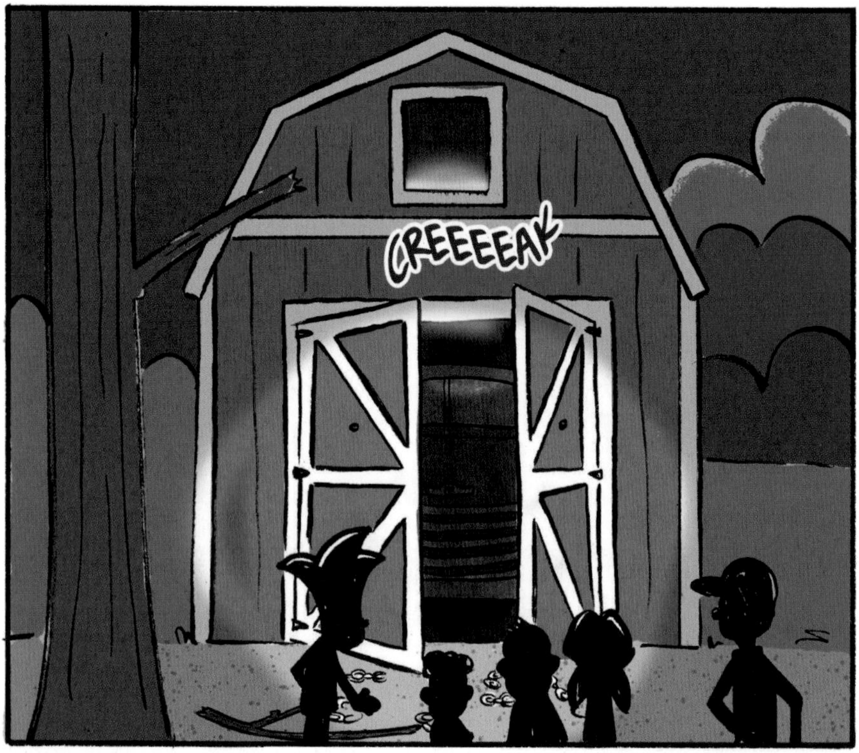
CREEEEAK

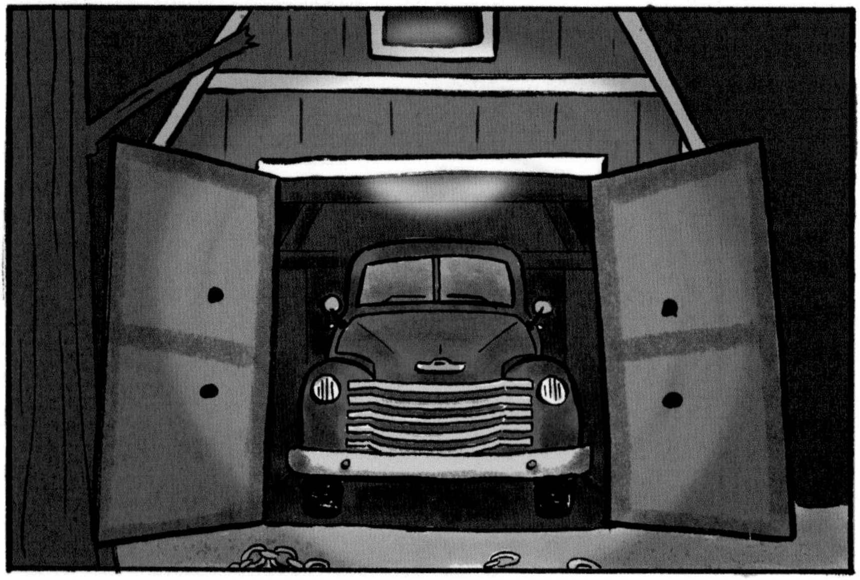

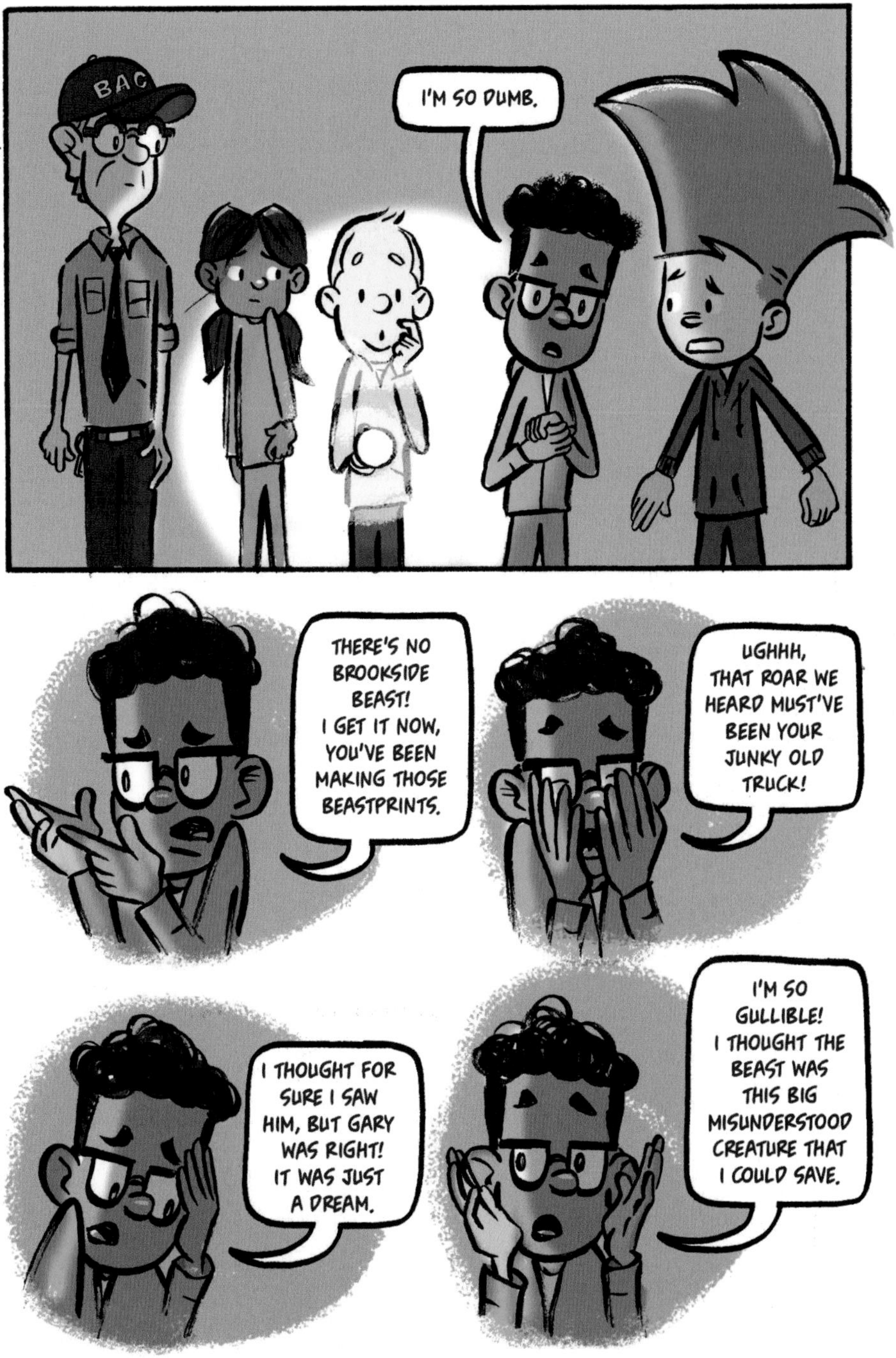
I'M SO DUMB.
THERE'S NO BROOKSIDE BEAST! I GET IT NOW, YOU'VE BEEN MAKING THOSE BEASTPRINTS.
UGHHH, THAT ROAR WE HEARD MUST'VE BEEN YOUR JUNKY OLD TRUCK!
I THOUGHT FOR SURE I SAW HIM, BUT GARY WAS RIGHT! IT WAS JUST A DREAM.
I'M SO GULLIBLE! I THOUGHT THE BEAST WAS THIS BIG MISUNDERSTOOD CREATURE THAT I COULD SAVE.

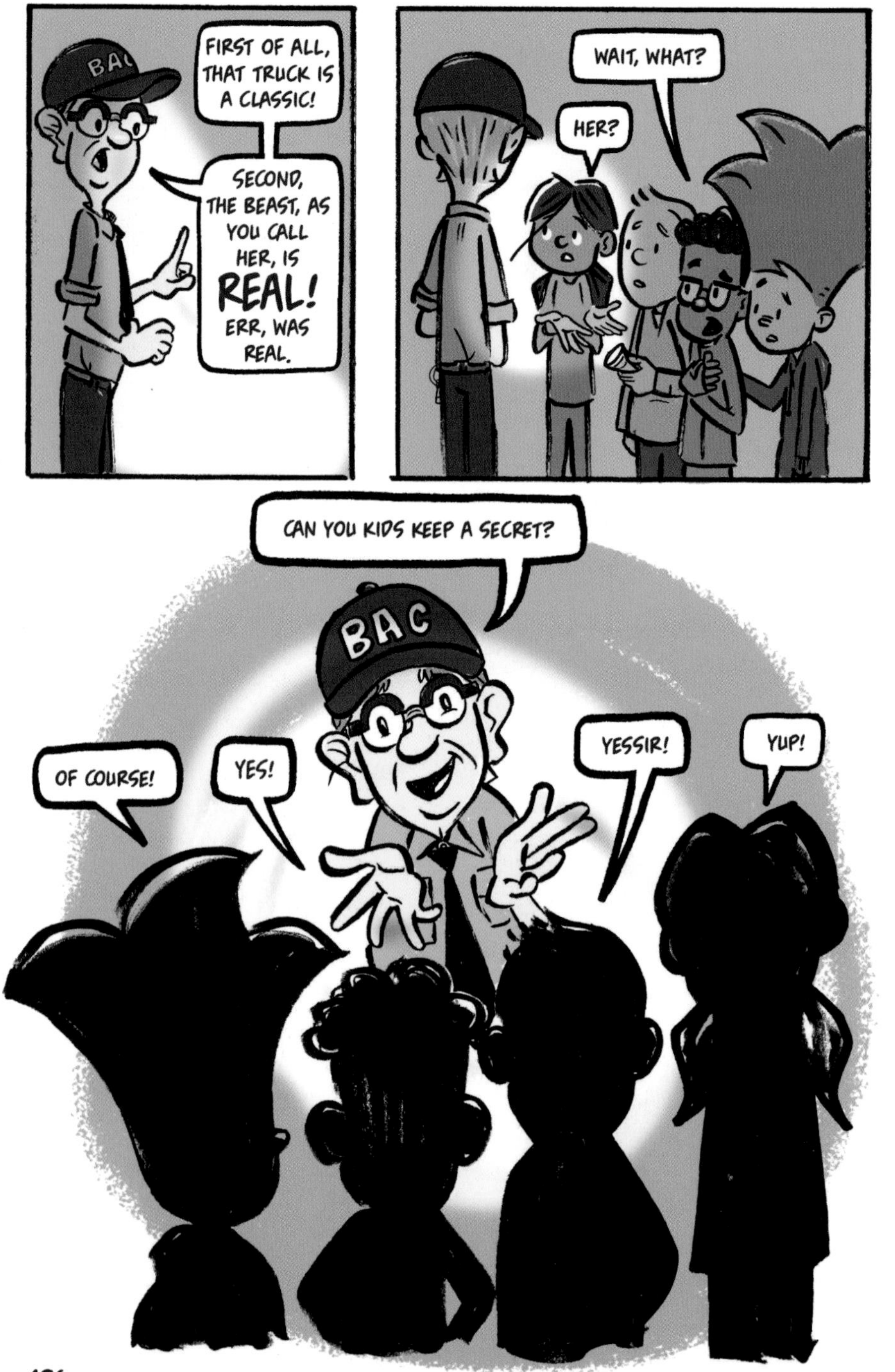

FIRST OF ALL, THAT TRUCK IS A CLASSIC!
SECOND, THE BEAST, AS YOU CALL HER, IS REAL! ERR, WAS REAL.
BAC
HER?
WAIT, WHAT?
CAN YOU KIDS KEEP A SECRET?
BAC
OF COURSE!
YES!
YESSIR!
YUP!

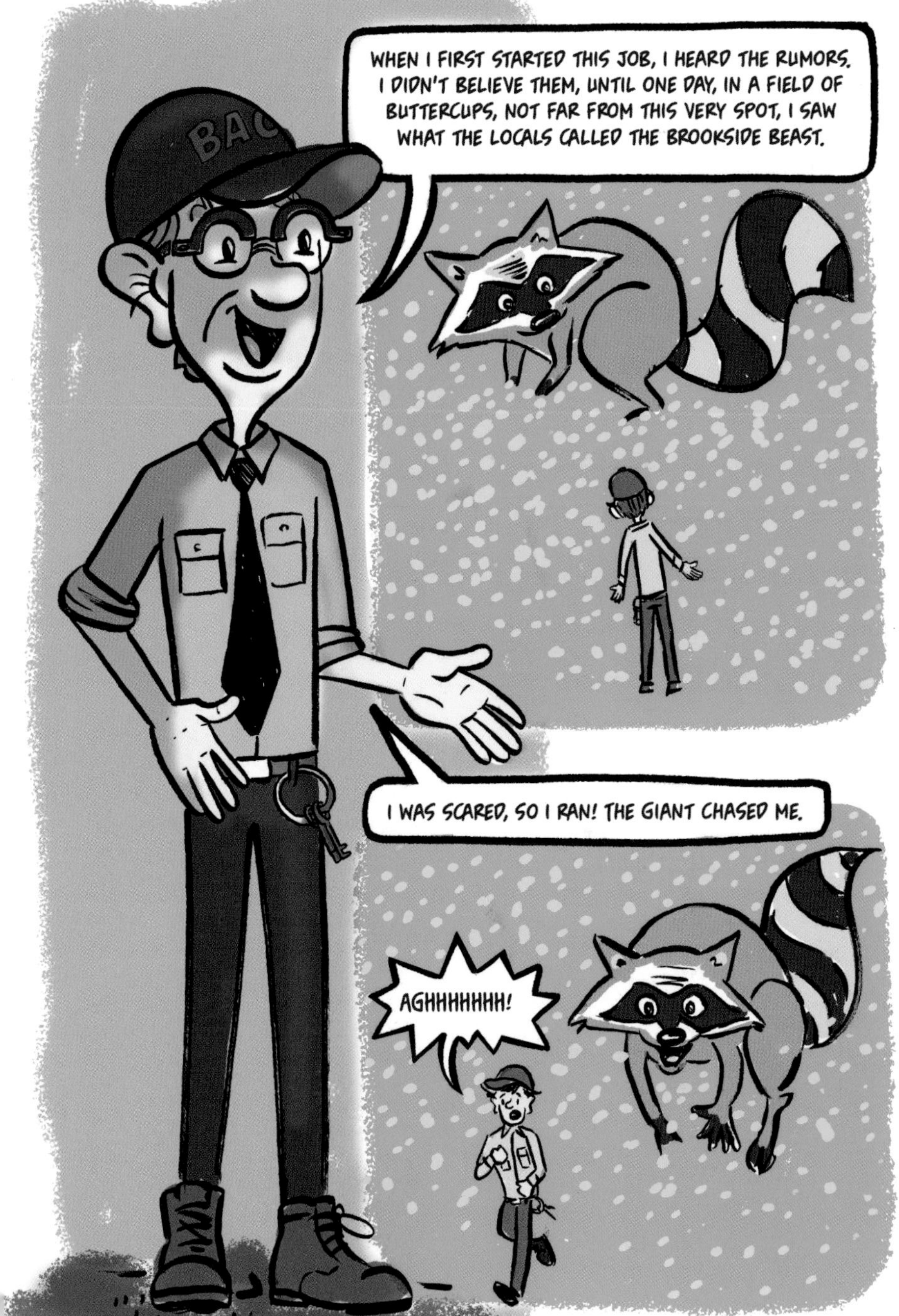
BAC
WHEN I FIRST STARTED THIS JOB, I HEARD THE RUMORS. I DIDN'T BELIEVE THEM, UNTIL ONE DAY, IN A FIELD OF BUTTERCUPS, NOT FAR FROM THIS VERY SPOT, I SAW WHAT THE LOCALS CALLED THE BROOKSIDE BEAST.
I WAS SCARED, SO I RAN! THE GIANT CHASED ME.
AGHHHHHHH!

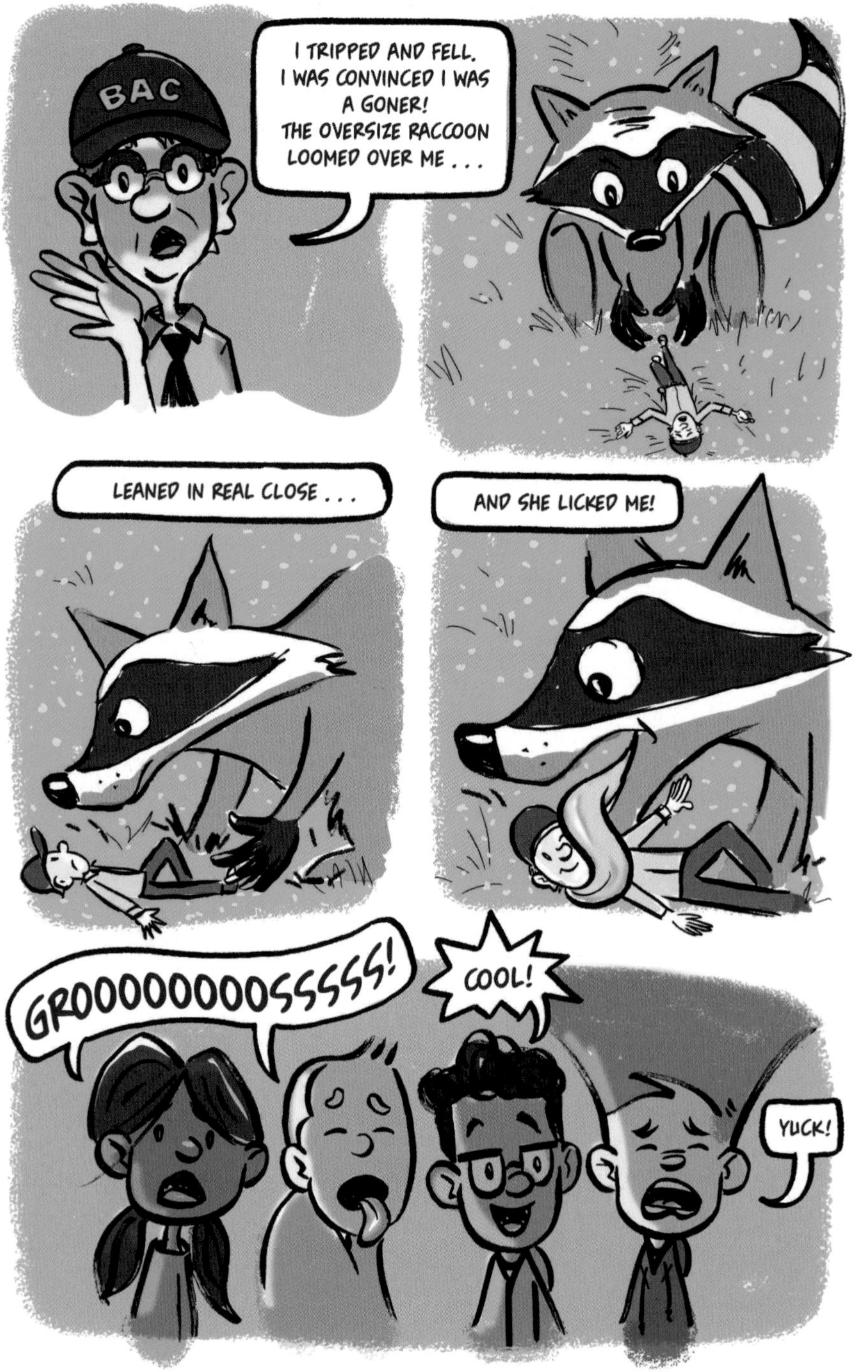
I TRIPPED AND FELL.
I WAS CONVINCED I WAS
A GONER!
THE OVERSIZE RACCOON
LOOMED OVER ME . . .
LEANED IN REAL CLOSE . . .
AND SHE LICKED ME!
GROOOOOOOOSSSSS!
COOL!
YUCK!

ONE THING I KNEW FOR SURE, THE GIGANTIC RACCOON WASN'T THE MONSTER EVERYONE THOUGHT SHE WAS.

I NAMED HER BUTTERCUP!

BUTTERCUP WAS LIKE A BIG OL' DOG. WE WOULD PLAY FETCH . . .

TOO BIG!

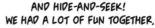

AND HIDE-AND-SEEK! WE HAD A LOT OF FUN TOGETHER.

FOUND YOU!

BUT AS HER LEGEND GREW, PEOPLE STARTED TALKING ABOUT CAPTURING HER, PUTTING BUTTERCUP IN A CAGE, AND SELLING TICKETS TO SEE HER.

SEE THE TERRIFYING
$5 BROOKSIDE BEAST $5

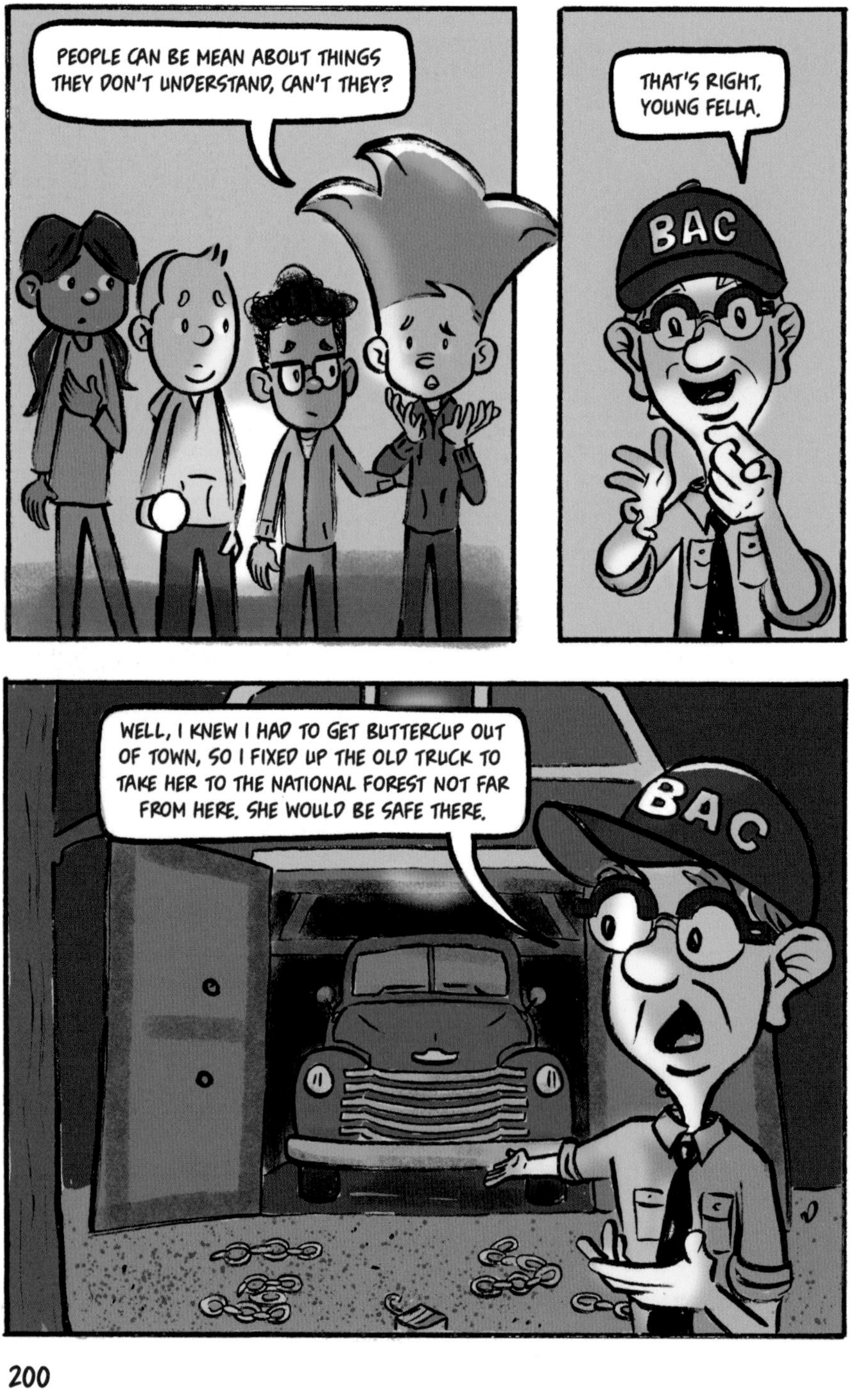
PEOPLE CAN BE MEAN ABOUT THINGS THEY DON'T UNDERSTAND, CAN'T THEY?
THAT'S RIGHT, YOUNG FELLA.
BAC
WELL, I KNEW I HAD TO GET BUTTERCUP OUT OF TOWN, SO I FIXED UP THE OLD TRUCK TO TAKE HER TO THE NATIONAL FOREST NOT FAR FROM HERE. SHE WOULD BE SAFE THERE.
BAC

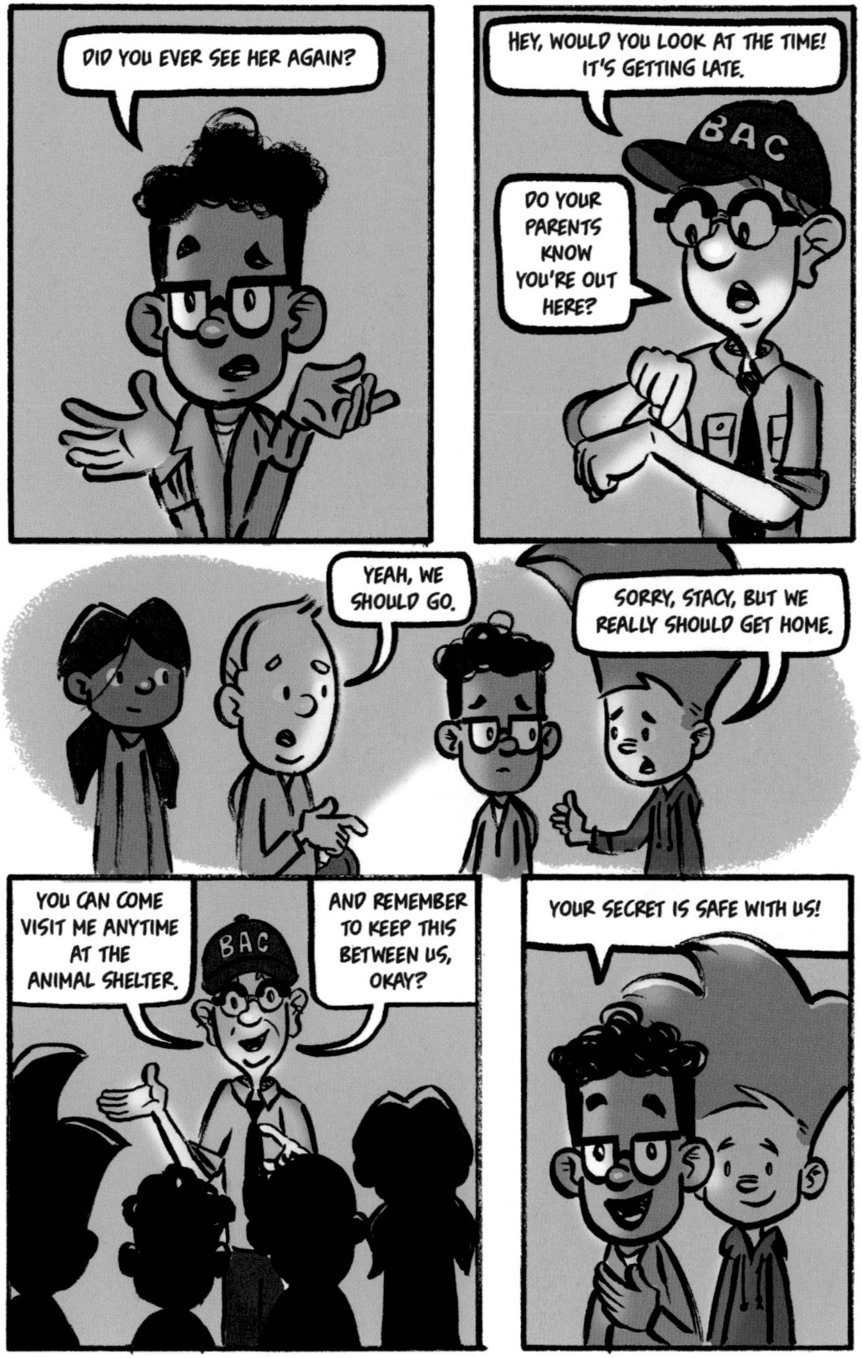
DID YOU EVER SEE HER AGAIN?
HEY, WOULD YOU LOOK AT THE TIME! IT'S GETTING LATE.
BAC
DO YOUR PARENTS KNOW YOU'RE OUT HERE?
YEAH, WE SHOULD GO.
SORRY, STACY, BUT WE REALLY SHOULD GET HOME.
YOU CAN COME VISIT ME ANYTIME AT THE ANIMAL SHELTER.
BAC
AND REMEMBER TO KEEP THIS BETWEEN US, OKAY?
YOUR SECRET IS SAFE WITH US!

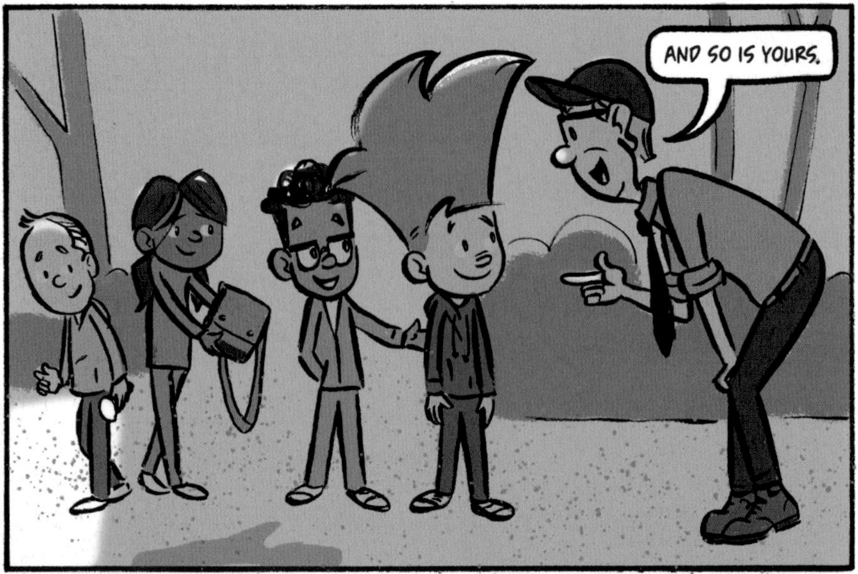
AND SO IS YOURS.

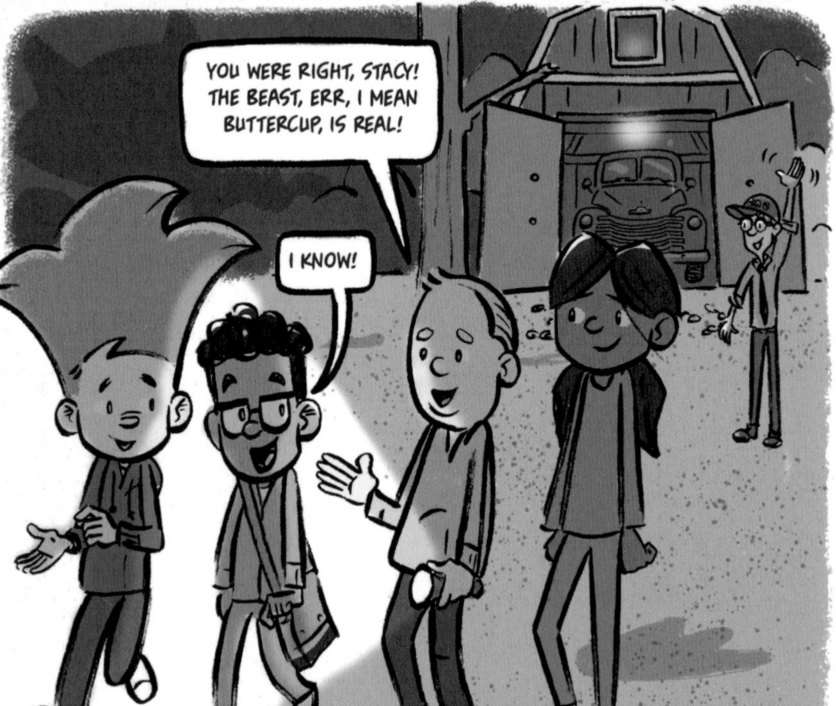
YOU WERE RIGHT, STACY! THE BEAST, ERR, I MEAN BUTTERCUP, IS REAL!
I KNOW!

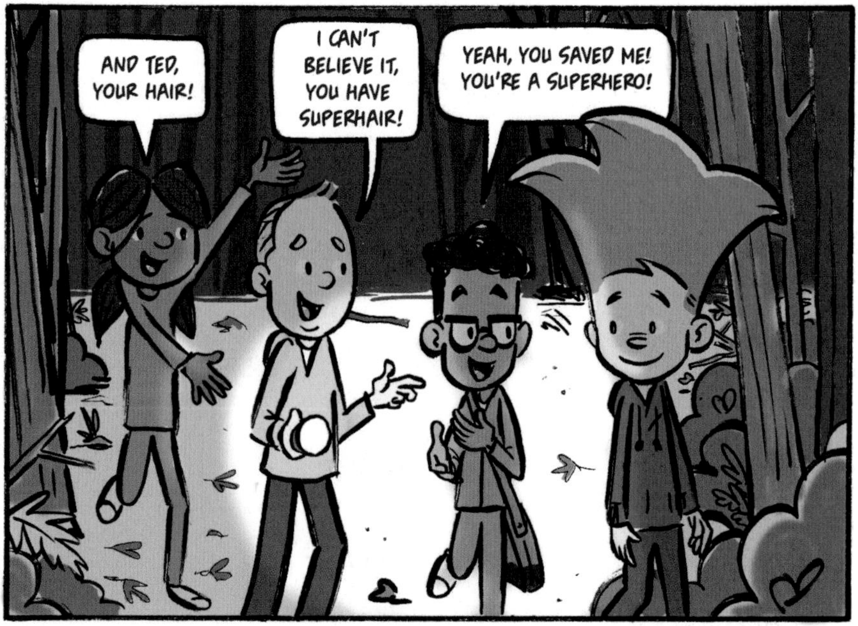
AND TED, YOUR HAIR!
I CAN'T BELIEVE IT, YOU HAVE SUPERHAIR!
YEAH, YOU SAVED ME! YOU'RE A SUPERHERO!

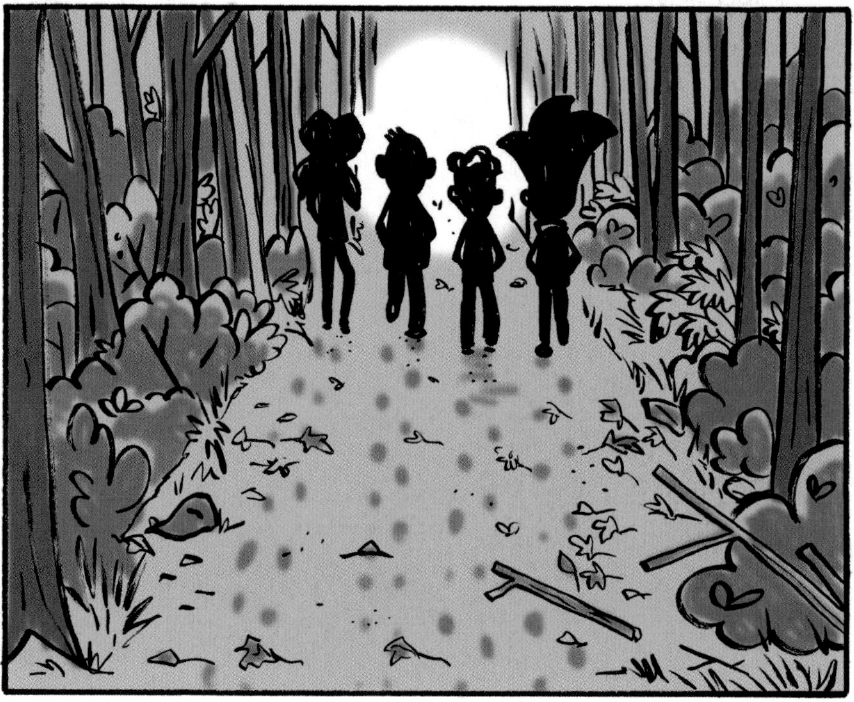

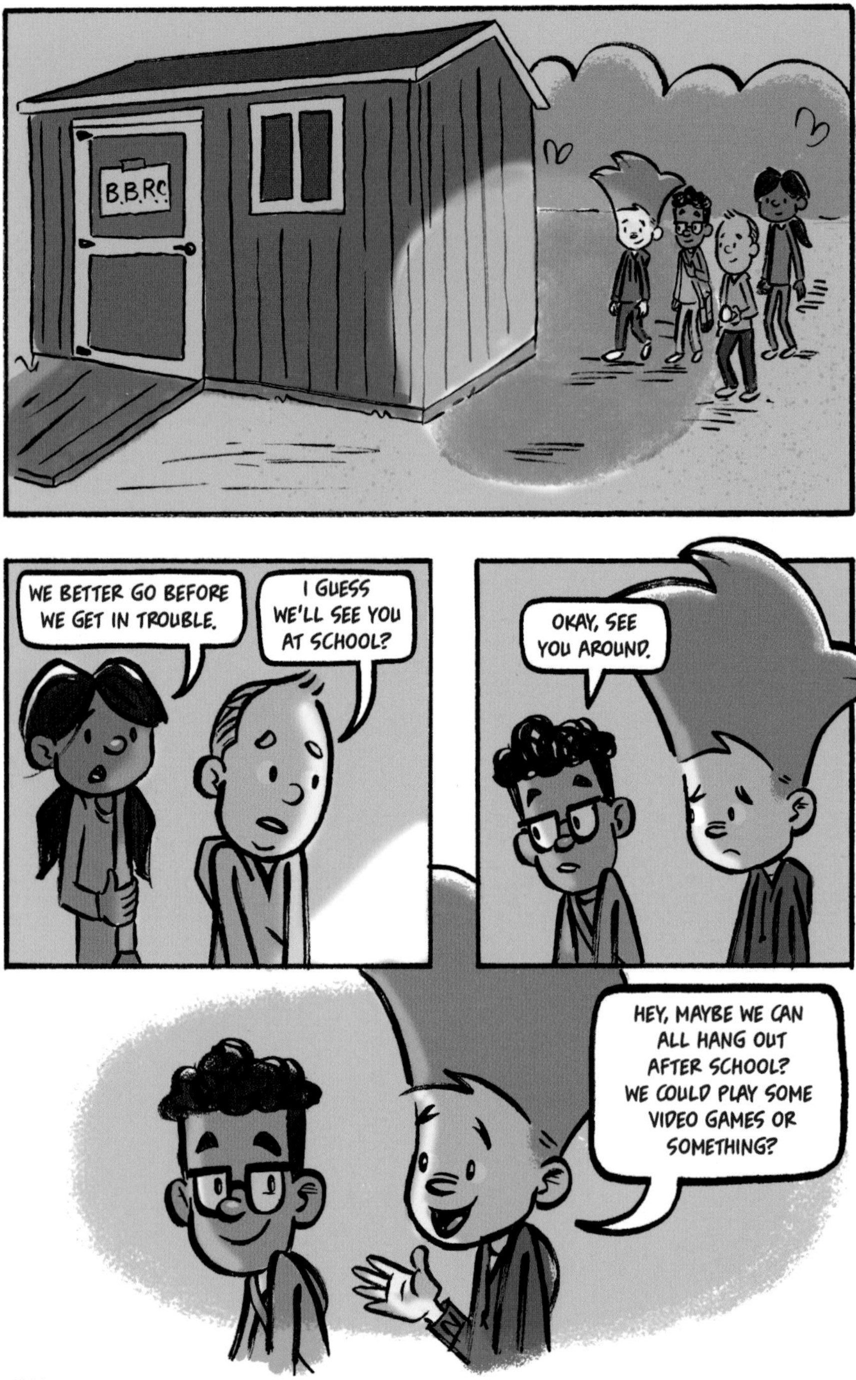
B.B.R.C.
WE BETTER GO BEFORE WE GET IN TROUBLE.
I GUESS WE'LL SEE YOU AT SCHOOL?
OKAY, SEE YOU AROUND.
HEY, MAYBE WE CAN ALL HANG OUT AFTER SCHOOL? WE COULD PLAY SOME VIDEO GAMES OR SOMETHING?

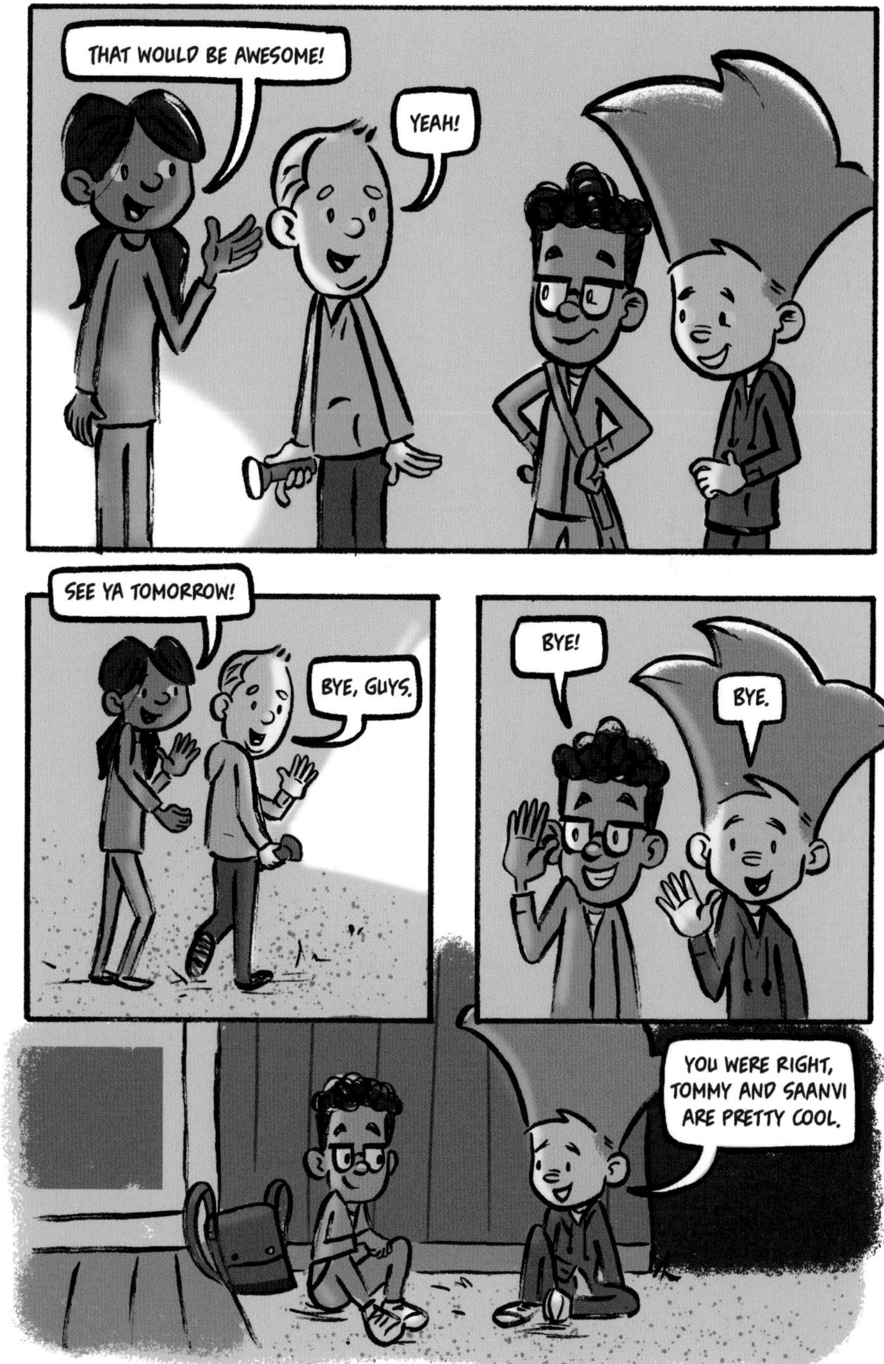
THAT WOULD BE AWESOME!
YEAH!
SEE YA TOMORROW!
BYE, GUYS.
BYE!
BYE.
YOU WERE RIGHT, TOMMY AND SAANVI ARE PRETTY COOL.

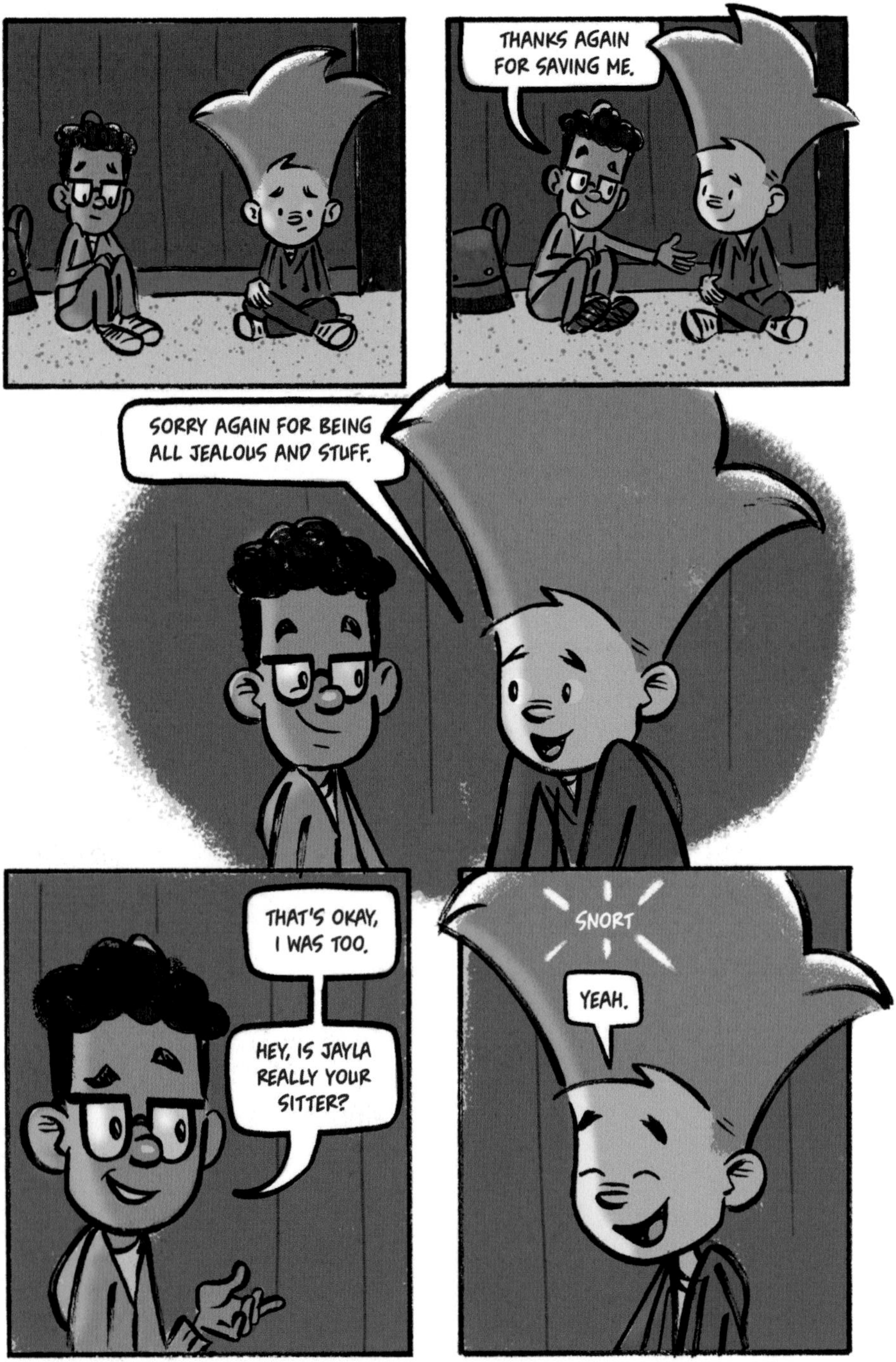
THANKS AGAIN FOR SAVING ME.
SORRY AGAIN FOR BEING ALL JEALOUS AND STUFF.
THAT'S OKAY, I WAS TOO.
HEY, IS JAYLA REALLY YOUR SITTER?
SNORT
YEAH.

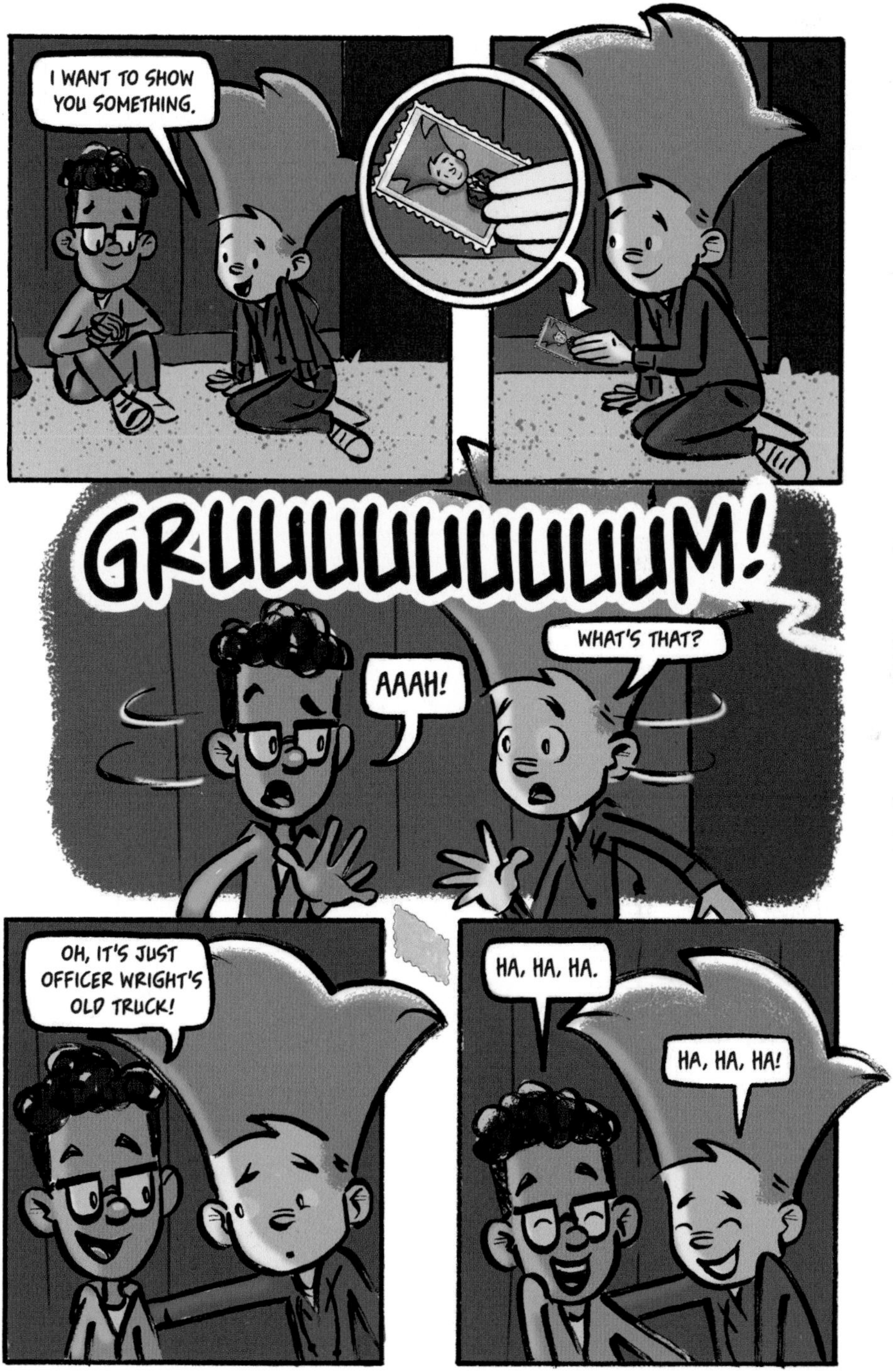
I WANT TO SHOW YOU SOMETHING.
GRUUUUUUUUUM!
AAAH!
WHAT'S THAT?
OH, IT'S JUST OFFICER WRIGHT'S OLD TRUCK!
HA, HA, HA.
HA, HA, HA!

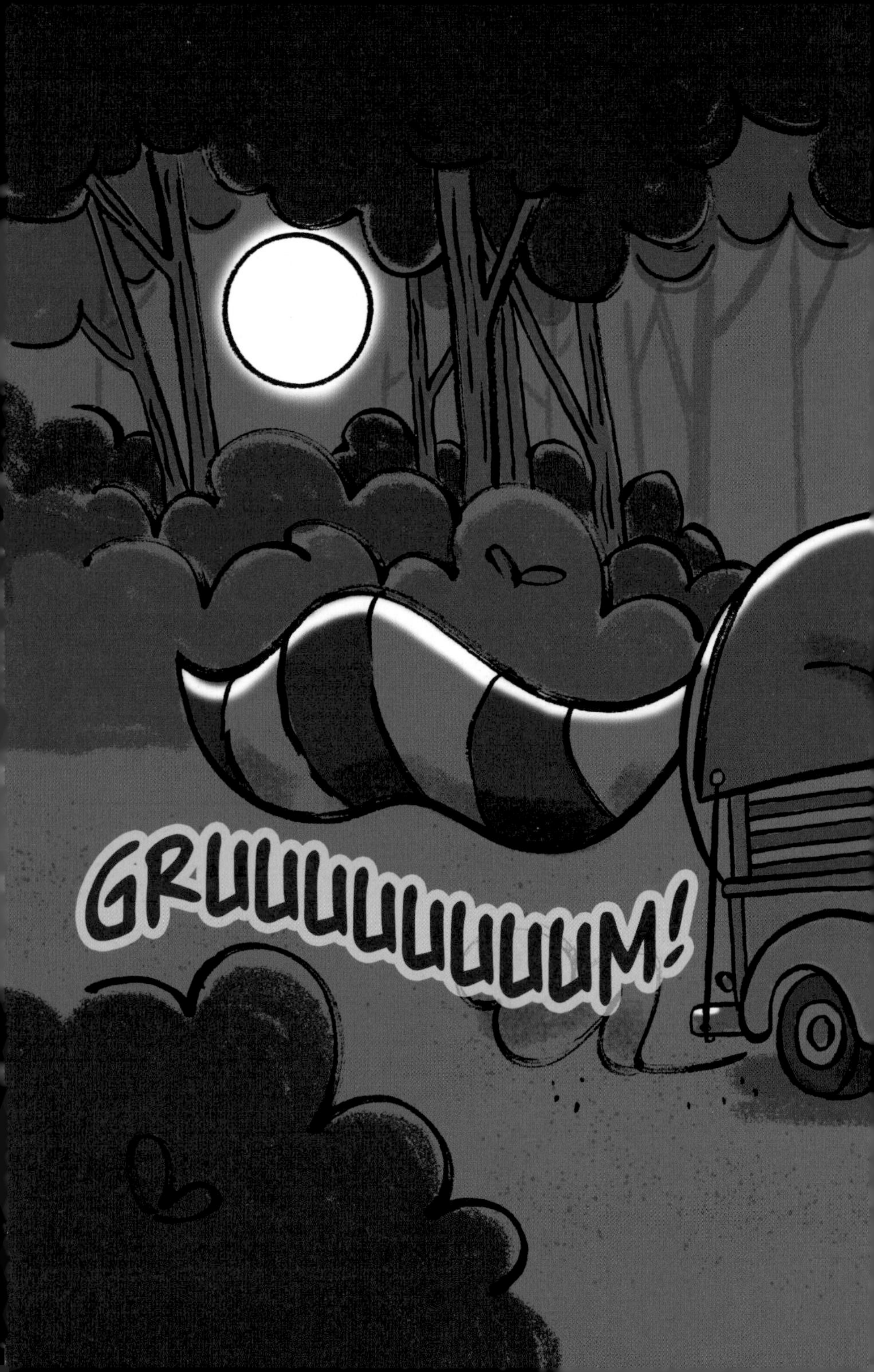
GRUUUUUUUUM!

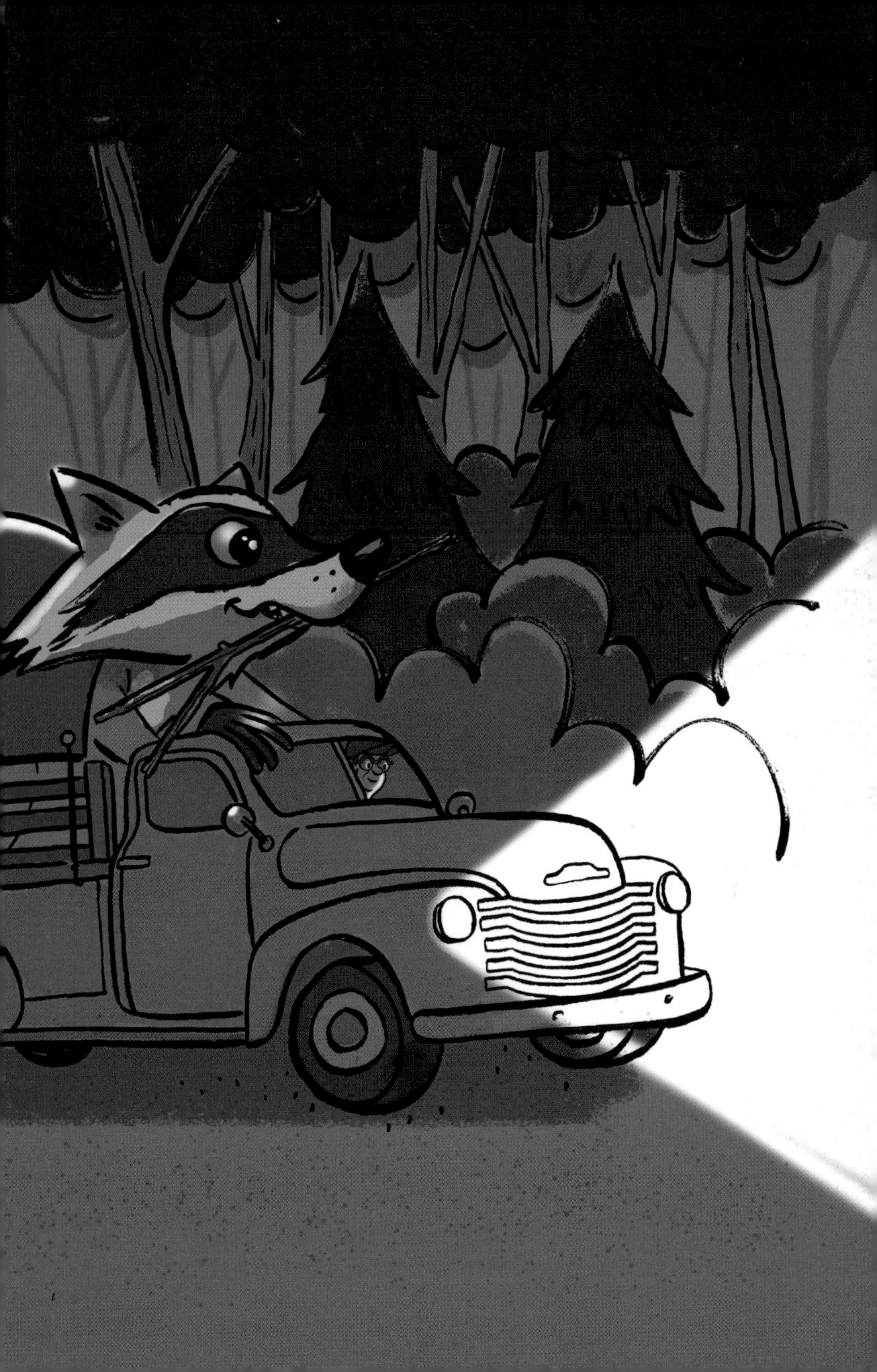

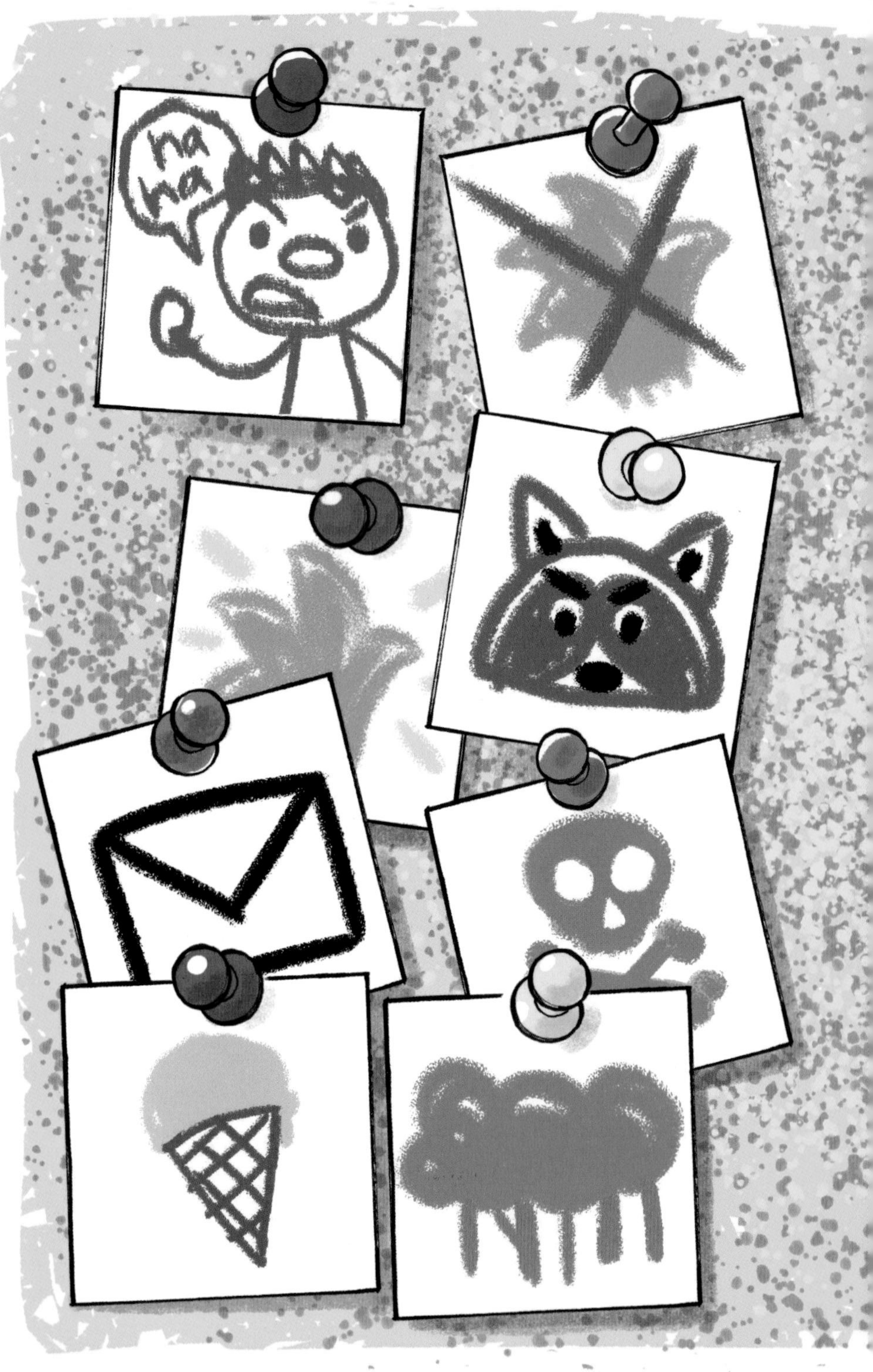
ha
ha

Thank You . . .

Peter Ryan, my agent, for believing in me.

My editor, Karen Chaplin, for nurturing this story
and making this book possible.

The amazing team at HarperCollins:
Molly Fehr, Senior Designer
Erin Fitzsimmons, Art Director
Rosemary Brosnan, Editorial Director (Quill Tree Books)
Andrew Arnold, Editorial Director (HarperAlley)
Caitlin Lonning, Production Editor
Jill Freshney, Copy Editor
Robby Imfeld, Marketing
Andrea Pappenheimer and the entire sales team

My dad, for his unwavering support and for instilling
in me a real love for drawing and storytelling.

Tom and Terry, my encouraging brother and sister-in-law.
My sister Kim White, for always lending an ear throughout
this book's long journey.
My brother-in-law, Joe, for his counsel.

My extended family and friends for their constant
support. Jane Savelli, for always checking up on me.

My artist pals, Karen McKeen, Ari Binus, and Sue Nally.

Christopher Harte and Darcy Evans, for the shots of
encouragement and wisdom when I needed it most.

And last, but not least, Linda and the sparks for this book,
Mea and Colin.

BEHIND THE PAGES

Like a lot of my ideas, it started with a doodle in my sketchbook. The name came quickly after—**Bedhead Ted**!

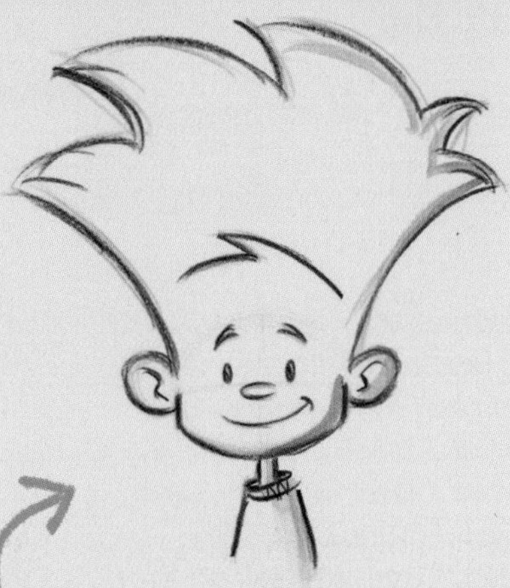

Early sketch of Ted.

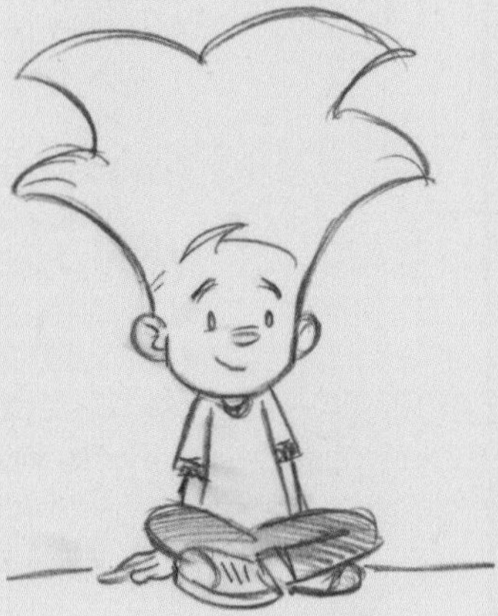

At first, I wasn't sure what to do with my new character with the silly name. Then I had an idea for a graphic novel . . . What if Ted is bullied for his unruly hair, and what if that hair is the key to a hidden superpower?

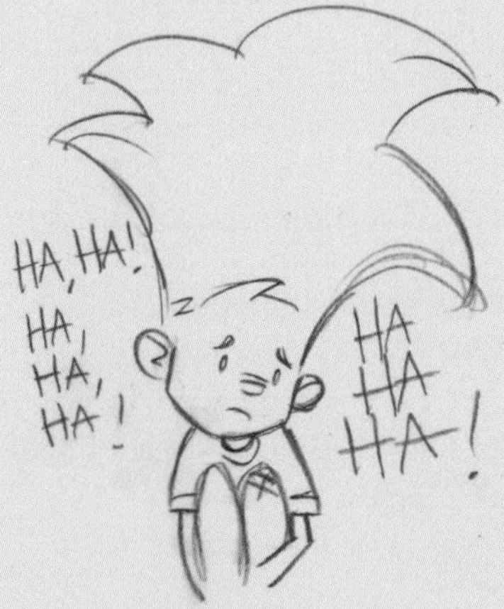
HA, HA!
HA, HA, HA!
HA HA HA!

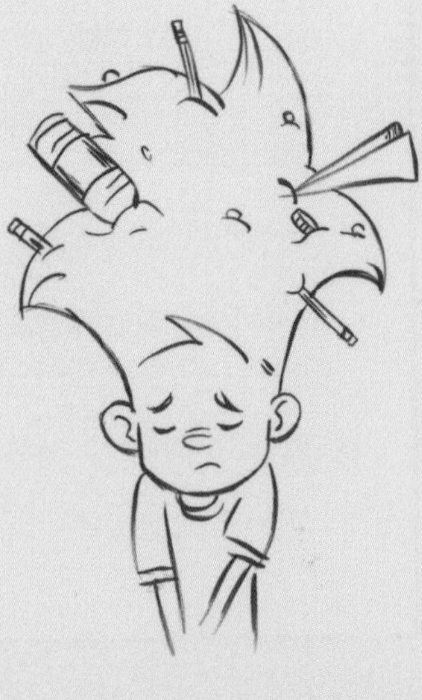

I had a lot of fun coming up with what his superhair could do.

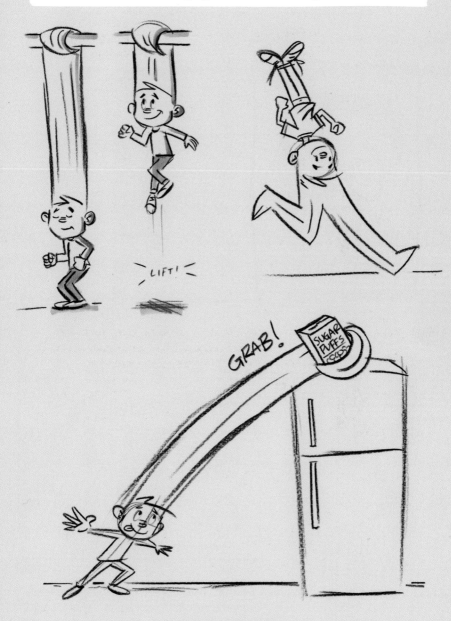

Unused hair gags.

The supporting characters just seemed to show up as I was writing the story. Stacy is a perfect example - he was fully formed from the get-go.

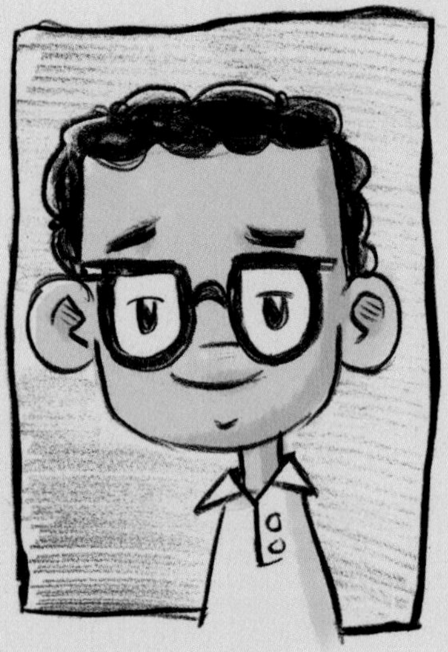

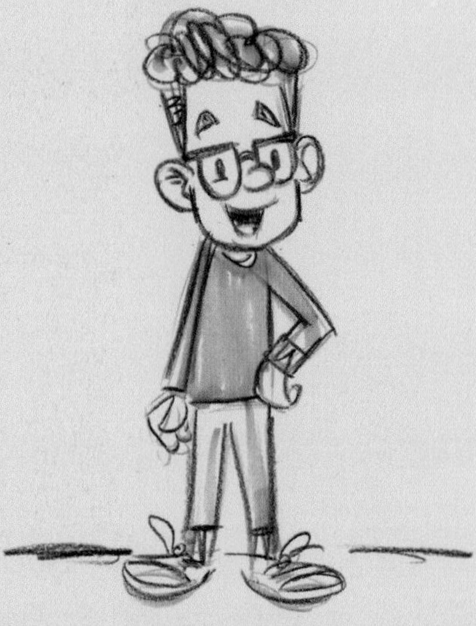

Early version of Stacy.

The look for Ted's mom and dad is based on my own parents.

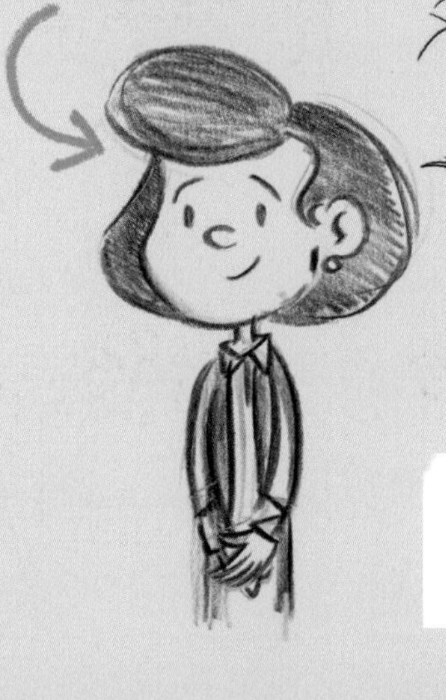

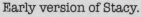

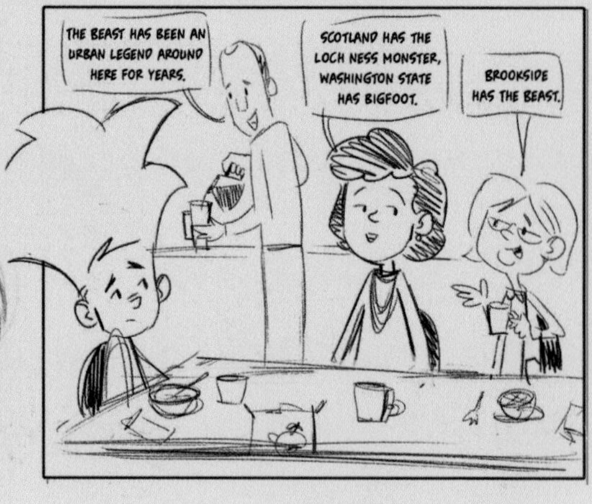
THE BEAST HAS BEEN AN URBAN LEGEND AROUND HERE FOR YEARS.
SCOTLAND HAS THE LOCH NESS MONSTER, WASHINGTON STATE HAS BIGFOOT.
BROOKSIDE HAS THE BEAST.

Before I start work on the final pages, I create rough sketches for every panel. Here is an example from page 6, panel 1.

Fun fact: Jayla and June were not in the original outline.
Now I can't imagine the story without them!

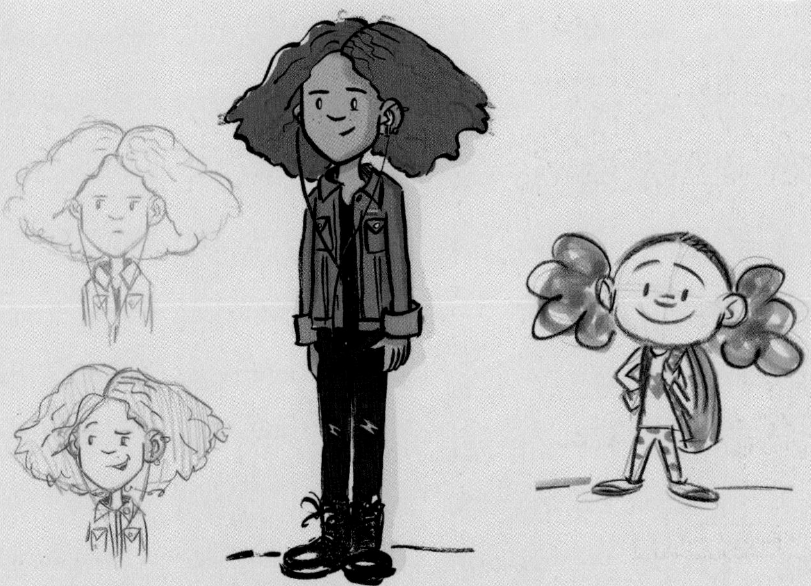

Jayla and June concept sketches.

Early sketch of Tommy, Gary, and Saanvi.

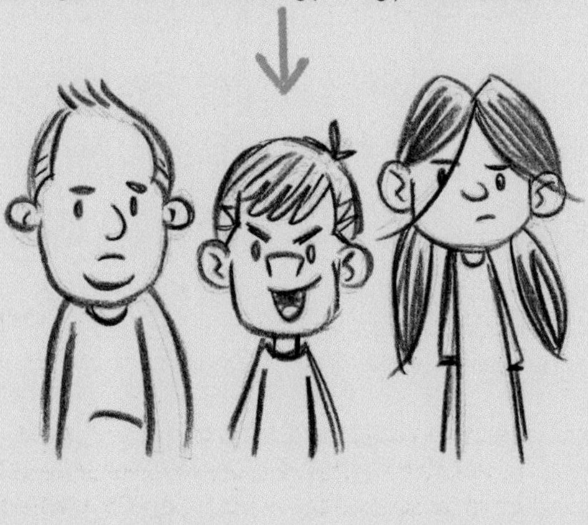

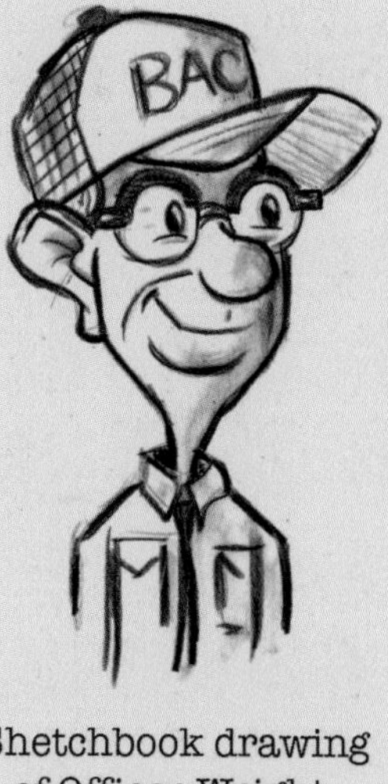
BAC

Shetchbook drawing
of Officer Wright.

Buttercup can be found hidden on several pages. Can you find her?